Bestselling author Tess Gerritsen is also a doctor, and she brings to her novels her first-hand knowledge of emergency and autopsy rooms.

But her interests span far wider than medical topics. As an anthropology undergraduate at Stanford University, she catalogued centuries-old human remains, and she continues to travel the world, driven by her fascination with ancient cultures and bizarre natural phenomena.

Now a full-time novelist, she lives with her husband in Maine.

For more information about Tess Gerritsen and her novels, visit her website at www.tessgerritsen.co.uk

D0300482

www.rbooks.co.uk

HAVE YOU READ THEM ALL?
The thrillers featuring
Jane Rizzoli and Maura Isles are:

THE SURGEON

Introducing Detective Jane Rizzoli of the Boston Homicide Unit

In Boston, there's a killer on the loose. A killer who targets lone women and performs ritualistic acts of torture before finishing them off...

'A read-in-one-go novel if ever there was one'
Independent on Sunday

THE APPRENTICE

The surgeon has been locked up for a year, but his chilling legacy still haunts the city, and especially Boston homicide detective Jane Rizzoli...

'Gerritsen has enough in her locker to seriously worry Michael Connelly, Harlan Coben and even the great Dennis Lehane. Brilliant'
Crime Time

THE SINNER

Long-buried secrets are revealed as Dr Maura Isles and detective Jane Rizzoli find themselves part of an investigation that leads to the awful truth.

'Gutsy, energetic and shocking'
Manchester Evening News

BODY DOUBLE

Dr Maura Isles has seen more than her share of corpses.
But never has the body on the autopsy table been her own...

'It's scary just how good Tess Gerritsen is. This is crime
writing at its unputdownable, nerve-tingling best'
Harlan Coben

VANISH

When medical examiner Maura Isles looks down at the body
of a beautiful woman she gets the fright of her life.
The corpse opens its eyes...

'A horrifying tangle of rape, murder and blackmail'
Guardian

THE MEPHISTO CLUB

Can you really see evil when you look into someone's eyes?
Dr Maura Isles and detective Jane Rizzoli encounter
evil in its purest form.

'Gruesome, seductive and creepily credible'
The Times

KEEPING THE DEAD

She's Pilgrim Hospital's most unusual patient – a mummy
thought to have been dead for centuries. But when Dr Maura
Isles attends the CT scan, it reveals the image
of a very modern bullet...

'A seamless blend of good writing and pulse-racing tension'
Independent

Have you read Tess Gerritsen's stand-alone thrillers?

GIRL MISSING

Her stunning first thriller

The first body is a mystery. The next body is
a warning. The final body might be hers...

'You are going to be up all night'
Stephen King

THE BONE GARDEN

Boston 1830: A notorious serial killer preys on his victims,
flitting from graveyards and into maternity wards.
But no one knows who he is...

'Fascinating...gory...a fast-paced novel that will leave
you with a real appreciation of just how far medicine
has come in the past century'
Mail on Sunday

HARVEST

How far would you go to save a life? A young surgical
resident is drawn into the deadly world of organ smuggling.

'Suspense as sharp as a scalpel's edge.
A page-turning, hold your breath read'
Tami Hoag

LIFE SUPPORT

A terrifying and deadly epidemic is about to be unleashed.

'If you like your crime medicine strong,
this will keep you gripped'
Mail on Sunday

LIFE SUPPORT

Tess Gerritsen

BANTAM BOOKS

LONDON • TORONTO • SYDNEY • AUCKLAND • JOHANNESBURG

TRANSWORLD PUBLISHERS
61-63 Uxbridge Road, London W5 5SA
A Random House Group Company
www.randomhouse.co.uk

LIFE SUPPORT
A BANTAM BOOK: 9780553824520

Originally published in the United States by Simon & Schuster, Inc.
First published in Great Britain by Headline Limited in 1997
Bantam edition published 2006
Bantam edition reissued 2010

Addresses for Random House Group Ltd companies outside the UK
can be found at: www.randomhouse.co.uk
The Random House Group Ltd Reg. No. 954009

The Random House Group Limited supports The Forest Stewardship
Council (FSC®), the leading international forest certification organisation.
Our books carrying the FSC label are printed on FSC® certified paper.
FSC is the only forest certification scheme endorsed by the leading
environmental organisations, including Greenpeace. Our
paper procurement policy can be found at
www.randomhouse.co.uk/environment

MIX
Paper from
responsible sources
FSC® C016897

Printed and bound in Great Britain by Clays Ltd, St Ives PLC

Typeset in Minion by Falcon Oast Graphic Art Ltd.

4 6 8 10 9 7 5 3

To Jacob, Adam, and Josh –
the guys in my life

Acknowledgments

With many thanks to:
  Emily Bestler, who can make any book shine
  Ross Davis, M.D., neurosurgeon and Renaissance man
  Jack Young, who cheerfully answers my oddest questions
  Patty Kahn, for all her research assistance
  Jane Berkey and Don Cleary, my navigators in the publishing world
  And most of all, to Meg Ruley, who always points me in the right direction. And then walks me there.

Introduction

Fans of my Jane Rizzoli crime series may not be aware that I am also the author of four best-selling medical suspense books. As a physician, I'm able to draw on my insider knowledge of medicine to bring my readers into the E.R. and the autopsy room, to show them what it's like to slice open a corpse or clamp a bleeding artery. In LIFE SUPPORT, published in 1997, you'll find the same forensic details that appear in my later crime thrillers, as well as the chilling twists that have become my trademark.

LIFE SUPPORT was inspired by my fascination with a disease that I'd first heard about in medical school. During eight-hour days filled with dry lectures, it's easy for a medical student to drift off into daydreams, and one afternoon in class, my mind was indeed wandering when I suddenly heard the professor say the words 'human cannibalism'. Instantly I snapped to attention. He was talking about a primitive tribe in New Guinea, where a bizarre epidemic had spread among the women and children. Wracked by seizures, suffering from spasms of weird laughter, the victims invariably died. The illness was Creutzfeldt-Jakob Disease, and in that particular tribe, the method of transmission was grotesque indeed: the women and children became infected because they practiced cannibalism. They had consumed their dead relatives.

That's just the sort of unforgettable little detail that a thriller writer can't wait to use. And that's what launched LIFE SUPPORT.

In this thriller, I introduce a courageous heroine named Dr. Toby Harper, a physician whose overnight shift in the emergency room suddenly erupts in crisis when a critically ill man arrives. Delirious and hallucinating from a possible viral infection of the brain, he barely responds to treatment . . . and then he disappears from the hospital without a trace. When a second patient turns up with the same symptoms, Toby realizes she has an epidemic on her hands. Tracking the source, she's soon on a dangerous trail that leads to a pregnant teenage prostitute. And to a macabre discovery: the fetus that the girl is carrying is bizarrely abnormal.

In fact, it may not even be human.

Tess Gerritsen, 2006

One

A scalpel is a beautiful thing.

Dr. Stanley Mackie had never noticed this before, but as he stood with head bowed beneath the OR lamps, he suddenly found himself marveling at how the light reflected with diamondlike brilliance off the blade. It was a work of art, that razor sharp lunula of stainless steel. So beautiful, in fact, that he scarcely dared to pick it up for fear he would somehow tarnish its magic. In its surface he saw a rainbow of colors, light fractured to its purest elements.

'Dr. Mackie? Is something wrong?'

He looked up and saw the scrub nurse frowning at him over her surgical mask. He had never before noticed how green her eyes were. He seemed to be seeing, really seeing, so many things for the very first time. The creamy texture of the nurse's skin. The vein coursing along her temple. The mole just above her eyebrow.

Or *was* it a mole? He stared. It was moving,

crawling like a many-legged insect toward the corner of her eye . . .

'Stan?' Dr. Rudman, the anesthesiologist, was speaking now, his voice slicing through Mackie's dismay. 'Are you all right?'

Mackie gave his head a shake. The insect vanished. It was a mole again, just a tiny fleck of black pigment on the nurse's pale skin. He took a deep breath and picked up the scalpel from the instrument tray. He looked down at the woman lying on the table.

The overhead light had already been focused on the patient's lower abdomen. Blue surgical drapes were clamped in place, framing a rectangle of exposed skin. It was a nice flat belly with a bikini line connecting the twin flares of the hip bones – a surprising sight to behold in this season of snowstorms and winter white faces. What a shame he would have to cut into it. An appendectomy scar would certainly mar any future Caribbean tans.

He placed the tip of the blade on the skin, centering his incision on McBurney's point, halfway between the navel and the protrusion of the right hip bone. The approximate location of the appendix. With scalpel poised to cut, he suddenly paused.

His hand was shaking.

He didn't understand it. This had never happened before. Stanley Mackie had always possessed rock steady hands. Now it took enormous effort just to maintain his grip on the handle. He swallowed and

14

lifted the blade from the skin. *Easy. Take a few deep breaths. This will pass.*

'Stan?'

Mackie looked up and saw that Dr. Rudman was frowning. So were the two nurses. Mackie could read the questions in their eyes, the same questions that people had been whispering about him for weeks. *Is old Dr. Mackie competent? At the age of seventy- four, should he still be allowed to operate?* He ignored their looks. He had already defended himself before the Quality Assurance Committee, had explained, to their satisfaction, the circumstances of his last patient's death. Surgery, after all, was not a risk-free proposition. When too much blood pools in the abdomen, it's easy to confuse one's landmarks, to make the wrong slice.

The committee, in their wisdom, had absolved him of blame.

Nevertheless, doubts had seeped into the minds of the hospital staff. He could see it in the nurses' expressions, in Dr. Rudman's frown. All those eyes watching him. Suddenly he sensed other eyes as well. He caught a fleeting glimpse of dozens of eyeballs floating in the air, all of them staring at him.

He blinked, and the terrible vision was gone.

My glasses, he thought. *I will have to get my glasses checked.*

A drop of sweat slid down his cheek. He tightened his grip on the scalpel handle. This was just a simple appendectomy, a procedure a lowly surgical intern could pull off. Surely he could manage this, even with shaking hands.

He focused on the patient's abdomen, on that flat belly with its golden tan. Jennifer Halsey, age thirty-six. A visitor from out of state, she had awakened this morning in her Boston motel room suffering from right lower quadrant pain. With the pain growing worse, she had driven through a blinding snowstorm to the ER at Wicklin Hospital, and had been referred to the surgeon on call for the day: Mackie. She knew nothing about the rumors concerning his competence, nothing about the lies and whispers that were slowly destroying his practice. She was merely a woman in pain who needed her inflamed appendix removed.

He pressed the blade to Jennifer's skin. His hand had steadied. He could do it. Of course he could do it. He made the incision, a smooth, clean slice. The scrub nurse assisted, sponging up blood, handing him hemostats. He cut deeper; through the yellow subcutaneous fat, pausing every so often to cauterize a bleeder. *No problem. Everything's going to be fine.* He would get in, remove the appendix, and get out again. Then he would go home for the afternoon. Maybe a little rest was all he needed to clear his head.

He slit through the glistening peritoneum, into the abdominal cavity. 'Retract,' he said.

The scrub nurse took hold of the stainless steel retractors and gently tugged open the wound.

Mackie reached into the gap and felt the

intestines, warm and slippery, squirm around his gloved hand. What a wondrous sensation, to be cradled in the heat of the human body. It was like being welcomed back into the womb. He exposed the appendix. One glance at the red and swollen tissue told him his diagnosis had been correct; the appendix would have to come out. He reached for the scalpel.

Only as he focused once again on the incision did he realize that something was not quite right.

There was far too much intestine crowded into the abdomen, twice as much as there should be. Far more than the woman needed. This wouldn't do. He tugged on a loop of small bowel, felt it glide, warm and slick, across his gloved hands. With the scalpel, he sliced off the excess length and set the dripping coil on the tray. There, he thought. That was much neater.

The scrub nurse was staring at him, her eyes wide over the surgical mask. 'What are you *doing*?' she cried.

'Too much intestine,' he answered calmly. 'Can't have that.' He reached into the abdomen and grasped another loop of bowel. No need for all this excess tissue. It only obscured his view of things.

'Dr. Mackie, no!'

He sliced. Blood pulsed out in a hot, arcing spray from the severed coil.

The nurse grabbed his gloved hand. He shook it off, outraged that a mere nurse would dare interrupt the procedure.

'Get me another scrub nurse,' he commanded. 'I need suction. Have to clear away all this blood.'

'Stop him! Help me stop him—'

With his free hand, Mackie reached for the suction catheter and plunged the tip into the abdomen. Blood gurgled up the tube and poured into the reservoir.

Another hand grasped his gown and pulled him away from the table. It was Dr. Rudman. Mackie tried to shake him off, but Rudman wouldn't let go.

'Put down the scalpel, Stan.'

'She has to be cleaned out. There's too much intestine.'

'*Put it down!*'

Struggling free, Mackie swung around to confront Rudman. He'd forgotten he was still holding the scalpel. The blade slashed across the other man's neck.

Rudman screamed and clapped his hand to his throat.

Mackie backed away, staring at the blood seeping out between Rudman's fingers. 'Not my fault,' he said. 'It's not my fault!'

A nurse yelled into the intercom: 'Send Security! He's going crazy in here! We need Security STAT!'

Mackie stumbled backward, through slippery pools of blood. Rudman's blood. Jennifer Halsey's blood. A spreading lake of it. He turned and bolted from the room.

They were chasing him.

He fled down the hallway, running in blind

panic, lost in a maze of corridors. Where was he? Why did nothing seem familiar? Then, straight ahead, he saw the window, and beyond it, the swirling snow. *Snow.* That cold, white lace would purity him, would cleanse this blood from his hands.

Behind him, footsteps pounded closer. Someone shouted, '*Halt!*'

Mackie took three running steps and leaped toward the rectangle of light.

Glass shattered into a million diamonds. Then the cold air whistled past him and everything was white. A beautiful, crystalline white.

And he was falling.

Two

It was a scorching day outside, but the driver had the air conditioner going full blast, and Molly Picker was feeling chilled as she rode in the back-seat of the car. The cold air blowing out of the vent by her knees seemed to knife straight up her miniskirt. She leaned forward and rapped on the Plexiglas partition.

'Excuse me?' she said. 'Hey, mister? Could you turn down that air conditioner? Mister?' She rapped again.

The driver didn't seem to hear her. Or maybe he was ignoring her. All she saw was the back of his blond head.

Shivering, she crossed her bare arms over her chest and scooted sideways, away from that vent. Staring out the car window, she watched the streets of Boston glide by. She didn't recognize this neighborhood at all, but she knew they were headed south. That's what the last sign had said, Washington Street, South. Now she looked out at boxy buildings and barred windows, at clumps of men sitting on front stoops, their faces glossed with sweat. Not even June, and already the temperature was in the eighties. Molly could read the day's heat just by looking at the people on the street. The languid slump of their shoulders, their slow-motion shuffle down the sidewalks. Molly enjoyed looking at people. Mostly she looked at women because she found them so much more interesting. She would study their dresses and wonder why some wore black in the heat of summer, why the fat ones with big butts chose bright stretch pants, why nobody wore hats these days. She would study how the pretty ones walked, their hips swaying ever so slightly, their feet perched, perfectly balanced, on high heels. She wondered what secrets pretty women knew that she didn't. What lessons their mamas had passed along to them, lessons that Molly had somehow missed. She would gaze long and hard at their faces, hoping for divine insight into what makes a woman beautiful. What special magic they possessed that she, Molly Picker, did not have.

The car stopped at a red light. A woman in platform heels was standing on the corner, one hip jutted out. Like Molly, a hooker, but older – maybe eighteen, with lustrous black hair that tumbled all over her bronzy shoulders. Black hair would be nice, thought Molly wistfully. It made a statement. It was not an in-between color, like Molly's limp hair, which was neither blond nor brown and made no statement at all. The car window was darkly tinted, and the black-haired girl couldn't see Molly staring at her. But she seemed to sense it, because she slowly pivoted on her platform heels to face the car.

She was not so pretty after all.

Molly sat back, feeling oddly disappointed.

The car turned left and continued southeast. They were far from Molly's neighborhood now, heading into territory that was both unfamiliar and threatening. The heat had driven people out of their apartments and they sat fanning themselves in shady doorways. Their gazes followed the car as it passed by. They knew it did not belong in this neighborhood. Just as Molly knew she did not belong here. Where was Romy sending her?

He hadn't given her any address. Usually a scrawled street number was thrust in her hand, and she was responsible for scrounging up her own taxi. This time, though, there'd been a car waiting at the curb for her. A nice car, too, with no telltale stains on the backseat, no stinky wads of tissue paper stuffed in the ashtray. It was all so clean. She'd never ridden in a car this clean.

The driver turned left, onto a narrow street. No people were sitting outside on the sidewalk here. But she knew they were watching her. She could feel it. She dug in her purse, fished out a cigarette, and lit up. She'd taken only two drags when a disembodied voice suddenly said: 'Please put it out.'

Molly glanced around, startled. 'What?'

'I said, put it out. We don't allow smoking in the car.'

Flushing with guilt, she quickly stubbed out the cigarette in the ashtray. Then she noticed the tiny speaker mounted in the partition.

'Hello? Can you hear me?' she said.

No reply.

'If you can, could you turn down the air conditioner? I'm freezing back here. Hello? Mister driver?'

The blast of cold air shut off.

'*Thank* you,' she said. And added under her breath: 'Asshole.'

She found the electric switch for the window and rolled it down a crack. The smell of summer in the city wafted in, hot and sulfurish. She didn't mind the heat. It felt like home. Like all the damp and sweaty summers of her childhood in Beaufort. Damn, she wanted a cigarette. But she didn't feel like arguing with that tinny little box.

The car rolled to a stop. The voice from the speaker said: 'This is the address. You can get out now.'

'What, here?'

'The building's right in front of you.'

Molly peered out at the four-story brownstone. The first-floor windows were boarded up. Broken glass glittered on the sidewalk. 'You've got to be kidding,' she said.

'The front door's open. Go up two flights to the third floor. It'll be the last door on your right. No need to knock, just walk right in.'

'Romy didn't say nothing about this.'

'Romy said you'd cooperate.'

23

'Yeah, well—'

'It's just part of the fantasy, Molly.'

'What fantasy?'

'The client's. You know how it is.'

Molly gave a deep sigh and stared out at the building again. Clients and their fantasies. So what was this guy's dream fuck? Doing it among the rats and cockroaches? A little danger, a little grunge to notch up the excitement? Why did clients' fantasies never match her own? A clean hotel room, a Jacuzzi. Richard Gere and Pretty Woman sipping champagne.

'He's waiting.'

'Yeah, I'm going, I'm going.' Molly shoved open the car door and stepped out onto the curb. 'You're gonna wait for me, right?'

'I'll be right here.'

She faced the building and took a deep breath. Then she climbed the steps and pushed into the entrance.

It was as bad inside as it looked on the outside. Graffiti all over the walls, the hallway littered with newspapers and a rusty box spring. Someone had trashed the place good.

She started up the stairs. The building was eerily silent, and the clatter of her shoes echoed in the stairwell. When she reached the second floor, her palms were sweaty.

This felt wrong. All wrong.

She paused on the landing and gazed toward the third floor. *What the hell did you get me into, Romy? Who is this client, anyway?*

She wiped her damp palms on her blouse. Then she took another breath and ascended the next flight of stairs. In the third floor hallway, she stopped outside the last door on the right. She heard a humming sound from the room beyond – an air conditioner? She opened the door.

Cool air spilled out. She stepped inside and was amazed to find herself in a room with pristine white walls. In the center was some sort of doctor's exam table, padded in maroon vinyl. Overhead hung an enormous lamp. There was no other furniture. Not even a chair.

'Hello, Molly.'

She spun around, searching for the man who'd just said her name. There was no one else in the room. 'Where are you?' she demanded.

'There's nothing to be afraid of. I'm just a little shy. First I'd like to get a look at you.'

Molly focused on a mirror, mounted in the far wall. 'You're back there, aren't you? Is that some kinda one-way glass?'

'Very good.'

'So what do you want me to do?'

'Talk to me.'

'Is that all?'

'There'll be more.'

Naturally. There was always more. She walked, almost casually, to the mirror. He'd said he was shy. That made her feel better. More in control. She stood with one hand propped on her miniskirted hip. 'Okay. If you want to talk, mister, it's your money.'

'How old are you, Molly?'

'Sixteen.'

'Are your periods regular?'

'What?'

'Your menstrual periods.'

She gave a laugh. 'I don't believe this.'

'Answer the question.'

'Yeah. They're sorta regular.'

'And your last period was two weeks ago?'

'How do you know *that*?' she demanded. Then, shaking her head, she muttered, 'Oh. Romy told you.' Romy would know, of course. He always knew when his girls were on the rag.

'Are you healthy, Molly?'

She glared at the mirror. 'Don't I look healthy?'

'No blood diseases? Hepatitis? HIV?'

'I'm clean. You won't catch anything, if that's what worries you.'

'Syphilis? Clap?'

'Look,' she snapped. 'Do you want to get laid or not?'

There was a silence. Then the voice said, softly: 'Take off your clothes.'

This was more like it. This was what she expected.

She stepped closer to the mirror, so close her breath intermittently steamed the glass. He would want to watch every detail. They always did. She reached up and began to unbutton her blouse. She did it slowly, drawing out the performance. As the fabric parted she let her thoughts go blank, felt herself withdrawing into some safe mental closet where men did not exist. She was moving her hips, swaying to imagined music. The blouse slid off her shoulders to the floor. Her breasts were exposed now, her nipples dimpling in the room's chill. She closed her eyes. Somehow that made it better. *Let's get this over with*, she thought. *Just screw him and get out of here*.

She unzipped her skirt and stepped out of it. Then she peeled off her panties. All this she did with her eyes closed. Romy had told her she had a good body. That if she used it right, no one would even notice how plain her face was. She was using that body now, dancing to a rhythm only she could hear.

'That's fine,' the man said. 'You can stop dancing.'

She opened her eyes and stared at the mirror in bewilderment. She saw her own reflection there. Limp brown hair. Breasts small but pointed. Hips as narrow as a boy's. When she'd been dancing with her eyes closed, she had been acting out a part. Now she confronted her own image. Her real self. She couldn't help crossing her arms over her naked chest.

'Go to the table,' he said.

'What?'

'The exam table. Lie down on it.'

'Sure. If that's what turns you on.'

'That's what turns me on.'

To each his own. She climbed onto the table. The burgundy vinyl was cold against her bare buttocks. She lay down and waited for something to happen.

A door opened, and she heard footsteps. She stared as the man approached the foot of the table and loomed above her. He was garbed entirely in green. All she could see of his face was his eyes, a cold steel blue. They were glazing at her over a surgical mask.

She sat up in alarm.

'Lie down,' he commanded.

'What the hell do you think you're doing?'

'I said, lie *down*.'

'Man, I'm getting out of here—'

He grabbed her arm. Only then did she notice he was wearing gloves. 'Look, I won't hurt you,' he said, his voice softer. Gentler. 'Don't you understand? *This* is my fantasy.'

'You mean – playing doctor?'

'Yes.'

'I'm supposed to be your patient?'

'Yes. Does that scare you?'

She sat thinking about it. Remembering all the other fantasies she'd endured on behalf of clients. This one, in the scheme of things, seemed relatively tame.

'All right,' she sighed, and lay back down.

He slid out the stirrups and extended the footrests so they jutted out from the end of the table. 'Come on, Molly,' he said. 'Surely you know what to do with your feet.'

'Do I have to?'

'I'm the doctor. Remember?'

She stared at his masked face, wondering what lay behind that rectangle of cloth. A perfectly ordinary man, no doubt. They were all *so* ordinary. It was their fantasies that repulsed her. Frightened her.

Reluctantly she raised her legs and positioned her feet in the stirrups.

He released the foot of the table and it swung down on hinges. She was lying with her thighs spread wide apart, her exposed bottom practically hanging off the table's edge. She displayed herself to men all the time, but there was something horribly vulnerable about this position. Those bright lights shining down between her legs. Her utter nakedness against the exam table. And the man, whose gaze was focused with clinical detachment on her most intimate anatomy.

He looped a Velcro strap around her ankle.

'Hey,' she said. 'I don't like being tied down.'

'I like it,' he murmured, fastening the other strap. 'I like my girls this way.'

She flinched as he inserted his gloved fingers. He leaned toward her, his gaze narrowed in concentration as his fingers probed deeper. She closed her eyes and tried to detach her thoughts from what was happening between her legs, but the sensations were difficult to ignore. Like a rodent burrowing deep inside her. He had one hand pressed down on top of her abdomen, and the fingers of his other hand were moving inside. Somehow this seemed a worse violation than any mere fuck, and she wanted it over and done with. *Is this turning you on, creep?* she wondered. *Are you stiff yet? When are you going to get on with it?*

He withdrew his hand. She gave a shudder of relief. Opening her eyes, she saw that he was not looking at her anymore. His gaze was focused instead on something beyond her field of vision. He nodded.

Only then did she realize there was someone else in the room.

A rubber mask was clamped over her mouth and nose. She tried to twist away, but her head was pressed hard against the table. She reached up, frantically clawing at the edges of the anesthesia mask. At once her hands were yanked away, and her wrists firmly and efficiently tied down. She gasped in a breath of acrid-smelling gas, felt it sear her throat. Her chest rebelled in a spasm of coughing. She bucked harder, but the mask would not go away. She took another breath; she could not help it. Now all sensation was draining from her limbs. The lights seemed dimmer. Bright white fading to gray.

To black.

She heard a voice say, 'Draw the blood now.'

But the words meant nothing to her. Nothing at all.

'Man, oh man, what a mess you've made.'

It was Romy's voice – that much she could figure out. But she could not seem to make sense of anything else. Where she was. Where she'd been.

Why her head ached and her throat felt so dry.

'Come on, Molly Wolly. Open your eyes.'

She groaned. Just the rumble of her own voice made her head vibrate.

'Open your fuckin' eyes, Molly. You're stinking up the whole room.'

She rolled onto her back. Light filtered, blood red, through her eyelids. She struggled to open them, to focus on Romy's face.

He was staring down at her with an expression of disgust in his dark eyes. His black hair was slicked back and shiny with pomade. It reflected light like a brass helmet. Sophie was there too, her face slightly sneering, her arms crossed over her balloon breasts. It made Molly even more miserable to see Sophie and Romy standing so close together, like the old lovers they were. Maybe still were. That horse-faced Sophie was always hanging around, trying to cut Molly out. And now she'd come into Molly's room, trespassing where she had no right to be.

Outraged, Molly tried to sit up, but her vision blanked out and she collapsed back on the bed. 'I feel sick,' she said.

'You've *been* sick,' said Romy. 'Now go get cleaned up. Sophie'll help you.'

'I don't want her to touch me. Get her out of here.'

Sophie gave a snort. 'Miss Titless, I wouldn't hang around your pukey room anyway,' she said and walked out.

Molly groaned. 'I don't remember what happened, Romy.'

'Nothing happened. You came back and went to bed. And threw up all over your pillow.'

Again she struggled to sit up. He didn't help her, or even touch her. She smelled that bad. Already he was heading for the door, leaving her to clean up her own filthy sheets.

'Romy,' she said.

'Yeah?'

'How did I get here?'

He laughed. 'Geez, you really did get wasted, didn't you?' And he left the room.

For a long time she sat on the side of the bed, trying to remember the last few hours. Trying to shake off her residual wooziness.

There had been a client – that much she remembered. A man all in green. A room with a giant mirror. And there had been a table.

But she couldn't remember the sex. Maybe she had blocked it out. Maybe it had been so disgusting an experience she'd shoved it into her subconscious, the way she'd successfully blocked out so much of her childhood. Only occasionally did she allow a wisp of a childhood memory to return. The good memories, mostly; she did have a few good memories of her years growing up in Beaufort, and she could conjure them up at will. Or suppress them at will.

But the events of this afternoon, she could hardly remember at all.

God, she stank. She looked down at her blouse and saw it was stained with vomit. The buttons had been done up wrong, and bare skin showed through an unfastened gap.

She began to strip. She peeled off the miniskirt, unbuttoned the blouse, and tossed them in a pile on the floor. Then she stumbled to the shower and turned on the water.

Cold. She wanted it cold.

Standing under the sputtering faucet, she felt her head begin to clear. As it did, another memory flickered into focus. The man in green, towering above her. Staring down at her. And the straps, pinching her wrists and ankles.

She looked down at her hands and saw the bruises, like circular cuff marks around her wrists. He had tied her down – not so unusual. Men and their crazy games.

Then her gaze focused on another bruise, in the crook of her left arm. It was so faint she'd almost missed the small blue circle. In the very center of the bruise, like the point of a bull's eye, was a single puncture mark.

She struggled to remember a needle, but she could not. All she remembered was the man in the surgeon's mask.

And the table.

Cold water dribbled down her shoulders. Shivering, Molly stared at the needle mark and she wondered what else she'd forgotten.

Three

A nurse's voice called to her from the wall intercom: 'Dr. Harper, we need you out here.'

Toby Harper awakened with a start to find that she had fallen asleep at her desk, with a stack of medical journals as her pillow. Reluctantly she raised her head, squinting against the light from the reading lamp. The brass desktop clock said 4:49 A.M. Had she really slept for almost forty minutes? It seemed as if she'd laid her head down just a moment ago. The words of the journal article she'd been reading had begun to blur, and she'd thought she'd allow her eyes a short rest. That was all she'd intended, just a moment's respite from dull writing and painfully small print. The journal was still open to the article she'd been trying to absorb, the page now crinkled with the imprint of her face. 'A randomized controlled study comparing the effectiveness of lamivudine and zidovudine in the treatment of HIV patients with less than 500 CD4+ cells per cubic centimeter.' She closed the journal. God. No wonder she'd fallen asleep.

There was a knock on the door, and Maudeen poked her head into the doctor's room. Ex-army major Maudeen Collins had a voice like a megaphone – not at all what one expected from a five-foot-two-inch pixie. 'Toby? You weren't asleep, were you?'

'I guess I dozed off. What've you got out there?'

'Sore toe.'

'At this hour?'

'Patient ran out of Colchicine and he thinks his gout's acting up.'

Toby groaned. 'Jesus. Why don't these crazy patients ever plan ahead?'

'They think we're just an all-night pharmacy. Look, we're still doing his paperwork. So why don't you take your time?'

'I'll be right out.'

After Maudeen left, Toby allowed herself a moment to fully wake up. She wanted to sound halfway intelligent when she spoke to the patient. She rose from the desk and crossed to the sink. She'd been on duty for ten hours now and so far it had been an uneventful shift. That was the nice part about working in a quiet suburb like Newton. There were often long periods when absolutely nothing happened in the Springer Hospital ER, periods when Toby could stretch out on the doctor's bed and take a nap, if she was so inclined. She knew the other ER doctors took naps, but Toby usually resisted the temptation. She was paid to work the twelve-hour night shift, and it seemed unprofessional to spend any of those hours in a state of unconsciousness.

So much for professionalism, she thought, staring at herself in the mirror. She'd fallen asleep on the job, and she could see the aftereffects in her face. Her green eyes were puffy. Newsprint from the medical journal had smudged words on her cheek. Her expensive salon haircut looked as though it had been whipped up by an eggbeater, and her hair stuck out in short blond spikes. This was the precise and elegant Dr. Harper as she really was – not so elegant after all.

In disgust Toby turned on the faucet and vigorously scrubbed the newsprint from her face. She splashed water on her hair as well, and combed it back with her fingers. So much for expensive haircuts. At least she no longer looked like a fuzzy blond dandelion. There was nothing she could do about the puffy eyes or the lines of exhaustion. At the age of thirty-eight, Toby couldn't bounce back from an all-nighter the way she did as a twenty-five-year-old medical student.

She left the room and walked down the hall to the ER.

No one was there. The front desk was unmanned, the waiting room deserted. 'Hello?' she called.

'Dr. Harper?' answered a voice over the intercom.

'Where is everyone?'

'We're in the staff room. Could you come back here?'

'Don't I have a patient to see?'

'We have a problem. We need you *now*.'

Problem? Toby didn't like the sound of that word. At once her pulse kicked into high gear. She hurried toward the staff room and pushed open the door.

A camera flashbulb went off. She froze in place as a chorus of voices began to sing:

'*Happy birthday to you! Happy birthday to you . . .*'

Toby looked up at the red and green streamers fluttering overhead. Then she looked at the cake, glittering with lit candles – dozens of them. As the last notes of 'Happy Birthday' faded away, she covered her face with her hand and groaned. 'I don't believe this. I completely forgot.'

'Well we didn't,' said Maudeen, snapping off another picture with her Instamatic. 'You're seventeen, right?'

'I wish. Who's the joker who put on a zillion candles?'

Morty, the lab tech, raised his pudgy hand. 'Hey, no one told me when to stop.'

'See, Morty wanted to test our sprinkler system—'

'Actually, this is a pulmonary function test,' said Val, the other ER nurse. 'In order to pass, Toby, you have to blow 'em all out with a single breath.'

'And if I don't?'

'Then we're gonna *intubate*!'

'C'mon, Toby. Make a wish!' urged Maudeen. 'And make him tall, dark, and handsome.'

'At my age, I'd settle for short, fat, and rich.'

37

Arlo, the security guard, piped up: 'Hey! I've got two out of three qualifications!'

'You've also got a wife,' shot back Maudeen.

'Go, Tobe! Make a wish!'

'Yeah, make a wish!'

Toby sat down in front of the cake. The other four gathered around her, giggling and jostling like rowdy kids. They were her second family, related to her not by blood but by years of shared crises in the Emergency Room. The Nanny Brigade was what Arlo called the night ER team. Maudeen and Val and the lady doc. God help the male patient who came in with a urologic complaint.

A wish, thought Toby. *What do I wish for? Where do I start?* She took a breath and blew. All the candles puffed out to a burst of applause.

'Way to go,' said Val, and she began plucking out the candles. Suddenly she glanced at the window. So did everyone else.

A Newton police car, blue lights flashing, had just pulled into the ER parking lot.

'We got a customer,' said Maudeen.

'Okay,' sighed Val, 'the ladies gotta go to work. Don't you boys eat all the cake while we're gone.'

Arlo leaned toward Morty and whispered, 'Aw, those girls are always on a diet anyway . . .'

Toby led the charge down the hall. The three women reached the front desk just as the automatic ER doors whisked open.

A young cop poked his head inside. 'Hey, we got this old guy out in the car. Found him wandering in the park. You ladies wanna take a look at him?'

Toby followed the cop outside, into the parking lot. 'Is he hurt?'

'Doesn't seem to be. But he's pretty confused. I didn't smell alcohol, so I'm thinking maybe Alzheimer's. Or diabetic shock.'

Great, thought Toby. A cop who thinks he's a doctor. 'Is he fully conscious?' she asked.

'Yeah. We got him in the backseat.' The cop opened the rear door of the patrol car.

The man was completely nude. He sat curled into a ball of thin arms and legs, his bald head bobbing back and forth. He was muttering to himself, but she could not quite make out what he was saying. Something about having to get ready for bed.

'Found him on a park bench,' said the other cop, who looked even younger than his partner. 'He was wearing his underwear then, but he took it off in the car. We found the rest of his clothes in the park. They're on the front seat.'

'Okay, we'd better get him inside.' Toby nodded to Val, who already had a wheelchair waiting.

'C'mon, buddy,' the cop urged. 'These nice ladies are gonna take care of you.'

The man hugged himself tighter and began to rock on his skinny buttocks. 'Can't find my pajamas . . .'

'We'll get you some pajamas,' said Toby. 'You come inside with us, sir. We'll give you a ride in this chair.'

Slowly the old man turned and focused on her. 'But I don't know you.'

'I'm Dr. Harper. Why don't you let me help you out of the car?' She held out her hand to him.

He studied it, as though he'd never seen a hand before. At last he reached for it. She slipped her arm around his waist and helped him out of the car. It was like lifting a bundle of dry twigs. Val scurried forward with the wheelchair just as the man's legs seemed to buckle beneath him. They strapped him into the chair and set his bare feet on the footrests. Then Val wheeled him through the ER doors. Toby and one of the baby-faced cops followed a few paces behind.

'Any history?' Toby asked him.

'No, Ma'am. He couldn't give us any. Didn't seem like he'd hurt himself or anything.'

'Does he have any ID?'

'There's a wallet in his pants pocket.'

'Okay, we'll need to contact his next of kin and find out if he has any medical problems.'

'I'll get his things out of the car.'

Toby walked into the exam room.

Maudeen and Val had already put the patient on the gurney and were now tying his wrist restraints to the siderails. He was still babbling about his pajamas and making half-hearted attempts to sit up. Except for a sheet discreetly draped across his groin, he was naked. Spasms of gooseflesh intermittently stippled his bare chest and arms.

'He says his name is Harry,' said Maudeen, slipping a blood pressure cuff around the man's arm. 'No wedding ring. No obvious bruises. Smells like he could use a bath.'

'Harry,' said Toby. 'Do you hurt anywhere? Are you in any pain?'

'Turn off the lights. I want to go to bed.'

'Harry—'

'Can't sleep with those damn lights on.'

'Blood pressure one fifty over eighty,' said Maudeen. 'Pulse is a hundred and regular.' She reached for the electronic thermometer. 'C'mon, sweetie. Put this in your mouth.'

'I'm not hungry.'

'You don't eat it, dear. I'm going to take your temperature.'

Toby stood back for a moment and just watched the man. He was moving all four limbs, and although he was on the thin side, he seemed adequately nourished, his muscles lean and wiry. It was his hygiene that bothered her. He had at least a week's worth of gray beard stubbling his face, and his fingernails were dirty and unclipped. Maudeen was right about that smell. Harry definitely needed a bath.

The electronic thermometer beeped. Maudeen took it out of the man's mouth and frowned at the reading. 'Thirty seven point nine. You feel okay, hon?'

'Where are my pajamas?'

'Boy, you do have a one-track mind.'

Toby shone a penlight in the man's mouth and saw the gleam of gold crowns – five of them. You could tell a lot about a patient's socioeconomic status just by looking at the teeth. Fillings and gold crowns meant middle class or better. Rotten teeth and gum disease said *empty bank account*. Or a morbid fear of dentists. She smelled no alcohol on his breath, no fruity odors that would indicate diabetic ketosis.

She began her physical exam at his head. Running her fingers across his scalp, she detected no obvious fractures or lumps. With her penlight she tested his pupillary reactions. Normal. So were his extraocular movements and gag reflex. All the cranial nerves seemed intact.

'Why don't you go away,' he said. 'I want to sleep.'

'Did you hurt yourself, Harry?'

'Can't find my damn pajamas. Did you take my pajamas?'

Toby looked at Maudeen. 'Okay, let's get some bloods cooking. CBC, lytes, glucose STAT. Couple of extra red tops for an SMA and tox screen. We'll probably have to cath him for a urine.'

'Gotcha.' Maudeen already had the tourniquet and Vacutainer syringe ready. While Val immobilized the man's arm, Maudeen drew the blood. The patient scarcely seemed to feel the needle going in.

'All right, honey,' said Maudeen, applying a bandage to the puncture site. 'You're a very good patient.'

'You know where I put my pajamas?'

'I'm gonna get you a fresh set, right now. You just wait.' Maudeen gathered up the blood tubes. 'I'll send these up under John Doe.'

'His name's Harry Slotkin,' said one of the cops. He had returned from the patrol car and now stood in the doorway, holding up Harry's trousers. 'Checked his wallet. According to the ID, he's seventy-two years old and he lives at 119 Titwillow Lane. That's right up the road, in that new Brant Hill development.'

'Next of kin?'

'There's an emergency contact here. Someone named Daniel Slotkin. It's a Boston phone number.'

'I'll give him a call,' said Val. She left the room, sliding the privacy curtains shut behind her.

Toby was left alone with the patient. She resumed the physical exam. She listened to the heart and lungs, felt the abdomen, tapped on tendons. She poked and prodded and squeezed, and found nothing out of the ordinary. Perhaps this is just Alzheimer's, she thought, standing back to study the patient. She knew the signs of Alzheimer's all too well: the crumbling memory, the nocturnal wanderings. The personality fracturing, breaking off a piece at a time. Darkness was distressing for these patients. As daylight faded, so did their visual links to reality. Perhaps Harry Slotkin was a victim of sundowning – the nighttime psychosis so common to Alzheimer's patients.

Toby picked up the ER clipboard and began to write, using the cryptic code of medical shorthand. VSS for vital signs stable. PERRL for pupils equal, round, and reactive to light.

'Toby?' called Val through the curtain. 'I've got Mr. Slotkin's son on the phone.'

'Coming,' said Toby. She turned to pull aside the curtain. She didn't realize an instrument stand was right on the other side. She knocked against the tray; a steel emesis basin fell off and clanged loudly to the floor.

As Toby bent down to pick it up, she heard another noise behind her – a strange, rhythmic rattling. She looked at the gurney.

Harry Slotkin's right leg was jerking back and forth.

Is he having a seizure?

'Mr. Slotkin!' said Toby 'Look at me. Harry, look at me!'

The man's gaze focused on her face. He was still conscious, still able to follow commands. Though his lips moved, silently forming words, no sound came out.

The jerking suddenly stopped, and the leg lay still.

'Harry?'

'I'm so tired,' he said.

'What just happened, Harry? Were you trying to move your leg?'

He closed his eyes and sighed. 'Turn off the lights.'

Toby frowned at him. Had it been a seizure? Or merely an attempt to free his restrained ankle? He seemed calm enough now, both legs lying motionless.

She stepped through the privacy curtain and went to the nurses' desk.

'The son's on line three,' said Val.

Toby picked up the receiver. 'Hello, Mr. Slotkin? This is Dr. Harper at Springer Hospital. Your father was brought to our ER a short time ago. He doesn't seem to be hurt, but he—'

'What's wrong with him?'

Toby paused, surprised by the sharpness of Daniel Slotkin's response. Was it irritation or fear that she heard in his voice? She answered calmly, 'He was found in a park and brought here by the police. He's agitated and confused. I can't find any focal neurologic problems. Does your father have a history of Alzheimer's? Or any medical problems?'

'No. No, he's never been sick.'

'And there's no history of dementia?'

'My father is sharper than I am.'

'When did you last see him?'

'I don't know. A few months ago, I guess.'

Toby absorbed that information in silence. If Daniel Slotkin resided in Boston, then he lived less than twenty miles away. Certainly not a distance that would explain such infrequent contact between father and son.

As though sensing her unspoken question, Daniel Slotkin added: 'My father leads a very busy life. Golf. Daily poker at the country club. It's not always easy for us to get together.'

'He was mentally sharp a few months ago?'

'Let's put it this way. The last time I saw my father, he gave me a lecture on investment strategies. Everything from stock options to the price of soybeans. It went over *my* head.'

'Is he on any medications?'

'Not that I know of.'

'Do you know the name of his doctor?'

'He goes to a specialist in that private clinic at Brant Hill, where he lives. I think the doctor's name is Wallenberg. Look, just how confused *is* my father?'

'The police found him on a park bench. He'd taken off his clothes.'

There was a long silence. 'Jesus.'

'I can't find any injuries. Since you say there's no history of dementia, there must be something acute going on. Maybe a small stroke. Or a metabolic problem.'

'Metabolic?'

'An abnormal blood sugar, for instance. Or a low sodium level. They can both cause confusion.'

She heard the man exhale deeply, a sound of weariness. And maybe frustration. It was five in the morning. To be awakened at such an hour, to face such a crisis, would exhaust anyone.

'It would be helpful if you came in,' said Toby. 'He might find a familiar face comforting.'

The man was silent.

'Mr. Slotkin?'

He sighed. 'I guess I'll have to.'

'If there's someone else in the family who can do it—'

'No, there's no one else. Anyway, he'll expect me to show up. To make sure everything's done right.'

As Toby hung up, Daniel Slotkin's last words

struck her as faintly threatening: *To make sure everything's done right.* And why *wouldn't* she do everything right?

She picked up the telephone and left a message with the Brant Hill Clinic answering service, telling them their patient Harry Slotkin was in the ER, confused and disoriented. Then she punched in the beeper for the Springer Hospital X-ray tech.

A moment later, the tech called back from home, his voice groggy with sleep. 'This is Vince. You beeped me?'

'This is Dr. Harper in the ER. We need you to come in and do a STAT CT head scan.'

'What's the patient's name?'

'Harry Slotkin. Seventy-two-year-old man with new-onset confusion.'

'Right. I'll be there in ten minutes.'

Toby hung up and stared at her notes. *What have I overlooked?* she wondered. *What else should I be searching for?* She reviewed all the possible causes of new-onset dementia. Strokes. Tumors. Intracranial bleeds. Infections.

She glanced again at the vital signs. Maudeen had recorded an oral temperature of 37.9 degrees centigrade. Not quite a fever, but not quite normal, either. Harry would need a spinal tap – but not until the CT scan was done. If there was a mass in his skull, a spinal tap could lead to a catastrophic shift in pressure on the brain.

The wail of a siren made her glance up.

'Now what?' said Maudeen.

Toby shot to her feet and was already waiting at

the ER entrance when the ambulance pulled up with a loud *whoop*. The vehicle's rear door flew open.

'We got a code in progress!' the driver yelled.

Everyone scrambled to unload the stretcher. Toby caught a quick glimpse of an obese woman, her face pale and limp-jawed. An ET tube was already taped in place.

'We lost her pressure en route – thought we'd better stop here instead of going on to Hahnemann—'

'What's the history?' snapped Toby.

'Found on the floor. Had an MI six weeks ago. Husband says she's on Digoxin—'

They rushed the patient through the ER doors, the driver pumping clumsily on the chest as the stretcher careened up the hall and swerved into the trauma room. Val hit the light switch. Overhead lamps flooded on, blindingly bright.

'Okay, you all got a grip? She's a big one. Watch that IV! One, two, three, *move!*' yelled Maudeen.

In one smooth transfer, four pairs of hands slid the patient off the ambulance stretcher and onto the treatment table. No one had to be told what to do. Despite the seeming confusion of a Code Blue, there was order in chaos. The driver resumed chest compressions. The other EMT continued bagging the lungs, pumping in oxygen. Maudeen and Val scrambled around the table untangling IV lines and connecting EKG wires to the cardiac monitor.

'We've got sinus rhythm,' said Toby, glancing at the screen. 'Stop compressions for a second.'

The driver stopped pumping on the chest.

'I'm barely getting a pulse,' said Val.

'Turn up that IV,' said Toby. 'We got any pressure yet?'

Val glanced up from the arm cuff. 'Fifty over zip. Dopamine drip?'

'Go for it. Resume compressions.'

The driver crossed his hands over the sternum and began to pump again. Maudeen scurried to the code cart and pulled out drug ampules and syringes.

Toby slapped her stethoscope on the chest and listened to the right lung field, then the left. She heard distinct breath sounds on both sides. That told her the ET tube was properly positioned and the lungs were filling with air. 'Hold compressions,' she said and slid the stethoscope over to the heart.

She could barely hear it beating.

Glancing up again at the monitor, she saw a fast sinus rhythm tracing across the screen. The heart's electrical system was intact. Why didn't the woman have a pulse? Either the patient was in shock from blood loss. Or . . .

Toby focused on the neck, and the answer instantly became apparent to her. The woman's obesity had obscured the fact that her jugular veins were bulging.

'You said she had an MI six weeks ago?' Toby asked.

'Yeah,' the driver grunted out as he resumed chest compressions. 'That's what the husband said.'

'Any other meds besides Digoxin?'

'There was a big bottle of aspirin on the night-stand. I think she's arthritic.'

That's it, thought Toby 'Maudeen, get me a fifty cc syringe and a cardiac needle.'

'Gotcha.'

'And toss me some gloves and a Betadine wipe!'

The packet flew toward her. Toby caught it in midair and ripped it open. 'Stop compressions,' she ordered.

The driver stepped back.

Toby gave the skin a quick swab of Betadine, then she pulled on the gloves and reached for the 50-cc syringe. She glanced one last time at the monitor. The rhythm was still a rapid sinus. She took a deep breath. 'Okay. Let's see if this helps . . .' Using the bony protrusion of the xiphoid process as her landmark, she pierced the skin and angled the needle tip straight toward the heart. She could feel her own pulse hammering as she slowly advanced the needle. At the same time she was pulling back on the plunger, exerting gentle negative pressure.

A flash of blood shot into the syringe.

She stopped right where she was. Her hands were absolutely steady. *God, let the needle be in the right place.* She pulled back on the plunger, gradually suctioning blood into the syringe. Twenty cc's. Thirty. Thirty-five

'Blood pressure?' she called out, and heard the rapid *whiff whiff* of the cuff being inflated.

'Yes! I'm getting one!' said Val. 'Eighty over fifty!'

'I guess we know what we've got now,' said Toby. 'We need a surgeon. Maudeen, get Dr. Carey on the line. Tell him we've got a pericardial tamponade.'

'From the MI?' asked the ambulance driver.

'Plus she's on high-dose aspirin, so she's prone to bleeding. She probably ruptured a hole in her myocardium.' Surrounded by blood in the closed sac of the pericardium, the heart would be unable to expand. Unable to pump.

The syringe was full. Toby withdrew the needle.

'Pressure's up to ninety-five,' said Val.

Maudeen hung up the wall phone. 'Dr. Carey's coming in now. So's his team. He says to keep her stabilized.'

'Easier said than done,' muttered Toby, her fingers probing for a pulse. She could feel one, but it remained thready. 'She's probably reaccumulating. I'll need another syringe and needle pretty quick. Can we get her typed and crossed? And let's get a STAT CBC and lytes while we're at it.'

Maudeen pulled out a fistful of blood tubes. 'Eight units?'

'At least. Whole blood if we can get it. And send down some fresh frozen plasma.'

'Pressure's falling to eighty-five,' said Val.

'Shit. We'll need to do it again.'

51

Toby ripped open a packet with a fresh syringe and tossed the wrapping aside. Already the floor was piling up with the debris of paper and plastic that accumulated during every code. *How many times will I have to repeat this?* she wondered as she positioned the needle. *Get your butt over here, Carey. I can't save this woman on my own . . .*

Toby wasn't sure Dr. Carey could save the patient either. If the woman *had* blown a hole in her ventricular wall, then she needed more than just a thoracic surgeon – she needed a full cardiac by-pass team. Springer Hospital was a small suburban facility perfectly capable of dealing with cesareans or simple gallbladder resections, but it was unequipped to deal with major surgery. Ambulance teams transporting serious trauma victims would normally bypass Springer Hospital and head straight for one of the larger medical centers like Brigham or Mass General.

This morning, though, the ambulance had unknowingly delivered a surgical crisis right to Toby's doorstep. And she didn't have the training – or the staff – to save this woman's life.

The second syringe was already filled with blood. Another fifty cc's of it – and it didn't clot.

'Pressure's going down again,' said Val. 'Eighty—'

'Doc, she's in V-tach!' one of the EMT's cut in.

Toby's gaze shot to the monitor. The rhythm had deteriorated to the jagged pattern of ventricular tachycardia. The heart was using only two of its four chambers now, beating too fast to be efficient.

'Defibrillator pads!' snapped Toby. 'We'll go with three hundred joules.'

Maudeen hit the charge button on the defibrillator. The needle climbed to three hundred watt-seconds.

Toby slapped two pads on the patient's chest. Coated with gel, the pads ensured electrical contact with the skin. She positioned the paddles. 'Back!' she said, and squeezed the discharge button.

The patient thrashed, all her muscles jerking simultaneously as the current shot through her body.

Toby glanced at the monitor. 'Okay, we're back in sinus—'

'No pulse. I've got no pulse,' said Val.

'Resume CPR!' said Toby. 'Hand me another syringe.'

Even as she opened the packet and twisted on the pericardiocentesis needle, Toby knew they were losing the fight. She could suction out liters of blood, but more would accumulate, compressing the heart. *Just keep her alive until the surgeon gets here*, thought Toby, and the words became her mantra. *Keep her alive. Keep her alive . . .*

'Back in V-Tach!' said Val.

'Charge to three hundred. Get a lidocaine bolus in—'

The wall phone rang. Maudeen answered it. A moment later she called out: 'Morty's having trouble crossmatching that blood I sent up! The patient's B negative!'

Shit. What else can go wrong? Toby slapped the paddles on the chest. 'Everyone back!'

Again the woman's body jerked. Again the rhythm settled back into rapid sinus.

'Getting a pulse,' said Val.

'Push that lidocaine *now*. Where's our fresh frozen plasma?'

'Morty's working on it,' said Maudeen.

Toby glanced at the clock. They'd been coding the patient for nearly twenty minutes. It seemed like hours. Surrounded by chaos, with the phone ringing and everyone talking at once, she felt a sudden flash of disorientation. Inside the gloves, her hands were sweating, and the rubber was clammy against her skin. The crisis was spiralling out of her control . . .

Control was the word Toby lived by. She strove to keep her life in order, her ER in order. Now this code was falling apart under her command, and there was nothing she could do to salvage it. She wasn't trained to crack a chest, to sew up a ruptured ventricle.

She looked at the woman's face. It was mottled, the flabby jowls deepening to purple. Even as she watched, she knew the brain cells were starving. Dying.

The ambulance driver, exhausted from chest compressions, switched places with his fellow EMT. A fresh pair of hands began pumping.

On the monitor, the heart tracing deteriorated

to a jaggedly chaotic line. Ventricular fibrillation. A fatal rhythm.

The team responded with the usual strategies. More boluses of antiarrhythmics. Lidocaine. Bretylium. Higher and higher jolts from the paddles. In desperation Toby withdrew another fifty cc's of blood from the pericardium.

The heart tracing flattened out to a meandering line.

Toby glanced around at the other faces. They all knew it was over.

'All right.' Toby released a deep breath, and her voice sounded chillingly calm. 'Let's call it. What time?'

'Six-eleven,' said Maudeen.

We kept her going forty-five minutes, thought Toby. That's the best we could do. The best anyone could do.

The EMT stepped back. So did everyone else. It was almost a reflex, that physical retreat, those few seconds of respectful silence.

The door banged open and Dr. Carey, the thoracic surgeon, made his usual dramatic entrance. 'Where's the tamponade?' he snapped.

'She just expired,' said Toby.

'What? Didn't you stabilize her?'

'We tried. We couldn't keep her going.'

'Well, how long did you code her?'

'Believe me,' said Toby. 'It was long enough.' She pushed past him and walked out of the room.

At the nurses' desk she sat down to gather her thoughts for a moment before filling out the ER sheet. She could hear Dr. Carey in the trauma room, his voice raised in complaint. They'd dragged him out of bed at five-thirty in the morning, and for what? A patient who couldn't be stabilized? Couldn't they *think* first before they ruined his night's sleep? Didn't they know he had a full day in the OR coming up?

Why are surgeons such assholes? Toby wondered, and she dropped her head in her hands. God, would the night never end? She had one more hour to go . . .

Through the fatigue clouding her brain, she heard the whoosh of the ER doors swinging open. 'Excuse me,' said a voice. 'I'm here to see my father.'

Toby looked up at the man standing across from her. Thin-faced, unsmiling, he regarded her with an almost bitter tilt to his mouth.

Toby rose from the chair. 'Are you Mr. Slotkin?'

'Yes.'

'I'm Dr. Toby Harper.' She held out her hand.

He shook it automatically, without any warmth. Even the touch of his skin was cold. Though he had to be at least thirty years younger than his father, the man's resemblance to Harry Slotkin was immediately obvious. Daniel Slotkin's face had the same sharply cut angles, the same narrow slash of a brow. But this man's eyes were different. They were small and dark and unhappy.

'We're still evaluating your father,' she said. 'I haven't seen any of his labs come back yet.'

He glanced around the ER and made a sound of

56

impatience. 'I need to be back in the city by eight. Can I see him now?'

'Of course.' She left the desk and led him to Harry Slotkin's room. Pushing open the door, she saw that the room was empty. 'They must have him in X-ray. Let me call over and see if he's done.'

Slotkin followed her back to the front desk and stood watching her as she picked up the phone. His gaze made her uneasy. She turned away from him and dialed.

'X-ray,' answered Vince.

'This is Dr. Harper. How's the scan coming?'

'Haven't done it yet. I'm still getting things set up here.'

'The patient's son wants to see him. I'll send him over.'

'The patient isn't here.'

'What?'

'I haven't gotten him in here yet. He's still in the ER.'

'But I just checked the room. He's not . . .' Toby paused. Daniel Slotkin was listening, and he'd heard the dismay in her voice.

'Is there a problem?' asked Vince.

'No. No problem.' Toby hung up. She looked at Slotkin. 'Excuse me,' she said, and headed up the hall to exam room three. She pushed open the door. There was no Harry Slotkin. But the gurney was there, and the sheet they'd used to cover him was lying crumpled on the floor.

Someone must have put him on a different gurney, moved him to a different room.

Toby crossed the hall to exam room four and shoved aside the curtain.

No Harry Slotkin.

She could feel her heart thudding as she moved down the hall to exam room two. The lights were off. No one would have put the patient in a dark room. Nevertheless she flicked on the wall switch.

Another empty gurney.

'Don't you people know where you put my father?' snapped Daniel Slotkin, who had followed her into the hall.

Pointedly ignoring his question, she stepped into the trauma room and yanked the curtain shut behind her. 'Where's Mr. Slotkin?' Toby whispered to the nurse.

'The old guy?' asked Maudeen. 'Didn't Vince take him to X-ray?'

'He says he never got him. But I can't find the man. And the son's right outside.'

'Did you look in room three?'

'I looked in *all* the rooms!'

Maudeen and Val glanced at each other.

'We'd better check the hallways,' said Maudeen, and she and Val hurried out into the corridor.

Toby was left behind to deal with the son.

'Where is he?' demanded Slotkin.

'We're trying to locate him.'

'I thought he was supposed to be in your ER.'

'There's been some kind of mix-up—'

'Is he or isn't he here?'

'Mr. Slotkin, why don't you have a seat in the waiting room? I'll bring you a cup of coffee—'

'I don't want a cup of coffee. My father's having some kind of medical crisis. And now you can't find him?'

'The nurses are checking X-ray.'

'I thought you just called X-ray!'

'Please, if you'll just have a seat in the waiting room, we'll find out exactly what . . .' Toby's voice trailed off as she caught sight of the two nurses hurrying back toward her.

'We called Morty,' said Val. 'He and Arlo are checking the parking lot.'

'You didn't find him?'

'He can't have gone far.'

Toby felt the blood slide from her cheeks. She was afraid to look at Daniel Slotkin. Afraid to meet his gaze. But she couldn't shut out the sound of his anger.

'What is going on around here?' he demanded.

The two nurses said nothing. Both of them looked at Toby. Both of them knew that in the ER, the doctor was the captain of the ship. The one on whose shoulders rested ultimate responsibility. Ultimate blame.

'Where is my father?'

Slowly Toby turned to Daniel Slotkin. Her answer came out in barely a whisper. 'I don't know.'

It was dark, and his feet hurt, and he knew he had to get home. The trouble was, he could not remember *how* to get home. Harry Slotkin could not even remember how he'd come to be

59

stumbling down this deserted street. He thought about stopping at one of the houses along the way to ask for help, but all the windows he passed were dark. Were he to knock at one of those doors and beg for help, there would be questions and bright lights and he would almost certainly be humiliated. Harry was a proud man. He was not a man to ask for anyone's assistance. Nor did he volunteer assistance to others – not even to his own son. He'd always believed that charity, in the long run, was crippling, and he had not wanted to raise a cripple. *Strength is independence. Independence is strength.*

Somehow, he would find his own way home.

If only the angel would reappear.

She had come to him in that place of horrors, where he'd been put on a cold table and lights had blinded his eyes, the place where strangers had poked him with needles and jabbed him with their probing fingers. Then the angel had appeared. She hadn't hurt him at all. Instead she had smiled at him as she untied his hands and feet, and she had whispered: 'Go, Harry! Before they come back for you.'

Now he was free. He'd escaped, good for him!

He continued down the street of dark and silent houses, searching for some familiar landmark. Anything to tell him where he was.

I must have gotten turned around, he thought. *Went out for a walk and lost my way.*

Pain suddenly bit into his foot. He looked down and halted in amazement.

Beneath the glow of a streetlamp, he saw that he was wearing no shoes. Or socks, either. He stared at his bare feet. At his bare legs. At his penis, hanging limp and shriveled and utterly pitiful.

I'm not wearing any clothes!

In panic he glanced around to see if anyone was looking at him. The street was deserted.

Cupping his hands over his genitals, he fled the streetlamp, seeking the cover of darkness. When had he lost his clothes? He couldn't remember. He squatted down on the cold, clipped lawn of a front yard and tried to think, but panic had crowded out all memories of what had happened earlier that night. He began to whimper soft little grunts and sobs as he rocked back and forth on his bare feet.

I want to go home. Please, oh please, if I could just wake up in my own bed . . .

He was hugging himself now, so lost in despair that he didn't notice the headlights rounding the far corner. Only when the van braked to a stop right beside him did Harry realize he'd been spotted. He clasped his arms tighter, curling into a shivering self-embrace.

A voice called softly through the darkness. 'Harry?'

He didn't raise his head. He was afraid to unfold his body, afraid to reveal his humiliating state of undress. He tried to squeeze himself into a tighter and tighter ball.

'Harry, I've come to take you home.'

Slowly he raised his head. He could not make

out the face of the driver, but the voice was one he knew. Or thought he knew.

'Step into the van, Harry.'

He rocked back and forth on his heels and felt the wet grass brush against his bare buttocks. His voice rose in a high, thin wail. 'But I have no clothes!'

'You have clothes at home. A whole closet of suits. Remember?' There was a soft clunk, the whine of metal sliding across metal.

Harry looked up and saw that the van door was open. Darkness gaped beyond. The silhouette of a man was standing beside the vehicle. The man extended his hand in a gesture of invitation.

'Come, Harry,' he whispered. 'Let's go home.'

Four

How hard can it be to find a naked man?

Toby sat in her car, squinting out at the hospital parking lot. It was already midmorning, and the sunlight seemed excruciatingly bright to her night-accustomed eyes. When had the sun come up? She hadn't seen it rise, hadn't enjoyed a single free moment to glance outside, and the daylight was a shock to her retinas. That's what came of choosing the graveyard shift. She was transforming into a creature of the night.

She sighed and started up the Mercedes. At last it was time to go home, time to leave behind the night's disasters.

But as she drove away from Springer Hospital, she was unable to shake off her gloom. Within the span of a single hour, she had lost two patients. She felt certain that the woman's death had been unavoidable, that there was nothing she could have done to save her.

Harry Slotkin was a different matter. Toby had left a confused patient unattended for nearly an hour. She was the last person to lay eyes on Harry, and try as she might, she could not remember whether she had restrained his wrists before she left the room. *I must have left him untied. It's the only way he could have escaped. It's my fault. Harry was my fault.*

Even if it *hadn't* been her fault, she was still the captain of the team, the person ultimately responsible. Now somewhere, an old man was wandering, naked and confused.

She slowed the car. Though she knew the police had already searched this area, she scanned the streets, hoping for a glimpse of her fugitive patient. Newton was a relatively safe suburb of Boston, and the neighborhood she was now driving through had the look of wealth. She turned onto a tree-lined residential street and saw well-kept houses, trimmed hedges, driveways fronted by iron gates. Not the sort of neighborhood where an old man would be assaulted. Perhaps someone had taken him in. Perhaps, right at this moment, Harry was sitting in a cozy kitchen, being fed breakfast.

Where are you, Harry?

She circled the neighborhood, trying to picture these streets from Harry's point of view. It would have been dark, confusing, cold without his clothes. Where did he think he was going?

Home. He would try to find his way home to Brant Hill.

Twice she had to stop and ask for directions. When at last she came to the turnoff for Brant Hill

Road, she almost drove right past it. There were no signs; the road was marked only by two stone pillars flanking the entrance. Between them, the gate hung open. She pulled to a stop between the pillars and saw that two letters were scrolled into the gate's cast iron design, an elegantly baroque *B* and *H*. Beyond the pillars, the road twisted away and vanished behind deciduous trees. So this is Harry's neighborhood, she thought.

She drove through the open gate, onto Brant Hill Road.

Though the road was newly paved, the maple and oak trees flanking it were fully mature. Some of the leaves were tinged with the first blazing hues of fall. Already September, she thought; when had the summer gone by? She followed the curving road, glancing at the trees on either side, noting the heavy undergrowth and all the shadowy places that might conceal a body. Had the police searched that shrubbery? If Harry had wandered this way in the dark, he might have gotten lost in those bushes. She would call the Newton police, suggest they take a closer look at this road.

Up ahead, the trees suddenly thinned, giving way to a panorama that was so unexpected Toby braked to a sudden stop. At the side of the road was a sign in green and gold.

BRANT HILL
RESIDENTS AND GUESTS ONLY

Beyond the sign stretched a landscape that might have been lifted from a lush painting of English countryside. She saw gently rolling fields of manicured grass, a topiary garden with fanciful animals, and autumn-tinged stands of birch and maple. Glistening like a jewel was a pond with wild irises. A pair of swans glided serenely among water lilies. Beyond the pond was a 'village,' an elegant cluster of homes, each with its own picket-fenced garden. The primary mode of transportation seemed to be golf carts with green and white awnings. The carts were everywhere, parked in driveways or gliding along village paths. Toby also spotted a few rolling about on the golf course, shuttling players from green to green.

She focused on the pond, suddenly wondering how deep the water was, and whether a man could drown in it. At night, in the dark, a confused man might walk straight into that water.

She continued driving down the road, toward the village. Fifty yards later, she saw a turnoff to the right, and another sign.

BRANT HILL CLINIC
AND RESIDENTIAL CARE FACILITY

She took the turnoff.

The road twisted through evergreen forest, to emerge suddenly and unexpectedly into a parking lot. A three-story building loomed ahead. To one side of it, construction on a new wing was about to start. Through the mesh fence ringing the side,

66

she saw the foundation pit had already been dug. At the edge of the pit, a circle of men in hardhats stood conferring over blueprints.

Toby parked in the visitors' lot and walked into the clinic building.

The whisper of classical music greeted her. Toby paused, impressed by her surroundings. This was not your usual waiting room. The couches were buttery leather, and original oil paintings hung on the walls. She looked down at the array of magazines. *Architectural Digest. Town & Country.* No *Popular Mechanics* on this coffee table.

'May I help you?' A woman in a pink nurse's uniform smiled from behind the reception window.

Toby approached her. 'I'm Dr. Harper from Springer Hospital. I examined one of your patients in the ER last night. I've been trying to contact the patient's physician for more medical history, but I can't seem to reach him.'

'Which doctor?'

'Dr. Carl Wallenberg.'

'Oh, he's away at a medical conference. He'll be back in clinic on Monday.'

'May I look at the patient's record? It might clear up a few medical questions for me.'

'I'm sorry, but we can't release records without authorization from the patient.'

'The patient's unable to give consent. Couldn't I talk to one of your other clinic doctors?'

'Let me pull the chart first.' The nurse crossed to a filing cabinet. 'The last name?'

'Slotkin.'

The nurse slid out a drawer and flicked through the folders. 'Harold or Agnes Slotkin?'

Toby paused. 'There's an Agnes Slotkin? Is she related to Harry?'

The nurse glanced at the chart. 'She's his wife.'

Why didn't Harry's son tell me there was a wife? she wondered. She reached in her purse and found a pen. 'Could you give me the wife's phone number? I really need to speak to her about Harry.'

'There's no phone in her room. You can just take that elevator there.'

'Where?'

'Agnes Slotkin is right upstairs in the skilled nursing facility. Room three four one.'

Toby knocked at the door. 'Mrs. Slotkin?' she called. There was no answer. She stepped into the room.

Inside a radio was playing softly, its station tuned to a classical program. White curtains hung at the window, and through the gauzy fabric, the morning sunlight shone in with a softly diffuse glow. On the nightstand roses in a vase shed pink petals. The woman in the bed lay unaware of any of this. Not the flowers nor the sunlight nor the presence of a visitor in her room.

Toby approached the bed. 'Agnes?'

The woman didn't stir. She was lying on her left side, facing the door. Her eyes were half-open but unfocused, her body positioned by pillows propped behind her back. Her arms were curled into a fetal self-embrace. Above the bed, a bag of creamy white liquid dripped into a feeding tube that snaked into the woman's nostril. Though the linens looked clean, an odor hung in the air, undisguised by the scent of roses. It was the smell of the stroke ward, of talcum powder and urine and Ensure. The smell of a body slowly involuting.

Toby reached for the woman's hand. Gently she tugged the arm straight. The elbow extended with only slight resistance. No permanent contractures had set in; the nursing staff had been diligent with the passive range-of-motion exercises. Toby lay the hand down, noting the plumpness of the flesh. Despite her comatose state, the patient had been kept well nourished, well hydrated.

Toby focused on the slack face and wondered if those eyes were looking at her. Could the woman see anything, comprehend anything?

'Hello, Mrs. Slotkin,' she murmured. 'My name is Toby.'

'Agnes can't answer you,' a voice said behind her. 'But I do believe she can hear you.'

Startled, Toby turned to face the man who'd just spoken. He was standing in the doorway – in truth, he *filled* the doorway, a giant of a man with a broad black face and a gleaming wedge of a nose. It was a nice face, she thought, because he had kind eyes. He was wearing a white doctor's coat, and he held a medical chart.

Smiling, he extended his hand. His arm was so long the wrist poked out beyond the sleeve's edge.

Did they make lab coats large enough for a man this size? she wondered.

'Dr. Robbie Brace,' he said. 'I'm Mrs. Slotkin's doc. Are you a relative?'

'No.' Toby shook the man's hand, felt it engulf hers like a warm brown glove. 'I'm an ER doc at Springer Hospital, down the road. Toby Harper.'

'Professional call?'

'In a way. I was hoping Mrs. Slotkin could tell me about her husband's medical history.'

'Is something wrong with Mr. Slotkin?'

'He was brought into the ER last night, confused and disoriented. Before I could finish my workup, Harry left the hospital. Now we can't find him, and I have no idea what was wrong with him. Would you know his history?'

'I just take care of nursing home inpatients. You might check with the doctors in the outpatient clinic downstairs.'

'Harry's a patient of Dr. Wallenberg's. But Wallenberg's out of town. And the clinic won't release records to me without his approval.'

Robbie Brace shrugged. 'That's the standing policy here.'

'Do you know Harry? Is there some medical problem I should be aware of?'

'I only know Mr. Slotkin in passing. I see him when he comes to visit Agnes.'

'So you have spoken to Harry.'

'Yeah, we'd say hello, that's all. I've only been working here a month, and I'm still trying to put names to faces.'

'Do you have the authority to release Harry's records to me?'

He shook his head. 'Only Dr. Wallenberg can, and he requires a patient's written consent before he'll release any information.'

'But this could affect his patient's medical care.'

He frowned. 'Didn't you say Harry walked out of your ER?'

'Well yes, he did—'

'So he's not really your patient anymore, is he?'

Toby paused, unable to contradict that statement. Harry *had* walked out of her ER. He *had* left her care. She had no pressing reason to demand his records.

She looked down at the woman in the bed. 'I guess Mrs. Slotkin can't tell me anything, either.'

'I'm afraid Agnes doesn't talk at all.'

'Was it a stroke?'

'Subarachnoid hemorrhage. According to her chart, she's been here a year. Seems to remain in a vegetative state. But every so often, she'll sort of look at me. Don't you, Agnes?' he said. 'Don't you look at me, honey?'

The woman in the bed didn't stir, didn't even flutter an eyelash. He moved to the bedside and began to examine his patient, his black hands a startling contrast against the woman's pallor. With his stethoscope he listened to her heart and lungs, and checked her abdomen for bowel sounds. He shone a light in her pupils. He extended her limbs, checking for resistance to range of motion. Finally he rolled her toward him and examined the skin on her back and buttocks. No bedsores. Gently he repositioned her against the pillows and folded the sheet over her chest.

'Lookin' good, Agnes,' he murmured, patting her on the shoulder. 'You have yourself a nice day.'

Toby followed him out of the room, feeling like a midget tagging at a giant's heels. 'She's in good condition for someone who's been vegetative for a year.'

He opened the chart and scribbled his progress note. 'Well, of course. We give genuine Rolls-Royce care.'

'At Rolls-Royce prices?'

Brace glanced up from the chart, the first hint of a grin on his lips. 'Let's just say, we don't have any Medicaid patients.'

'They're all private pay?'

'They can afford it. We've got some pretty wealthy residents.'

'Is this place exclusively for retirees?'

'No, we have a few active professionals who've bought into Brant Hill just to guarantee that their future needs are taken care of. We provide housing, meals, medical care. Long-term care, if it becomes necessary. You probably saw we're already expanding the nursing home.'

'I also noticed a very nice golf course.'

'Along with tennis courts, a movie theater, and an indoor pool.' He closed the chart and grinned at her. 'Sorta makes you want to retire early, doesn't it?'

'I don't think I could afford to retire here.'

'I'll let you in on a secret: neither one of us could.' He glanced at his watch. 'It was nice meeting you, Dr. Harper. If you'll excuse me, I've got a lot of patients to see.'

'Is there any way I could find out more about Harry?'

'Dr. Wallenberg's back on Monday. You can talk to him then.'

'I'd like to know *now* what I was dealing with. It's really bothering me. Couldn't you review the outpatient record? Call me if you find anything relevant?' She scribbled her home phone number on a business card and handed it to him.

Reluctantly, he took the card. 'I'll see what I can do,' was all he said. Then he turned and walked into a patient's room, leaving Toby standing alone in the hallway.

She turned from the closed door and sighed. She'd done her best to track down the information, but Brant Hill wasn't cooperating. Now hunger and fatigue were dragging her down, and she could feel her body issuing demands. *Food. Sleep. Now.* In slow motion, legs sluggish, she began to walk toward the elevators. Halfway there, she halted.

Someone was screaming.

It came from one of the patient rooms at the end of the hall – not a cry of pain, but of fear.

As Toby ran toward the screams, she heard other voices spilling into the hallway behind her, heard footsteps following at a run. Toby reached the room ahead of everyone else and shoved open the door.

At first all she saw was the elderly man crouching on hands and knees on the bed. He was naked below the waist, and his wrinkled buttocks were bobbing up and down in a doglike mating dance.

Then Toby saw the trapped woman underneath him, her frail body almost hidden among the tangle of blankets and sheets.

'Get him off me! Please get him off me!' the woman cried.

Toby grabbed the man's arm and tried to drag him away. He responded with a shove so powerful it sent Toby sprawling backward to the floor. A nurse ran into the room.

'Mr. Hackett, stop it! *Stop it!*' The nurse tried to pull the man away, but she too was flung aside.

Toby scrambled back to her feet. 'You grab one arm, I'll get the other!' she said, circling around to the far side of the bed. Together, she and the nurse took hold of the man's arms. Even as he was dragged off the woman, he kept thrusting like a grotesque sexual robot without an off switch. The woman on the bed curled up into a fetal position and began to cry as she hugged herself among the blankets.

Suddenly the man twisted, elbowing Toby under the chin. The jab slammed her jaw shut, ramming a bolt of pain straight through her skull. She saw a burst of white and almost released him, but sheer rage kept her holding on. He lashed out at her again. They were grappling like animals now, and she could smell his sweat, could feel every muscle in his body straining against her. The nurse

74

lost her footing and stumbled, releasing her grip. The old man reached behind Toby's head and grabbed a fistful of her hair. He was thrusting at *her* now, his erect penis stabbing at her hip. Disgust and fury boiled up in her throat. She tensed her thigh, preparing to knee him in the groin.

Then her target was gone. The man was lifted away by a pair of huge black hands. Robbie Brace hauled the man halfway across the room and barked to the nurse: 'Get me some Haldol! Five milligrams IM STAT!'

The nurse ran from the room. She came back a moment later, syringe in hand.

'C'mon, I can't hold him forever,' said Brace.

'Let me get at his butt—'

'Do it, do it!'

'But he keeps squirming away—'

'Man, this guy's strong. What've you been feeding him?'

'He's a protocol patient – plus he's got Alzheimer's – I can't get at him!'

Brace shifted his grip, turning the man's rear end toward the nurse. She pinched a fold of bare buttock and stabbed it with the needle. The old man shrieked. Bucking, he yanked away from Brace. In a blur of motion, he grabbed a water glass from the nightstand and swung it at the doctor's face.

The glass shattered against Brace's temple.

Toby lunged, catching the old man's wrist before he could swing again. Viciously she twisted

75

his hand and the broken shard tumbled from his grasp.

Brace wrapped giant arms around the man's shoulders and yelled, 'Give him the rest of the Haldol!'

Again the nurse jabbed the needle into the man's buttock and squeezed the plunger. 'It's all in! God, I hope this works better than the Mellaril.'

'This guy's on Mellaril?'

'Around the clock. I *told* Dr. Wallenberg it wasn't holding him. These Alzheimer's patients need to be watched every second or they—' The nurse took in a sharp breath. 'Dr. Brace, you're bleeding!'

Toby glanced up and was alarmed to see blood trickling down Brace's cheek and splattering his white coat. The broken glass had sliced open the skin on his temple.

'We have to stop that bleeding,' said Toby. 'It's obvious you'll need stitches.'

'First let me get this guy into a nice tight Posey restraint. Come on, sir. Let's get you back to your room.'

The old man let fly a glob of spit. 'Nigger! Let me go!'

'Oh man,' said Brace. 'You're trying to get on my good side, aren't you?'

'Don't like niggers.'

'Yeah, you and everyone else,' said Brace, sounding more tired than angry. He half-dragged, half-marched the old man out of the room and

76

into the hall. 'Buddy, it looks like you've earned yourself a date with a straitjacket.'

'Ouch. Don't make me look like Frankenstein's monster, okay?'

Gently Toby emptied the syringe of Xylocaine and withdrew the needle. She had injected local anesthetic along both edges of Robbie's laceration and now she gave the skin a gentle prick. 'Feel that?'

'Nope. It's numb.'

'Are you sure you wouldn't rather have a plastic surgeon stitch you up?'

'You're an ER doc. Don't you do this all the time?'

'Yes, but if you're concerned about the cosmetic result—'

'Why would I be? I'm already so damn ugly. A scar will be an improvement.'

'Well, it'll give your face character,' she said and reached for the needle forceps and suture. She'd found all the supplies she needed in the well-stocked treatment room. Like everything else at Brant Hill, the equipment was spanking new and top of the line. The table where Robbie Brace lay could be adjusted to a wide variety of positions, which made it convenient for treating anything from scalp wounds to hemorrhoids. The overhead lights were bright enough for surgery. And in the corner, ready for emergencies, was the cardiac crash cart, a state-of-the-art model, of course.

She swabbed the wound again with Betadine

and poked the curved suture needle through the edges of the laceration. Robbie Brace lay on his side, perfectly still. Most patients would have closed their eyes, but he kept his wide open and staring at the opposite wall. Though his size was intimidating, his eyes seemed to neutralize any threat. They were a soft brown, the lashes thick as a child's.

She took another stitch and drew the suture through his skin. 'The old guy cut pretty deep,' she said. 'You're lucky he missed your eye.'

'I think he was trying for my throat.'

'And he's on round-the-clock sedation?' She shook her head. 'You'd better double the dose and keep him locked up.'

'He usually is. We keep the Alzheimer's patients in a separate ward, where we can control their movements. I guess Mr. Hackett slipped out. And you know sometimes those old guys can't handle the libido. The self-control's gone, but the body's still willing.'

Toby snipped off the needle and tied the last stitch. The wound was closed now, and she began wiping the site with alcohol. 'What protocol is he on?' she asked.

'Hm?'

'The nurse said Mr. Hackett was on some kind of protocol.'

'Oh. It's something Wallenberg's testing. Hormone injections in elderly men.'

'For what purpose?'

'The fountain of youth, what else? We've got a

wealthy clientele, and most of them want to live forever. They're all eager to volunteer for the latest treatment fad.' He sat up on the side of the table and gave his head a shake, as though to dispel a sudden rush of dizziness. Toby thought with sudden panic: The bigger they are, the harder they fall. And the harder they are to pick up off the floor.

'Lie back down,' she said. 'You got up too fast.'

'I'm fine. I've gotta get back to work.'

'No, you sit there, okay? Or you'll fall and I'll just have to stitch up the other side of your face.'

'Another scar,' he grunted. 'More character.'

'You're already a character, Dr. Brace.'

He smiled, but his gaze looked a little unfocused. Warily she watched him for a moment, ready to catch him if he passed out, but he managed to stay upright.

'So tell me more about the protocol,' she said. 'Which hormones is Wallenberg injecting?'

'It's a cocktail. Growth hormone. Testosterone. DHEA. A few others. There's plenty of research to back it all up.'

'I know growth hormone increases muscle mass in the elderly. But I haven't seen many studies using it in combination.'

'It makes sense though, doesn't it? As you get older, your pituitary starts to fade out. Doesn't produce all those juicy young hormones. The theory is, that's the reason we age. Our hormones conk out.'

'So Wallenberg replaces them.'

'It seems to be having *some* effect. Look at Mr. Hackett. Plenty of get up and go.'

'Too much. Why're you giving hormones to an Alzheimer's patient? He can't give consent.'

'He probably gave consent years ago, while he was still competent.'

'The study's been going on that long?'

'Wallenberg's research dates back to '92. Check out the *Index Medicus*. You'll see his name pop up on a dozen published papers. Everyone working in geriatrics knows Wallenberg's name.' Gingerly he lowered himself from the table. After a moment, he nodded. 'Steady as a rock. So when do these stitches come out?'

'Five days.'

'And when do I get the bill?'

She smiled. 'No bill. Just do me a favor.'

'Uh, oh.'

'Look up Harry Slotkin's medical record. Call me if there's anything I should know. If there's anything I might have missed.'

'You think you might have missed something?'

'I don't know. But I hate screwing up, I really do. Harry may be lucid enough to find his way back to Brant Hill. Maybe even to his wife's room. Keep an eye out for him.'

'I'll tell the nurses.'

'He shouldn't be hard to miss.' She reached for her purse. 'He's not wearing a stitch of clothes.'

* * *

Toby pulled into her driveway, parked next to Bryan's Honda, and turned off the engine. She didn't climb out of her car but simply sat there for a moment, listening to the *tick-tick* of the engine cooling off, enjoying these quiet moments, undisturbed by the demands of others. So many, many demands. She took a deep breath and leaned back against the neck rest. It was nine-thirty, a quiet hour in this neighborhood of suburban professionals. Couples had left for work, the kids were packed off to school or day care, and houses stood empty, awaiting the arrival of domestics who would vacuum and scrub and then vanish, leaving behind their telltale scent of lemon wax. It was a safe neighborhood of well-tended homes, not the most elegant section of Newton, but it satisfied Toby's need for some sort of order in her life. After the unpredictability of a shift in the ER, a manicured lawn had its attractions.

Down the street, a leaf blower suddenly roared to life. Her moment of silence had ended. The yard service trucks had begun their daily invasion of the neighborhood.

Reluctantly she stepped out of the Mercedes and climbed the porch steps.

Bryan, her mother's hired companion, was already waiting at the front door, arms crossed, eyes narrowed in reproval. He was jockey size, a trim young man in miniature, but he presented an imposing barrier.

'Your mama's been bouncing off the walls this morning,' he said. 'You shouldn't do this to her.'

'Didn't you tell her I'd be late getting home?'

'Doesn't do any good. You know she can't understand. She expects you home early, and when you don't get here, she does her thing at the windows. You know, back and forth, back and forth, watching for your car.'

'I'm sorry, Bryan. It couldn't be helped.' Toby walked past him, into the house and set her purse down on the hall table. She took her time hanging up her jacket, thinking: *Don't get annoyed. Don't lose your temper. You need him. Mom needs him.*

'It doesn't matter to me if you're two hours late,' he said. 'I get paid. I get paid a lot, thank you very much. But your mama, poor thing, she doesn't get it.'

'We had some problems at work.'

'She wouldn't touch her breakfast. So now she's got a plate of cold eggs.'

Toby shut the closet door, hard. '*I will make her another breakfast.*'

There was a silence.

She stood with her back to him, her hand still pressed to the closet, thinking: I didn't mean to sound so angry. But I'm tired. I'm so very tired.

'Well,' said Bryan, and in that one word he communicated everything. Hurt. Withdrawal.

She turned to face him. They had known each other for two years now, yet they had never gone beyond the relationship of employer-employee, had never crossed that barrier into real friendship. She'd never visited his house, had never met Noel, the man with whom he lived. Yet she realized, at

82

that moment, that she had come to depend on Bryan more than she depended on anyone else. *He* was the one who kept her life sane, and she couldn't afford to lose him.

She said, 'I'm sorry. I just can't handle another crisis right now. I've had a really shitty night.'

'What happened?'

'We lost two patients. In one hour. And I'm feeling pretty awful about it. I didn't mean to take it out on you.'

He gave a slight nod, a grudging acceptance of her apology.

'And how was your night?' she asked.

'She slept all the way through. I just took her out to the garden. That always seems to quiet her down.'

'I hope she hasn't picked all the lettuce.'

'I hate to break this to you, but your lettuce went to seed a month ago.'

All right, so I'm a failure as a gardener too, thought Toby as she headed through the kitchen to the back door. Every year, with high hopes, she started a vegetable patch. She would plant rows of lettuce and zucchini and green beans, would successfully nurture them along to seedling stage. Then, inevitably, her life would get too busy and she'd neglect the garden. The lettuce would bolt, and the beans would hang yellow and woody from the vines. In disgust she'd yank it all out and promise herself a better garden next year, knowing that the next year would produce only another crop of zucchinis as inedible as baseball bats.

She stepped outside into the yard. At first she didn't see her mother. The summer flower garden had grown into a weedy jungle of chin-high flowers and vines. There had always been a pleasant randomness to this garden, as though the beds had been dug with no plan in mind, but rather had been expanded by the original gardener's whim, season by season. When Toby had bought the house eight years ago, she'd planned to tear out the more unruly plants, to ruthlessly enforce some form of horticultural discipline. It was Ellen who'd talked her out of it, Ellen who'd explained that, in the garden, disorder was to be cherished.

Now Toby stood by the back door, surveying a yard so overgrown she could not even see the brick pathway. Something rustled among the flower stalks, and a straw hat bobbed into view. It was Ellen, crawling on her knees in the dirt.

'Mom, I'm home.'

The straw hat tipped up, revealing Ellen Harper's round, sunburned face. She saw her daughter and waved, something dangling from her hand. As Toby crossed the yard and stepped through the tangle of vines, her mother rose to her feet, and Toby saw that she was clutching a fistful of dandelions. It was one of the ironies of Ellen's illness that although she had forgotten so many things – how to cook, how to bathe herself – she had not forgotten, would probably never forget, how to distinguish a weed from a flower.

'Bryan says you haven't eaten yet,' said Toby.

'No, I think I did. Didn't I?'

'Well, I'm going to make some breakfast. Why don't you come inside and eat with me?'

'But I have so much work to do.' Sighing, Ellen looked around at the flower beds. 'I never seem to get it all done. You see these things here? These bad things?' She waved the limp plants she was holding.

'Those are dandelions.'

'Yes. Well, these things are taking over. If I don't pull them up, they'll get into those purple things over there. What do you call them . . .'

'The purple flowers? I really don't know, Mom.'

'Anyway, there's only so much room, then things have to be cleaned out. It's a fight for more room. I have so much work, and I never have enough time.' She gazed around the garden, her cheeks ruddy from the sun. *So much to do, never enough time.* That was Ellen's mantra, a recurrent loop of words that remained intact while the rest of her memory disintegrated. Why had that particular phrase persisted in Ellen's mind? Had her life as a widowed mother of two girls been so stamped by the pressures of time, of tasks undone?

Ellen dropped back to her knees and began rooting around in the dirt again. For what, Toby didn't know; perhaps more of those hated dandelions. Toby looked up and saw that the sky was cloudless, the day pleasantly warm. Ellen would be fine out here, unsupervised. The gate was locked, and she seemed content. This was their routine during the summertime. Toby would make her mother a sandwich and leave it on the kitchen countertop, and then she would go to bed. At four in the afternoon, she'd wake up, and she and Ellen would eat supper together.

She heard the rattle of Bryan's car driving away. At six-thirty he would be back to stay with Ellen for the night. And Toby would leave, once again, for her usual shift at the hospital.

So much to do, never enough time. It was becoming Toby's mantra as well. Like mother, like daughter, never enough time.

She took a deep breath and slowly released it. The adrenaline from this morning's crisis had worn off and now she felt the fatigue weighing down on her like so many stones on her shoulders. She knew she should go straight up to bed, but she couldn't seem to move. Instead she stood watching her mother, thinking how young Ellen looked, not elderly at all, but more like a round-faced girl in a floppy hat. A girl happily making mud pies in the garden.

I'm the mother now, thought Toby. And like any mother, she was suddenly aware of how quickly time passed, moments passed.

She knelt down beside her mother in the dirt.

Ellen looked sideways at her, a trace of bewilderment in her light blue eyes. 'Do you need something, dear?' she asked.

'No, Mom. I just thought I'd help you pull a few weeds.'

'Oh.' Ellen smiled and lifted a dirt-stained hand

to stroke back a tendril of hair off Toby's cheek. 'Are you certain you know which ones to pull?'

'Why don't you show me?'

'Here.' Gently, Ellen guided Toby's hand to a clump of green. 'You can start with these.'

And, side by side, mother and daughter knelt in the dirt and began to pull dandelions.

Five

Angus Parmenter turned up the speed on the treadmill and felt the moving belt give a little jerk under his feet. He accelerated his stride to a brisk six miles per hour. His pulse sped up as well; he could see it on the digital readout, mounted on the treadmill hand-grips. 112. 116. 120. Had to get that heart rate up, the blood flowing. *Push yourself! Oxygen in, oxygen out. Get those muscles pumping.*

On the movie screen mounted in front of him, the 'boredom-buster' video played scenes from the cobbled streets of a Greek village. But his gaze remained focused on the digital readout. He watched his pulse climb to 130. At last, target heart rate. He would try to keep it there for the next twenty minutes, give himself a good aerobic workout. Then he would cool down, letting his pulse gradually drop to a hundred, then eighty, then down to his usual resting pulse of sixty-eight. After that, it was time for a session on the Nautilus, an upper-body workout, and afterward he'd hit the showers. By then it would be time for lunch, a low-fat, high-protein, high-roughage meal served in the country club dining room. With the meal would come a few of his daily pills: vitamin E, vitamin C, zinc, selenium. An arsenal of magic remedies to keep the years at bay.

It all seemed to be working. At eighty-two years old, Angus Parmenter had never felt better in his life. And he was enjoying the fruits of his labors. He had worked hard for his fortune, harder than any of these whining kids would ever work in *their* lives. He had money, and he intended to live long enough to spend it, every last goddamn penny. Let the next generation earn their own fortunes. This was *his* time to play.

After lunch, there'd be a round of golf with Phil Dorr and Jim Bigelow, his friendly rivals. Then he had the option of riding the Brant Hill van into the city. Tonight they were planning a trip to the Wang Center for a performance of *Cats*. He'd probably skip that one. All those ladies might go wild over singing kitty cats, but not him; he'd seen the show on Broadway, and once was more than enough.

He heard the stationary bicycle begin to whir beside him and he glanced sideways. Jim Bigelow was frantically pedaling away.

Angus nodded. 'Hey, Jim.'

'Hello, Angus.'

For a moment they sweated side by side, too focused on their exercise to speak. On the screen ahead, the video changed from a Greek village to a muddy road in a rain forest. Angus's heart rate remained steady at 130 beats per minute.

'Have you heard anything yet?' asked Bigelow over the whir of his bicycle. 'About Harry?'

'Nope.'

'I saw them . . . the police . . . they're dragging the pond.' Bigelow was panting, having trouble talking and pedaling at the same time. His own fault, thought Angus. Bigelow liked his desserts, and he came to the gym only once a week. He hated exercise, hated healthy foods. At seventy-six, Bigelow looked his age.

'I heard . . . at breakfast . . . they haven't found him yet . . .' Bigelow leaned forward, his face a bright pink from exertion.

'That's the last I heard, too,' said Angus.

'Funny. Not like Harry.'

'No, it's not.'

'Wasn't acting right . . . over the weekend. Did you notice?'

'What do you mean?'

'Had his shirt inside out. Socks didn't match. Not like Harry at all.'

Angus kept his gaze straight ahead on the video screen. Jungle saplings parted before him. A boa constrictor slithered on a tree branch overhead.

'And did you notice . . . his hands?' panted Bigelow.

'What about them?'

'They were shaking. Last week.'

Angus said nothing. He gripped the treadmill bar and concentrated on his stride. *Walk, walk.*

Pump those calves, keep them firm and young.

'Funniest damn thing,' said Bigelow. 'This business about Harry. You don't suppose . . .'

'I don't suppose anything, Jim. Let's just hope he turns up.'

'Yeah.' Bigelow stopped pedaling. He sat catching his breath and staring at the video screen, where a tropical rainstorm was now pounding the jungle ferns. 'Trouble is,' he said quietly, 'I don't expect he will turn up all right. It's been two days.'

Angus abruptly switched off the treadmill. Forget the cooldown. He'd move straight to the upper body workout. He slung his towel over his shoulder and crossed the room to the Nautilus. To his annoyance, Bigelow got off the bike and followed him.

Ignoring Bigelow, Angus sat down on the bench and started with his latissimus dorsi workout.

'Angus,' said Bigelow, 'Doesn't it worry you?'

'There's nothing we can do about it, Jim. The police are looking.'

'No, I mean doesn't it remind you of . . .' Bigelow's voice dropped to a murmur. 'What happened to Stan Mackie?'

Angus went still, his hands gripping the Nautilus pulleys. 'That happened months ago.'

'Yes, but it was the same thing. Remember how he showed up with his fly unzipped? And then he forgot Phil's name. You don't forget the name of your best friend.'

'Phil's quite forgettable.'

'I can't believe you're so flippant about this.

First we lose Stan. And now Harry. What if—'
Bigelow paused and glanced around the gym, as
though afraid someone else might be listening.
'What if something's going wrong? What if we're
all getting sick?'

'Stan's death was a suicide.'

'That's what they *say*. But people don't go
jumping out of windows for no reason.'

'Did you know Stan well enough to say he
didn't have a reason?'

Bigelow looked down. 'No . . .'

'Well, then.' Angus resumed working at the
pulleys. *Pull, release. Pull, release. Keep those
muscles young . . .*

Bigelow sighed. 'I can't help wondering. I never
felt right about it. Maybe this is some sort of . . . I
don't know. Divine consequence. Maybe it's what
we deserve.'

'Don't be so Catholic, Jim! You're always waiting for a lightning bolt to hit you. It's been a year
and a half, and I've never felt better in my life.' He
stretched out his leg. 'Look at my quadriceps! See
the muscle definition? It wasn't there two years
ago.'

'My quadriceps hasn't improved any,' Bigelow
noted glumly.

'That's because you're not working at it. And
you worry too damn much.'

'Yes, I suppose I do.' Bigelow sighed and looped
his towel around his neck. It made him look like
some old tortoise poking its head out of its shell.
'Are we still on for this afternoon?'

'Phil hasn't said otherwise.'

'Right. Then see you at the first tee.'

Angus watched his friend lumber out of the gym. Bigelow was looking old, and no wonder; he'd spent only ten minutes on the bike, hardly an aerobic workout. Some people just couldn't commit to their own health. Instead they wasted their energy worrying about things they could do nothing about.

His latissimus dorsi muscles were burning with that pleasant ache of a thorough workout. He released the pulleys and rested for a moment. Looking around the gym, he saw that all the other machines were in use, mostly by women, the granny set in their sweat suits and tennis shoes. A few of the ladies glanced his way, flashing him the come-hither look he found so ridiculous in women their age. They were far too old for his taste. A woman of, say, fifty might be more to his liking. But only if she was slim and fit enough to keep up with him, in every way.

It was time to work on the pectorals.

He reached up for the appropriate arm grips and was about to make the first squeeze when he noticed that something was wrong with the machine. The right-hand grip seemed to be vibrating.

He released his hold and stared at the grip. It was perfectly still, no vibrations at all. Then he looked down, and felt a sudden chill. *What is going on?*

His right hand was shaking.

* * *

Molly Picker raised her head from the toilet and pulled the flush lever. There was nothing left in her stomach; she'd thrown it all up. Pepsi, Fritos, and Lucky Charms. Dizzy, she sat down on the floor, leaned her back against the bathroom wall, and listened to the water whoosh down the pipes. Three weeks, she thought. I been sick for three weeks now.

She dragged herself to her feet and stumbled back to bed. Curling up on the lumpy mattress, she fell quickly and deeply asleep.

At noon, she woke up when Romy walked into her room. He didn't bother to knock first; he sat down on the bed and gave her a shake. 'Hey, Molly Wolly. Still got the ol' stomach bug?'

Groaning, she looked at him. Romy reminded her of a reptile, his hair all slicked back and shiny, his eyes so dark you couldn't see the pupils. Lizard man. But the hand stroking her hair was gentle – an aspect of Romy she hadn't seen in such a very long time. He gave her a smile. 'Not so good today, huh?'

'I threw up again. I can't stop throwing up.'

'Yeah, well, I finally got you something for that.' He placed a bottle of pills on the nightstand. It had a label with handwritten instructions: *Take one pill every eight hours for nausea*. Romy went into the bathroom, filled a glass with water, and returned to Molly's bed. He opened the bottle, shook a pill out, and helped her sit up. 'Down the hatch,' he said.

She frowned at the pill. 'What is this?'

'Medicine.'

'Where'd you get it?'

'It's okay. It's what the doctor ordered.'

'What doctor?'

'Here I'm trying to be nice, trying to make you feel better, and you talk back. I don't really give a shit if you take the pill or not.'

She turned away and felt his hand pressing against her back, tightening into a fist. Then, unexpectedly, he relaxed and began to rub her back in warm, coaxing strokes.

'C'mon, Moll. You know I look out for you. Always have, always will.'

She gave a bitter laugh. 'Like that makes me special.'

'You are. You're my special babe. My own best girl.' He slid his hand under her shirt and stroked across her skin. 'You been so prickly lately. Didn't feel like showing you no favors. But you know I'm always watching out for you, Molly lollipop.' He tasted her earlobe and murmured: 'Yum.'

'So what's in the pill?'

'I told you. It's so you'll stop puking and start eating again. A growing girl's gotta eat.' His lips slid down her neck, to graze her shoulder. 'If you don't eat, pretty soon I'll have to bring you to some hospital. You want to wind up in a hospital? Bunch of strange doctors?'

'I don't want to see no doctors.' She regarded the pill in her hand and felt a sudden sense of wonder, not about the pill, but about Romy. He hadn't been this sweet to her in months, hadn't paid her much attention at all. Not like before, when she *had* been his special girl. When they'd spent nights together in bed, watching MTV, eating ice cream, drinking beer. When he was the only one who'd touch her. Who was *allowed* to touch her. Before everything between them had changed.

He was smiling, not his usual small, mean smile, but one that actually touched his eyes.

She swallowed the pill and washed it down with a sip of water.

'That's my girl.' He eased her back down to the pillow and tucked her in. 'You go to sleep now.'

'Stay with me, Romy.'

'I got things to do, babe.' He stood up. 'Business.'

'I have to tell you something. I think I know why I been sick—'

'We'll talk about it later, okay?' He gave her a pat on the head and left the room.

Molly stared at the ceiling. *Three weeks is too long for the stomach flu*, she thought. She placed her hands on her belly and imagined she could already feel the swelling there. *When did I mess up? Which guy pumped in a live one?* She was always careful, always carried her own rubbers, had learned to apply them with the silky strokes of foreplay. She wasn't stupid; she knew a girl could get sick out there.

Now she really *was* sick, and she couldn't remember when she'd made the mistake.

Romy would blame *her*.

Rising from the bed, she felt light-headed. It was the hunger. These days she was always hungry, even when she felt nauseated. As she dressed, she munched on some more Fritos. The salt tasted good. She could have devoured handfuls, but there were only a few chips left. She tore the bag open and licked the crumbs, then saw herself in the mirror, her lips crusted with salt, and she was so disgusted by the image she tossed the bag into the rubbish and left her room.

It was only one-fifteen, and there was no action coming down yet. She saw Sophie up the street, leaning in a doorway as she chugged from a Pepsi can. Sophie was all butt and no brains. Determined to ignore her, Molly walked right past, her eyes focused straight ahead.

'If it isn't Miss Titless,' said Sophie.

'Bigger the tits, smaller the brain.'

'Then girl, you must have one *hell* of a big brain.'

Molly kept walking, quickening her pace to escape Sophie's whinnying laughter. She didn't stop walking until she'd reached the phone booth two blocks away. She searched the tattered copy of the Yellow Pages, then slipped a quarter into the slot and dialed.

A voice answered: 'Abortion Counseling.'

'I need to talk to someone,' said Molly. 'I'm pregnant.'

A black car glided to a stop at the curb. Romy got into the back seat and shut the door.

The driver didn't turn to look at him; he never did. Most of the time Romy found himself staring at the back of the man's head, a narrow head with white-blond hair. You didn't see that color of hair very often, not on a guy. Romy wondered if the bitches went for it. But the way he figured it, bitches didn't really care if you had any hair on your head, as long as you had money in your wallet.

Romy's wallet was feeling pretty thin these days.

He looked around at the car, admiring it as he always did, yet resentful of the fact the guy in the driver's seat was the man on top in more ways than one. Didn't need to know the man's name or what he did; you could *smell* his superiority like you could smell the fact these seats were leather. To a guy like him, Romulus Bell was just a scrap of litter that had blown into the car and would soon be ejected. Not worth a backward glance.

Romy looked at the man's exposed neck and thought how easy it'd be to turn the tables. If he wanted to. That made him feel better.

'You have something to tell me?' the driver said.

'Yeah. I got another one knocked up.'

'Are you certain?'

'Hey, I know my girls, inside and out. I know it before they do. I been right every other time, haven't I?'

'So you have.'

'What about the money? I'm supposed to get my money.'

'There's a problem.'

'What problem?'

The driver reached up and adjusted the rearview mirror. 'Annie Parini didn't show up for her appointment this morning.'

Romy stiffened, his hand gripping the seat in front of him. 'What?'

'I couldn't find her. She wasn't waiting on the Common as we agreed.'

'She was there. I walked her there myself.'

'Then she must have left before I arrived.'

The stupid bitch, he thought. How could you keep a business going when the bitches were always going against him, always screwing things up? Bitches had no brains. And now they were making *him* look bad.

'Where is Annie Parini, Mr. Bell?'

'I'll find her.'

'Do it soon. We can't let her go more than another month.' The man waved his hand. 'You can get out of the car now.'

'What about my money?'

'There's no payment today.'

'But I told you, I got another one knocked up.'

'This time we want delivery first. The last week of October. And don't lose the merchandise. Now get out, Mr. Bell.'

'I need—'

'*Get out.*'

Romy climbed out and slammed the door. At once the car drove away, leaving him staring after it in fury.

He began to walk up Tremont Street, his

agitation mounting with every step. He knew where Annie Parini hung out; he knew he could find her, and he would.

The words of the driver kept playing in his head. *This time, don't lose the merchandise.*

The phone rang, waking Toby from a sleep so deep she felt as if she was surfacing through layers of mud. She fumbled for the receiver and knocked it off its cradle. It thudded to the floor. As she rolled over in bed to retrieve the phone, she caught sight of the bedside clock. It was twelve noon – for her, the equivalent of the middle of the night. The receiver had tumbled onto the other side of the nightstand. She used the cord to haul it back up.

'Hello?'

'Dr. Harper? It's Robbie Brace.'

She lay in a stupor, struggling to remember who this man was and why his voice sounded familiar.

'Brant Hill Nursing Home?' he said. 'We met two days ago. You asked me about Harry Slotkin.'

'Oh. Yes.' She sat up, her mind suddenly swept clear of sleep. 'Thanks for calling.'

'I'm afraid there's not much to report. I have Mr. Slotkin's clinic chart in front of me and I see a clean bill of health.'

'There's nothing at all?'

'Nothing that would explain his illness. Physical exam's unremarkable. Labs look good . . .' Over the receiver, Toby could hear the rustle of pages being turned. 'He had a full endocrine panel, totally normal.'

'When was this?'

'A month ago. So whatever you saw in the ER must've been fairly acute.'

She closed her eyes and felt her stomach knotting up again with tension. 'Have you heard anything new?' she asked.

'They dragged the pond this morning. Haven't found him. Which is good, I guess.'

Yes. It means he could still be alive.

'Anyway, that's all I have to report.'

'Thank you,' she said, and hung up. She knew she should try to fall back to sleep. She was scheduled for another shift tonight, and she'd had only four hours of rest. But Robbie Brace's call had left her agitated.

The phone rang again.

She grabbed the receiver and said, 'Dr. Brace?'

The voice on the other end sounded startled. 'Uh, no. This is Paul.' Paul Hawkins was chief of Springer ER. Officially he was her boss; unofficially, he was a sympathetic ear and one of her few close friends on the medical staff.

'Sorry, Paul,' she said. 'I thought you were someone else calling back. What's up?'

'We have a problem here. We need you to come in this afternoon.'

'But I got off just a few hours ago. I'm scheduled for another shift tonight.'

'This isn't for a shift. It's for a meeting with Administration. Ellis Corcoran's asked for it.'

In the hierarchy of doctors at Springer Hospital, Corcoran, chief of the Med-Surg staff, was at the

101

top of the authority pyramid. Paul Hawkins, and every other department chief, answered to Corcoran.

Toby sat up. 'What's this meeting all about?'

'A couple of things.'

'Harry Slotkin?'

A pause. 'Partly. There are other issues they want to discuss.'

'They? Who else is going to be there?'

'Dr. Carey. Administration. They have questions about what happened that night.'

'I told you what happened.'

'Yes, and I've tried to explain it to them. But Doug Carey's got some goddamn bee in his bonnet. He's complained to Corcoran.'

She groaned. 'You know what this is really about, Paul? It has nothing to do with Harry Slotkin. It's about the Freitas boy. The one who died a few months ago. Carey's trying to get back at me.'

'This is an entirely separate issue.'

'No it's not. Carey screwed up and the kid died. I called him on it.'

'You didn't just call him on a mistake. You got him *sued* for it.'

'The boy's family asked for my opinion. Was I supposed to lie to them? Anyway, he *should* have been sued. Leaving a kid with a splenic rupture on an unmonitored floor? I'm the one who had to code the poor kid.'

'All right, so he screwed up. But you could've been more discreet with your opinions.'

And therein lay the real problem. Toby had not been discreet.

It had been the sort of code every doctor dreads: a dying child. The parents shrieking in the hallway. During her struggle to revive the boy, Toby had blurted out in frustration: *'Why isn't this boy in the ICU?'*

The parents had heard it. Eventually, the lawyers heard it too.

'Toby, right now we have to focus on the issue at hand. The meeting's scheduled for two o'clock this afternoon. They weren't going to invite you, but I insisted.'

'Why wasn't I invited? Is this a secret lynching?'

'Just try to get here, okay?'

She hung up and glanced at the clock. It was already twelve thirty; she couldn't leave until she found someone to stay with her mother. Immediately she picked up the phone again and called Bryan. She heard it ring four times, and then the answering machine picked up. *Hi, this is Noel! And this is Bryan! We're absolutely dying to hear from you, so leave a message . . .*

She hit the disconnect button and dialed another number – her sister's. *Please be home. For once, Vickie, please be there for me . . .*

'Hello?'

'It's me,' said Toby, releasing a sigh of relief.

'Can you hold on a minute? I've got something on the stove . . .'

Toby heard the receiver clunk down, and the

rattle of a pot lid. Then Vickie came back on the line.

'Sorry. Steve's partners are coming for dinner tonight and I'm trying out this new dessert—'

'Vickie, I'm up against a wall. I need you to watch Mom for a few hours.'

'You mean . . . *now*?' Vickie's laugh was sharp and incredulous.

'I've got an emergency meeting at the hospital. I'll drop her off with you and pick her up again as soon as the meeting's over.'

'Toby, I've got company coming tonight. I'm cooking, the house still needs to be cleaned, and the kids're coming home from school.'

'Mom's no trouble, really. She'll keep herself busy in the backyard.'

'I can't have her wandering in the yard! We just put in new grass—'

'Then set her in front of the TV. I've got to leave now or I'm not going to make it.'

'Toby—'

She slammed the receiver down. She didn't have the time or patience to argue; Vickie's house was half an hour's drive away.

She found Ellen outside, happily mucking round in the compost heap.

'Mom,' said Toby. 'We have to go to Vickie's house.'

Ellen straightened, and Toby was dismayed to see her mother's hands were filthy, her dress soiled. There was no time to get her bathed and changed. Vickie would pitch a fit.

'Let's get in the car,' urged Toby. 'We have to hurry.'

'We shouldn't bother Vickie, you know.'

'You haven't seen her in weeks.'

'She's busy. Vickie is a very busy girl. I don't want to bother her.'

'Mom, we have to leave now.'

'You go. I'll just stay home.'

'It's only for a few hours. Then we'll come right back.'

'No, I think I'll just tidy up here in the garden.' Ellen squatted down and thrust her trowel deep into the black mound of compost.

'Mom, we have to *go*!' In frustration, Toby grabbed her mother's arm, and hauled her back to her feet so abruptly Ellen gave a gasp of shock.

'You're hurting me!' Ellen wailed.

Instantly Toby released her. Ellen took a step backward, rubbing her arm as she stared in bewilderment at her daughter.

It was Ellen's silence, and the glimmer of tears in her eyes, that cut straight to Toby's heart.

'Mom.' Toby shook her head, sick with shame. 'I'm sorry. I'm really sorry. I just need you to cooperate with me right now. Please.'

Ellen looked down at her hat, which had fallen and now lay on the grass, the straw brim trembling in the wind. Slowly she bent down to retrieve it, then straightened, hugging the hat to her chest. In a gesture of sorrow, she lowered her head and nodded. Then she walked to the garden gate and stood waiting for Toby to open it.

On the drive to Vickie's, Toby tried to make up with Ellen. With forced cheerfulness she talked about what they would do this weekend. They'd put up another rose trellis against the house and plant a bush of New Dawn, or perhaps Blaze. Ellen did love red roses. They would spread compost and plan a bulb garden. They would eat fresh tomato sandwiches and drink lemonade. There was so much to look forward to!

Ellen stared at the hat in her lap and said nothing.

They pulled into Vickie's driveway, and Toby steeled herself for the ordeal to come. Vickie, of course, would make a noisy deal about just how big an imposition this was. Vickie and all her responsibilities! A faculty position in the biology department at Bentley College. A snooty executive husband whose favorite word was *me*. A son and daughter, both in sullen adolescence. Lucky Toby, single and childless! Of course she was the obvious one to take care of Mom.

What else would I do with my life?

Toby helped Ellen out of the car, and up the front steps to the house. The door swung open and Vickie appeared, her face flushed with annoyance.

'Toby, this is the *worst* possible time.'

'For both of us, believe me. I'll try to pick her up as soon as I can.' Toby urged her mother forward. 'Go on, Mom. Have a nice visit.'

'I'm cooking,' said Vickie. 'I can't watch her—'

'She'll be fine. Sit her in front of the TV. She likes the Nickelodeon channel.'

Vickie frowned at Ellen's dress. 'What happened to her clothes? She's filthy. Mom, is something wrong with your arm? Why're you rubbing it?'

'Hurts.' Ellen shook her head sadly. 'Toby got mad at me.'

Toby felt her face redden. 'I had to get her into the car. She wouldn't leave the garden. That's why she's so dirty.'

'Well, I can't have her looking like *that*. I have company coming at six!'

'I promise, I'll be back before then.' Toby gave Ellen a kiss on the cheek. 'See you later, Mom. You listen to Vickie.'

Without a backward glance, Ellen walked into the house. *She's punishing me*, thought Toby. *Making me feel guilty for having lost my temper*.

'Toby,' said Vickie, following her down the front steps to the car. 'I need more warning next time. Isn't this what we pay Bryan for?'

'Not available. Your kids'll be home soon. They can watch her.'

'They don't want to!'

'Then try *paying* them. Your kids certainly seem to value the almighty buck.' Toby slammed the car door shut and started the engine. *Why the hell did I say that?* she thought as she drove away. *I have to cool down. I have to get back in control and get ready for this meeting*. But she'd already blown it with Vickie. Now her sister was pissed at her, and so was Ellen. Maybe the whole goddamn world was pissed at her.

She had the sudden impulse to step on the gas

and keep driving, to leave this all behind. Find a new identity, a new town, a new life. The one she had now was a mess, and she didn't know whose fault that was. Certainly not all hers; she was simply trying to do the best she could.

It was 2:10 when she pulled into a parking stall at Springer Hospital. She had no time to collect her thoughts; the meeting was already under way, and she didn't want Doug Carey shooting off his mouth in her absence. If he was going to attack her, she wanted to be there to defend herself. She hurried straight to the administrative wing on the second floor and stepped into the conference room.

Inside, all conversation ceased.

Glancing around the table, she saw friendly faces among the six people sitting there. Paul Hawkins. Maudeen and Val. Toby sat down in the chair next to Val, and across from Paul, who gave her a silent nod of greeting. If she had to stare at someone, it might as well be at a good-looking man. She barely glanced at Dr. Carey, who was at the far end of the table, but his hostile presence was impossible to ignore. A small man – in more ways than one – Carey compensated for his short stature by a ramrod posture and a gaze that was threateningly direct. A mean little Chihuahua. At that moment he was looking straight at Toby.

She ignored Carey and focused instead on Ellis Corcoran, the chief of the Med-Surg staff. She didn't know Corcoran very well; she wondered if anyone at Springer did. It was hard to get past his

Yankee reserve. He seldom showed emotion, and he was showing none now. Neither did the hospital administrator, Ira Beckett, who sat with bulging abdomen crammed up against the table. The silence went on a little too long for comfort. Her palms were damp; under the table, she wiped her hands on her slacks.

Ira Beckett spoke. 'You were telling us, Ms. Collins?'

Maudeen cleared her throat. 'I was trying to explain to you that everything happened at once. We had that code in the trauma room. That took all our attention. We figured Mr. Slotkin was stable enough—'

'So you ignored him?' said Carey.

'We didn't ignore him.'

'How long *did* you leave him unattended?' asked Beckett.

Maudeen glanced at Toby with a silent plea of *help me out here.*

'I was the last one to see Mr. Slotkin,' Toby said. 'That was around five, five-fifteen. It was sometime after six when I realized he was gone.'

'So you left him unattended for almost an hour?'

'He was waiting for a CT scan. We'd already called in the X-ray tech. There was nothing else we were doing for him at that point. We still don't know how he managed to leave the room.'

'Because you people didn't keep an eye on him,' said Carey. 'You didn't even have him restrained.'

'He *was* restrained,' said Val. 'Both ankles and wrists!'

'Then he must be some kind of Houdini. Nobody gets out of four-point restraints. Or did someone forget to tie the straps down?'

Neither nurse spoke; they were both staring at the table.

'Dr. Harper?' said Beckett. 'You said you were the last one to see Mr. Slotkin. Were his restraints tied?'

She swallowed. 'I don't know.'

Paul frowned at her across the table. 'You told me they were.'

'I *thought* they were. I mean, I assumed I tied them. But it was such a confusing shift. Now I'm – I'm not so sure. If he was tied down, it seems impossible that he could have escaped.'

'At least we're finally being honest about this,' said Carey.

'I've never *not* been honest!' she shot back. 'If I screw up, at least *I* admit it.'

Paul cut in, 'Toby—'

'Sometimes we're juggling half a dozen crises at once. We don't remember every single detail of what goes wrong during a shift!'

'You see, Paul?' said Carey. 'This is what I'm talking about. I run into this defensiveness all the time. And it's *always* the night shift.'

'You're the only one who seems to complain,' said Paul.

'I can name half a dozen other docs who've had problems. We get called in at all hours of the night to admit patients who don't need to be admitted. It's a judgment problem.'

110

'Which patients are you referring to?' asked Toby.

'I don't have the names in front of me now.'

'Then you get the names. If you're going to question my judgment, I want specifics.'

Corcoran sighed. 'We're getting off the subject.'

'No, this *is* the subject,' said Carey. 'The competence of Paul's ER staff. Do you know what was going on in the ER that night? They were having a goddamn birthday party! I went into the staff room for a cup of coffee and they had streamers hanging all over the place! A cake and a bunch of burned candles. *That's* probably what happened. They were so busy partying in the back room, they didn't bother to—'

'That is a bunch of *crap*,' said Toby.

'There *was* a party, wasn't there?' said Carey.

'Earlier in the shift, yes. But it didn't distract us from our jobs. Once that tamponade case came in, we were up to our asses in alligators. She required all our attention.'

'And you lost her too,' said Carey.

His comment felt like a slap, and heat flooded Toby's cheeks. The worst part of it was, he was right. She *had* lost the patient. Her shift *had* turned into a disaster – and a very public one. New patients had walked into the waiting room to hear an angry monologue by Harry Slotkin's son. Then an ambulance had pulled up with a chest pain, and the police had arrived – two squad cars called in to help search for the missing patient. The first law of physics had taken over as Toby's tightly regulated ER had devolved into a state of chaos.

She leaned forward, her hands pressed to the table, her gaze not on Carey, but on Paul. 'We didn't have the backup to deal with a tamponade. That patient belonged in a trauma center. We kept her alive as long as we could. I doubt even the wonderful Dr. Carey could have saved her, either.'

'You called me way too late in the game to do anything,' said Carey.

'We called you as soon as we realized she had a tamponade.'

'And how long did it take you to realize that?'

'Within minutes of her arrival.'

'According to the ambulance record, the patient arrived at five-twenty. You didn't call me until five-forty-five.'

'No, we called you earlier.' She glanced at Maudeen and Val, who both nodded in agreement.

'It's not in the code record,' said Carey.

'Who had time to take any notes? We were scrambling to save her life!'

Corcoran cut in: 'Everybody, *please!* We're not here to get in a fistfight. We need to talk about how to handle this new crisis.'

'What new crisis?' said Toby.

Everyone looked at her in surprise.

'I didn't get a chance to tell you,' said Paul. 'I just heard about it myself. Some newspapers picked up the story. Something along the lines of "Forgotten patient vanishes from ER." A reporter called a little while ago, asking for details.'

'What makes this newsworthy?'

'It's like that surgeon cutting off the wrong leg. People want to hear about things that go wrong in hospitals.'

'But who told the newspapers?' She looked around the table, and just for an instant, her gaze met Carey's. He looked away.

'Maybe the Slotkin family told them,' said Beckett. 'Maybe they're laying the groundwork for a lawsuit. We really don't know *how* the newspaper got word of it.'

Carey said, with a quiet note of venom, 'Screwups do get noticed.'

'Yours usually manage to get buried,' said Toby.

'*Please*,' said Corcoran. 'If the patient's found unharmed, then we'll be okay. But it's going on two days now, and as far as I know, there's been no sighting. We're just going to have to hope they find him alive and well.'

'A reporter's already called the ER twice this morning,' said Maudeen.

'No one talked to him, I hope?'

'No. In fact the nurses hung up on him.'

Paul gave a rueful laugh. 'Well, that's one way of handling the press.'

Corcoran said, 'If they can just find the man, we might squeeze through this without any damages. Unfortunately, these Alzheimer's patients can wander for miles.'

'He's not an Alzheimer's,' said Toby. 'The

113

medical history wasn't consistent with that.'

'But you said he was confused.'

'I don't know why. I didn't find anything focal when I examined him. All the blood work came back normal. Unfortunately, we never got the CT scan. I wish I could tell you his diagnosis, but I never finished the workup.' She paused. 'I *did* wonder, though, if he might be having seizures.'

'Did you witness one?'

'I noticed his leg jerking. I couldn't tell if it was a voluntary movement or not.'

'Oh, God.' Paul sank back in his chair. 'Let's hope he doesn't wander onto some highway, or near a body of water. He could be in trouble.'

Corcoran nodded. 'So could we.'

After the meeting ended, Paul asked Toby to join him in the hospital cafeteria. It was three o'clock and the food line had closed down an hour ago, so they resorted to the vending machines, which were stocked with crackers and chips and a never-ending supply of coffee as strong as battery acid. The cafeteria was deserted, and they had the choice of any table in the room, but Paul crossed to the corner table, farthest from the doorway. Farthest from any listening ears.

He sat down without looking at her. 'This isn't easy for me,' he said.

She took one sip of coffee, then set the cup down with careful concentration. He was still focused not on her but on the tabletop. Neutral territory. It was not like Paul to avoid her gaze.

114

Over the years they'd settled into a comfortable, plainspoken friendship. As with all friendships between men and women, there were, of course, the small dishonesties between them. She would never admit how strongly attracted she was to him because it served no purpose, and she liked his wife, Elizabeth, too well. But in almost every other way, she and Paul could be honest with each other. So it hurt her now, to see him staring down at the table, because it made her wonder when he had stopped being entirely truthful.

'I'm glad you were there,' he said. 'I wanted you to see what I'm up against.'

'You mean Doug Carey?'

'It's not just Carey. Toby, I've been asked to attend the Springer board meeting next Thursday. I know this business is going to come up. Carey has friends on that board. And he's out for blood.'

'He has been, for months, ever since the Freitas boy died.'

'Well, this is the payback he's been waiting for. Now the Slotkin case is out in the open, and the hospital board's primed to hear all of Carey's complaints about you.'

'Do you think his complaints are valid?'

'If I did, Toby, you wouldn't be on my staff. I mean that.'

'The problem is,' she sighed, 'I'm afraid I did screw up this time. I don't see how Harry Slotkin could have escaped with his restraints tied down. Which means I must have left him untied. I just can't remember . . .' Her eyes felt gritty from lack

115

of sleep, and the coffee was churning in her stomach. Now I'm losing *my* memory, she thought. Is this the first sign of Alzheimer's disease? Is this the beginning of the end for me as well?' 'I keep thinking about my mother,' she said. 'About how I'd feel if *she* was lost somewhere on the streets. How angry I'd be at the people responsible. I got careless and I put a helpless old guy in danger. Harry Slotkin's family has every right to come after me with their lawyers. I'm just waiting for it to happen.'

It was Paul's silence that made her look up.

He said, quietly, 'I guess now's the time to tell you.'

'What?'

'The family's asked for a copy of the ER record. The request came through their attorney's office this morning.'

She said nothing. The churning in her stomach had turned to nausea.

'It doesn't mean they're going to sue,' said Paul. 'For one thing, the family hardly needs the money. And the circumstances may prove too embarrassing to air. A father wandering naked in the park—'

'If Harry's found dead, I'm sure they *will* sue.' She dropped her head in her hands. 'Oh, God. It's my second lawsuit in three years.'

'The last suit was a crock, Toby. You beat it.'

'I won't beat this one.'

'Slotkin's seventy-two years old – not much of a life span left. That could lessen the monetary damages.'

116

'Seventy-two is young! He could still have years ahead of him.'

'But he was obviously sick in the ER. If they find his body, if they can show he already had a terminal illness, it'll work to your advantage in court.'

She rubbed her face. 'That's the last place I want to end up. In court.'

'Let's worry about that if and when it happens. Right now we've got other political issues brewing. We know the news has already reached the media, and they love nightmare stories about doctors. If the hospital board starts to feel any pressure from the public, they'll be on *my* back to take action. I'll do everything I can to protect you. But Toby. I can be replaced, too.' He paused. 'Mike Esterhaus has already expressed interest in being ER chief.'

'He'd be a disaster.'

'He'd be a yes-man. He wouldn't fight them the way I do. Every time they try to cut another RN from our staff, I scream bloody murder. Mike will politely bend right over.'

For the first time it occurred to her: *I'm taking Paul down with me.*

'The one thing we have to hope for,' he said, 'is that they find the patient. That will defuse this crisis. No more media interest, no threat of a lawsuit. He has to be found – alive and well.'

'Which gets less and less likely every hour.'

They sat in silence, their coffee growing cold, their friendship strained to its weakest point. This is why doctors should never marry each other, she thought. Tonight, Paul will go home to Elizabeth, whose work has nothing to do with medicine. They'll have none of these tensions hanging between them, no shared worries about Doug Carey or lawsuits or hospital boards to ruin their supper. Elizabeth will help him escape this crisis, at least for an evening.

And whose help do I have?

Six

No rubber chicken tonight, observed Dr. Robbie Brace as a waitress set a plate before him. He looked down at the rack of spring lamb and new potatoes and glazed baby vegetables. Everything looked tender and so very young. As his knife sliced through the meat, he thought: The privileged prefer to dine on babies. But he did not feel particularly privileged tonight, despite the fact he sat at a candlelit table, a flute of champagne beside his plate. He glanced at his wife, Greta, sitting beside him and saw her pale forehead etched with a frown. He suspected that frown had nothing to do with the quality of her meal; her request for a vegetarian plate had been graciously filled, and the food was artistically presented. As she gazed around at the two dozen other tables in the banquet room, perhaps she was taking note of what her husband had already observed: They'd been seated at the table farthest from the dais. Banished to a corner where they'd be scarcely noticed.

Half the chairs at their table were vacant, and the other three chairs were occupied by nursing home administrators and an extremely deaf Brant Hill investor. Theirs was the Siberia of tables. Scanning the room, he saw that all the other physicians were seated in better locations. Dr. Chris Olshank – who'd been hired the same week Robbie was – rated a table far closer to the dais. *Maybe it means nothing, maybe it's just a screwup in the seating arrangements.* But he could not help noting the essential difference between Chris Olshank and himself.

Olshank was white.

Man, you're just screwing around with your own head.

He took a swallow of champagne, drinking it down in a resentful gulp, the whole time intensely aware that he was the only black male guest at the banquet. There were two black women at another table, but he was the only black man. It was something he never failed to take stock of, something that was always in the forefront of his consciousness whenever he walked into a room full of people. How many were white, how many Asian, how many black? Too many, one way or the other, made him uneasy, as though it violated some privately acceptable racial quota. Even now, as a doctor, he couldn't get away from that painful awareness of his own skin color. The M.D. after his name had changed nothing.

Greta reached for him, her hand small and pale against his blackness. 'You're not eating.'

'Sure I am.' He looked at her plate of vegetables. 'How's the rabbit food?'

'Very good, as a matter of fact. Have a taste.' She slipped a forkful of garlicky potatoes into his mouth. 'Nice, isn't it? And better for your arteries than that poor lamb is.'

'Once a carnivore—'

'Yes, always a carnivore. But I keep hoping you'll see the light.' At last he smiled, reflecting on the beauty of his own wife. Greta had more than just eye-of-the-beholder beauty; one saw fire and intelligence in her face. Though she seemed oblivious to her effect on the opposite sex, Brace was painfully aware of how other men looked at her. Aware, too, of how they looked at *him*, a black man married to a redhead. Envy, resentment, puzzlement – he saw it in men's eyes as they glanced between husband and wife, between black and white.

A tap on the microphone drew their attention. Brace looked up and saw that Kenneth Foley, the CEO of Brant Hill, was standing behind the podium.

The lights dimmed and a slide appeared on the projector screen over Foley's head. It was the Brant Hill logo, a curly baroque *B* intertwined with an *H*, and beneath it the words:

WHERE LIVING WELL IS THE BEST REWARD.

'That is a disgusting slogan,' whispered Greta. 'Why don't they just say, *Where the rich folk live*?'

Brace gave her knee a squeeze of warning. He agreed with her, of course, but one didn't spout off Socialist opinions in the presence of the mink and diamonds set.

At the podium, Foley began his presentation. 'Six years ago, Brant Hill was only a concept. Not a unique concept, of course; across the country, as Americans grow older, retirement communities are springing up in every state. What makes Brant Hill unique isn't the concept. It's the *execution*. It's the degree to which we carry out the *dream*.'

A new slide flashed onto the screen: a photograph of the Brant Hill common, with the swan pond in the foreground and the rolling hills of the golf course stretching into a soft shroud of mist.

'We know that the *dream* has nothing to do with a comfortable old age followed by a comfortable death. The dream has to do with *life*. With beginnings, not endings. *That* is what we offer our clients. We've made the dream a reality. And look how far we've come! Brant Hill, Newton, is expanding. Brant Hill, La Jolla, is sold out. Last month we started construction on our third development, in Naples, Florida, and already, seventy-five percent of those unbuilt units have been sold. And tonight, on the sixth anniversary of our first groundbreaking, I'm here to announce the most *exciting* news of all.' He paused, and on the screen above him, the Brant Hill logo reappeared on a background of royal blue. 'At eight A.M. tomorrow,' he said, 'we will be making our initial public offering of stock. I think you all understand what *that* means.'

Money, thought Brace as he heard the murmurs of excitement in the room. A fortune for the initial investors. And for Brant Hill itself, it meant an infusion of cash that would spur construction of new developments in other states. No wonder there was champagne on the table; as of tomorrow morning, half the people in this room were going to be even more wealthy than they already were.

The audience burst out in applause.

Greta did not, which Robbie noted with some discomfort. The old stereotype about stubborn redheads held true for his wife. She was sitting with arms folded, her chin jutting out, the very picture of a pissed-off Socialist.

More slides appeared on-screen, reflecting a changing collage of colors on Greta's face. Photos of La Jolla's Brant Hill, designed as a cluster of Mediterranean-style villas overlooking the Pacific. A photo of the health club in Newton, where a dozen aging women in snazzy warm-up suits danced aerobics. A shot of Newton's fifth green, with two men posing beside their canopied golf cart. Then a photo of residents dining in the country club restaurant, a bottle of champagne chilling in a silver ice bucket.

Where the rich folk live.

Brace shifted in his chair, uncomfortably attuned to what Greta must be thinking of all this. Taking care of rich folk was not what he'd planned for his life's work when he'd been a medical student. But then, he hadn't anticipated the pressures of student loans or a home mortgage or saving for their kid's college fund. He hadn't imagined he would be forced to sell out.

Greta uncrossed her legs, and as her thigh brushed against his, he felt an unexpected dart of anger that she couldn't see his side of this. She was the wife; she could hang on to *her* principles. He was the one who had to keep their family fed and housed. And where was the sin in taking care of the rich? Like everyone else, the rich got sick, they needed doctors, they needed compassion.

They paid their bills.

He crossed his arms, withdrawing both physically and emotionally from Greta, and stared at the projector screen. So this was Ken Foley's real purpose for the dinner – to drum up excitement about the initial public offering, to fire up demand for the new stock. Foley's speech was intended for a far wider audience of investors than was now in this room. Already, Brant Hill must be showing up on radar screens of brokerage firms across the country. Every word he said tonight would be piped straight to the business media.

A new slide appeared, an artist's rendition of the new nursing home wing now under construction. Yesterday the concrete foundation had been poured, and next week excavation started on yet a second addition. They were building as fast as they could, yet the demand would only keep growing.

Foley had described the product; now he

explained the market for it. The next slide was a bar graph representing the growth of the elderly population in the United States, the surge of baby boomers progressing into old age like a pig swallowed and digested as it moves through a snake. The me-generation was graduating from skis to walkers. Here's our target population, Foley said, his laser pointer circling the statistical pig in the snake. Our future clients. By the year 2005, boomers will start retiring, and Brant Hill is just the sort of development they'll turn to. We're talking growth – and extraordinary returns on your investment. Boomers will be looking toward an exciting new phase in their lives. They don't want worries about sickness or infirmity. Many of them will have money saved up – a lot of it. They'll be getting old, but they don't want to *feel* old.

And who does? thought Brace. Which one of us doesn't look in the mirror and feel a sense of dismay that the face staring back is too old to be *me*?

Dessert and coffee finally arrived at their wilderness table. Greta, tasting artificial something-or-other in the whipped topping, didn't eat hers. Brace ate both their desserts in a depressing orgy of calories. He had his mouth full of whipped cream when he heard his name spoken over the microphone.

Greta gave him a nudge. 'Stand up,' she whispered. 'They're introducing the new doctors.'

Brace shot to his feet, accidentally flicking a glob of cream across the front of his suit. He stood for only a second, fumbling with a napkin as he waved to the audience, then quickly sank back into his chair. The other three new doctors rose to their feet, waving as they were introduced, no one else wearing whipped cream on their clothes, no one else tight-faced with embarrassment. *I graduated second highest in my med school class,* he thought. *I was voted intern of the year. I did it against all odds, and without a penny of help from my family and I am sitting here feeling like a god-damn imbecile.*

Under the table, Greta touched his knee. 'The air's too rich in here,' she whispered. 'I think I'm choking on the gold dust.'

'Do you want to leave?'

'Do you?'

He looked at the dais, where Foley was still talking about money. Returns on investment, growth of the retiree market. There's gold in them thar old folks.

He threw his napkin on the table. 'We're outta here.'

Angus Parmenter was not feeling well, not feeling well at all. Since Thursday the trembling in his right hand had come and gone twice. He found that if he concentrated, he could suppress it, but it took great effort, and it left his arm aching. Both times the twitching stopped of its own accord. For the last two days, it had not recurred at all, and he'd managed to convince himself the attacks meant nothing. Too much coffee, perhaps. Or too much time at the Nautilus machine, overexerting those arm muscles. He had stopped using the Nautilus, and the movement had not returned, which was a good sign.

But now something *else* was wrong.

He had noticed it upon awakening from his afternoon nap. It was dark, and he had switched on the lamp and looked around at his bedroom. All the furniture seemed tilted. When had that happened? Had he moved things around today? He couldn't recall. But there was the nightstand, way beyond arm's reach. It was tottering on its edge, ready to fall. He stared at it, trying to understand why it didn't topple over, why the glass of water set on top of it was not sliding to the floor.

He turned and looked at the window. It, too, had shifted position. It was now far in the distance, a receding square at the end of a long tunnel.

He stepped out of bed and immediately swayed. *Was that an earthquake?* The floor seemed to roll like swells on the open sea. He stumbled one way, then the other, and finally caught himself on the dresser. There he paused, clinging to the edge, trying to regain his sense of balance. He felt something dribble onto his foot. He looked down and saw that the carpet was wet, and he smelled the warm, sour odor of urine. Who the hell had peed in his bedroom?

He heard a chiming. The notes seemed to float around the room, like tiny black balloons. Church bells? A clock? No, someone was ringing the door-bell.

He staggered out of the bedroom, holding on to the walls, doorways, anything he could cling to. The hallway seemed to elongate, the door gliding away from his outstretched hand. Suddenly his fingers closed around the knob. With a grunt of triumph, he yanked open the door.

In astonishment he stared at the two midgets standing on his front porch.

'Go away,' he said.

The midgets stared at him and made mewing sounds.

Angus started to swing the door shut but couldn't get it to close. A woman had appeared and was holding it open.

'What are you doing, Dad? Why aren't you dressed?'

'Go. Get out of my house.'

'Dad!' The woman was forcing her way in now.

'Get out!' said Angus. 'Leave me alone!' He turned and staggered up the hall, trying to flee the woman and the two midgets. But they pursued him, the midgets whimpering, the woman yelling: 'What's wrong? What's wrong with you?'

He tripped on the carpet. What happened next went by gracefully, like a slow dance underwater. He felt his body flying forward, gliding. Felt his arms stretching out like wings as he soared through liquid air.

He did not even feel the impact.

'Dad! Oh my God.'

Those damn midgets were screeching and pawing at his head. Now the woman crouched over him. She turned him over on his back.

'Dad, are you hurt?'

'I can fly,' he whispered.

She looked at the midgets. 'Get the telephone. Call nine one one. *Go!*'

Angus moved his arm, flapping it like a wing.

'Hold still, Dad. We're getting an ambulance.'

I can fly! He was floating. Gilding. *I can fly.*

'I've never seen him like this. He doesn't recognize me, and he doesn't seem to know his own grandchildren. I didn't know what else to do, so I called the ambulance.' The woman shot an anxious glance into the exam room, where the nurses were trying to take Angus Parmenter's vital signs. 'It's a stroke or something. Isn't it?'

'I'll be able to tell more after I examine him,' said Toby.

'But does it sound like a stroke?'

'It's possible.' Toby gave the woman's arm a squeeze. 'Why don't you sit in the waiting room, Mrs. Lacy? I'll be out to talk to you as soon as I know more.'

Edith Lacy nodded. Hugging herself, she went into the waiting area and sank onto the couch between her two daughters. The three of them hugged one another, arms forming a warm and compact universe.

Toby turned and entered the exam room.

Angus Parmenter was strapped down on the

gurney in four-point restraints, babbling something about strangers in his house. For an
eighty-two-year-old man, his limbs were taut and
surprisingly muscular. He was dressed only in his
undershirt. That's the way his daughter had found
him, naked from the waist down.

Maudeen peeled off the blood pressure cuff and
slid it neatly into the wall basket. 'Vitals are fine.
One thirty over seventy. Pulse is ninety-four and
regular.'

'Temp?'

'Thirty-eight degrees,' said Val.

Toby stood by the man's head and tried to
engage his attention. 'Mr. Parmenter? Angus? I'm
Dr. Harper.'

'. . . came right into my house . . . wouldn't
leave me alone . . .'

'Angus, did you fall down? Did you hurt
yourself?'

'. . . goddamn midgets, came to steal my money.
Everyone's after my money.'

Maudeen shook her head. 'I can't get a word of
history out of him.'

'The daughter says he's been healthy. No recent
illnesses.' Toby shone her penlight into the man's
eyes. Both pupils constricted. 'She spoke to him on
the phone only two weeks ago and he sounded
fine. Angus! Angus, what happened to you?'

'. . . always trying to take my damn money . . .'

'We have a one-track mind,' sighed Toby, flicking off the penlight. She continued her exam,
searching first for evidence of head trauma, then

130

moving on to her exam of the cranial nerves. She found no localizing signs, nothing to pinpoint the cause of the man's confusion. The daughter had described a staggering gait. Had the man suffered a stroke of the cerebellum? That would affect coordination.

She unstrapped his right wrist. 'Angus, can you touch my finger?' She held her hand in front of his face. 'Reach up and touch my finger.'

'You're too far away,' he said.

'It's right here, right in front of you. Come on, try and touch it.'

He raised his arm. It wobbled in midair, like a dancing cobra.

The phone rang. Maudeen reached for the receiver.

Angus Parmenter's arm began to twitch, a violently rhythmic shaking that rattled the gurney.

'What's he doing?' said Val. 'Is he having a seizure?'

'Angus!' Toby grasped the man's face and stared straight at him. He wasn't looking at her; he was gazing at his own arm.

'Can you talk, Angus?'

'There it goes again,' he said.

'What? You mean the shaking?'

'That hand – whose hand is that?'

'It's *your* hand.'

The shaking suddenly ceased. The arm flopped down like a deadweight onto the gurney. Angus closed his eyes. 'There now,' he said. 'All better.'

'Toby?' It was Maudeen, turning from the

131

telephone. 'There's a Dr. Wallenberg on the line. He wants to talk to you.'

Toby took the receiver. 'Dr. Wallenberg? This is Toby Harper. I'm the ER doctor on duty tonight.'

'You have my patient there.'

'You mean Mr. Parmenter?'

'I just got beeped about the ambulance transfer. What happened?'

'He was found confused at home. Right now he's awake and the vitals are stable. But he's got ataxia, and he's disoriented times three. He doesn't even recognize his own daughter.'

'How long has he been there?'

'The ambulance brought him in around nine.'

Wallenberg was silent for a moment. In the background, Toby heard the sound of laughter and voices. A party.

'I'll be there in an hour. Just keep him stable till I arrive.'

'Dr. Wallenberg—'

The line had already gone dead.

She turned to the patient. He was lying very still, his eyes focused intently on the ceiling. Now his gaze shifted, first right, then left, as though he were watching a slow-motion tennis match.

'Let's get this man a STAT CT scan,' said Toby. 'And we'll need some bloods drawn.'

Val pulled a fistful of glass tubes out of the drawer. 'The usual? CBC and SMA?'

'Add a drug screen. He seems to be hallucinating.'

'I'll call X-ray,' said Maudeen, reaching once again for the phone.

'Ladies,' said Toby. 'One more thing.'

Both nurses looked at her.

'Whatever happens tonight, we're *not* going to leave this guy alone, not for a second. Not till he's transferred out of our ER.'

Val and Maudeen nodded.

Toby took hold of Angus Parmenter's unrestrained hand and tied it firmly to the gurney siderail.

'Here come the cuts,' said the CT tech.

Toby stared at the computer screen as the pixels formed the first image, an oval with different shades of gray. She was looking at a cross section of Angus Parmenter's brain. Thousands of X-ray beams directed at his cranium had been analyzed by computer, and the different densities of bone and fluid and brain matter had produced this image. The skull appeared as a thick white rim, like the rind of a fruit. Inside the rind, the brain showed up as grayish pulp, indented by black wormlike sulci.

A succession of images materialized on the screen, each one a slightly different cut of the patient's cranium. She saw the anterior horns, two black ovals filled with cerebrospinal fluid. The caudate nuclei. The thalamus. There appeared to be no anatomical shifts, no asymmetry. No evidence of blood leakage into any part of the brain.

'I don't see anything acute,' Toby said. 'What do you think?'

Vince was not a physician, but he'd seen far

more CT scans as an X-ray tech than Toby had. He frowned at the screen as a fresh cut appeared. 'Wait,' he said. 'That shot looks a little funny.'

'What?'

'Right there.' He pointed to a smudge at the center. 'That's the sella turcica. See how it's not very clearly demarcated on this edge?'

'Could it be patient movement?'

'No, the rest of the shot's perfectly clean. He didn't move.' Vince picked up the phone and dialed the radiologist at home. 'Hi, Dr. Ritter? Are the cuts coming across okay on your computer? Great. Dr. Harper and I are looking at them right now. We're wondering about that last cut' – he typed on the keyboard, and the image reverted back to the previous screen – 'that slice right there, see it? What do you think about the sella turcica?'

As Vince conferred with Dr. Ritter, Toby bent closer to the screen. What Vince had spotted was a very subtle change – so subtle she herself would have missed it. The sella turcica was a tiny pocket of thin bone housing the pituitary gland at the base of the brain. The gland itself was vital; the hormones it produced controlled a wide variety of functions, from fertility to childhood growth to the daily sleep-wake cycle. Could that tiny erosion of the sella turcica be the cause of the patient's symptoms?

'Okay, I'll do the coronal thin slices,' said Vince. 'Anything else you want me to do?'

'Let me talk to Ritter,' said Toby. She took the

receiver. 'Hi, George, this is Toby. What do you think about that sella?'

'Not much,' said Ritter. She heard the squeak of his chair – probably leather. George Ritter liked his luxuries. She could imagine him ensconced in his study, surrounded by the latest in computer technology. 'In a man this age, pituitary adenomas aren't uncommon. Twenty percent of eighty-year-olds have them.'

'Big enough to erode the sella?'

'Well, no. This one's gotten a little large. What's his endocrine status?'

'I haven't checked it. He just came in the ER with acute confusion. Could this be the cause?'

'Not unless the adenoma's produced a secondary metabolic abnormality. Have you checked the electrolytes?'

'They've been drawn. We're waiting for results.'

'If those are normal, and the endocrine status is okay, I think you're going to have to look for some other reason for his confusion. This is too small a tumor to exert much anatomical pressure. I've asked Vince to do some thin-slice cuts on the coronal plane. That should define it a little better. You'll probably want to send the patient out for an MRI, too. Who's admitting him?'

'Dr. Wallenberg.'

There was a silence. 'This is a Brant Hill patient?'

'Yes.'

Ritter gave an irritated sigh. 'I wish you'd told me this earlier.'

'Why?'

'I don't read X rays on Brant Hill patients. They use their own radiologist to interpret all their films. Which means I won't get paid for this.'

'I'm sorry, I didn't know that. Since when did this arrangement start?'

'Springer signed a subcontract agreement with them a month ago. Their patients aren't supposed to go through the ER. The Brant Hill docs admit directly to the wards. How did this patient end up with you?'

'The daughter panicked and called nine one one. Wallenberg's on his way in now.'

'Okay. Then let Wallenberg decide what to do about the coronal slices. I'm going to bed.'

Toby hung up and looked at Vince. 'Why didn't you tell me Brant Hill had a closed referral system?'

Vince gave her a sheepish look. 'You didn't tell me this was a Brant Hill patient.'

'Don't they trust our radiology staff?'

'Our hospital techs shoot the films, but the Brant Hill radiologist interprets them. I guess they're trying to keep the professional fees within their group.'

Hospital politics again, she thought. Everyone fighting for the same shrinking health care dollar.

She rose and looked through the viewing window into the CT scan room. The patient was still lying on the table, his eyes closed, his lips moving silently. The twitching of his right hand had not recurred. Nevertheless, he would need an

EEG to rule out seizures. And probably a lumbar puncture. Wearily she leaned against the glass, trying to think of what she might have missed, what she could not afford to miss.

Ever since Harry Slotkin had vanished from her ER two weeks ago, she knew her performance was under scrutiny by the hospital board, and she had been even more compulsively thorough than usual. Every afternoon, she'd wake up wondering if this was the day they'd find Harry Slotkin's body, if this was the day her name would once again be thrust into the public eye. The initial news coverage had been painful enough. The week of Harry's disappearance, the tale of the missing patient had aired on all the local television stations. She'd managed to ride out that storm, and now it was old news, probably forgotten by the general public. But the minute they find Harry's body, she thought, it will once again be a hot story. And I'll be in the hot seat, battling both lawyers and reporters.

Behind her, a door opened and a voice said: 'Is that my patient on the table?'

Toby turned and was startled to see a strikingly tall man in a tuxedo. He glanced at Vince, his gaze quickly taking in the CT tech, and just as quickly dismissing him. Then he strode to the viewing window and stared through the glass at Angus Parmenter. 'I didn't ask for a CT. Who ordered it?'

'I did,' said Toby.

Now Wallenberg focused on *her*, as though finally realizing she was worth his attention. He was no older than forty, yet he regarded her with an expression of clear superiority. Perhaps it was the tuxedo; a man who looked as if he'd stepped off the pages of GQ had every reason to feel superior. He reminded Toby of a young lion, his brown hair perfectly clipped and swept back like a mane, his eyes like amber, alert and not particularly friendly. 'Are you Dr. Harper?'

'Yes. I wanted to save you some time on the workup. I thought I'd order the CT.'

'Next time, let me order my own tests.'

'But it seemed more efficient to get it done now.'

The amber eyes narrowed. He seemed about to make a retort, then thought better of it. Instead he simply nodded and turned to Vince. 'Please get my patient back on the gurney. He's being admitted to the third floor, medical wing.' He started to leave the room.

'Dr. Wallenberg,' said Toby. 'Did you want to hear the results of your patient's CT scan?'

'Was there anything to report?'

'A small erosion of the sella turcica. It appears he has a pituitary adenoma growing.'

'Was there anything else?'

'No, but you'll probably want to order thin-slice tomography. Since he's already lying on the CT table—'

'It won't be necessary. Just get him upstairs and I'll write the admitting orders.'

'What about the lesion? I know the adenoma's not an emergency, but it may require surgical removal.'

With a sigh of impatience he turned to face her. 'I am *fully* aware of the adenoma, Dr. Harper. I've been following it for two years now. Thin-slice tomography would be a waste of money. But *thank* you for your suggestion.' He walked out of the room.

'Geez,' muttered Vince. 'Who shoved the pole up *his* ass?'

Toby looked through the viewing window at Angus Parmenter, who was still babbling quietly to himself. She didn't agree with Wallenberg; she thought further X-ray studies were indicated. But the patient was no longer her responsibility.

She looked at Vince. 'Come on. Let's get him on the gurney.'

Seven

The sign on the door was stenciled in soft blue on gray: PRENATAL COUNSELING. Molly could hear the sound of a telephone ringing in the room beyond, and she hesitated in the hallway, her hand clutching the knob as she listened to the faint murmur of a woman's voice beyond the closed door.

She took a breath and walked in.

The receptionist didn't see her at first; she was too busy talking on the phone. Afraid to interrupt this very busy woman, Molly stood on the other side of the desk, waiting to be noticed. At last the receptionist hung up and looked at her. 'Can I help you?'

'Um, I'm supposed to talk to someone . . .'

'Are you Molly Picker?'

'Yeah.' Molly gave a relieved nod. They were expecting her. 'That's me.'

The receptionist smiled, the sort of smile that starts off at the mouth, but then gets no further. 'I'm Linda. We spoke on the phone. Why don't we go in the other room?'

Molly glanced around the reception area. 'Am I gonna see a nurse or something? 'Cause maybe I'm s'posed to pee first.'

'No, today we're just going to talk, Molly. The rest room's out in the hall if you need to use it right away.'

'I guess I can wait.'

She followed the woman into the adjoining room. It was a small office with a desk and two chairs. On one wall was a giant poster of a pregnant woman's belly, drawn as if that belly were sliced right down the middle, so you could see the baby resting inside, its chubby little arms and legs curled up, its eyes closed in sleep. On the desk was a plastic model of a pregnant womb, a 3-D puzzle that could be taken apart layer by layer, belly, womb, and then baby. There was also a big picture book open to a drawing of an empty baby stroller, which seemed like a strange image to display.

'Why don't you have a seat?' Linda said. 'Would you like a cup of tea? A glass of apple juice?'

'No, Ma'am.'

'Are you sure? It's really no trouble.'

'I'm not thirsty, thank you, Ma'am.'

Linda sat down across from Molly so that the two of them were looking directly at each other. The woman's smile had changed to an expression of concern. She had light blue eyes that, with a little makeup, might have been pretty were they not staring from a face that was so bland and humorless. Nothing about this woman – not her suburban housewife perm or her high-necked dress or her tight little mouth – set Molly at ease. She might as well be from another planet, for all the ways they were different. She knew the other woman sensed that difference as well, could see it by the way Linda sat behind her desk, her shoulders squared, her bony hands folded before her. Molly suddenly felt the need to tug down the hem of her skirt, to cross her arms over her chest. And she felt a twinge of something she hadn't felt in a long time.

She felt ashamed.

'Now,' said Linda. 'Tell me about your situation, Molly.'

'My, uh, situation?'

'You said on the phone you're pregnant. Are you having symptoms?'

'Yes, Ma'am. I think so.'

'Can you tell me what they are?'

'I, uh . . .' Molly looked down at her lap. The short skirt was riding up her thighs. She squirmed a little in her chair. 'In the morning, I'm sick to my stomach. I gotta pee all the time. And I haven't had my monthly in a while.'

'How long since your last period?'

Molly shrugged. 'I'm not real sure. I think it was back in May.'

'That's over four months ago. Didn't it worry you, being so late?'

'Well, I didn't really keep track, you know. And then I got that stomach flu and I thought that's why I was late. And also, I – I guess I didn't want to think about it. About what it might mean. You know how it is.'

Linda obviously didn't know. She just kept looking at Molly with those pinched eyes. 'Are you married?'

Molly gave a startled laugh. 'No, Ma'am.'

'But you did have . . . sex.' The word came out like a throat clearing, a low, choked sound.

Molly fidgeted in her chair. 'Well, yeah,' she answered. 'I've had sex.'

'Unprotected?'

'You mean like do I use rubbers? Yeah, sure. But I guess I . . . had an accident.'

Again, the woman made that throat-clearing sound. She folded her hands on the desk. 'Molly, do you know what your baby looks like right now?'

Molly shook her head.

'You do understand it *is* a baby you're carrying?' The woman slid the picture book toward Molly and flipped to a page near the beginning. She pointed to an illustration, a miniature baby all wrapped around itself in a small fleshy ball. 'At four months, this is what he looks like. He has a little face and little hands and feet. See how perfect he is already? He's a real baby. Isn't he cute?'

Molly shifted uneasily.

'Do you have a name for him yet? You should give him a name, don't you think? Because you're going to start feeling him move around inside you real soon, and you can't just call him *hey you*. Do you know the father's name?'

143

'No, Ma'am.'

'Well, what was *your* daddy's name?'

Molly swallowed. 'William,' she whispered. 'My daddy's name is William.'

'Now that's a nice name! Why don't we call the baby Willie? Of course, if it's a little girl, we'd have to change it.' She smiled. 'There are so many nice names for girls these days! You could even name her after yourself.'

Molly looked at her in bewilderment. Softly she asked: 'Why're you doing this to me?'

'Doing what, Molly?'

'What you're doing . . .'

'I'm trying to offer you a choice. The only choice. You've got a baby in there. A four-month-old fetus. The Good Lord has given you a sacred responsibility.'

'But, Ma'am, it wasn't the Good Lord who fucked me.'

The woman gasped, her hand flying to her throat.

Molly squirmed in her chair. 'I think maybe I should go—'

'No. No, I'm only trying to lay out the options for you – all of them. You do have choices, Molly, and don't let anyone tell you differently. You can choose life for that baby. For little Willie.'

'Please don't call him that.' Molly stood up.

So did Linda. 'He has a name. He is a *person*. I can put you in touch with an adoption agency. There are people who want your baby – thousands of families just waiting for one. It's time to think about someone besides yourself.'

'But I gotta think about myself,' whispered Molly. ''Cause no one else does.' She walked out of the office, out of the building.

In a phone booth she found a Boston directory. In the Yellow Pages was a listing for a Planned Parenthood clinic, on the other side of town.

I've gotta think about myself. Because no one else does. No one ever has.

She rode the bus, transferring twice, and got off a block away from her destination.

There was a crowd of people standing on the sidewalk. Molly could hear them chanting, but she couldn't understand the words. It was just a noisy chorus of voices, rhythmically punching the air. Two cops stood off to the side, arms crossed, looking bored.

Molly halted, uncertain whether to approach. The crowd suddenly turned its attention to the street, where a car had just pulled up at the curb. Two women emerged from the building and moved swiftly, defiantly, through the gathering. They helped a frightened-looking woman out of the car's passenger seat. Locking arms around her, they started back toward the building.

The two cops finally moved into action, pushing into the fray, trying to clear a path for the three women.

A man yelled: 'This is what they do to babies in that building!' and he threw a jar down on the sidewalk.

Glass shattered. Blood splashed across the

pavement in a bright, shocking spray of crimson.

The crowd began to chant: '*Baby killers. Baby killers. Baby killers.*'

The three women, heads ducked, blindly followed the cop up the steps and into the building. The door slammed shut.

Molly felt a tug on her arm, and a man shoved a brochure in her hand.

'Join us in the fight, sister,' he said.

Molly looked down at the brochure she was holding. It was a printed photo of a smiling child with wispy blond hair. *We are all God's angels*, it said.

'We need new soldiers,' the man said. 'It's the only way to combat Satan. We'd welcome you.' He reached out to her; fingers bony as a skeleton's.

Molly fled in tears.

She caught a bus back to her own neighborhood.

It was nearly five when she climbed the stairs to her room. She was so tired she could barely move her legs, could barely drag herself up that last flight of stairs.

A moment after she'd flopped onto her bed, Romy shoved open the door and walked in. 'Where you been?'

'For a walk.'

He gave her bed a kick. 'You're not doing a little on the side, are you? I got my eye on you, girl. I'm keeping track.'

'Leave me alone. I want to sleep.'

'You fucking around on your own time? That what you been doing?'

146

'Get *out* of my room.' With her foot, she shoved him off the bed.

Bad mistake. Romy grabbed her wrist and twisted it so savagely she thought she could feel her bones snapping.

'Stop it!' she screamed. 'You're breaking my arm—'

'And you're forgetting who you are, Molly Wolly. Who I am. Don't like it when you go off without telling me where you are.'

'Let me go. C'mon, Romy. Please stop hurting me.'

With a grunt of disgust he released her. He crossed to the old rattan dresser where she'd left her purse. Turning the purse upside down, he emptied the contents on the floor. From her wallet he pulled out eleven dollars – all the money she had. If she'd been turning tricks on the side, she sure wasn't getting paid for it. As he stuffed the bills in his pocket, he suddenly noticed the brochure – the one with the picture of the little blond child. *We are all God's angels.*

He snatched it up and laughed. 'What's this angel shit?'

'It's nothing.'

'Where'd you get it?'

She shrugged. 'Some guy gave it to me.'

'Who?'

'I don't know his name. It was over by the Planned Parenthood. There was a whole bunch of crazy people out on the street, yelling and shoving folks.'

'So what were *you* doing there?'

'Nothing. I wasn't doing nothing.'

He crossed back to her bed and grabbed her under the chin. Softly he said, 'You didn't go and do something without telling me?'

'What do you mean?'

'No one *touches* you without my permission. You got that?' His fingers dug into her face and suddenly she felt afraid. Romy was speaking softly, and when he got quiet was when he got mean. She'd seen the bruises he left on other girls' faces. The bloody gaps where their teeth had been. 'Thought we got that straight a long time ago.'

The pressure of his fingers brought tears to her eyes. She whispered, 'Yeah. Yeah, I . . .' She closed her eyes, steeling herself for the blow. 'Romy, I messed up. I think I'm pregnant.'

To her surprise the blow never came. Instead he released her and made a sound almost like a chuckle. She didn't dare look at him but kept her head bowed in supplication.

'I don't know how it happened,' she said. 'I was scared to tell you. I figured I'd just, you know, take care of it. And then I wouldn't have to tell you nothing.'

His hand came down on her head, but the contact was gentle. A caress. 'Now you know that's not the way we do things. You know I take care of you. Gotta learn to *trust* me, Molly Wolly. Gotta learn to *confide* in me.' His fingers slid down her cheek, soft as a tickle. 'I know a doctor.'

She stiffened.

'I'll take care of it, Moll, just like I take care of everything else. So don't you go making other arrangements. You got that?'

She nodded.

After he left the room, she slowly unfolded her limbs and let out a deep sigh. She'd gotten off easy this time. Only now, after the encounter was over, did she realize how close she'd come to getting hurt. You didn't go against Romy, not if you wanted to hold on to your teeth.

She was hungry again; she was always hungry. She reached under the bed for the bag of Fritos, then remembered she'd eaten them all that morning. She got up and rooted around the room for something else to eat.

Her gaze fell on the picture of the blond baby. The brochure was lying on the floor, where Romy had tossed it.

We are all God's angels.

She picked up the brochure and studied the baby's face. Was it a girl or a boy? She couldn't tell. She didn't know much about babies, hadn't been around one in years, not since she was a girl. She had only a vague recollection of holding her younger sister on her lap. She remembered the crackle of plastic pants over Lily's diaper, the sweet powdery smell of her skin. How Lily had no neck, just that soft little hump between her shoulders.

She lay down and placed her hands on her belly, felt her own womb, firm as an orange, bulging under the skin. She thought of the drawing in

Linda's picture book – the baby with the perfect fingers and toes. A Polly Pocket baby you could hold in one hand,

We are all God's angels.

She closed her eyes and thought wearily: *What about me? You forgot me, God.*

Toby stripped off her gloves and tossed them in the rubbish can. 'All stitched up. Now you'll have something to show the other kids at school.'

The boy finally got up the nerve to look at his elbow. He'd had his eyes closed tight, had not dared even a single peek while Toby was suturing. Now he stared in awe at the nubbins of blue nylon thread. 'Wow. How many stitches?'

'Five.'

'Is that a lot?'

'It's five too many. Maybe you should retire the old skateboard.'

'Nah. I'd just bang myself up some other way.' He sat up and slid off the treatment table. Immediately he swayed sideways.

'Uh oh,' said Maudeen. She scooped him up under the arms and lowered him into a chair. 'You're moving too fast, kid.' She shoved the boy's head between his knees and rolled her eyes at Toby. Teenagers. All brag and no backbone. This one would probably strut into school tomorrow morning and proudly wave his new battle scar. He wouldn't bother to mention the part about nearly fainting into a nurse's arms.

The intercom buzzed. It was Val. 'Dr. Harper,

they've got a Code Blue up on Three West!'

Toby shot to her feet. 'I'm on my way.'

She jogged up the hall toward the stairwell, bypassing the elevator. She could make it faster on her own two feet.

Two flights up, she emerged in the Three West corridor and spotted a nurse wheeling a crash cart through a doorway. Toby followed her into the patient's room.

Two ward nurses were already at the bedside, one holding a mask to the patient's face and bagging oxygen into the lungs, the other nurse administering chest compressions. The nurse with the crash cart pulled out EKG leads and slapped contact pads onto the patient's chest.

'What happened?' said Toby.

The nurse pumping on the chest answered. 'Found him seizing. Then he went flaccid – stopped breathing—' Her words came out in rhythmic bursts as she leaned forward, released. 'Dr. Wallenberg's on his way.'

Wallenberg? Toby glanced at the patient's head. She hadn't recognized him because the oxygen mask had obscured her view of the face. 'Is this Mr. Parmenter?'

'Hasn't been doing so well the last few days. I tried to get him transferred to the ICU this morning.'

Toby squeezed around to the head of the bed. 'Get those EKG leads on. I'll put the airway in. Number seven ET tube.'

The crash cart nurse passed her the

laryngoscope and ripped open the ET tube packet.

Toby crouched down by the patient's head. 'Okay, let's do it.'

The oxygen mask was removed. Tilting the head back, Toby slid the laryngoscope blade into the patient's throat. At once she identified the vocal cords and slid the plastic ET tube into place. The oxygen line was reconnected, and the nurse resumed bagging.

'I've got a tracing,' said the crash cart nurse. 'Looks like V. fib.'

'Charge to a hundred joules. Hand me the defib paddles! And get a lidocaine bolus ready – a hundred milligrams.'

It was too many orders at once, and the crash cart nurse was looking overwhelmed. In the ER, every task would have been done in the blink of an eye, without a doctor uttering a single word. Now Toby wished she'd brought Maudeen upstairs with her.

Toby placed the paddles on the chest. 'Back!' she ordered and pressed the discharge buttons.

A hundred joules of electricity coursed through Angus Parmenter's body.

Everyone's gaze snapped to the monitor.

The heart tracing shot straight up, then slid back to baseline. A blip appeared, the narrow peak of a QRS complex. Then another, and another.

'*Yes!*' said Toby. She reached down to feel the carotid. There was a pulse, faint but definitely present.

'Someone call ICU,' said Toby. 'We'll need a bed.'

'I'm getting a BP – eighty-five systolic—'

'Can we draw some stat electrolytes? And hand me a blood gas syringe.'

'Here, Doc.'

Toby uncapped the blood gas needle. She didn't waste her time on the wrist searching for the radial artery; she went straight for the femoral. Piercing the groin, she angled the needle toward the pulse. A flash of bright red blood told her she'd found her target. She collected 3 cc's in the syringe, then handed it to a nurse.

'Okay. Okay.' Applying pressure to the groin puncture, Toby took a deep breath and allowed herself a precious moment to review the situation. They had a patent airway, a heart rhythm, and an adequate blood pressure. They were doing all right. Now she could address the question: Why had the patient coded?

'You said he was seizing before he lost his blood pressure?' she asked.

A nurse answered, 'I'm pretty sure it was a seizure. I found him on my ten o'clock med rounds. His arm was jerking and he was un-responsive. We have a standing order to give him IV Valium as needed, and I was getting the dose ready when he stopped breathing.'

'IV Valium? Did Wallenberg order that?'

'For the seizures.'

'How many has he had?'

'Since he was admitted? Maybe six. About once

a day. It's usually his right arm that's affected. He's been having trouble with his balance, too.'

Toby frowned at the patient. She had a sudden, vivid memory of Harry Slotkin's jerking leg. 'What's their diagnosis? Do they know?'

'He's still being worked up. They've had a neurology consult, but I don't think he's figured out the problem yet.'

'He's been here a whole week and they have no idea?'

'Well, nobody's told *me*.' The RN glanced at the other nurses, and they all shook their heads.

They heard Wallenberg's voice before they realized he had walked into the room. 'What's the status here?' he said. 'Have you got him stabilized?'

Toby turned to face him. As their gazes met, she thought she saw a flash of dismay in his eyes. It was just as quickly gone.

'He was in V. fib,' said Toby. 'Preceded by a seizure and respiratory arrest. We cardioverted him, and he's now in sinus rhythm. We're waiting for an ICU bed.'

Wallenberg nodded and automatically reached for the patient's chart. Was he avoiding her gaze? She watched him flip through the pages and couldn't help envying his unflappability. His elegance. Not a hair out of place, not one unseemly crease in his white coat. Toby, dressed in her usual baggy scrubs, felt like something dragged up from the dirty clothes hamper.

'I understand he's had a number of seizures,' said Toby.

'We're not certain they are seizures. The EEG didn't confirm it.' He set down the chart and gazed at the cardiac monitor, where a normal sinus rhythm continued to trace across the oscilloscope. 'It looks like everything's under control. I can take over from here, thank you.'

'Have you ruled out toxins? Infectious agents?'

'We've had a neurology consult.'

'Has he looked specifically for those things?'

Wallenberg shot her a puzzled look. 'Why?'

'Because Harry Slotkin presented in exactly the same way. He had focal seizures. Acute onset of confusion—'

'Confusion, unfortunately, is something that happens in this age group. I hardly think it's something you can catch like the common cold.'

'But they both lived at Brant Hill. They both presented with the same clinical picture. Maybe there's a common toxin involved.'

'Which toxin? Can you be specific?'

'No, but a neurologist might be able to narrow it down.'

'We have a neurologist on the case.'

'Does he have a diagnosis?'

'Do you, Dr. Harper?'

She paused, startled by his hostile tone. She glanced at the nurses, but they studiously avoided her gaze.

'Dr. Harper?' A nurse's aide poked her head in

155

the doorway. 'ER's on the line. They have a patient downstairs. Headache.'

'Tell them I'll be right down.' Toby turned back to Wallenberg, but he had put on his stethoscope, effectively cutting off any further discussion. In frustration, she left the room.

As she descended the stairwell, she kept reminding herself that Angus Parmenter was not her patient, not her concern. Dr. Wallenberg specialized in geriatrics; surely he was better qualified to manage the patient's care than she was.

But she could not stop fretting over it.

For the next eight hours she attended to the usual night-shift parade of ailments, the chest pains and the stomachaches and the babies with fevers. But every so often there would be a lull in the pace and her thoughts would snap right back to Angus Parmenter.

And to Harry Slotkin, who had not yet been found. It had been over three weeks since his disappearance. Last night the temperature had dropped into the thirties, and she had sat up thinking about the cold, had imagined what it would be like to wander naked in that wind. She knew it was just another way of punishing herself. Harry Slotkin was not suffering on that cold night. He was, almost certainly, dead.

At dawn, the ER waiting room finally emptied out, and Toby retreated to the doctor's room. Over the desk was a bookshelf of medical texts. She perused the titles, then pulled out a neurology textbook. In the index, she looked up *Confusion*. There were over twenty entries, and the different diagnoses included everything from fevers to alcoholic DT's. She scanned the subheadings: *Metabolic. Infectious. Degenerative. Neoplastic. Congenital.*

She decided that *Confusion* was too broad a term; she needed something more specific, a physical sign or a lab test that would point her to the right diagnosis. She remembered Harry Slotkin's leg, thrashing on the gurney. And she remembered what the nurse had said about Mr. Parmenter's jerking arm. Seizures? According to Wallenberg, the EEG had ruled that out.

Toby closed the textbook and rose, groaning, to her feet. She needed to review Mr. Parmenter's chart. There might be some abnormal lab test, some physical finding that had not been pursued.

It was seven o'clock; her shift was finally over.

She rode the elevator to the fourth floor and walked into the ICU. At the nurses' station seven EKG tracings fluttered across monitor screens. A nurse sat staring at them as though hypnotized.

'Which bed is Mr. Parmenter in?' asked Toby.

The nurse seemed to shake herself out of her trance. 'Parmenter? I don't know that name.'

'He was transferred here last night from Three West.'

'We didn't get any transfers. We got that MI you sent us from the ER.'

'No, Parmenter was a post-Code Blue.'

'Oh, I remember. They canceled that transfer.'

157

'Why?'

'You'd have to ask Three West.'

Toby took the stairwell down to the third floor. The nursing station was deserted and the telephone was blinking on hold. She went to the chart rack and scanned the names but couldn't find Parmenter. With mounting frustration, she went up the hall to the patient's room and pushed open the door.

She froze, stunned by what she saw.

Morning light shone through the window, its hard glare focused on the bed where Angus Parmenter lay. His eyes were half open. His face was bluish white, the jaw sagging limply to his chest. All the IVs and monitor lines had been disconnected. He was quite obviously dead.

She heard a door whish open and turned to see a nurse wheeling a medication cart out of the patient's room across the hall. 'What happened?' Toby asked her. 'When did Mr. Parmenter expire?'

'It was about an hour ago.'

'Why wasn't I called for the code?'

'Dr. Wallenberg was here on the ward. He decided not to code him.'

'I thought the patient was being moved to the IGU.'

'They canceled the transfer. Dr. Wallenberg called the daughter, and they both agreed it didn't make sense to move the patient. Or use extraordinary measures. So they let him go.'

It was a decision with which Toby could not argue; Angus Parmenter had been eighty-two years old and comatose for a week, with little hope of recovery.

She had one more question to ask: 'Has the family given permission for the autopsy?'

The nurse looked up from her medication cart. 'They're not doing an autopsy.'

'But there has to be an autopsy.'

'The funeral arrangements are all made. The mortuary's coming to pick up the body.'

'Where's the chart?'

'The ward clerk's already broken it down. We're just waiting for Dr. Wallenberg to fill out the death certificate.'

'So he's still in the hospital?'

'I believe so. He's seeing a consult on the surgery floor.'

Toby went straight to the nurses' station. The ward clerk was away from her desk, but she'd left the loose pages from Mr. Parmenter's chart on the countertop. Quickly Toby flipped to the last progress note and read Dr. Wallenberg's final entry.

Family notified. Respirations ceased – nurses unable to detect pulse. On exam, no heartbeat noted on auscultation. Pupils midposition and fixed. Pronounced dead 0558.

There was no mention of an autopsy, no speculation about the underlying illness.

The squeak of rolling wheels made her glance up as two hospital orderlies came out of the

159

elevator, pushing a gurney. They wheeled it toward room 341.

'Wait,' said Toby. 'Are you here for Mr. Parmenter?'

'Yeah.'

'Hold on. Don't take him *anywhere* yet.'

'The hearse is already on its way over.'

'The body stays where it is. I have to talk to the family.'

'But—'

'Just *wait*.' Toby picked up the phone and paged Wallenberg to Three West. There was no answer. The orderlies stood waiting in the hallway, glancing at each other, shrugging. Again she picked up the phone and this time she called the patient's daughter, whose number was listed in the chart. It rang six times. She hung up, her frustration now at a boil, and saw that the orderlies had wheeled the gurney into the patient's room.

She ran after them. 'I told you, the patient *stays*.'

'Ma'am, we were ordered to pick him up and bring him downstairs.'

'There's been a mistake, I know it. Dr. Wallenberg's still in the hospital. Just wait until I can talk to him about this.'

'Talk to me about what, Dr. Harper?'

Toby turned. Wallenberg stood in the doorway.

'An autopsy,' she said.

He stepped into the room, letting the door slowly whoosh shut behind him. 'Are you the one who paged me?'

'Yes. They're taking the body to the mortuary. I told them to wait until you could arrange for the autopsy.'

'There's no need for an autopsy.'

'You don't know why he coded. You don't know why he became confused.'

'A stroke is the most likely cause.'

'The CT scan didn't show a stroke.'

'The CT may have been done too early. And you wouldn't necessarily see a brain stem infarct.'

'You're guessing, Dr. Wallenberg.'

'What would you have me do? Order a head scan on a dead patient?'

The orderlies were watching the heated exchange with fascination, their gazes bouncing back and forth. Now the men's eyes were focused on Toby, waiting for her answer.

She said, 'Harry Slotkin presented with identical symptoms. Acute onset of confusion and what appeared to be focal seizures. Both these men lived at Brant Hill. Both of them were previously healthy.'

'Men in that age group are prone to strokes.'

'But there could be something else going on. Only an autopsy can determine that. Is there some reason you're opposed to one?'

Wallenberg flushed, his anger so apparent Toby almost took a step backward. They eyed each other for a moment, then he seemed to regain his composure.

'There'll be no autopsy,' he said, 'because the daughter has refused. And I'm honoring her wishes.'

'Maybe she doesn't understand how important this is. If I spoke to her—'

'Don't even think about it, Dr. Harper. You'd be invading her privacy.' He turned to the orderlies, his dominance fully reasserted. 'You can bring him downstairs now.' He shot a last dismissive glance at Toby, then he left the room.

In silence Toby watched as the orderlies wheeled the gurney toward the bed and braked it in place.

'One, two, three, move.'

They slid the corpse onto the gurney and secured it in place with a chest strap. It was not for safety but for aesthetics. Gurneys could be bumped, ramps could be steep, and one didn't want dead bodies accidentally tumbling onto floors. Above the corpse, a false mattress pad was clamped into place, then a long sheet draped over the whole contraption. A casual observer passing it in the hall would think it was merely an empty stretcher.

They wheeled the body out of the room.

Toby stood alone, listening to the receding squeak of the wheels. She thought of what would happen next. Downstairs, in the morgue, there would be paperwork to complete, authorization forms and releases to be signed. Then the deceased would be loaded into a hearse and transported to the mortuary, where the body fluids would be drained and replaced with embalming fluid.

Or would it be a cremation? she wondered. A fiery reduction to carbon ash and trace elements, leaving behind no answers?

This was her last chance to learn Angus Parmenter's diagnosis. And maybe Harry Slotkin's diagnosis as well. She picked up the phone and once again called the patient's daughter.

This time a voice answered with a soft 'Hello?'

'Mrs. Lacy? This is Dr. Harper. We met last week, in the Emergency Room.'

'Yes. I remember.'

'I'm very sorry about your father. I just learned the news.'

The woman gave a sigh, more a sound of weariness than of grief. 'We were expecting it, I suppose. And to be perfectly honest, it's something of a . . . well, a relief. That sounds awful. But after a week of watching him . . . like that . . .' Again she sighed. 'He wouldn't have wanted to live that way.'

'Believe me, none of us would.' Toby hesitated, searching for the right words. 'Mrs. Lacy, I know this is a bad time to talk to you about this, but there's really no other time to do it. Dr. Wallenberg told me you didn't want an autopsy. I understand how hard it is for the family to give permission for something like this. But I really feel, in this case, it's vital. We don't know what your father died of, and it may turn out to be—'

'I didn't object to an autopsy.'

'But Dr. Wallenberg said you refused one.'

'We never discussed it.'

Toby paused. *Why did Wallenberg lie to me?* She said, 'May I have your permission for an autopsy, then?'

163

Mrs. Lacy hesitated only a few seconds. Softly she said: 'If you think one is necessary. Yes.'

Toby hung up. She started to call the Pathology Department next, then decided against it. Even with the family's permission, no Springer pathologist would perform the postmortem – not when the attending physician objected.

Why is Wallenberg so determined to avoid an autopsy? What is he afraid they'll find?

She looked at the telephone. *Decide. You have to decide now.* She picked it up and dialed directory assistance. 'City of Boston,' she said. 'The office of the medical examiner.'

It took a moment to obtain the phone number, another few moments to get through to the right extension. While she waited, she could picture the progress of Angus Parmenter's body toward the morgue. The ride down the elevator. The door whishing open to the basement level. The corridor with its groaning water pipes.

'Medical examiner's office. This is Stella.'

Toby snapped to attention. 'I'm Dr. Harper at Springer Hospital in Newton. May I speak to the chief medical examiner?'

'Dr. Rowbotham is on vacation, but I can connect you with our deputy chief, Dr. Dvorak.'

'Yes, please.'

There were a few clicks, and then a man's voice, flat and weary, said: 'This is Dr. Dvorak.'

'I have a patient who just expired,' she said. 'I think an autopsy is indicated.'

'May I ask why?'

164

'He was admitted here a week ago. I saw him in the ER when he came in by ambulance—'

'Were there traumatic injuries?'

'No. He was confused, disoriented. There were cerebellar signs. Early this morning he had a respiratory arrest and died.'

'Do you suspect foul play of any kind?'

'Not really, but—'

'Then your own hospital pathologist can certainly perform the autopsy. You don't have to report a death to our office unless the patient dies within twenty-four hours of being admitted.'

'Yes, I realize it's not your usual coroner's case. But the attending physician refuses to order a postmortem, which means our pathologist won't do it. That's why I'm calling you. The family has already agreed to it.'

She heard a long sigh and the shuffle of papers, could almost see the man at his desk, tired and overworked, surrounded by countless reminders of death. A joyless profession, she thought, and Dr. Dvorak had the voice of an unhappy man.

He said, 'Dr. Harper, I don't think you're quite clear on the role of our office here. Unless there's a question of foul play or public health—'

'This *could* be a public health issue.'

'How so?'

'It's the second case I've seen in my ER this month. Two elderly men, both presenting with acute confusion, cerebellar signs, and focal seizures. And here's what troubles me: these two patients lived in the same retirement complex.

They drank the same water, ate in the same dining room. They probably knew each other.'

Dr. Dvorak said nothing.

'I don't know what we're dealing with here,' said Toby. 'It could be anything from viral meningitis to garden pesticides. I would hate to overlook a preventable illness. Especially if other people are at risk.'

'You say there were two patients.'

'Yes. The first one was in my ER three weeks ago.'

'Then the autopsy on that first patient should provide your answers.'

'There was no autopsy on the first patient. He vanished from the hospital. His body's never been recovered.'

The man's silence gave way to a soft exhalation. When he spoke again, she could hear the new undertone of interest. 'You said you're at Springer Hospital? What's the patient's name?'

'Angus Parmenter.'

'And is the body still there?'

'I'll make sure it is,' she said.

She ran four flights down the stairwell and emerged in the basement. One of the overhead fluorescents was flickering like a strobe light, and her legs seemed to move in a jerky click-click-click of freeze frames as she hurried down the hall to a door labeled: AUTHORIZED PERSONNEL ONLY. She stepped into the morgue.

The lights were on, and a radio on the

attendant's desk was playing, but there was no one in the anteroom.

Toby entered the autopsy lab. The stainless steel table was empty. Next she checked the cold room, the refrigerated locker where bodies were stored prior to autopsy. A chill vapor, faintly malodorous, swirled out of the locker. The smell of dead meat. She flipped on the light and saw two gurneys. She went to the first one and unzipped the shroud, revealing the face of an elderly woman, eyes open, the sclerae shockingly red from hemorrhages. Shuddering, she closed the shroud and went to the second gurney. It was a large corpse, and a foul odor rose up as she slid the zipper open. At her first sight of the man's face, she jerked away, fighting nausea. The flesh of the corpse's right cheek had melted away.

Necrotizing streptococcus, she thought, the flesh devoured by bacteria.

'This area is off limits,' a voice said.

Turning, she saw the morgue attendant. 'I'm looking for Angus Parmenter. Where is he?'

'They wheeled him out to the loading bay.'

'They're taking him already?'

'The hearse just arrived.'

'Shit,' she muttered and dashed out of the morgue.

A quick jog down the hall brought her to the loading bay doors. She pushed through, and the morning sunlight caught her full in the face. Blinking against the glare, she quickly took in the situation: the orderly, standing by the empty

167

gurney. The hearse, as it pulled away. She dashed past the orderly and ran alongside the moving hearse, rapping at the driver's window.

'Stop. Stop the car!'

The driver braked and rolled down his window. 'What is it?'

'You can't take the body.'

'It's been authorized. The hospital released it.'

'It's going to the medical examiner.'

'No one told me. As far as I know, the family's already made arrangements with the mortuary.'

'This is now a medical examiner's case. You can check with Dr. Dvorak at the ME's office.'

The driver glanced back at the loading bay, where the orderly stood watching in puzzlement. 'Gee, I don't know . . .'

'Look, I'll take full responsibility,' she said. 'Now back up. We have to unload the body.'

The driver shrugged. 'Whatever you say,' he muttered and shifted into reverse. 'But someone's gonna catch hell for this. And I sure hope it isn't me.'

Eight

Lisa was flirting with him again. It was one of the daily irritations that Dr. Daniel Dvorak had learned to tolerate: his female assistant's eyelash-batting glances through the protective goggles, her insatiable curiosity about his private life, and her obvious frustration that he chose to ignore her advances. He didn't understand why she should find him so interesting; he suspected her attraction to him was nothing more than the challenge of a silent man.

An older man, he admitted to himself with resignation as he eyed his youthful assistant. Lisa had no wrinkles, no gray hairs, no sagging epidermis. At twenty-six she was, in the immortal words of his own teenage son, a blond babe. And what does my boy call *me* behind my back? he wondered. Old fart? Fuddy duddy? To a fourteen-year-old like Patrick, forty-five must seem as distant as the next ice age.

But we're all closer to death than we realize, thought Dvorak, gazing at the naked body on the morgue table. The overhead lights shone down, harsh and unforgiving, emphasizing every wrinkle and mole on the corpse's skin. The gray hairs on the chest. The black seborrheic keratoses on the neck. The inevitable changes of aging. Even blond and buff Lisa would someday have liver spots.

'Looks like we have an outdoorsman,' he commented, running a gloved finger across a rough patch of skin on the corpse's forehead. 'Actinic keratoses. He has sun damage here.'

'But pretty nice pectorals for an old guy.' Lisa, of course, noticed such details. She was a health club addict, had started the gym craze two years ago, and her quest for physical perfection had reached the point where she talked incessantly about abs and lats and reps. It was the code of the muscle obsessed, who seemed to prefer one-syllable words. Often Dvorak would see Lisa glancing at her own reflection in the mirror over the sink. Was the hair perfect? Did that blond forelock curl just so? Was the tan holding, or would she need another twenty minutes on her apartment rooftop? Dvorak found her youthful preoccupation with good looks both amusing and bewildering.

Dvorak seldom looked in a mirror anymore, and that was only to shave. When he did look at himself, he was always surprised to see that his hair was now as much silver as black. He could see the passage of years in his face, the deepening lines around his eyes, the permanent frown etched between his eyebrows. He also saw how tired and

170

drawn he'd become. He'd lost weight since his divorce three years ago, had lost even more weight since his son, Patrick, had left for boarding school two months ago. As layers of his personal life had peeled away, so had the pounds.

This morning, Lisa had commented on his new gauntness. *Lookin' good these days, Doc!* she'd chirped, which only confirmed how blind the young were. Dvorak didn't think he looked good. When he looked in the mirror, what he saw was a candidate for Prozac.

This autopsy was not going to improve his mood.

He said to Lisa, 'Let's turn him over. I want to examine his back first.'

Together they log-rolled the corpse sideways. Dvorak redirected the light and observed dependent mottling, consistent with the post-mortem pooling of blood, as well as pale areas on the buttocks where the weight of the body had compressed the soft tissues. He pressed a gloved finger against the bruiselike discoloration. It blanched.

'Livor mortis not fixed,' he noted. 'We've got an abrasion here, over the right scapula. But nothing impressive.'

They rolled the corpse onto its back again.

'He's in complete rigor mortis,' said Lisa.

Dvorak glanced at the medical record. 'Time of death recorded at five-fifty-eight. It's consistent.'

'What about those bruises on the wrists?'

'Looks like restraints.' Dvorak flipped through

the record again and saw the nurse's note: *Patient remains agitated and in four-point restraints*. If only all his postmortems came with the circumstances of death so well documented. When a body was wheeled into his autopsy room, he felt fortunate just to have a positive identification, even more fortunate if the body was both intact and free of odors. To deal with the worst odors, he and his assistants donned protective suits and oxygen units. Today, though, they were working with standard gloves and goggles, on a cadaver that had already been screened in the hospital for HIV and hepatitis. While autopsies were never pleasant, this one would be relatively benign. And probably unrewarding.

He redirected the light straight down on the table. The corpse had pincushion arms – typical for a hospital death. Dvorak counted four different puncture sites on the left upper extremity, five on the right. There was also a needle puncture wound in the right groin – probably from an arterial blood gas draw. This patient had not gone peacefully into that good night.

He picked up the scalpel and made his Y incision. Lifting the sternum in one piece, he exposed both the chest and abdominal cavities to view.

The organs looked unremarkable.

He began to remove them, dictating his findings as he worked.

'This is the body of a well-nourished white male, age eighty-two . . .' He paused. That age couldn't be right. He flipped to the front of the chart and checked the birth date. The age was correct.

'I would've guessed sixty-five,' said Lisa.

'It says here, eighty-two.'

'Could that be a mistake?'

Dvorak studied the corpse's face. The variability of aging was a matter of both genetics and lifestyle. He had seen eighty-year-old women who could pass for sixty. He had also seen a thirty-five-year-old alcoholic who'd appeared ancient. Perhaps Angus Parmenter was merely the beneficiary of youthful genes.

'I'll confirm the age later,' he said, and continued dictating. 'Decedent expired today at five-fifty-eight in Springer Hospital, Newton, Massachusetts, where he was admitted as a patient seven days ago.' Once again, he picked up the scalpel.

Dvorak had gone through these motions so many times before that much of it was automatic for him. He severed the esophagus and trachea, as well as the great vessels, and removed the heart and lungs. Lisa slid them onto the scale and called out the weights, then placed the heart on the cutting board. Dvorak sliced along the coronary vessels.

'I don't think we have an MI,' he said. 'Coronaries look pretty clean.'

He resected the spleen, then the small intestine. The seemingly endless coils of bowel felt chill and slippery. The stomach, pancreas, and liver were resected in one block. He saw no signs of peritonitis, nor did he detect the odor of anaerobic bacteria. The joys of working on a fresh corpse. No foul smells, only the butcher-shop scent of blood.

On the cutting board, he sliced open the stomach and found it was empty.

'Hospital food must've sucked,' said Lisa.

'He wasn't able to eat, according to the record.'

So far, Dvorak had seen nothing on gross inspection that would point to the cause of death.

He circled around to the cadaver's head, made his incision, then folded the scalp forward over the face like a rubber mask. Lisa had the Stryker saw ready. Neither of them spoke as the saw whined, opening up the skull.

Dvorak lifted off the cap of bone. The brain looked like a mass of gray worms under its delicate covering of meningeal membrane. The meninges did not appear in any way unusual, which argued against infection. Neither did Dvorak see any signs of epidural bleeding.

The brain would have to be removed for closer inspection. He picked up the scalpel and worked quickly, severing optic nerves and blood vessels. As he reached deeper, to free the brain from the spinal cord, he felt a sharp bite of pain.

At once he withdrew his hand and stared at the cut glove. 'Shit,' he muttered and crossed to the sink.

'What happened?' said Lisa.

'Cut myself.'

'Are you bleeding?'

Dvorak ripped off the gloves and examined his left middle finger. A fine line of blood welled up along the razor-thin laceration. 'Scalpel went right through both gloves. Shit, shit, *shit*.' He grabbed a bottle of Betadine from the counter and squirted a stream of disinfectant on his finger. 'Die, buggers.'

'He's HIV negative, right?'

'Yeah. Lucky for me,' he said, blotting his finger dry. 'That shouldn't have happened. I just got careless.' Angry at himself now, he regloved and went back to the cadaver. The brain had already been severed of all its connections. Gingerly he scooped it up in both hands, swished it in saline to wash off the blood, and lay the dripping organ on the cutting board. He gave the organ a visual inspection, turning it to examine all the surfaces. The lobes appeared normal, without any masses. He slid the brain into a bucket of Formalin, where it would fix for a week before it was ready to be sliced and mounted on slides. The answers would most likely be found under the microscope.

'Dr. Dvorak?' It was his secretary, Stella, speaking over the intercom.

'Yes?'

'There's a Dr. Carl Wallenberg on the line.'

'I'll call him back. I'm in the middle of an autopsy.'

'Actually, that's why he insists on talking to you now. He wants the autopsy stopped.'

Dvorak straightened. 'Why?'

'Maybe you should talk to him yourself.'

'Guess I have to take this call,' he muttered to Lisa, stripping off his gloves and apron. 'Go ahead with the muscle biopsies and liver sections.'

'Shouldn't I wait until you talk to him?'

'We've gone this far. Let's finish the tissue sections.'

He went to his office to take the call. Even with the door shut, the room was pervaded by the odor of Formalin, carried in on his clothes, his hands. He himself smelled like some preserved specimen, hidden away in this windowless office.

A man in a jar, trapped.

He picked up the phone. 'Dr. Wallenberg? This Is Dr. Dvorak.'

'I believe there's been a misunderstanding. Mr. Parmenter was my patient, and I'm at a complete loss as to why you're performing an autopsy.'

'It was requested by one of the doctors at Springer Hospital.'

'You mean Dr. Harper?' The sound that came through the line was clearly a snort of disgust. 'She wasn't involved with the patient's care. She had no authority to call you.'

'According to the record, she did see the patient in the ER.'

'That was a week ago. Since then, the patient has been under my care, as well as the care of several subspecialists. None of us felt an autopsy was necessary. And we certainly didn't think it was a case for the medical examiner.'

'She led me to believe this was a public health issue.'

Again, that snort of disgust. 'Dr. Harper's not exactly a reliable source of information. Maybe you haven't heard. Springer Hospital has her under investigation for mistakes she's made in the ER, serious mistakes. She may soon be out of a job, and I wouldn't trust her opinion on anything. Dr. Dvorak, this is a chain-of-command issue. I'm the attending physician, and I'm telling you an autopsy is a waste of your time. And a waste of my taxes.'

Dvorak stifled a groan. *I don't want to be dealing with this. I'm a pathologist. I'd rather work with dead bodies than live egos.*

'Also,' said Wallenberg, 'there's the family. The daughter would be very upset about her father being mutilated. She may even consider legal action.'

Slowly Dvorak straightened, his head coming up in puzzlement. 'But Dr. Wallenberg, I've spoken to the daughter.'

'What?'

'This morning. Mrs. Lacy called to discuss the autopsy. I explained the reasons for it, and she seemed to understand. She didn't argue against it.'

There was silence on the line. 'She must have changed her mind since I spoke to her,' said Wallenberg.

'I guess so. At any rate, the autopsy has been done.'

'Already?'

'It's been a relatively quiet morning here.'

Again there was a pause. When Wallenberg

spoke again, his voice was oddly subdued. 'The body – it will be returned, complete, to the family?'

'Yes. With all the organs.'

Wallenberg cleared his throat. 'I suppose that will satisfy them.'

Interesting, thought Dvorak as he hung up. *He never asked what I found on autopsy.*

He replayed the conversation in his head. Had he simply been sucked into the petty politics of a suburban hospital? Wallenberg had characterized Dr. Harper as a marginal physician, a woman under scrutiny, perhaps a woman at odds with her colleagues. Was her request for an autopsy merely an attempt to embarrass another physician on the staff?

This morning, he should have exercised a little Machiavellian reasoning, should have sought out her real agenda. But Dvorak's logic tended toward the concrete. He gathered information from what he could see and touch and smell. A cadaver's secrets are easily laid bare with a knife; human motives remained a mystery to him.

The intercom buzzed. 'Dr. Dvorak?' said Stella. 'Dr. Toby Harper's on the line. Want me to put her through?'

Dvorak thought it over and decided he was in no mood to talk to a woman who'd already ruined his day. 'No,' he said.

'What shall I tell her?'

'I've gone home for the day.'

'Well, if that's what you really want . . .'

178

'Stella?'

'Yes?'

'If she calls back again, give her the same answer. I'm not available.'

He hung up and returned to the morgue.

Lisa was bent over the cutting board, her scalpel slicing off a section of liver. She looked up as he walked in. 'Well?' she asked. 'Do we finish the biopsies?'

'Finish them. Then return the organs to the cavity. The family wants it all back.'

She made another cut, then paused. 'What about the brain? It still needs to be fixed for another week.'

He looked at the bucket where Angus Parmenter's brain lay in its bath of Formalin. Then he looked down at his bandaged finger and thought of how the scalpel had sliced through two gloves and into his own flesh.

He said, 'We'll keep it. I'll just replace the skull cap and sew the scalp shut.' He pulled on a fresh pair of gloves and reached into a drawer for a needle and suture. 'They'll never know it's missing.'

Toby hung up the telephone in frustration. Had the autopsy been completed or hadn't it? For two days she'd been trying to get through to Daniel Dvorak, but each time his secretary had told her he was not available, and her tone of voice had made it clear that Toby's calls were not welcome.

The oven alarm buzzed. Toby turned off the gas

179

and removed the casserole dish. She was copping out tonight – lasagna from the frozen food section, and a sadly wilted salad. She'd had no chance to shop for groceries and there was no milk left, so she poured two glasses of water and set them on the kitchen table. Her whole life, it seemed, had been reduced to a mad scramble for shortcuts. Frozen dinners and dishes stacked in the sink and wrinkled blouses pulled straight from the dryer. She wondered if her profound weariness was due to some incubating flu virus, or if it was mental exhaustion that was dragging her down. She opened the kitchen door and called out:

'Mom, dinner's ready! Come in and eat.'

Ellen emerged from behind a clump of bee balm and obediently shuffled into the kitchen. Toby washed her mother's hands at the sink and sat her down at the table. She tied a napkin around Ellen's neck and slid the plate of lasagna in front of her. She cut the lasagna into bite-size pieces. She did this to the salad as well. She placed a fork in Ellen's hand.

Ellen did not eat but sat waiting and watching her daughter.

Toby sat down with her own plate of food and took a few bites of lasagna. She noticed Ellen wasn't eating. 'It's your dinner, Mom. Put it in your mouth.'

Ellen slid the empty fork into her mouth and tasted it with great concentration.

'Here. Let me help you.' Toby glided Ellen's fork to the plate, scooped up a lasagna noodle, and raised it to Ellen's mouth.

180

'Pretty good,' said Ellen.

'Now take another bite. Go on, Mom.'

Ellen looked up as the doorbell rang.

'That must be Bryan already,' said Toby, rising from the table. 'You keep eating now. Don't wait for me.'

She left her mother in the kitchen and went to answer the front door. 'You're early.'

'I thought I'd help out with dinner,' Bryan said as he came into the house. He held out a paper bag. 'Ice cream. Your mama does like her strawberry ice cream.'

As she took the bag, she noticed Bryan wasn't looking at her; in fact he seemed to be avoiding her gaze, turning his back to her as he removed his jacket and hung it up in the closet. Even when he turned to face her, his eyes were focused elsewhere. 'So how're we doing with dinner?' he asked.

'I just sat her down at the table. We're having a little trouble eating today.'

'Again?'

'She didn't touch the sandwich I left her. And she looks at the lasagna like it's something from outer space.'

'Oh. I can take care of that—'

From the kitchen came a loud crash followed by the clatter of broken china skittering across the floor.

'Oh my God,' said Toby as she ran into the kitchen.

A bewildered Ellen stood staring down at the

broken casserole dish. Lasagna had splattered all over the floor and against one wall in a shocking spray of cheese and tomato sauce.

'Mom, what are you *doing*?' yelled Toby.

Ellen shook her head and mumbled: 'Hot. Didn't know it was hot.'

'Christ, *look* at this mess! All this cheese . . .' Toby grabbed the trash can. In rage and frustration she dragged it across the floor to the broken dish. As she knelt down to clean up the ruined meal she realized she was dangerously close to tears. *I'm losing it. Everything in my life is so fucking screwed up. I can't deal with this, too. I just can't.*

'Come on, Ellen sweetie,' she heard Bryan say. 'Let's have a look at those hands. Oh dear, you're going to need some cold water on that. No no, don't pull away, sweetheart. Let me make them feel better. That's nasty, isn't it?'

Toby looked up. 'What is it?'

'Your mama burned her hands.'

'Ouch, ouch, *ouch!*' Ellen squealed.

Bryan led Ellen to the sink and ran cold water over her hands. 'Isn't that better? Now, we're going to have ice cream after this and that'll make you feel even better. I brought strawberry. Yum yum.'

'Yum,' murmured Ellen.

Cheeks flushing with shame, Toby watched as Bryan tenderly dabbed Ellen's hands with a towel. Toby hadn't even noticed her mother was hurt. In silence she resumed picking up the pieces of crockery and the lumps of congealing cheese. She sponged up the sauce and wiped down the wall. Then she sat down at the table and watched Bryan coax Ellen into eating the ice cream. His patience, his gentle wheedling, made Toby feel more guilty. It was Bryan who had noticed Ellen's burned hands, Bryan who'd seen to her needs; Toby had seen only the broken dish and the mess on the floor.

Now it was already six-fifteen, time for Toby to get ready for work.

She didn't have the energy to rise from the table. She sat with her hand against her forehead, delaying just a little while longer.

'I have something to tell you,' said Bryan. He put down the spoon and gently wiped Ellen's mouth with a napkin. Then he met Toby's gaze. 'I'm really sorry about this. It wasn't an easy decision but . . .' He placed the napkin carefully on the table. 'I've been offered another position. It's something I can't pass up. Something I've wanted to do for so long. I wasn't *looking* for another job – it just sort of happened.'

'*What* happened?'

'I got a call from Twin Pines nursing home, out in Wellesley. They're looking for someone to start up a new recreational art therapy program. Toby, they made me an offer. I couldn't turn it down.'

'You didn't say a word about this to me.'

'I only got the call yesterday. I had the interview this morning.'

183

'And you took the job, just like that? Without even talking to me?'

'I had to make a decision on the spot. Toby, it's a nine-to-five job. It means I can rejoin the rest of the human race.'

'How much are they offering you? I'll pay you more.'

'I've already accepted.'

'How *much*?'

He cleared his throat. 'It's not the money. I don't want you to think that's the reason. It's . . . everything combined.'

Slowly she sank back. 'So I can't make you a better offer.'

'No.' He looked down at the table. 'They want me to start as soon as possible.'

'What about my mother? What if I can't find anyone to watch her?'

'I'm sure you will.'

'Exactly how much time do I have to find someone?'

'Two weeks.'

'Two *weeks*? Do you think I can pull someone out of thin air? It took me months to find *you*.'

'Yes, I know, but—'

'What the hell am I supposed to *do*?' The desperation in her voice seemed to hang like an ugly pall between them.

Slowly he looked up at her, his gaze unexpectedly detached. 'I like Ellen. You know that. And I've always given her the best care I could. But Toby, she's not my mother. She's yours.'

The simple truth of that statement silenced any response she could have made. *Yes, she is my mother. My responsibility.*

She looked at Ellen and saw that her mother was paying attention to none of this. Ellen had picked up a napkin and was folding it over and over, her forehead wrinkled in concentration.

Toby said, 'Do you know anyone who might want the job?'

'I can get you some names,' he said. 'I know a few people who might be interested.'

'I would appreciate it.'

They looked at each other across the table, not as employer and employee this time, but as friends. 'Thank you, Bryan,' she said. 'For all you've done for us.'

In the living room, the clock struck the half hour. Toby gave a sigh and dragged herself out of the chair.

It was time to go to work.

'Toby, we have to talk.'

She looked up from a wheezing three-year-old and saw Paul Hawkins standing in the exam room doorway. 'Can you wait a minute?' she asked.

'It's pretty urgent.'

'Okay, let me give this epinephrine shot and I'll be right out.'

'I'll wait in the staff kitchen.'

As Maudeen handed her the vial of epinephrine, Toby saw the nurse's questioning look. They were both wondering the same thing: Why was the ER chief here at 10 P.M. on a Thursday night? He'd been dressed in a suit and tie – not his usual hospital garb. Already feeling uneasy, Toby drew two-tenths of a cc of epinephrine into a TB syringe, then forced a cheerful note into her voice as she said to the child, 'We're going to make your breathing much, much better. You have to sit very still. This will feel like a beesting, but it'll be over quick, okay?'

'Don't wanna beesting. Don't wanna beesting.'

The child's mother tightened her grip around the boy. 'He hates these shots. Just go ahead and do it.'

Toby nodded. Bargaining with a three-year-old was a hopeless proposition anyway. She injected the drug, eliciting a shriek that could peel paint off a wall. Just as suddenly, the screaming was over, and the boy, though still sniffling, was eyeing the syringe with a covetous look.

'I want it.'

'You can have a new one,' said Toby, and she handed him a fresh syringe, minus the needle. 'Bathtub fun.'

'Gonna give my sister a shot.'

The mother rolled her eyes. 'She's gonna love that.'

Already the boy's wheezing seemed to be better, so Toby left Maudeen in charge and went to find Paul in the staff kitchen.

He stood up as she walked in but didn't speak until she'd closed the door.

'We had a hospital board meeting tonight,' he

said. 'It just wrapped up. I thought I should come right over and explain what happened.'

'I assume this has to do with Harry Slotkin again.'

'That was one of the issues we discussed.'

'There were others?'

'The matter of the autopsy came up as well.'

'I see. I have a feeling I should sit down for this.'

'Maybe we both should.'

She took a chair across the dining table from him. 'If it was a "torch Dr. Harper" session, why wasn't I invited for the barbecue?'

Paul sighed. 'Toby, you and I could have toughed out the crisis with Harry Slotkin. In fact, so far you're lucky on that case. The Slotkin family isn't talking lawsuit yet. And the negative publicity seems to be over. From what I hear, any fresh news stories were squelched by Brant Hill. And Dr. Wallenberg.'

'Why would Wallenberg do me any favors?'

'I guess it wasn't good for Brant Hill, having it known that one of their wealthy residents was wandering around like some street person. You know, they're not your usual Sun City of retirees. Their success depends on their platinum status, on being the best and charging the bucks for it. You can't attract new people if there's any question about the well-being of your clients.'

'So Wallenberg was protecting his cash cow and not me.'

'Whatever the reason, he helped you out. But now you've gone and pissed him off. What was going through your head? Calling in the medical examiner? Turning it into a coroner's case?'

'It was the only way to get a diagnosis.'

'The man was no longer your patient. An autopsy should have been Wallenberg's decision.'

'But he was avoiding the issue. Either he didn't want to know the cause of death or he was afraid to find out. I couldn't think of anything else to do.'

'You made him look bad. You made it look like some sort of criminal case.'

'I was concerned about the public health issue—'

'This isn't a public health issue. This is a political *mess*. Wallenberg was at the meeting tonight. So were Doug Carey's allies. It was a barbecue all right, and you were the main course. Now Wallenberg's threatening to admit all Brant Hill patients to Lakeside Hospital instead of Springer. Which is going to hurt us. Maybe you don't realize that Brant Hill's just one link in a big chain. They're affiliated with a dozen other nursing homes, and all of them refer their patients to us. Do you have any idea how much money we make on their hip surgeries alone? Add the TURPs, the cataracts, and the hemorrhoids, and you're talking a lot of patients, most of them with supplemental insurance on top of Medicare. We can't afford to lose those referrals. But that's what Wallenberg's threatening.'

'All because of the autopsy?'

'He has a pretty good reason to be upset. When you called the ME, you made Wallenberg look incompetent. Or worse. Now we're getting calls from newspapers again. It could be another round of bad publicity.'

'Doug Carey's tipping them off. It's just the sneaky kind of thing he'd do.'

'Yeah, well, now Wallenberg's pissed that his name could be dragged into the public eye. The board's pissed that they could lose all their Brant Hill referrals.'

'And of course everyone's pissed at me.'

'Are you surprised?'

Slowly she let out a breath. 'Okay, so you had a barbecue and now I'm a crispy critter.'

Paul nodded. 'Wallenberg wants your contract terminated. Of course it has to go through me first, since I'm ER chief. I wasn't left with a lot of maneuvering room.'

'What did you tell them?'

'That there was a problem firing you.' He gave an uneasy laugh. 'I used a delaying tactic that you might not approve of. I told them you might fight back by filing a sex discrimination suit. That made them nervous. If there's anything they didn't want to deal with, it's a whiny feminist.'

'How flattering.'

'It was the only thing I could think of.'

'Funny. It's something I never would have considered. And *I'm* the woman.'

'Remember that sexual harassment suit one of the nurses filed? It dragged on for two years, and Springer ended up paying a fortune in attorney's fees. This was one way I could make them stop and consider their actions. And buy you some time until things cool down.' He dragged his fingers through his hair. 'Toby, I'm in the hot seat. They're pressuring me to resolve the situation. And I don't want to hurt you, I really don't.'

'Are you asking me to resign?'

'No. No, that's not why I'm here.'

'What are you asking me to do?'

'I'm thinking maybe you should take a leave of absence for a few weeks. In the meantime, the ME's report will come back. I'm sure it'll show natural causes. That will let Wallenberg off the hook.'

'And all will be forgiven.'

'I hope so. You're scheduled to go on vacation next month anyway. You could take it now. Extend it by three or four weeks.'

For a moment she sat thinking it over, playing a mental game of dominoes. One action produces a result that produces another result. 'Who'll fill in for me?' she asked.

'We can pull Joe Severin in to take your shifts. He's only a part-timer now. I'm sure he'd be willing.'

She looked straight at Paul. 'And I'd never get my job back. Would I?'

'Toby—'

'Wasn't it Doug Carey who brought Severin on staff? Aren't they buddies or something? You're not taking all the personalities into account. If I go on leave, Joe Severin steps right in. I won't have a job to come back to, and you know it.'

He said nothing. He just looked at her, his expression unfathomable. For too many years, she had let her attraction for Paul Hawkins obscure the relationship. She'd read more into his smiles, his friendliness, than had really existed. That she realized it only now, at her most vulnerable moment, made the blow even more painful.

She stood up. 'I'll take my vacation as scheduled. No earlier.'

'Toby, I'm doing what I can to protect you. You have to understand, *my* position isn't secure either. If we lose those Brant Hill referrals, Springer's going to be hurt. And the board will be looking for fall guys.'

'I'm not blaming you, Paul. I understand why you're doing this.'

'Then why won't you do what I suggest? Take the leave of absence. Your job will still be here.'

'Can I have that in writing?'

He was silent.

She turned toward the door. 'That's what I thought.'

Nine

Molly Picker stood looking at the pay phone, trying to scrape up the courage to pick up the receiver. It was the second visit she'd made to this phone booth today. The first time she hadn't even stepped inside but had turned around and walked away. Now she was standing right in front of the phone and the door was shut behind her, and there was nothing to stop her from making the call.

Her hands shook as she picked up the receiver and dialed.

'Operator.'

'I want to make a collect call. To Beaufort, South Carolina.'

'Who shall I say is calling?'

'Molly.' She gave the number, then leaned back with eyes closed, heart pounding, as the operator put through the call. She heard it ring. Her fear was so intense she thought she might throw up, right there in the booth. *Sweet Jesus, help me.*

'Hello?'

Molly's back snapped straight. It was her mother's voice. 'Mama,' she blurted out, but then the operator cut in:

'You have a collect call from Molly. Will you accept?'

There was a long silence on the other end.

Please, please, please. Talk to me.

'Ma'am? Will you accept the charges?'

A long sigh, then: 'Oh, I guess so.'

'Go ahead,' said the operator.

'Mama? It's me. I'm calling from Boston.'

'So you're still up there.'

'Yeah. I been wantin' to call—'

'You need money or something. Is that it?'

'No! No, I'm doin' okay. I'm, uh . . .' Molly cleared her throat. 'I'm holdin' my own.'

'Well, that's good.'

Molly closed her eyes, wishing her mother's voice didn't sound so flat. Wishing this conversation would go the way she'd fantasized it would. That Mama would break down crying and then ask her to come home. But there were no tears in Mama's voice, only that lifeless tone that cut straight to Molly's heart.

'So is there a reason you're calling?'

'Uh . . . no.' Molly rubbed a hand across her eyes. 'Not really.'

'You wanna say something or what?'

'I just – I guess I wanted to say hello.'

'Okay. Well, look. I gotta finish cookin' here. If you don't have much more to say—'

'I'm pregnant,' whispered Molly.

There was no response.

'Did you hear me? I'm gonna have a baby. Think of it, Mama! I'm hopin' it's a girl, so I can dress her all up like a princess. 'Member how you used to stitch up those dresses for me? I'm gonna get me a sewing machine, learn how to sew.' She was laughing now, talking rapidly and desperately through her tears. 'But you gotta teach me, Mama, because I never could get it right. Never did learn how to do those blind hems—'

'Is it gonna be colored?'

'What?'

'Is the baby gonna be colored?'

'I don't know—'

'What do you mean, you don't *know*?'

Molly clapped her hand over her mouth to stifle a sob.

'You mean you don't have any idea?' said her mother. 'You lost count or what?'

'Mama,' whispered Molly. 'Mama, it doesn't really matter. It's still my baby.'

'Oh, it matters. It matters to people round here. What you think they're gonna say? And your daddy – it's gonna kill your daddy.'

Someone was rapping on the phone booth door. Molly turned to see a man pointing at his watch, waving at her to get out of the booth. She turned her back on him.

'Mama,' she said. 'I want to come home.'

'You can't come home. Not in your condition.'

'Romy's tellin' me to get rid of it, to kill my baby. He's sending me to the doctor today, and I

194

don't know what to do. Mama, I need you to tell me what to do . . .'

Her mother released a weary sigh. Quietly she said: 'Maybe it would be for the best.'

'What?'

'If you got rid of it.'

Molly shook her head in bewilderment. 'But it's your *grandbaby*—'

'That's no grandbaby of mine. Not the way you got it.'

The man knocked at the door again and yelled at Molly to get off the phone. She pressed her hand over her ear to block out his voice.

'Please,' Molly whimpered. 'Let me come home.'

'Your daddy can't deal with this right now, you know he can't. After the shame you put us through. After I told you and told you what to expect. But you never listen, Molly, you never have.'

'I won't cause no more trouble. Romy and me, we're all through. I just want to come home now.'

The man was pounding on the booth now, shouting at her to get the fuck off the phone. Desperately Molly braced her back against the door to keep him out.

'Mama?' she said. 'Mama?'

The answer came back with a note of triumph. 'You made your bed. Now you go lie in it.'

Molly stood clutching the receiver to her ear, knowing that her mother had already hung up yet unable to believe the link was broken. *Talk to me.*

Tell me you're still there. Tell me you'll always be there.

'Hey, *bitch*! Get off the fucking *phone*!'

Wordlessly she let the receiver drop from her hand. It swung free, clattering against the booth. In a daze she stepped outside, not really seeing the man who was still cussing her out, not hearing a word he said. She just walked away.

Can't go home. Can't go home. Not now, not ever.

She walked without seeing, without feeling her own legs moving, her own feet stumbling in their platform shoes. Her anguish had blocked out all physical sensation.

She never saw Romy coming at her.

The blow struck her under the chin and sent her stumbling against the building. She caught herself on the window bars and clung to the wrought iron to keep from falling. She didn't understand what had just happened; all she knew was that Romy was yelling at her and that her whole head was ringing with pain.

He grabbed her arm and hauled her through the front door. In the foyer, he hit her again. This time she did fall, sprawling onto the steps.

'Where the fuck you been?' he shouted.

'I had – I had things to do—'

'You had an appointment, remember? They want to know why you aren't there.'

She swallowed and stared at the step. She didn't dare look him in the face. She only hoped he'd accept a lie. 'I forgot,' she said.

'What?'

'I said I forgot.'

'You are one *dumb* bitch. I told you this morning where you had to be.'

'I know.'

'You must have shit for brains.'

'I got to thinking 'bout other things.'

'Well, they're still waiting on you. You get your ass in the car.'

She looked up. 'But I'm not ready—'

'Ready?' Romy laughed. 'All you gotta do is get on the table and spread your legs.' He pulled her to her feet and thrust her toward the door. 'Go on. They sent you the fuckin' limousine.'

She stumbled outside onto the sidewalk.

A black car was parked at the curb, waiting for her. She could barely make out the driver's silhouette through the tinted glass.

'Go on, get in.'

'Romy, I don't feel so good. I don't want to do this.'

'Don't mess with me. Just get in the car.' He opened the door, shoved her into the backseat, and slammed the door shut.

The car pulled away from the curb.

'Hey!' she said to the driver. 'I want to get out!' There was a barrier of Plexiglas between her and the front seat. She pounded on it, trying to get his attention, but he didn't react. She looked at the tiny speaker mounted in the partition and suddenly felt a chill of recognition. She remembered this car. She had ridden in it once before.

'Hello?' she said. 'Do I know you?'

The driver didn't even turn his head.

She sat back against the leather seat. The same car. The same driver. She remembered that blond, almost silvery hair. The last time, when he had driven her to Dorchester, there had been another man waiting for her, a man in a green mask. And there had been a table with straps.

Her chill turned to panic. She glanced ahead and saw that an intersection was coming up. The last one, before the expressway turnoff. She stared at the traffic light, praying: *Turn red. Turn red!*

Another car cut in front of them. Molly lurched forward as her driver slammed on the brakes. Behind them horns blared and traffic screeched to a halt.

Molly shoved open the door and leaped out of the car.

The driver yelled: 'Get back here! You get back here *now!*'

She darted between two idling cars and scrambled to the sidewalk, her platform shoes clacking on the pavement. Goddamn heels almost tripped her up. She recovered her balance and began running down the street.

'*Hey!*'

Molly glanced back and was startled to see that the blond man had left his car parked near the curb and was chasing her on foot, dodging through a river of honking traffic.

She ran, a clumsy, clacking gait, crippled by her shoes. At the end of the block she glanced back.

The driver was gaining.

Why won't he leave me alone?

She reacted with the automatic response of prey – she fled.

Darting right, she turned onto a narrow street and struggled up the bumpy brick sidewalk leading up Beacon Hill. Only a block of running uphill and she was out of breath. And her calves ached – these damn shoes.

She looked back.

The driver was scrambling up the hill in pursuit.

Fresh panic sent Molly scrambling faster. She turned left, then right, worming deeper into the maze of Beacon Hill. She didn't stop to look back; she knew he was there.

By now her feet were bruised from the shoes and stinging with fresh blisters. *I can't outrun him.*

Rounding another corner, she spotted a taxi idling at the curb. She made a dash for it.

The driver glanced up in surprise as Molly threw herself into the backseat and pulled the door shut.

'Hey! I'm not available,' he snapped.

'Just go. *Go!*'

'I'm waiting for a fare. Get out of my cab.'

'Someone's after me. Please, can't you drive around the block?'

'I'm not driving nowhere. Get out or I radio for a cop.'

Cautiously Molly lifted her head and peered out the window.

Her pursuer was standing only a few yards away, his gaze scanning the street.

At once she dropped back down to the floor. 'It's him,' she whispered.

'I don't give a shit who it is. I'm calling a cop.'

'Okay. Go ahead! For once in my life I could *use* a fucking cop.'

She heard him reach for the radio mike, then heard him mutter 'Shit!' as he racked it again.

'You gonna call one or what?'

'I don't want to talk to no cops. Why can't you just get out like I'm telling you?'

'Why can't you drive around the block?'

'Okay, *okay*.' With a grunt of resignation he let out the parking brake and pulled away from the curb. 'So who's the guy?'

'He was driving me someplace I didn't want to go. So I bailed out.'

'Driving you where?'

'I don't know.'

'You know what? I don't want to know either. I don't want to know nothing 'bout your messed-up life. I just want you outta my cab.' He swerved to a stop. 'Now get *out*.'

'Is the guy around?'

'We're on Cambridge Street. I brought you a few blocks over. He's way the other side.'

She lifted her head and took a quick look. There were plenty of people around, but no sign of her pursuer. 'Maybe I'll pay you sometime,' she said and stepped out of the cab.

'Maybe I'll fly to the moon.'

Quickly she walked, first down Cambridge, then onto Sudbury. She didn't stop until she was deep in the maze of streets in the North End.

There she found a cemetery with a public bench in front. COPP'S BURYING GROUND, the sign said. She sat down and took off her shoes. Her blisters were raw, her toes bruised purple. She was too tired to walk even another block, so she just sat there in her bare feet watching tourists wander by with their Freedom Trail brochures, all of them enjoying a surprisingly mild October afternoon.

I can't go back to my room. I can't go back for my clothes. Romy sees me, he'll kill me.

It was almost four o'clock, and she was hungry; she hadn't eaten anything except grapefruit juice and two strawberry doughnuts for breakfast. The delicious smells from an Italian restaurant across the street were driving her crazy. She looked in her purse but saw only a few dollars inside. She'd hidden more money back in her room; somehow she'd have to get it without Romy seeing her.

She put her shoes back on, wincing at the pain. Then she hobbled up the street to a pay phone. *Please do this for me, Sophie*, she thought. *For once, please be nice to me.*

Sophie answered, her voice low and cautious. 'Yeah?'

'It's me. I need you to go into my room—'

'No way. Romy's going fucking nuts around here.'

'I need my money. Please get it for me, and I'll be outta there. You won't have to see me again.'

'I'm not going anywhere near your room.

201

Romy's in there right now, tearing things apart. There's not gonna be nothing left.'

Molly sagged against the phone booth.

'Look, just stay away. Don't come back here.'

'But I don't know where to go!' Molly's voice suddenly shattered into sobs. In despair, she curled up against the booth, her hair falling over her eyes, the strands wet with tears. 'I don't have anyplace to go . . .'

There was a silence. Then Sophie said, 'Hey, Titless? Listen to me. I think I know someone who might help you out. It'd have to be for just a few nights. Then you're on your own again. Hey, are you listening?'

Molly took a deep breath. 'Yeah.'

'It's over on Charter Street. There's this bakery on the corner with a boarding house next door. She's got a room on the second floor.'

'Who?'

'Just ask for Annie.'

'You're one of Romy's girls. Aren't you?'

The woman stared out over the door chain, and through the narrow opening, Molly could make out only half her face – curlicue bangs of brilliant red hair, a blue eye smudged with a dark circle of fatigue.

'Sophie told me to come,' said Molly. 'She said you might have room for me—'

'Sophie should've asked me first.'

'Please – can't I sleep here – just for tonight?' Shivering, Molly wrapped her arms around her

shoulders and glanced up and down the dark hallway. 'I don't have anywhere to go. I'll be real
quiet. You won't even know I'm here.'

'What'd you do to piss off Romy?'

'Nothin'.'

The woman started to shut the door.

'Wait!' cried Molly. 'Okay, okay I guess I *did*
piss him off. I didn't want to see that doctor
again . . .'

Slowly the door cracked open. The red-haired
woman's gaze shifted downward, to Molly's waist.
She said nothing.

'I'm so tired,' whispered Molly. 'Can I just sleep
on your floor? Please, just for tonight.'

The door swung shut.

Molly gave a soft whimper of despair. Then she
heard the chain rattle free and the door swung
open again. The woman stood in full view, her
belly swollen under a flowered print dress. 'Come
in,' she said.

Molly entered the apartment. At once the
woman shut the door and refastened the chain.

For a moment they looked at each other. Then
Molly's gaze dropped to the other woman's belly.

The woman saw Molly staring, and she gave a
shrug. 'I'm not fat. It's a baby.'

Molly nodded and placed her hands on her own
gently rounded abdomen. 'I've got one too.'

'I spent twenty-two years looking after old people.
Worked at four boarding homes in New Jersey. So
I know 'bout how to keep them out of trouble.'

203

The woman pointed to the résumé lying on Toby's kitchen table. 'I been at this a long time.'

'Yes, I can see you have,' said Toby, scanning the work history of Mrs. Ida Bogart. The pages reeked of cigarette smoke. So did the woman, who had carried the stench in on her baggy clothes and infected the whole kitchen with the smell. *Why am I going through the motions?* Toby wondered. *I don't want this woman in my house. I don't want her anywhere near my mother.*

She lay the pages down on the table and forced herself to smile at Ida Bogart. 'I'll keep your résumé on file until I make a decision.'

'You need someone right away, don't you? That's what the ad said.'

'I'm still looking at applicants.'

'Mind my asking if you got many?'

'Several.'

'Not many people want to work nights. I never had a problem with it.'

Toby stood up, a clear signal that the interview was over. She herded the woman out of the kitchen and down the hallway. 'I'll keep your name under consideration. Thank you for coming, Mrs. Bogart.' She practically pushed the woman out of the house and closed the front door. Then she stood with her back propped against it, as though to barricade her home from any more Mrs. Bogarts. *Six more days*, she thought. *How will I find someone in six days?*

In the kitchen, the phone rang.

It was her sister calling. 'So how are the

interviews going?' Vickie asked.

'They're not going anywhere.'

'I thought you got responses to the ad.'

'One who's a chain-smoker, two who barely understand English, and one who made me want to lock up the liquor. Vickie, this isn't working. I can't leave Mom with any of these people. You're going to have to keep her at your house at night until we can find someone.'

'She wanders, Toby. She might turn on the stove while we're sleeping. I have my kids to think of.'

'She never turns on the stove. And she usually sleeps all night.'

'What about the temp agency?'

'It would only be a short-term solution. I can't have new faces coming in and out all the time. It would confuse Mom.'

'At least it'd be some sort of solution. It's gotten to the point where it's either that or a nursing home.'

'No way. No nursing home.'

Vickie sighed. 'It was just a suggestion. I'm thinking of you, too. I wish there was more I could do . . .'

But there isn't, thought Toby. Vickie already had two children greedily vying for attention. To force Ellen on their family would be one more burden on an already overwhelmed Vickie.

Toby crossed to the kitchen window and looked out at the garden. Her mother was standing by the toolshed, holding a leaf rake. Ellen didn't seem to remember what to do with a rake, and she kept scraping the teeth across the brick path.

'How many other applicants are you interviewing?' asked Vickie.

'Two.'

'Do their résumés look okay?'

'They look fine. But they *all* look fine on paper. It's only when you meet them face-to-face that you smell the booze.'

'Oh, it can't be that bad, Toby. You're too negative about the whole process.'

'*You* come and interview them. The next one should be here any minute—' She turned at the sound of the doorbell. 'That must be him.'

'I'm coming over right now.'

Toby hung up and went to answer the front door.

On the porch stood an elderly man, face drawn and gray, shoulders slumped forward. 'I'm here about the job,' was all he managed to get out before he was seized by a fit of coughing.

Toby hurried him inside and sat him down on the sofa. She brought him a glass of water and watched while he hacked, cleared his throat, and hacked some more. Just a leftover cold, he told her in fits and starts. Over the worst of it now, only this bronchitis hanging on. Didn't interfere with his ability to do a job, no sir. He'd worked while much sicker than this, had worked all his life, since he was sixteen years old.

Toby listened, more out of pity than interest, her gaze fixed on the résumé lying on the coffee table.

Wallace Dugan, sixty-one years old. She knew she was not going to hire him, had known it from the instant she'd seen him, but she didn't have the heart to cut him short. So she sat in passive silence, listening to how he had come to this sad point in his life. How badly he needed the job. How hard it was for a man his age.

He was still sitting on her sofa when Vickie arrived. She walked into the living room, saw the man, and halted.

'This is my sister,' said Toby. 'And this is Wallace Dugan. He's applying for the job.'

Wallace stood up to shake Vickie's hand but quickly sank back down again, seized by a new fit of coughing.

'Toby, can I talk to you for a minute?' said Vickie, and she turned and walked into the kitchen.

Toby followed her, closing the door behind her.

'What's wrong with that man?' whispered Vickie. 'He looks like he's got cancer. Or TB.'

'Bronchitis, he says.'

'You're not thinking of *hiring* him, are you?'

'He's the best applicant so far.'

'You're kidding. Please tell me you're kidding.'

Toby sighed. 'Unfortunately, I'm not. You didn't see the others.'

'They were worse than *him*?'

'At least he seems like a nice man.'

'Oh, sure. And when he keels over, Mom's going to do CPR?'

'Vickie, I'm not going to hire him.'

'Then why don't we send him on his way, before he croaks in your living room?'

The doorbell rang.

'Jesus,' said Toby, and she pushed out of the kitchen. She shot an apologetic glance at Wallace Dugan as she walked past him, but he had his head bent over a handkerchief, coughing again. She opened the front door.

A petite woman smiled at her. She was in her midthirties, with trim brown hair in a Princess Di cut. Her blouse and slacks appeared neatly pressed. 'Dr. Harper? I'm sorry if I'm early. I wanted to make sure I could find your house.' She extended her hand. 'I'm Jane Nolan.'

'Come in, I'm still talking to another applicant, but—'

'I can interview her,' cut in Vickie, pushing forward to shake Jane Nolan's hand. 'I'm Dr. Harper's sister. Why don't we go talk in the kitchen?' Vickie looked at Toby. 'In the meantime, why don't you finish up with Mr. Dugan?' In a whisper, she added: 'Just get *rid* of him.'

Wallace Dugan already knew the verdict. When Toby walked back into the living room, she found him gazing down at the coffee table with a look of defeat. His résumé lay before him, three pages chronicling forty-five years of labor. A chronicle that had most likely reached its end.

They chatted a moment longer, more out of politeness than necessity. They would never meet again; they both knew it. When at last he walked out of her house, Toby closed the door with a sense of relief. Pity, after all, did not get the job done.

She went into the kitchen.

Vickie was alone in the room, gazing out the doorway. 'Look,' she said.

Outside, in the garden, Ellen shuffled along the brick path. At her side was Jane Nolan, nodding as Ellen pointed to one plant, than another. Jane was like a small, swift bird, alert to every move her companion made. Ellen halted and frowned at something near her feet. She bent down to pick it up – a garden claw. Now she turned it around in her hands, as though searching for some clue to its purpose.

'Now what did you find there?' asked Jane.

Ellen held up the claw. 'This thing. A brush.' At once Ellen seemed to know that was the wrong word and she shook her head. 'No, it's not a brush. It's – you know – you know.'

'For the flowers, right?' prompted Jane. 'A claw, to loosen up the dirt.'

'Yes.' Ellen beamed. 'A claw.'

'Let's put it in a safe place, where it won't get lost. And you won't accidentally step on it.' Jane took the claw and set it in the wheelbarrow. She looked up and, seeing Toby, smiled and waved. Then she took Ellen's arm, and the two of them continued along the path and vanished around the corner of the house.

Toby felt an invisible burden seem to tumble from her shoulders. She looked at her sister. 'What do you think?'

'Her résumé looks good. And she has excellent references from three different nursing homes. We'll have to go up on the hourly rate, since she's an LPN. But I'd say she's worth it.'

'Mom seems to like her. That's the most important thing.'

Vickie gave a sigh of satisfaction. Mission accomplished. Vickie the efficient. 'There,' she said, shutting the back door. 'That wasn't so hard.'

Another day, another dollar. Another corpse.

Daniel Dvorak stepped back from the autopsy table and stripped off his gloves. 'There you have it, Roy. Penetrating wound to the left upper quadrant, laceration of the spleen resulting in massive hemorrhage. Definitely not natural causes. No surprises.' He tossed the gloves into the contaminated rubbish bin and looked at Detective Sheehan.

Sheehan was still standing by the table, but his gaze wasn't on the hollowed-out body cavity. No, Sheehan was making moo eyes at Dvorak's assistant, Lisa. How romantic. Romeo and Juliet meeting over a corpse.

Dvorak shook his head and went to wash his hands in the sink. In the mirror he glimpsed the progress of the incipient romance. Detective Sheehan standing a little straighter, tucking in his gut. Lisa laughing, flicking back her blond bangs. Even in the autopsy room, nature will have its way.

Even when one of the parties is a married, middle-aged, overweight cop.

If Sheehan wants to play lover boy to a pair of blue eyes, it's none of my business, thought Dvorak as he calmly dried off his hands. But I should warn him he's not the first cop whose hormones got tweaked down here. Autopsies had become surprisingly popular events lately, and it wasn't because of the corpses.

'I'll be in my office,' Dvorak said, and he walked out of the lab.

Twenty minutes later Sheehan knocked at Dvorak's office door and came in, wearing the sheepishly happy face of a man who's been acting foolish, knows it, knows everyone else knows it, but doesn't care.

Dvorak decided he didn't care, either. He went to his file cabinet, took out a folder, and handed it to Sheehan. 'There's that final tox report you wanted. You need anything else?'

'Uh, yeah. The prelim on that baby.'

'Consistent with SIDS.'

Sheehan pulled out a cigarette and lit up. 'That's what I thought.'

'Mind putting that out?'

'Huh?'

'It's a smoke-free building.'

'Your office too?'

'The smell hangs around.'

Sheehan laughed. 'In your line of work, Doc, you can hardly complain about smells.' But he put out the cigarette, crushing it on the coffee saucer that Dvorak slid across to him. 'You know, that Lisa's a nice girl.'

Dvorak said nothing, figuring that silence was safer.

'She got a boyfriend?' asked Sheehan.

'I wouldn't know.'

'You mean you never asked?'

'No.'

'Not even curious?'

'I'm curious about a lot of things. But that's not one of them.' Dvorak paused. 'By the way, how're the wife and kids?'

A pause. 'They're fine.'

'So things're good at home?'

'Yeah. Sure.'

Dvorak nodded gravely. 'Then you're a lucky man.'

Face reddening, Sheehan stared down at the tox report. Cops see too much death, thought Dvorak, and they run around grabbing at all the highs in life they can get. Sheehan was struggling, a smart guy, a basically decent guy, dealing with the first glimpse of middle age in his mirror.

Lisa chose that moment to walk into the office, carrying two trays of microscope slides. She flashed Sheehan a smile and seemed taken aback when he simply looked away.

'Which slides are these?' asked Dvorak.

'Top tray's liver and lung sections from Joseph Odette. Bottom tray has brain sections from Parmenter.' Lisa stole another glance at Sheehan, then pulled her dignity back together again. In a businesslike tone she said: 'You just wanted H and E and PAS stains on the brain, right?'

'Did you do Congo-Red?'

'That's in there too. Just in case.' She turned and walked out, pride intact.

After a moment, Sheehan left as well, a temporarily chastened Romeo.

Dvorak brought the trays of new slides back to the lab and turned on his microscope. The first slide was of Joey Odette's lung. Smoker, he thought, focusing on the alveoli. No surprise; he'd already recognized the emphysematous changes at autopsy. He flipped through a few more lung sections, then moved onto the liver slides. Cirrhosis and fatty infiltration. A boozer, too. Had Joey Odette not shot himself in the head, either his liver or his lungs would have failed him eventually. There are many ways to commit suicide.

He dictated his findings, then set aside the Odette slides and reached for the next tray.

The first slide of Angus Parmenter's brain appeared through the lens. The microscopic exam of brain sections was a routine part of the autopsy. This slide showed a section of cerebral cortex, stained a hot pink with periodic-acid-Schiff. He focused, and the field came sharply into view. For a full ten seconds he stared through the eyepiece, trying to make sense of what he was seeing.

Artifact, he thought. That must be the problem. A distortion of tissue from the fixing or staining process.

He took out the slide and put in another. Again he focused.

Again, everything looked all wrong. Instead of a

uniform field of neuronal tissue stippled with occasional purple nuclei, this looked like pink and white froth. There were vacuoles everywhere, as though the brain matter had been eaten away by microscopic moths.

Slowly he lifted his head from the eyepieces. Then he looked down at his finger – the finger he'd cut with the scalpel. The laceration was healed now, but he could still see the fine line on the skin, where the wound had recently closed. *I was working with the brain when it happened. I've been exposed.*

The diagnosis would have to be confirmed. A neuropathologist consulted, electron microscopy performed, the clinical record reviewed. He should not be planning his own funeral quite yet.

His hands were sweating. He turned off the microscope and released a deep breath. Then he picked up the telephone.

It took his secretary only a moment to locate Toby Harper's number in Newton. The phone rang six times before it was answered by an irritated 'Hello?'

'Dr. Harper? This is Dan Dvorak at the ME's office. Is this a good time to talk?'

'I've been trying to reach you all week.'

'I know,' he admitted. And could think of no excuse to give her.

'Do you have a diagnosis on Mr. Parmenter?' she asked.

'That's why I'm calling. I need some more medical history from you.'

'You have his hospital record, don't you?'

'Yes, but I wanted to talk to you about what you saw in the ER. I'm still trying to interpret the histology. What I need is a better clinical picture.'

Over the line, he heard what sounded like water running from a faucet, and then Toby called out: 'No, turn it off! Turn it off, the water's getting all over the floor!' The phone clattered down and there were running footsteps. She came back on the line. 'Look, this isn't a good time for me right now. Can we discuss this in person?'

He hesitated. 'I suppose that's a better idea. This afternoon?'

'Well, it's my night off, but I have to make arrangements for a sitter. What time do you leave work?'

'I'll stay as late as I need to.'

'Okay, I'll try to get there by six. Where are you located?'

'Seven twenty Albany Street, across from City Hospital. It'll be after hours, so the front door will be locked. Park around in back.'

'I'm still not sure what this is all about, Dr. Dvorak.'

'You'll understand,' he said. 'After you see the slides.'

Ten

It was nearly six-thirty when Toby pulled into the parking lot behind the two-story brick building at 720 Albany Street. She drove past three identical vans, each labeled on the side with COMMON-WEALTH OF MASSACHUSETTS, CHIEF MEDICAL EXAMINER, and she parked in a stall near the building's rear door. The rain, which had threatened all day, was finally beginning to fall in a gentle sprinkling that silvered the gloom. It was late October, and darkness fell so early these days; already she missed the long warm twilights of summer. The building looked like a crypt walled in by red brick.

She stepped out of the car and walked across the lot, head bent under the rain. Just as she reached the rear entrance, the door swung open. Her head snapped up in surprise.

A man was standing in the doorway, his tall frame silhouetted against the hall light. 'Dr. Harper?'

'Yes.'

'I'm Dan Dvorak. They usually lock the doors by six, so I was watching for your arrival. Come in.'

She stepped into the building and wiped the rain from her eyes. Blinking against the light, she focused on Dvorak's face, reconciling the mental image she'd formed from his telephone voice with the imposing man who stood before her. He was about as old as she'd expected, in his mid-forties, his black hair generously streaked with silver and tousled, as though he'd been nervously running his fingers through it. His eyes, an intense blue, were so deeply set they seemed to gaze at her from dark hollows. Though he did manage a small smile, she sensed it was forced; it flickered only briefly but attractively across his lips, and then was gone, replaced by an expression she could not quite fathom. Anxiety, perhaps. Worry.

'Most everyone's gone home for the day,' he said. 'So it really is as quiet as a morgue in here right now.'

'I tried to get here as soon as I could, but I had to make arrangements with the sitter.'

'You have children, then?'

'No, the sitter's for my mother. I don't like to leave her alone.'

They took the stairs up, Dvorak slightly in the lead, white lab coat flapping at long legs. 'I'm sorry to ask you here on such short notice.'

'You've been refusing all my calls, and then suddenly you *have* to talk to me tonight. Why?'

'I need your clinical opinion.'

217

'I'm not a pathologist. You're the one who did the autopsy.'

'But you examined him while he was still alive.'

He pushed through the stairwell door onto the second floor and started up the hall, moving with such nervous energy that Toby had to trot to keep up.

'There was a neurologist consulting on the case,' she said. 'Did you talk to him?'

'He didn't perform his exam until after the patient became comatose. By then there were few signs and symptoms to go on. Other than coma.'

'What about Wallenberg? He was the attending physician.'

'Wallenberg maintains it was a stroke.'

'Well, was it?'

'No.' He opened a door and flipped on the wall switch. It was an office furnished with a utilitarian steel desk, chairs, and a filing cabinet. The office of a thoroughly organized man, thought Toby, looking at the neatly stacked papers, at the textbooks lined up on the shelf. The only personal touch to the office was an obviously neglected fern perched on the filing cabinet, and a photo on the desk. A teenage boy, shaggy-haired and squinting into the sunlight as he held up a prize trout. The boy's face was a clone of Dvorak's. She sat down in a chair by the desk.

'Would you like some coffee?' he asked.

'I'd rather have some information. What, exactly, *did* you find on autopsy?'

'On gross exam, nothing.'

'No evidence of a stroke?'

'Neither thrombotic nor hemorrhagic.'

'What about the heart? The coronaries?'

'Patent. In fact, I've never seen such a clean left anterior descending artery in a man his age. No evidence of infarction, fresh or otherwise. It wasn't a cardiac death.' He sat down behind the desk, his gaze so intense on hers she had to force herself to maintain eye contact.

'Toxicology?'

'It's been only a week. The preliminary screen shows diazepam and Dilantin. Both were given in the hospital to treat seizures.' He leaned forward. 'Why did you insist on the autopsy?'

'I told you. He was the second patient I'd seen with that presentation of symptoms. I wanted a diagnosis.'

'Tell me the symptoms again. Everything you remember.'

She found it difficult to concentrate while those blue eyes were so intently focused on her face. She sat back, shifting her gaze to the stack of papers on his desk. She cleared her throat. 'Confusion,' she said. 'They both came into the ER disoriented to time and place.'

'Tell me first about Mr. Parmenter.'

She nodded. 'The ambulance brought him in after his daughter found him stumbling around at home. He didn't recognize her or his own grand-daughters. From what I gathered, he was having visual hallucinations. Thought he could fly. When

I examined him, I didn't find any evidence of trauma. Neurologically, the only localizing sign seemed to be an abnormal finger-to-nose test. I thought at first it might be a cerebellar stroke. But there were other symptoms I couldn't explain.'

'Such as?'

'He seemed to have some visual distortion. He had trouble judging how far away I was standing.' She paused, frowning. 'Oh. That explains the midgets.'

'Excuse me?'

'He complained about midgets being in his house. I guess he was referring to his grand-daughters. They're about ten years old.'

'Okay, so he had distorted vision and cerebellar signs.'

'And there were seizures.'

'Yes, I saw you mentioned them in your ER notes.' He reached for a folder on his desk and opened it. She saw it was a photocopy of the patient's Springer Hospital record. 'You described a focal seizure of the right upper extremity.'

'The seizures recurred on and off during his hospitalization, despite anticonvulsants. That's what the nurses told me.'

He flipped through the chart. 'Wallenberg hardly mentions them. But I do see an order sheet here, for Dilantin. Which he signed.' He looked up at her. 'Obviously, you're correct about the seizures.'

Why wouldn't I be? she thought with sudden irritation. Now she was the one who leaned forward. 'Why don't you just tell me which diagnosis you're fishing for?'

'I don't want to influence your memory of the case. I need your unbiased recollection.'

'Being straight with me would save us both a lot of time.'

'Are you pressed for time?'

'This is my night off, Dr. Dvorak. I could be home doing other things right now.'

He regarded her for a moment in silence. Then he sat back and released a heavy sigh. 'Look, I'm sorry for being evasive, but this has shaken me up quite a bit.'

'Why?'

'I think we're dealing with an infectious agent.'

'Bacterial? Viral?'

'Neither.'

She frowned at him. 'What else is there? Are we talking parasites?'

He rose to his feet. 'Why don't you come down to the lab? I'll show you the slides.'

They rode the elevator to the basement and stepped out into a deserted hallway. It was after seven now. She knew there had to be someone else on duty in the morgue, but at that moment, walking along the silent corridor, it seemed that she and Dvorak were utterly alone in the building. He led her through a doorway and flipped on the wall switch.

Fluorescent panels flickered on, the harsh light reflecting off gleaming surfaces. She saw a refrigerator, stainless steel sinks, a countertop with quantitative analysis equipment and a computer terminal. Lined up on a shelf were jars of human organs, suspended in preservative. The faint tang of Formalin hung in the air.

He crossed to one of the microscopes and flipped on the switch. It had a teaching eyepiece; they could both examine the field at the same time. He put a slide under the lens and sat down while he focused. 'Take a look.'

She pulled up a stool. Bending her head close to his, she peered into the twin eyepiece. What she saw looked like white bubbles in a sea of pink.

'It's been a long time since I took histology,' she admitted. 'Give me a hint.'

'Okay. Can you identify the tissue we're looking at?'

She flushed with embarrassment. If only she *could* rattle off the answer. Instead she was painfully aware of her ignorance. And of the silence stretching between them. With her face pressed to the eyepiece, she said: 'I hate to admit it, but no, I can't identify this.'

'It's no reflection on your training, Dr. Harper. This slide is so abnormal the tissue *is* hard to recognize. What we're looking at is a slide of Angus Parmenter's cerebral cortex, PAS stained. The pink is background neuropil, with the nuclei stained purple.'

'What are all those vacuoles?'

'That was exactly my question. Normal cortex doesn't have all those tiny holes.'

'Weird. It looks like my pink kitchen sponge.'

He didn't respond. Puzzled, she raised her head and saw that he was looking at her. 'Dr. Dvorak?'

'You saw it right away,' he murmured.

'What?'

'That's exactly what it looks like. *A pink sponge.*' He sat back and rubbed his hand over his eyes. Under the harsh lab lights, she saw the lines of fatigue in his face, the shadow of dark beard. 'I think we're dealing with a spongiform encephalopathy,' he said.

'You mean like Creutzfeldt-Jakob disease?'

He nodded. 'It would account for the pathologic changes on the slide. As well as the clinical picture. The mental deterioration. Visual distortion. Myoclonic jerks.'

'So they weren't focal seizures?'

'No. I think what you saw was startle myoclonus. Violently repetitive spasms, set off by a loud noise. It can't be controlled with Dilantin.'

'Isn't Creutzfeldt-Jakob extremely rare?'

'One in a million. It tends to strike the elderly on a sporadic basis.'

'But there *are* clusters of cases. Last year, in England—'

'You're thinking of mad cow disease. That seems to be a variant of Creutzfeldt-Jakob. Maybe it's the same disease, we're not really sure. The English victims got infected by eating beef with the bovine spongiform strain. That was a rare outbreak, and it hasn't been seen since.'

Her gaze shifted back to the microscope. Softly she said, 'Is it possible we have a cluster *here*?

Angus Parmenter wasn't the first patient I saw with those symptoms. Harry Slotkin was. He came in weeks before Parmenter did, with the same presentation. Confusion, visual distortion.'

'Those are nonspecific signs. You'd need an autopsy to confirm it.'

'That's not possible with Mr. Slotkin. He's still missing.'

'Then there's no way to make the diagnosis.'

'They both lived in the same residential complex. They could've been exposed to the same pathogen.'

'You don't catch CJD the way you catch the common cold. It's transmitted by a prion. An abnormal cellular protein. It requires direct tissue exposure. A corneal transplant, for instance.'

'Those people in England caught it from eating beef. Couldn't it happen here? They could have shared a meal—'

'The American herd is clean. We don't have mad cow disease.'

'How do we know that for certain?' She was intrigued now, feverishly pursuing this new line of thought. She remembered that night in the ER, when Harry had come in. Recalled the clang of the steel basin crashing to the floor, and then the sound of Harry's leg rubbing against the gurney. 'We have two men from the same housing complex. Presenting with the same symptoms.'

'Confusion isn't specific enough.'

'Harry Slotkin had what I *thought* were focal

seizures. Now I realize it might have been startle myoclonus.'

'I need a body to autopsy. I can't diagnose Harry Slotkin without brain tissue.'

'Well, how certain are you of Angus Parmenter's diagnosis?'

'I've sent the slides to a neuropathologist for confirmation. He'll examine the sections under electron microscopy. The results may take a few days.' Quietly he added: 'I'm just hoping I'm wrong.'

She studied him and realized she was seeing more than weariness in his face. What she saw was fear.

'I cut myself,' he said. 'During the autopsy while I was removing the brain.' He shook his head, gave a strangely ironic laugh. 'I've cut open a thousand skulls. Worked on bodies with HIV, hepatitis, even rabies. But I've never cut myself. Then I get Angus Parmenter on the table, and it looks like natural causes. A weeklong hospital stay, no evidence of infection. And what do I do? I cut my finger. While I'm working on the god-damn *brain*.'

'The diagnosis isn't confirmed. It could be artifact. Maybe the slides weren't prepared correctly.'

'That's what I keep hoping.' He stared at the microscope, as though regarding his mortal enemy. 'I had my hands around the brain. I couldn't have chosen a worse time to nick myself.'

'It doesn't mean you're infected. Your chances

of actually getting the disease have to be extremely small.'

'But still there. The chance is still there.' He looked at her, and she couldn't contradict him. Nor could she offer any false reassurance. Silence, at least, was honest.

He turned off the microscope lamp. 'It has a long incubation period. So it will be a year, two years until I know. Even at five years, I'll still be wondering. Waiting for the first signs. At least it's a relatively painless end. You start with dementia. Visual distortion, maybe hallucinations. Then you progress to delirium. And finally you slip into a coma . . .' He gave a weary shrug. 'I guess it beats dying of cancer.'

'I'm sorry,' she murmured. 'I feel responsible . . .'

'Why?'

'I insisted on the autopsy. I put you in a hazardous position.'

'I put myself in that position. We both do, Dr. Harper. It comes with the job. You work in the ER, someone coughs on you, you catch TB. Or you stick yourself with a needle and you get hepatitis or AIDS.' He removed the slide and set it in a tray. Then he pulled a plastic cover over the microscope. 'There are hazards to every job, just like there are hazards to getting up in the morning. Driving to work, walking to the mailbox. Boarding a plane.' He looked at her. 'The surprise isn't that we die. The surprise is how and when we die.'

'There could be some way to stop the infection

at this stage. Maybe a shot of immunoglobulin—'

'Doesn't work. I checked the literature.'

'Have you discussed it with your doctor?'

'I haven't mentioned this to anyone yet.'

'Not even your family?'

'There's just my son, Patrick, and he's only fourteen. At that age, he's got enough things to worry about.'

She remembered the photo on the desk, the shaggy-haired boy holding up his prize trout. Dvorak was right; a boy of fourteen was too young to be confronted with a parent's mortality.

'So what are you going to do?' she asked.

'Make sure my life insurance is paid up. And hope for the best.'

He stood up and reached for the light switch. 'There's nothing more I can do.'

Robbie Brace answered the door wearing a Red Sox T-shirt and ratty sweatpants. 'Dr. Harper,' he said. 'You got here quick.'

'Thanks for seeing me.'

'Yeah, well, you're not exactly catching us at our finest hour. Bedtime, you know. Lots of whining and bargaining going on.'

Toby stepped in the front door. Somewhere upstairs, a child was screaming. Not a distressed scream, but an angry one, accompanied by the sound of stamping feet and the crash of something hard hitting the floor.

'We are three years old and learning the meaning of power,' explained Brace. 'Man, don't

227

you just love parenthood?' He latched the front door and led her up a hallway, toward the living room. Once again she was impressed by how big he was, his arms so muscular they could not hang straight from his shoulders. She sat down on a couch, and he settled into a well-worn recliner.

Upstairs the screaming continued, hoarser and punctuated by loud, dramatic snuffles. There was also a woman's voice speaking, calm but determined.

'It's the clash of the titans,' said Brace, glancing upward. 'My wife, she stands a lot tougher than I do. Me, I just roll over and play dead.' He looked at Toby and his smile faded. 'So what's this about Angus Parmenter?'

'I've just come from the ME's office. They have a preliminary diagnosis: Creutzfeldt-Jakob disease.'

Brace gave an amazed shake of his head. 'Are they sure?'

'It still needs confirmation by a neuropathologist. But the symptoms do match the diagnosis. Not just for Parmenter. For Harry Slotkin as well.'

'Two cases of CJD? That's sort of like having lightning strike twice. How could you possibly confirm it?'

'Okay, we can't confirm Harry's case because there's no body. But what if two residents from Brant Hill did have CJD? It makes you wonder if there's a common source of infection.' She leaned

228

forward. 'You told me Harry had a clean bill of health on his out patient record.'

'That's right.'

'Did he have any surgery in the past five years? A corneal transplant, for instance?'

'I don't remember seeing anything like that in the record. I guess you could catch CJD that way.'

'It's been reported.' She paused. 'There's another way it can be transmitted. By injections of human growth hormone.'

'So?'

'You told me Brant Hill's doing studies on hormone injections in the elderly. You said your patients have shown improvement in muscle mass and strength. Is it possible you're injecting tainted growth hormone?'

'Growth hormone doesn't come from cadaver brains anymore. It's manufactured.'

'What if Brant Hill is using an old supply? Growth hormone infected with CJD?'

'The old growth hormone's been off the market for a long time. And Wallenberg's been using this protocol for years, ever since he was at the Rosslyn Institute. I've never heard of a case of CJD in any of his patients.'

'I'm not familiar with the Rosslyn Institute. What is that?'

'Center for geriatric research, in Connecticut. Wallenberg worked as a research fellow there for a few years, before he came to Brant Hill. Check out the geriatric literature – you'll find a number of studies originating at Rosslyn. And half a dozen papers with Wallenberg's name as author. He's the guru of hormone replacement.'

'I didn't know that.'

'You'd have to be in geriatrics to know that.' He rose from the chair, disappeared into an adjoining room, and came back out with some papers, which he set down on the coffee table in front of Toby. On top was a photocopied article from *Journal of the American Geriatrics Society*, 1992. There were three authors listed, and the first name was Wallenberg's. The title of the article was: 'Beyond the Hayflick Limit: Extending Longevity at the Cellular Level.'

'It's research at its most basic,' said Brace. 'Taking a cell's maximum life span – the Hayflick Limit – and trying to prolong it with hormonal manipulation. If you accept the idea that our senescence and death is a cellular process, then you want to work toward prolonging cell life.'

'But a certain amount of cell death is necessary for health.'

'Sure. We shed dead cells all the time, in our mucous membranes and our skin. But we regenerate those. What we don't regenerate are cells like bone marrow and brain and other vital organs. They grow old and die. And we die as a result.'

'And with this hormonal manipulation?'

'That's the point of the study. Which hormones – or combination of hormones – prolong cell life span? Wallenberg's been researching this since 1990. And he's finding some promising results.'

She looked up at him. 'That old man in the nursing home – the one who put up such a good fight?'

Brace nodded. 'He probably has the muscle mass and strength of a much younger man. Unfortunately, Alzheimer's has messed up his brain. Hormones can't help that.'

'Which hormones are we talking about? You mentioned a combination.'

'The accepted research shows promise for growth hormone, DHEA, melatonin, and testosterone. I think Wallenberg's current protocol involves various proportions of those hormones, plus maybe a few others.'

'You're not certain?'

'I'm not involved with the protocol. I take care of only their nursing home patients. Hey, it's all pie in the sky right now. No one knows what works. All we know is, our pituitaries stop producing certain hormones as we get older. Maybe the fountain of youth is some pituitary hormone we haven't discovered yet.'

'So Wallenberg's giving replacement injections.' She laughed. 'Literally a shot in the dark.'

'It might work. Seems to me Brant Hill's got some pretty healthy-looking eighty-year-olds zipping around on that golf course.'

'They're also wealthy, they exercise, and they live a carefree life.'

'Yeah, well, who knows? Maybe the best predictor of longevity is a healthy bank account.'

Toby flipped through the research article, then

lay it on the coffee table. Once again she looked at the publication date. 'He's been doing hormone injections since 1990, with no recorded case of CJD?'

'The protocol ran four years at Rosslyn. Then he came to Brant Hill and resumed the studies.'

'Why did he leave Rosslyn?'

Brace laughed. 'Why do you suppose?'

'Money.'

'Hey, it's the reason I came to Brant Hill. Nice paycheck, no hassles with insurance companies. And patients who actually listen to my advice.' He paused. 'In Wallenberg's case, I hear there were other things going on. Last geriatrics conference I attended, there was some gossip circulating. About Wallenberg and a female research associate at Rosslyn.'

'Oh. If it's not money, it's sex.'

'What else is there?'

She thought of Carl Wallenberg in his tuxedo, the young lion with amber eyes, and she could easily imagine him being the object of female desire. 'So he had an affair with a research associate,' she said. 'That's not particularly shocking.'

'It is if there are three people involved.'

'Wallenberg, the woman, and who else?'

'Another M.D. at Rosslyn, a man. I understand things got pretty tense between them, and all three of them resigned. Wallenberg came to Brant Hill and resumed his research. Anyway, that makes it a full six years he's been injecting hormones, with no catastrophic side effects.'

'And no cases of CJD.'

'None reported. Try again, Dr. Harper.'

'Okay, let's look at other ways these two men might've gotten infected. A surgical procedure. Something relatively minor, like a corneal transplant. You might have overlooked that history in their outpatient charts.'

Brace made an exasperated sound. 'Why are you hung up on this, anyway? Patients die on me all the time, and I don't obsess over it.'

Sighing, she sank back on the couch. 'I know it doesn't change things. I know Harry's probably dead. But if he *did* have Creutzfeldt-Jakob, then he was already dying when I saw him. And nothing I did could have saved him.' She looked at Brace. 'Maybe I wouldn't feel so responsible for his death.'

'So it's guilt, is it?'

She nodded. 'And a certain amount of self-interest. The lawyer representing Harry's son is already taking depositions from the ER staff. I don't think there's any way I *can* avoid a lawsuit. But if I could prove Harry already *had* a fatal illness when I saw him—'

'Then the damages wouldn't seem so severe in court.'

She nodded. And felt ashamed. *Your dad was already dying, Mr. Slotkin. What's the big deal?*

'We don't know Harry's dead,' said Brace.

'He's been missing for a month. What else

would he be? It's just a matter of finding his body.'

Upstairs, the crying had stopped, the battle finally won. The silence only accentuated their uneasy lapse in conversation. Footsteps creaked down the stairs, and a woman appeared. She was a redhead, so fair-skinned her face seemed translucent in the glow of the living room lamp.

'My wife, Greta,' said Brace. 'And this is Dr. Toby Harper. Toby just dropped by for some shop talk.'

'I'm sorry about all the screaming,' said Greta. 'It's our daily tantrum. Tell me again, Robbie. Why *did* we have a kid?'

'To pass on the gift of our superior DNA. Trouble is, babe, she got *your* temper.'

Greta sat down on the armrest next to her husband. 'That's called *determination*. Not temper.'

'Yeah, well, whatever you call it, it's hard on the ears.' He patted his wife on the knee. 'Toby's an ER doc over at Springer Hospital. She's the one who stitched up my face.'

'Oh.' Greta nodded in appreciation. 'You did a very nice job. He'll hardly have a scar.' She suddenly frowned at the coffee table. 'Robbie, I hope you offered our guest something to drink. Shall I put on some tea?'

'No, babe, that's all right,' said Robbie. 'We're all finished here.'

I guess that's my signal to leave, thought Toby. Reluctantly she stood up.

So did Robbie. He gave his wife a quick kiss and

said, 'This won't take long. I'm just running over to the clinic.' Then he turned to Toby, who was looking at him in surprise. 'You want to see those outpatient records, don't you?' he asked.

'Yes. Of course.'

'Then I'll meet you there. Brant Hill.'

Eleven

'I knew you were gonna keep bugging me about this,' said Robbie as he unlocked the front door to the Brant Hill Clinic building. '*Check this out, check that out.* Man, I figured I'd just let you see the damn charts for yourself, so you'd know I wasn't holding out on you.' They walked into the building and the front door slammed shut behind them, setting off echoes down the empty hallway. He turned right, and unlocked a door labeled: MEDICAL RECORDS.

Toby flipped on the lights and blinked in surprise at six aisles of filing cabinets. 'Alphabetical?' she asked.

'Yeah. *A*s are that way, *Z*s the other way. I'll find Slotkin's chart, you find Parmenter.'

Toby headed toward the *P*s. 'I can't believe how many records you have. Does Brant Hill really have this many patients?'

'No. This is central records storage for all of Orcutt Health's nursing homes.'

'Is that like a conglomerate?'

'Yeah. We're their flagship facility.'

'So how many nursing homes do they run?'

'A dozen, I think. We all share billing and referral services.'

Toby found the cabinet for the *P*s and thumbed through the charts. 'I can't find it,' she said.

'I found Slotkin's.'

'Well where's Parmenter?'

Brace reappeared in her aisle. 'Oh, I forgot. He's deceased, so they probably moved that file to the inactives.' He walked to a set of cabinets at the back of the room. A moment later he closed the drawer. 'Must've been culled. I can't find it. Why don't you just concentrate on Harry's chart? Look it over to your heart's content and prove to yourself I haven't missed anything.'

She sat down at an empty desk and opened Harry Slotkin's file. It was organized in a problem-oriented format, with Current Illnesses listed on the first page. She saw nothing surprising here: benign prostatic hypertrophy. Chronic back pain. Mild hearing loss secondary to otosclerosis. All the expected ravages of old age.

She flipped to the past medical history. Again, it was a typical list: Appendectomy, age thirty-five. Transurethral resection of the prostate, age sixty-eight. Cataract surgery, age seventy. Harry Slotkin had been, for the most part, a healthy man.

She turned to the clinic visits record, which contained the doctors' notes. Most were routine checkups, signed by Dr. Wallenberg, with an occasional subspecialist note by Dr. Bartell, a urologist. Toby turned the pages until she paused over an entry dated two years before. She could barely decipher the doctor's name.

'Who wrote this?' she asked. 'The signature looks like a Y something.'

Brace squinted at the illegible handwriting. 'Beats me.'

'You don't recognize the name?'

He shook his head. 'Occasionally we get outside docs coming in for specialty clinics. What's the visit for?'

'I think it says "deviated nasal septum." Must be ENT.'

'There's an ENT specialist named Greeley here in Newton. That signature must be a G, not a Y.'

She knew the name. Greeley occasionally consulted in the Springer ER.

She turned to the lab section, where Harry's most recent blood counts and chemistries were recorded on a computer printout. All were in the normal ranges.

'Pretty good hemoglobin for a guy his age,' she noted. 'Fifteen's better than mine.' She turned to the next page and paused, frowning at a printout with the letterhead: *Newton Diagnostics*. 'Wow, you guys don't believe in cost control, do you? Look at all these labs. Radioimmunoassays for thyroid hormone, growth hormone, prolactin, melatonin, ACTH. The list goes on and on.' She flipped to the next page. 'And on. The panel was

238

done a year ago, and three months ago as well. Some lab in Newton is raking it in.'

'That's the panel Wallenberg orders on all his hormone-injection patients.'

'But the hormone protocol's not mentioned anywhere in this chart.'

Brace fell silent for a moment. 'It does seem strange, doesn't it? To be ordering all these tests if Harry wasn't on the protocol.'

'Maybe Brant Hill's padding the pockets of Newton Diagnostics. This patient's endocrine panel probably cost a few thousand dollars.'

'Did Wallenberg order it?'

'Doesn't say on the lab report.'

'Look at the order sheets. Cross-check the dates.'

She flipped to the section labeled: Physician's Orders. The sheets were carbon copies of the doctors' handwritten orders, each signed and dated.

'Okay, the first endocrine panel was ordered by Wallenberg. The second panel was ordered by that guy with the bad handwriting. Dr. Greeley – if that's who this is.'

'Why would an ENT order an endocrine panel?'

She scanned the rest of the order sheets. 'Here's that signature again, dated almost two years ago. He ordered preop Valium and six A.M. van transport to Howarth Surgical Associates in Wellesley.'

'Preop for what?'

'I think this says "Deviated nasal septum." '

Sighing, she closed the chart. 'That wasn't very helpful, was it?'

'So can we get out of here? Greta's probably getting pissed at me about now.'

Ruefully she handed back the chart. 'Sorry for dragging you out here tonight.'

'Yeah, well, I can't believe I went along with it. You don't really need to look at Parmenter's record, do you?'

'If you can find it for me.'

He stuffed Harry Slotkin's chart in the cabinet and slid the drawer shut with a bang. 'To tell you the truth, Harper, it's not high on my list of priorities.'

A light was burning in the living room. As Toby pulled into the driveway next to Jane Nolan's Saab, she saw the warm glow through the curtains, saw the silhouette of a woman standing in the window. It was a reassuring sight, that vigilant figure peering out at the darkness. It told her someone was home, someone was keeping watch.

Toby let herself in the front door and walked into the living room. 'I'm back.'

Jane Nolan had turned from the window to gather up her magazines. On the sofa, a *National Enquirer* lay open to a spread on 'Shocking Psychic Predictions.' Quickly Jane scooped it up and turned to Toby with an embarrassed smile. 'My intellectual stimulation for the night. I know I'm supposed to be improving my mind

240

with serious reading. But honestly' – she held up the tabloid – 'I can't resist anything with Daniel Day-Lewis on the cover.'

'Neither can I,' admitted Toby. They both laughed, a comfortable acknowledgment that among women, some fantasies are universal.

'How did the evening go?' asked Toby.

'Very well.' Jane turned and quickly straightened the sofa cushions. 'We had dinner at seven, and she pretty much devoured everything. Then I gave her a bubble bath. I guess I shouldn't have, though,' she added ruefully.

'Why? What happened?'

'She had such a good time she refused to get out. I had to drain the tub first.'

'I don't think I've ever given Mom a bubble bath.'

'Oh, it's really funny to watch! She puts the foam on her head and blows it all over. You should've seen the mess on the floor. It's like watching a kid play. Which, in a way, she is.'

Toby sighed. 'And the kid is getting younger every day.'

'But she's such a *nice* kid. I've worked with so many Alzheimer's patients who aren't nice. Who just get *mean* as they get older. I don't think your mother will.'

'No, she won't.' Toby smiled. 'She never was.'

Jane picked up the rest of her magazines, and Daniel Day-Lewis disappeared into her backpack. There was a *Modern Bride* in the stack as well. The magazine of dreamers, thought Toby.

241

According to Jane's résumé, she was single. At thirty-five, Jane seemed like so many other women Toby knew, unattached but hopeful. Anxious but not yet desperate. Women for whom images of dark-haired movie idols would have to suffice until a flesh-and-blood man came into their lives. If one appeared at all.

They walked to the front door.

'So you think everything went well,' said Toby.

'Oh, yes. Ellen and I will get along just fine.' Jane opened the door and stopped. 'I almost forgot. Your sister called. And there was a call from some man at the ME's office. He said he'd call back.'

'Dr. Dvorak? Did he say what he wanted?'

'No. I told him you'd be home later.' She smiled and gave a wave. 'Good night.'

Toby latched the front door and went to the bedroom to call her sister.

'I thought it was your night off,' said Vickie.

'It is.'

'I was surprised when Jane answered.'

'I asked her to watch Mom for a few hours. You know, I *do* enjoy having one night out every six months.'

Vickie sighed. 'You're pissed at me again. Aren't you?'

'No, I'm not.'

'Yes you are. Toby, I *know* you're getting stuck with Mom. I know it doesn't seem fair. But what am I supposed to do? I've got these kids driving me crazy. I have a job, and I still end up with most of the housework. I feel like I'm barely treading water.'

'Vickie, is this a contest? Who's suffering the most?'

'You have no idea what it's like trying to deal with kids.'

'No, I guess I don't.'

There was a long pause. And Toby thought: *I have no idea because I never got the chance.* But she couldn't blame that on Vickie. It was ambition that had kept Toby focused so squarely on her career. Four years of medical school, three years of residency. There'd been no time for romance. And then Ellen's memory had deteriorated, and Toby had gradually assumed responsibility for her mother's affairs. It had not been planned. It was not a path she'd deliberately chosen. It was simply the way her life had turned out.

She had no right to be angry at her sister.

'Look, can you come for dinner on Sunday?' asked Vickie.

'I'm working that night.'

'I can never keep your schedule straight. Is it still four nights on, three nights off?'

'Most of the time. I'll be off Monday and Tuesday next week.'

'Oh, God. Neither of those nights will work for us. Monday's open house at school. And Tuesday is Hannah's piano recital.'

Toby said nothing, merely waited for Vickie to finish her usual litany of how full her calendar was, how difficult to coordinate the schedules of four different people. Hannah and Gabe were so busy these days, like all kids, filling up every spare moment of their childhoods with music lessons, gymnastics, swimming, computer classes. It was drive them here, drive them there, and by the end of the day, Vickie didn't know which end was up.

'It's all right,' Toby finally interrupted. 'Why don't we try for another day?'

'I really *did* want you to come over.'

'Yes, I know. I'm off the second weekend of November.'

'Oh, I'll put that down. First let me make sure it's okay with the troops. I'll call you back next week, okay?'

'Fine. Good night, Vickie.' Toby hung up and wearily ran her hand through her hair. Too busy, too busy. We can't even find the time to mend our bridges. She went down the hall to her mother's room and peeked in the door.

By the soft glow of the night-light, Toby could see that Ellen was asleep. She looked childlike in her bed, her lips slightly parted, her face smooth and unworried. There were times, like this one, when Toby glimpsed the ghost of the little girl that once was Ellen, when she could picture the child with Ellen's face and Ellen's fears. What became of that child? Did she retreat, to become entombed in all the numbing layers of adulthood? Was she reemerging only now, at the end of life, as those same layers peeled away?

She touched her mother's forehead, brushing aside her tendrils of gray hair. Stirring, Ellen opened her eyes and regarded Toby with a look of confusion.

'It's just me, Mom,' said Toby. 'Go back to sleep.'

'Is the stove turned off?'

'Yes, Mom. And the doors are locked. Good night.' She gave Ellen a kiss and left the room.

She decided not to go to bed yet. No sense confusing her circadian rhythm – in another twenty-four hours she'd be back on the night shift. She poured herself a glass of brandy and carried it into the living room. She turned on the stereo and slipped in a Mendelssohn CD. A single violin sang out, pure and mournful. It was Ellen's favorite concerto, and now it was Toby's as well.

At the peak of a crescendo, the phone rang. She turned down the music and reached for the receiver.

It was Dvorak. 'I'm sorry to call so late,' he said.

'It's all right. I just got home a little while ago.' She settled back on the sofa cushions, the brandy glass in hand. 'I heard you tried to reach me earlier.'

'I spoke to your housekeeper.' He paused. In the background, she could hear opera music playing on his end. *Don Giovanni.* Here we are, she thought, two unattached people, each of us sitting at home, keeping company with our stereos. He said, 'You were going to check the history on those Brant Hill patients. I was wondering if you'd learned anything more.'

'I saw Harry Slotkin's chart. There was no surgical exposure to Creutzfeldt-Jakob.'

'And the hormone injections?'

'None. I don't think he was on the protocol. At least, it wasn't mentioned in his chart.'

'What about Parmenter?'

'We couldn't locate his record. So I don't know about surgical exposure. You might ask Dr. Wallenberg tomorrow.'

He said nothing. She realized that *Don Giovanni* was no longer playing, that Dvorak was sitting in silence.

'I wish I could tell you more,' she said. 'This waiting around for a diagnosis must be awful.'

'I've had more enjoyable evenings,' he admitted. 'I've discovered that life insurance policies make very dull reading.'

'Oh, no. That's not how you spent your evening, was it?'

'The bottle of wine helped.'

She gave a sympathetic murmur. 'Brandy is what I generally recommend after a bad day. In fact, I'm holding a glass of it right now.' She paused, and added recklessly: 'You know, I'll be awake all night. I always am. You're welcome to come over and have a glass with me.'

When he didn't answer right away, she closed her eyes, thinking: *God, why did I say that? Why do I sound so desperate for company?*

'Thank you, but I wouldn't be much fun tonight,' he said. 'Another time, maybe.'

'Yes. Another time. Good night.' As she hung

up, she thought, *And what was I expecting?* That he'd drive right over, that they'd spend the night together gazing into each other's eyes?

She sighed and restarted the Mendelssohn concerto. As the violin played, she sipped her brandy and counted the hours until dawn.

Twelve

James Bigelow was tired of funerals. He had attended so many of them in the last few years, and lately they had become more and more frequent, like an accelerating drumbeat marking the passage of time. That so many of his friends had died was to be expected; at seventy-six years old, he had already outlived most of them. Now death was catching up with him as well. He could sense its stalking footsteps, could envision, quite clearly, his own stiff form lying in the open coffin, face powdered, hair combed, gray woolen suit neatly pressed and buttoned. This very same crowd filing by, silently paying their last respects. The fact it was Angus Parmenter and not Bigelow lying in the coffin was merely a matter of timing. Another month, another year, and it would be his coffin on display in this funeral parlor. The journey comes to an end for all of us.

The line moved forward; so did Bigelow. He came to a stop beside the coffin and gazed down at his friend. *Even you were not immortal, Angus.*

He moved past, headed up the center aisle, and took a seat in the fourth row. From there he watched the procession of familiar faces from Brant Hill. There was Angus's neighbor Anna Valentine, who had recklessly pursued him with phone calls and casseroles. There were golfing buddies from the club, and couples from the wine-tasting circle, and musicians from the Brant Hill amateur band.

Where was Phil Dorr?

Bigelow scanned the room, looking for Phil, knowing he should be here. Only three days ago, they had shared a few drinks at the club, had spoken in hushed tones about their old poker buddies, Angus and Harry and Stan Mackie. All three of them gone now, and only Phil and Bigelow remaining. A game of poker with just two of them didn't seem worth the effort, Phil had said. He'd been planning to slip a deck of cards into Angus's coffin, a sort of going-away gift for the great poker table in the sky. Would the family mind? he'd wondered. Would they think it un-dignified to have such a cheap token tucked in with the satin lining? They'd shared a sad laugh about that, another round of tonic water. Hell, Phil had said, he'd do it anyway; Angus would appreciate the gesture.

But Phil had not shown up today with his deck of cards.

Anna Valentine edged into his row and sat down in the chair next to him. Her face was thickly powdered, grotesquely so, every fine wrinkle emphasized by the attempt to camouflage her age. Another hungry widow; he was surrounded by them. Normally he would have avoided striking up a conversation with her, for fear of stirring up mistaken notions of affection in her one-track mind, but at the moment there was no one else close enough to talk to.

Leaning toward her, he murmured: 'Where's Phil?'

She looked at him, as though surprised he'd spoken to her. 'What?'

'Phil Dorr. He was supposed to be here.'

'I think he's not feeling well.'

'What's wrong with him?'

'I don't know. He begged off the theater trip two nights ago. Said his eyes were bothering him.'

'He didn't tell me.'

'He only noticed it last week. He was going to see the doctor about it.' She gave a deep sigh and gazed straight ahead, at the coffin. 'It's terrible, isn't it, how everything's falling apart. Our eyes, our hips, our hearing. I realized today that my voice has changed. I hadn't noticed. I saw the videotape of our trip to Faneuil Hall, and I couldn't believe how old I sounded. I don't *feel* old, Jimmy. I don't recognize myself in the mirror anymore . . .' Again she sighed. A tear slid down her cheek, carving a trail through that dusting of face powder. She wiped it away, leaving a chalky smear.

Phil's eyes were bothering him.

Bigelow sat thinking about this as the line of

250

mourners filed past the coffin, as chairs creaked and voices murmured around him: *'Remember when Angus ...' 'Can't believe he's gone ...' 'Said it was some kind of stroke ...' 'No, that's not what I heard ...'*

Abruptly Bigelow rose to his feet.

'Aren't you staying for the service?' asked Anna.

'I – I have to go talk to someone,' he said and squeezed past her, into the aisle. He thought he heard her calling after him, but he didn't glance back; he headed straight out the front door.

He drove first to Phil's cottage, which was only a few houses away from his. The door was locked; no one answered the bell. Bigelow stood on the porch peering in through the window, but all he could see was the foyer with the little cherry wood table and the brass umbrella holder. There was a single shoe lying on the floor – that struck him as odd. Wrong. Phil was so persnickety about orderliness.

Walking back out through the garden gate, he noticed the mailbox was full. That, too, was unlike Phil.

His eyes were bothering him.

Bigelow climbed back in his car and drove the winding half mile to the Brant Hill Clinic. By the time he walked up to the receptionist's window his palms were sweating, his pulse hammering.

The woman didn't notice he was there – she was too busy yammering on the phone.

He rapped at the window. 'I have to see Dr. Wallenberg.'

251

'I'll be right with you,' she answered.

He watched with surging frustration as she turned away from him and began typing on the keyboard as she talked on the phone, something about insurance copayments and authorization numbers.

'This is important!' he said. 'I have to know what happened to Phil Dorr.'

'Sir, I'm on the telephone.'

'Phil's sick too, isn't he? He's having trouble with his eyes.'

'You'll have to talk to his doctor.'

'Then let me see Dr. Wallenberg.'

'He's at lunch right now.'

'When will he get back? *When?*'

'Sir, you really do have to calm down—'

He reached in through the window and stabbed the disconnect button on her phone. '*I have to see Wallenberg!*'

She pushed her chair back from the window, retreating beyond his reach. Two other women suddenly appeared from the file room. They were all staring at him, at the crazy man ranting in their waiting room.

A door opened and one of the doctors appeared. A big black man, he towered over Bigelow. His name tag said: ROBERT BRACE, M.D.

'Sir, what seems to be the problem?'

'I have to see Wallenberg.'

'He's out of the building at the moment.'

'Then *you* tell me what happened to Phil.'

'Who?'

252

'You know! Phil Dorr! They said he's sick – something wrong with his eyes. Is he in the hospital?'

'Sir, why don't you have a seat while the ladies check the files for—'

'I don't want to sit down! I just want to know if he's got the same thing Angus had. The same thing Stan Mackie had.'

The front door opened and a woman patient walked in. She froze, stared at Bigelow's flushed face, sensing at once that some crisis was under way.

'Why don't we talk in my office?' said Dr. Brace, his voice low and gentle. He reached out toward Bigelow. 'It's just up the hall.'

Bigelow gazed at the doctor's broad hand, the surprisingly pale palm across which a lifeline traced thick and black. He looked up at Dr. Brace. 'I just want to know,' he said softly.

'Know what, sir?'

'Am I going to get sick like the others?'

The doctor shook his head – not an answer to the question, but an expression of bewilderment. 'Why would you get sick?'

'They said there was no risk – they said the procedure was safe. But then Mackie got sick, and—'

'Sir, I don't know Mr. Mackie.'

Bigelow looked at the receptionist. 'You remember Stan Mackie. Tell me you remember Stan.'

'Of course, Mr. Bigelow,' she answered. 'We were so sorry when he passed on.'

'Now Phil's gone too, isn't he? I'm the only one left.'

'Sir?' It was one of the other clerks, calling through the window. 'I just checked Mr. Dorr's chart. He's not sick.'

'Why didn't he go to Angus's funeral? He was supposed to be there!'

'Mr. Dorr had to leave town for a family emergency. He asked for his medical records to be transferred to his new doctor in La Jolla.'

'What?'

'That's what it says here.' She held up the chart, with a note clipped to the cover. 'The authorization's dated yesterday. It says "Patient has moved due to family emergency – will not be returning. Transfer all records to Brant Hill West, La Jolla, California."'

Bigelow moved to the window and stared at the signature on the authorization: *Carl Wallenberg, M.D.*

'Sir?' It was the doctor, his hand resting on Bigelow's shoulder. 'I'm sure you'll be hearing from your friend soon. It sounds like he got called away.'

'But how can he have a family emergency?' Bigelow said softly.

'Maybe someone got sick. Someone died.'

'Phil doesn't *have* a family.'

Dr. Brace was staring at him now. So were the women in the office. He could see them standing behind the glass window, like spectators gazing into a zoo enclosure.

'Something's wrong here,' said Bigelow. 'You're not telling me, are you?'

'We can talk about it,' said the doctor.

'I want to see Dr. Wallenberg.'

'He's at lunch. But you can talk to me, Mr.—'

'Bigelow. James Bigelow.'

Dr. Brace opened the door to the clinic hallway. 'Why don't we go to my office, Mr. Bigelow? You can tell me everything.'

Bigelow stared at the long white corridor that stretched beyond the doorway. 'No,' he said, and he backed away. 'No, never mind—'

He fled the building.

Robbie Brace knocked on the door and stepped into Carl Wallenberg's office. The room, like the man, showed snooty good taste. Brace wasn't up on fancy furniture brands, but even he could spot quality. The massive desk was made of some warm and exotically reddish wood he didn't recognize. The art hanging on the walls was that fartsy-abstract stuff for which one usually paid a fortune. Through the window, behind Wallenberg's back, was a view of the setting sun. The light glared in, forming a halo around the man's head and shoulders. *Jesus H. Wallenberg*, thought Brace as he stood before the desk.

Wallenberg looked up from his papers. 'Yes, Robbie?' *Robbie. Not Dr. Brace. Guess we know who's in charge here.*

Brace said, 'Do you remember a patient named Stan Mackie?'

255

Against the backlight, Wallenberg's expression was unreadable. Slowly he leaned back in his chair, eliciting the rich creak of leather. 'How did Stan Mackie's name come up?'

'From one of your patients, James Bigelow. You do know Mr. Bigelow?'

'Yes, of course. He was one of the first patients on my panel here. One of the first to move into Brant Hill.'

'Well, Mr. Bigelow was over in the clinic this afternoon, very upset. I'm not sure I got a coherent story out of him. He kept ranting about all his friends getting sick, wondering whether he'd be next. He mentioned Mr. Mackie's name.'

'That would be Dr. Mackie.'

'He was a physician?'

Wallenberg gestured to a chair. 'Why don't you have a seat, Robbie? It's hard to discuss this with you when you're towering over me.'

Brace sat down. He realized at once it was a tactical error; he had lost his advantage of height, and they were facing each other directly across the desk. Now Wallenberg held all the advantages. Seniority. Race. A better tailor.

'What was Mr. Bigelow talking about?' asked Brace. 'He seemed terrified of getting sick.'

'I haven't the faintest idea.'

'He mentioned some sort of procedure that he and his friends had.'

Wallenberg shook his head. 'Maybe he meant the hormone protocol? The weekly injections?'

'I don't know.'

256

'If he did, he's worrying needlessly. There's nothing revolutionary about our protocol. You know that.'

'So Mr. Bigelow and his friends *were* getting hormone injections?'

'Yes. It was one of the reasons they came to Brant Hill. For the benefits of our cutting-edge research.'

'Interesting you should use the term *cutting edge*. Mr. Bigelow didn't say anything about injections. He specifically used the term *procedure*. Like some sort of surgery.'

'No, no. He hasn't had any surgery. In fact, the only time I recall him needing a surgeon was to get a nasal polyp removed. It was benign, of course.'

'Well, what about that hormone protocol, then? Have there been *any* serious side effects?'

'None.'

'So there's no chance it caused Angus Parmenter's death?'

'The diagnosis hasn't been determined yet.'

'It was Creutzfeldt-Jakob disease. That's what Dr. Harper told me.'

Wallenberg went very still, and Brace suddenly realized he shouldn't have mentioned Toby Harper's name. Shouldn't have revealed any contact with her.

'Well,' said Wallenberg quietly. 'It does explain the patient's symptoms.'

'What about Mr. Bigelow's concerns? That his other friends had the same illness?'

Wallenberg shook his head. 'You know, it's hard

for our patients to accept the fact they've reached the end of their life spans. Angus Parmenter was eighty-two. Senescence and death are what happen to all of us.'

'How did Dr. Mackie die?'

Wallenberg paused. 'That was a particularly upsetting event. Dr. Mackie had a psychotic break. He jumped out of a window at Wicklin Hospital.'

'Jesus.'

'It stunned us all. He was a surgeon, and a very good one, too. Never retired from the OR, even at the age of seventy-four. He worked right up until the day of his . . . accident.'

'Was an autopsy done?'

'The cause was clearly from trauma.'

'Yes, but was an autopsy done?'

'I don't know. He was under the care of surgeons at Wicklin. He died about a week after the fall.' He regarded Robbie with a thoughtful gaze. 'You seem bothered by all this.'

'I guess it's because Mr. Bigelow was so upset. There's one more name he mentioned, another friend who's fallen ill. A Phillip Dorr.'

'Mr. Dorr's fine. He moved to Brant Hill West, in La Jolla. I just received his signed authorization to transfer his records.' He shuffled through the files on his desk and finally produced a sheet of paper. 'Here's his fax from California.'

Brace glanced at the sheet, and saw Phillip Dorr's signature at the bottom. 'So he's not sick.'

'I saw Mr. Dorr in clinic a few days ago, for a routine checkup.'

'And?'

Wallenberg looked straight at him. 'He was in perfect health.'

Back at his own desk, Brace finished up the day's medical charts and dictations. At six-thirty, he finally shut off the microcassette recorder and looked down at his newly cleared desk. He found himself staring at the name he'd scrawled on the back of a lab report: *Dr. Stanley Mackie.* The incident that afternoon in the clinic still bothered him. He thought of the other names James Bigelow had mentioned: *Angus Parmenter. Phillip Dorr.* That two of those three men were now dead was not in itself alarming. All of them were elderly; all of them had reached their statistically apportioned life spans.

But old age was not in itself a cause of death.

Today he'd seen fear in James Bigelow's eyes, real fear, and he could not quite shake off his uneasiness.

He picked up the phone and called Greta, telling her he'd be home late because he had to make a stop at Wicklin Hospital. Then he packed up his briefcase and left the office.

By now the clinic was deserted, the corridor lit by only one fluorescent panel at the end of the hall. As he walked beneath it, he heard a faint humming and looked up to see the shadow of an insect trapped behind the opaque plastic, wings fluttering against its own doom. He flipped off the wall switch. The hallway went dark, but he could still hear the humming overhead, the frantic thrashing of wings.

He walked out of the building, into a damp and windblown night.

His Toyota was the only car left in the clinic lot. Parked beneath the sulfurous glow of a security lamp, it looked more black than green, like the shiny carapace of a beetle. He paused to fish the car keys from his pocket. Then he gazed up at the lit windows of the nursing facility, at the unmoving silhouettes of patients in their rooms, the flicker of TV screens barely watched. He was gripped by a sudden and profound depression. What he was seeing, in those windows, was the end of life. A shadowbox of his own future.

He slid into his car and drove out of the lot, but he could not leave behind that sense of depression. It clung to him like cold mist on his skin. *I should have chosen pediatrics*, he thought. Babies. Beginnings. Growing, not decaying flesh. But in medical school he'd been advised that the future of medical practice lay in geriatrics, with baby boomers gone gray, a vast army of them, marching toward senility, sucking up medical resources along the way. Ninety percent of the health care dollar was spent on sustaining a person's last year of life. That's where the money would flow; that's where doctors would make their livings.

Robbie Brace, a practical man, had chosen a practical field.

Oh, but how it depressed him.

As he drove toward Wicklin Hospital, he

260

considered what his life would be like had he chosen pediatrics. He thought of his own daughter, and remembered his joy at looking into her wrinkled newborn face as she'd wailed in fury in the delivery room. He remembered the exhaustion of 2 A.M. feedings, the smell of talcum powder and sour milk, the silky baby skin in a warm bath. In so many ways, infants were like very old people. They needed to be bathed and fed and dressed. They needed their diapers changed. They could neither walk nor talk. They lived only at the mercy of people who cared about them.

It was seven-thirty when he reached Wicklin, a small community hospital just inside the Boston City limits. He pulled on his white coat, made sure his name tag with ROBERT BRACE, M.D. was clipped on, and walked into the building. He didn't have hospital privileges here, nor did he have the authority to request any of their medical charts; he was gambling that no one would bother to question him.

In the medical records department, he filled out a request form for Stanley Mackie's chart and handed the slip to the clerk, a petite blond. She glanced at his name tag and hesitated, no doubt realizing he was not on their staff.

'I'm from Brant Hill Clinic,' he said. 'This patient was one of ours.'

She brought him the chart, and he carried it to an empty desk and sat down. Across the chart cover was written in black marker: *Deceased*. He opened the file and looked at the first page, listing the identifying data: name, birth date, Social Security number. The address caught his eye at once: 101 Titwillow Lane, Newton, MA.

It was a Brant Hill address.

He turned to the next page. The record covered only a single hospitalization – the one in which Stanley Mackie had died. With a growing sense of dismay he read the admitting surgeon's dictated history and physical, dated March ninth.

74-year-old previously healthy white male physician admitted with massive head trauma via ER after falling from fourth-floor window. Just prior to accident, patient had been scrubbed and gowned and was performing a routine appendectomy. According to OR nurses, Dr. Mackie displayed marked tremors of both hands. Without explanation, he proceeded to resect several feet of normal-appearing small bowel, resulting in massive hemorrhage and death. When the OR staff attempted to pull him away from the table, he slashed the anesthesiologist's jugular vein, then fled the OR.

Witnesses in the hallway saw him dive head-first through window. He was found in the parking lot, unresponsive and bleeding from multiple lacerations.

After being intubated and stabilized in the ER, patient was admitted to trauma service with multiple skull fractures as well as probable spinal compression fractures . . .

The physical exam had been recorded in typically terse surgical style, a rapid rundown of the patient's injuries and neurologic findings. Lacerated scalp and face. Open fractures of the parietal and coronal bones with extrusion of gray matter. A blown pupil on the right. No spontaneous respirations, no response to painful stimuli. The patient's injuries, thought Brace, were consistent with a head-first landing in the parking lot.

Flipping further, he saw the surgeon's note: 'X-ray report: spinal compression fractures C6, C7, T8.' That, too, indicated a headfirst landing with the force of the fall transmitted straight down the spinal column.

Stanley Mackie's hospital course was a week-long deterioration of multiple organ systems. Comatose and on a ventilator, he never re-awakened. First his kidneys shut down, probably due to the shock of his injuries. Then he developed pneumonia and his BP dropped out twice, causing a bowel infarct. Finally, seven days after his plunge through the fourth-story window, his heart went into arrest.

He flipped to the back of the chart, where the lab results were filed. There were seven days' worth of computer printouts, a running log of electrolytes and blood chemistries, cell counts, and urinalyses. He kept turning pages, scanning thousands of dollars' worth of lab tests done on a man whose death had been, from the very first day, inevitable.

He paused at a lab report marked: *Pathology*.

Liver (postmortem):
  Gross appearance: Weight: 1600 gm., pale, pinpoint surface areas of acute hemorrhage. No evidence chronic fibrotic changes.
  Microscopic: On H and B stain, there are scattered areas of poorly stained mummified hepatocytes. This is consistent with focal coagulative necrosis, probably secondary to ischemia.

Brace turned the page and found a blood count report, out of sequence. He turned another page, and found himself staring at the back cover. There were no pages left.

He flipped toward the front of the record, searching for other postmortem reports, but could find only the page describing the liver. This didn't make sense. Why would Pathology do a postmortem on a single organ? Where were the reports for lungs, the heart, the brain?

He asked at the desk if there were more files for Stanley Mackie.

'That's the only one,' said the clerk.

'But some of the Pathology reports are missing.'

'You can check directly with Path. They keep copies of all their reports.'

The Pathology Department, located in the basement, was a low-ceilinged warren of rooms, the walls painted white and decorated with lushly photographed travel posters. Mist over the

Serengeti. A rainbow arching above Kauai. An island of mangroves in a turquoise sea. A radio was playing soft rock music. The lone technician at work in that room seemed absurdly cheerful, considering the nature of her job. She herself was another bright splash of color, with rouged cheeks and eyelids powdered a sparkly green.

'I'm trying to locate an autopsy report done back in March,' said Brace. 'It's not in the patient's file. Medical Records suggested I check with you.'

'What was the patient's name?'

'Stanley Mackie.'

The technician shook her head as she crossed to a filing cabinet. 'He was such a nice man. We all felt awful about that.'

'You knew him?'

'The surgeons always come down to check path reports on their patients. We got to know Dr. Mackie pretty well.' She pulled open a drawer and began thumbing through files. 'He bought us our department coffeemaker for Christmas. We call it the Mackie Memorial Mr. Coffee. 'She straightened and stood frowning at the open drawer. 'That's frustrating.'

'What?'

'I can't find it.' She closed the drawer. 'I'm sure an autopsy was done on Dr. Mackie.'

'Could it be misfiled? Under *S* for *Stanley*?'

She opened a different drawer, searched the files, then closed it again. She turned as another technician entered the lab. 'Hey, Tim, have you seen the autopsy report for Dr. Mackie?'

'Wasn't that done way back?'

'It was early this year.'

'Then it should still be in the files.' He set a tray of slides on the countertop. 'Try checking Herman.'

'Why didn't I think of Herman?' she sighed, and crossed the lab into one of the offices.

Brace followed her. 'Who's Herman?'

'He's not a *who* but a *what*.' She flipped on the lights, revealing a desk with a personal computer. 'That's Herman. It's Dr. Seibert's pet project.'

'What does Herman do?'

'He – it – is supposed to make retrospective studies a snap. Say you want to know how many perinatal deaths involved mothers who smoked. You type in the keywords *smoker* and *perinatal* and you'll get a list of relevant patients who've been autopsied.'

'So all your autopsy data's in there?'

'Some of it. Dr. Seibert started inputting our data only two months ago. He's a long way from finishing.' She sat down at the keyboard, typed in the name Mackie, Stanley, and clicked on Search.

A new screen appeared with identifying data. It was Stanley Mackie's autopsy report.

The technician vacated the seat. 'It's all yours.'

Brace sat down in front of the computer. According to the data on the screen, this report had been input six weeks ago; the actual file must have been lost since then. He hit Page Down and began to read.

The report described the body's gross

appearance at post-mortem: the multiple IV lines, the shaved head, the incision marks on the scalp left by the neurosurgeon's blade. The report continued with a description of the internal organs. The lungs were congested and swollen with inflammation. The heart showed a fresh infarct. The brain had multiple areas of hemorrhage. The findings at gross examination were consistent with the surgeons' diagnosis: massive head trauma with bilateral pneumonia. The fresh myocardial infarct had probably been the terminal event.

He clicked to the microscopic reports and found a summary of the same page he'd seen in the medical record, describing the liver. In addition there were reports that had not appeared in the medical record – microscopics of the liver, the heart, the lungs. No surprises, he thought. The man fell headfirst onto the pavement, he crushed his skull, and the neurologic trauma led to multiple organ failure.

He clicked to the microscopic report on the brain, and his eyes suddenly focused on a sentence buried within the description of traumatic injuries:

'. . . variable vacuolation in the background neuropil. Some neuronal loss and reactive astrocytosis with kuru plaques, Congo-red positive, as seen in cerebellar sections.'

At once he clicked to the last page and his gaze flew down to the final diagnoses:

1.   Multiple intracerebral hemorrhages secondary to trauma.

2.   Preexisting Creutzfeldt-Jakob disease.

In the parking lot, Robbie Brace sat in his car, wondering what he should do next. Whether he should do anything next. He weighed all the possible consequences of his actions. This would be a devastating blow to Brant Hill's reputation. Surely the media would pick this up, and there'd be screaming headlines: RITZ AND DEATH. MONEY BUYS MAD COW DISEASE.

He'd be out of a job.

You can't stay silent, man. Toby Harper is right. We have a deadly outbreak on our hands, and we don't know the source. The hormone injections? The food?

He reached under the seat for his cellular phone. He was still carrying Toby Harper's card; he punched in her home phone number.

A woman answered, 'Harper residence.'

'This is Dr. Brace from Brant Hill. May I speak to Toby Harper?'

'She's not here, but I can take a message. What's your number?'

'I'm in my car right now. Just tell her she was right. Tell her we've got a second case of CJD.'

'Excuse me?'

'She'll know what it means.' Headlights flickered in his rearview mirror. He turned and saw that a car was slowly moving along the next row. 'What time's she getting home?' he asked.

'She's at work right now—'

'Oh. Then I'll swing by Springer Hospital. Never mind about the message.' He disconnected, slid the phone under the seat, and started the car. As he pulled out of the driveway, he noticed those same headlights moving toward the parking lot exit. He quickly lost sight of them in the busy flow of traffic.

It was a half hour drive to Springer Hospital. By the time he turned into the parking lot, he'd developed a headache from hunger. He pulled into a stall in the visitors' area. With the engine off, he sat for a moment in his car, massaging his temples. It was just a mild headache, but it reminded him he hadn't eaten since breakfast. He'd stay only a few minutes, just long enough to tell her what he'd learned, and then he'd let *her* carry the ball from there. All he wanted to do now was go home, eat supper. Play with his little girl.

He climbed out of the car, locked it, and started toward the ER entrance. He'd taken only a few steps when he heard the growl of a car behind him. Turning, he squinted at the slowly approaching headlights. The car came to a stop beside him. He heard the electric hum of the driver's window as it rolled down.

A man with hair so blond it looked silvery under the parking lot light smiled at him. 'I think I'm lost.'

'Where you trying to get to?' asked Brace.

'Irving Street.'

'You're nowhere near it.' Brace took a step toward the open car window. 'You'll have to go back out to the road, turn right, and drive about four or five—'

The *pop, pop* took him by surprise. So did the punch in the chest.

Brace jerked away, startled by the unprovoked blow. He touched his hand to his chest, where the pain was just beginning to assert itself, and found he could not draw in a deep breath. Warmth seeped from his shirt and dribbled onto his fingers. He looked down and saw that his hand was wet and glistening with dark liquid.

There was another *pop*, another punch in the chest.

Brace staggered. He tried to regain his footing, but his legs seemed to fold up beneath him. He dropped to his knees and saw the streetlamp begin to waver like water.

The last bullet slammed into his back.

He collapsed with his face pressed against the cold pavement, the gravel biting into his cheek. The car drove off, the purr of its engine fading into the night. He could feel his life spilling away in a hot stream. He pressed his hand to his chest, trying to stanch the flow, but the strength had left his arm. All he could manage was a feeble clasp.

God, not here, he thought. *Not now.*

He began to crawl toward the ER doors, at the same time trying to maintain pressure on his chest wound, but with every beat of his heart, he felt more heat gush out. He tried to keep his gaze fixed on the sign: EMERGENCY, brightly lit in red, but his vision kept going out of focus, and the word began to waver like seeping blood.

The glass doors of the ER were straight ahead. Suddenly a figure appeared from that warm rectangle of light. It came to a halt only a few feet away. Desperately Brace reached out and whispered: 'Help me. Please.'

He heard the woman yell: 'There's a man bleeding out here! I need assistance STAT!'

And then he heard footsteps running toward him.

Thirteen

'Get a third IV in!' yelled Toby. 'Sixteen gauge! Ringer's lactate, wide open—'

'Lab says O-negative blood's on its way.'

'Where the hell is Carey?'

'He was just in the hospital,' said Maudeen. 'I'll page him again.'

Toby pulled on a pair of sterile gloves and reached for the scalpel. Under the bright trauma room lights, Brace's face was glistening with sweat and fear. He stared up at her, his eyes wide above the hissing oxygen mask, his breaths coming in short, desperate puffs. The bandage over his chest was slowly seeping with red again. A nurse-anesthetist, called down from the obstetrics ward, was already preparing to intubate.

'Robbie, I'm going to put in a chest tube,' said Toby. 'You're getting a tension pneumothorax.' She saw him give a quick nod of comprehension, saw his jaw tighten in anticipation of more pain. But he didn't even flinch as her blade sliced through the skin above his rib; a subcutaneous

272

injection of Xylocaine had already numbed the nerve endings. Toby heard a rush of escaping air and knew she was now in the chest cavity. She also knew she'd been correct; the bullet had punctured a lung, and with each breath Robbie took, air was leaking from the ruptured lung into the pleural space, building up enough pressure to shift the heart and great vessels, compressing whatever pulmonary tissue was still intact.

She slipped her finger through the incision to widen it, then slipped in the clear plastic chest tube. Val connected the other end to low-pressure suction. Immediately a stream of bright red shot into the tube and collected in the drain reservoir.

Toby and Val glanced at each other, both of them sharing the same thought: *He's bleeding into his chest – and fast.*

She looked at Robbie's face and saw he was watching her, that he'd registered her look of dismay.

'It's . . . not good,' he whispered.

She squeezed his shoulder. 'You're doing fine, Robbie. The surgeon'll be here any minute.'

'Cold. Feel so cold . . .'

Maudeen threw a blanket over him.

'Where's that O-neg blood?' called Toby.

'Just arrived. I'll hang it now—'

'Toby,' whispered Val. 'Systolic's down to eighty-five.'

'Come on, come on. Let's pour in that blood!'

The door sprang open and Doug Carey walked it. 'What've you got here?' he snapped.

273

'Gunshot wounds to chest and back,' said Toby. 'Three bullets show up on X ray, but I counted four entry holes. Tension pneumothorax. And that' – she pointed to the chest tube reservoir, where 100 cc's of blood had already accumulated – 'that's just in the last few minutes. Systolic's slipping.'

Carey glanced at the X ray hanging on the light box. 'Let's crack the chest,' he said.

'We'd need a full cardiac team – maybe bypass—'

'Can't wait. Have to stop the bleeding *now*.' He looked straight at Toby, and she felt the old dislike welling up inside her. Doug Carey was a bastard, but right now she needed him. Robbie Brace needed him.

Toby nodded to the nurse-anesthetist. 'Go ahead and intubate. We'll get him prepped. Val, open that thoracotomy tray . . .'

As everyone scurried around the room in preparation, the anesthetist drew a dose of Etomidate into a syringe. The drug would render Robbie fully unconscious for the intubation.

Toby loosened Robbie's oxygen mask and saw that he was gazing up, his eyes focused desperately on hers. So many times before she had seen terror in a patient's eyes and had forced herself to suppress her own emotions, to concentrate on her job. This time, though, she could not ignore the fear in her patient's eyes. This was a man she knew, a man she'd grown to like.

'Everything will be all right,' she said. 'You have

to believe me. I won't let *anything* go wrong.'
Gently she cradled his face between her hands and
smiled.

'Counting . . . on you . . . Harper,' he
murmured.

She nodded. 'You do that, Robbie. Now, are
you ready to go to sleep?'

'Wake me . . . when it's over . . .'

'It'll seem like no time at all.' She nodded to the
anesthetist, who injected the Etomidate into the IV
line. 'Go to sleep, Robbie. That's it. I'll be right
here when you wake up . . .'

His gaze remained focused on her. She would be
the last image he'd register, the last face he'd see.
She watched as consciousness faded from his eyes,
as his muscles slowly went slack and his eyelids
drifted shut.

I won't let anything go wrong.

She removed the oxygen mask. At once the
anesthetist tipped Robbie's head back and slid
the laryngoscope blade into the throat. It took her
only seconds to identify the vocal cords, to thread
the ET tube into the trachea. Then the oxygen was
connected and the tube taped into place. The
ventilator would take over now, breathing for
him, forcing into his lungs a precise mixture of
oxygen and halothane.

I won't let anything go wrong.

Toby released a tense breath of her own. Then
she quickly gowned up. She knew they were
breaking sterile conditions left and right, but
it couldn't be helped. No time to scrub –

she snapped on gloves and moved to the table.

She stood right across from Doug Carey. The patient's chest had been hastily painted with Betadine and sterile drapes were laid over the operative site.

Carey made his incision, a single clean slice down the sternum. There was no time to be elegant; the blood pressure was falling – down to seventy systolic with three big-bore IVs pouring in saline and whole blood. Toby had witnessed emergency thoracotomies before, and the brutality of it never failed to appall her. She watched with a twinge of nausea as Carey wielded the saw, as the sternum was split in a mist of bone dust and flying blood.

'Shit,' said Carey, looking into the chest cavity. 'There's at least a liter of blood in here. Suction! Hand me some sterile towels!'

The gurgle of the suction catheter was so loud Toby could barely hear the *beep-beep* of Robbie's heartbeat on the cardiac monitor. As Val suctioned, Maudeen ripped open the sterile seal on a bundle of towels. Carey stuffed one into the chest cavity. When he pulled it out, it was sopping red. He tossed it on the floor, thrust in another towel. Again it came out soaked with blood.

'Okay. Okay, I think I see where it's coming from. Looks like the ascending aorta – leaking fast. Toby, I need more exposure . . .'

The suction catheter was still gurgling. Though most of the blood had been cleared out, a steady stream of it was spilling out of the aorta.

'I don't see a bullet,' said Carey. He glanced at the X ray, then stared into the open chest. 'There's the leak, but where's the fucking bullet?'

'Can't you just patch it?'

'It could still be lodged somewhere in the aortic wall. We patch and close, another hole could rip open later.' He reached for the needle clamp and sutures. 'Okay, let's shut off this leak first. Then we'll look around . . .'

Toby retracted the lung while Carey worked. He sewed quickly, his suture needle nipping in and out of the aortic wall. As he tied off and the bleeding stopped, everyone in the room gave a simultaneous sigh of relief.

'BP?' he called out.

'Holding at seventy-five,' said Val.

'Keep that O-neg going in. We got more units?'

'On the way.'

'Okay.' Carey took a breath. 'Let's see what else we got in here . . .' He suctioned off the pooled blood, clearing the field for easier inspection. Then, gently applying traction for a better view, he took a sponge and dabbed along the aorta.

Suddenly his hands froze. 'Fuck,' he said. 'The bullet—'

'What?'

'It's right here! It's almost through the opposite wall!' He started to withdraw his hand.

A fountain of blood suddenly exploded upward, splattering them both in the face.

'*No!*' cried Toby.

Panicked, Carey grabbed a clamp off the tray

and reached in through the rushing blood, but he was working blind, groping in a shimmering sea of red. It spilled out of the thorax and soaked into Toby's gown.

'Can't stop it – feels like he's got a rip along the whole fucking wall—'

'Clamp it! Can't you clamp it?'

'Clamp *what*? The aorta's shredded—'

The cardiac monitor squealed. The anesthetist said: 'Asystole! We've got asystole!'

Toby's gaze shot to the screen. The heart tracing had gone flat.

She reached into that hot pool of blood and grasped the heart. She squeezed, once, twice, her hand taking over for Robbie's heartbeat.

'Don't!' said Carey. 'You're only making him bleed out!'

'He's in arrest—'

'You can't change that.'

'Then what the fuck do we *do*?'

The monitor was still squealing. Carey looked down at the open chest. At the glistening pool of red. Since Toby had ceased cardiac massage, the fountaining had stopped. There was only the slow drip, drip of blood spilling out of the open thorax onto the floor.

'It's over,' he said. Quietly he stepped away from the body. His gown was saturated to the waist. 'There was nothing to sew up, Toby. The whole aorta was dissecting. It just blew apart.'

Toby looked at Robbie's face. His eyelids were

partly open, his jaw slack. The ventilator was still cycling, automatically blowing air into a dead body.

The anesthetist flipped off the switch. Silence fell over the room. Toby lay her hand on Robbie's shoulder. Through the sterile drapes, his flesh felt solid, and still warm.

I won't let anything go wrong.

'I'm sorry,' she whispered. 'I'm so sorry . . .'

The police showed up before Robbie's wife did. Within minutes of their arrival, the first two patrolmen had secured the crime scene and were busy cordoning off half the parking lot. By the time Greta Brace hurried into the ER, the parking lot was already awash in the flashing lights of half a dozen police cars from both the Newton and the Boston PD. Toby was standing by the front desk taking to one of the detectives when she spotted Greta stepping through the ER doors, her red hair in windblown disarray. The waiting area was filled with cops, plus a few bewildered ER patients, and Greta sobbed and cursed as she pushed her way across the room.

'Where is he?' she cried.

Toby broke off her conversation with the detective and crossed toward Greta. 'I'm so sorry—'

'*Where is he?*'

'He's still in the trauma room. Greta, no! Don't go back there yet. Give us some time to—'

'He's my husband. I have to see him.'

'Greta—'

But the other woman pushed past her and headed into the treatment area with Toby in pursuit. Greta didn't know which way to go; she zigzagged back and forth, frantically searching the rooms. At last she spotted the door labeled: TRAUMA. She pushed straight into the room.

Toby was right behind her. Dr. Daniel Dvorak, gowned and gloved, looked up from the body as the two women entered. Robbie lay undraped, his chest gaping open, his face slack with death.

'No,' said Greta, and her voice rose from a moan to a high, keening wail. '*No . . .*'

Toby reached for her arm and tried to lead her out of the room, but Greta shook her off and stumbled to her husband's side. She cradled his face in her hands, kissed his eyes, his forehead. The ER tube was still in place, the tip of it protruding from his mouth. She tried to unpeel the tape, to remove the offending piece of plastic.

Daniel Dvorak put his hand on hers to stop her. 'I'm sorry,' he said quietly. 'It has to remain.'

'I want this thing out of my husband's throat!'

'It has to stay for now. I'll remove it when I finish my exam.'

'Who the fuck are *you*?'

'I'm the medical examiner. Dr. Dvorak.' He looked at the homicide detective, who'd just stepped into the trauma room.

'Mrs. Brace?' said the cop. 'I'm Detective Sheehan. Why don't you and I go someplace quiet. Where we can sit down.'

280

Greta didn't move. She stood murmuring softly, cradling Robbie's face in her hands, her expression hidden behind that fountain of red hair.

'We need your help, Mrs. Brace, to find out what happened.' Gently the cop touched her shoulder. 'Let's go sit in another room. Where we can talk.'

At last she allowed herself to be led away from the table. At the doorway she halted and looked at her husband.

'I'll be right back, Robbie,' she said. Then she walked slowly out of the room.

Toby and Dvorak were left alone. 'I didn't realize you were here,' she said.

'I arrived about ten minutes ago. With so many people out there, you probably missed me in the crowd.'

She looked at Robbie, wondering if his flesh was still warm. 'I wish we could just shut down the ER. I wish I could go home. But patients keep walking in. With their stomachaches and their sniffles. And their goddamn piddly complaints . . .' Her vision suddenly blurred with tears. She wiped her face and turned toward the door.

'Toby?'

She halted, not answering. Not looking back.

'I need to talk to you. About what happened tonight.'

'I've already spoken to half a dozen cops. No one on the staff saw what happened. We found him in the parking lot. He was crawling toward the building . . .'

'Do you agree with Dr. Carey that death resulted from aortic exsanguination?'

She took a breath and reluctantly turned to face him. 'Whatever Dr. Carey says.'

'What do you remember about the surgery?'

'There was . . . a small nick in the aorta. He patched it up. But then we saw the bullet . . . had passed through . . . there was an intimal tear. An aortic dissection. Then the wall blew open . . .' She swallowed and looked away. 'It was a nightmare.'

He said nothing.

'I *knew* him,' she whispered. 'I'd been to his house. I'd met his wife. Oh Jesus.' She pushed out of the room.

The only refuge she could find was the doctor's sleeping quarters. She closed the door behind her and sat down on the bed, crying, rocking back and forth. She didn't even hear the knock on the door.

Dvorak came quietly into the room. He'd stripped off the gown and gloves, and now he stood by the bed, unsure of what to say.

'Are you all right?' he finally asked.

'No. I am not all right.'

'I'm sorry about the questions. I had to ask them.'

'You were so fucking cold-blooded about it.'

'I needed to know, Toby. We can't help Dr. Brace, not now. But we can find the answers. We owe it to him.'

She dropped her face in her hands and struggled to regain control, to stop crying. Her tears felt all the more humiliating because *he* was standing there, watching her. She heard the chair give a squeak as he sat down. When at last she managed to raise her head, she found herself looking straight into his eyes.

'I didn't realize you and the victim were acquainted,' he said.

'He's not *the victim*. His name was Robbie.'

'Okay. Robbie.' He hesitated. 'Were you good friends?'

'No. Not . . . not *good* friends.'

'You seem to be taking this pretty hard.'

'And you don't understand. Do you?'

'Not entirely.'

She took a breath and slowly released it. 'It catches up with us, you know. Most of the time, when we lose a patient, we can deal with it. Then there'll be a child. Or someone we know. And suddenly we realize we can't handle it at all . . .' She wiped her hand across her eyes. 'I have to get back to work. There must be patients waiting out there—'

He grasped her hand. 'Toby, if it makes a difference to you, I don't think there's anything you could have done to save him. The damage to his aorta was devastating.'

She looked down at his hand, feeling faintly surprised that he was still touching her. He, too, seemed taken aback by that spontaneous contact, and he quickly released her wrist. They sat in silence for a moment.

'This hits too close to home,' she said. Hugging

herself, she found her gaze drawn, once again, to his. 'I walk through that parking lot every evening. So do all the nurses. If this was a robbery attempt, any one of us would have made an easier target.'

'Have there been other attacks at Springer?'

'Only one I can think of. A few years ago – a nurse was raped. But this isn't like downtown Boston. We don't worry about our safety here.'

'Monsters live in the suburbs too.'

The knock on the door startled them both. Toby opened the door to find Detective Sheehan.

'Dr. Harper, I need to ask you a few questions,' he said and stepped inside, shutting the door behind him. The room suddenly seemed very crowded. 'I just spoke to Mrs. Brace. She thinks her husband might have come here to see *you*.'

Toby shook her head. 'Why?'

'That's what we're wondering. He called her around six-thirty and told her he was driving to Wicklin Hospital, and that he'd be home late.'

'Did he go to Wicklin?'

'We're checking that now. What we don't know is why he ended up *here*. Do you know?'

She shook her head.

'When was the last time you saw Dr. Brace?'

'Last night.'

Sheehan's eyebrow twitched upward. 'He came to Springer?'

'No. I went to his house. He helped me look up a medical record.'

'You got together to look at medical records?'

'Yes.' She looked at Dvorak. 'It was right after I

saw *you*. You'd just told me Angus Parmenter's diagnosis. I wondered about Harry Slotkin – whether he had Creutzfeldt-Jakob disease as well. So Robbie and I looked up Slotkin's outpatient record.'

'*What* disease?' interjected Sheehan.

'Creutzfeldt-Jakob. It's a fatal brain infection.'

'Okay. So you and Dr. Brace got together last night. And then what?'

'We drove to Brant Hill. We looked at the medical chart. Then we both went home.'

'You didn't stop somewhere? He didn't go to your house?'

'No. I got home around ten-thirty, alone. He didn't call me afterward, and I didn't call him. So I don't know why he'd come to see me tonight.'

There was a knock. *How many more people can fit in this room?* wondered Toby as she opened the door.

It was Val. 'We've got a guy with left-sided weakness and slurred speech. BP's two fifty over one thirty. He's in room two.'

Toby glanced back at Sheehan. 'I don't have anything more to tell you, Detective. Now if you'll excuse me, I have patients to see.'

At eight o'clock the next morning, Toby pulled into her driveway next to Jane's dark blue Saab and turned off the engine. She was too exhausted to climb out of the car and deal with Ellen just yet, so she sat for a moment, staring out at the dead leaves blowing across the lawn. It had been one of the worst nights of her life, first Robbie's death, and then a succession of seriously ill patients – a stroke, a myocardial infarction, and a case of end-stage emphysema so critical the patient had required intubation. Added to that was the general sense of confusion from all those cops milling about with their chattering walkie-talkies. Was it a full moon last night? she wondered. Some crazy juxtaposition of the planets that had blown chaos into her ER? And then there'd been Detective Sheehan, ambushing her at every opportunity to ask *just one more* question.

A gust of wind buffeted the car. With the heater turned off, she was starting to feel cold. It was the chill that finally drove her out of the car and into the house.

She was greeted by the smell of coffee and the pleasant clatter of chinaware from the kitchen. 'I'm home,' she called out, and hung her jacket in the closet.

Jane appeared in the kitchen doorway, her smile warm and welcoming. 'I've just made a pot – would you like a cup?'

'I would, but I won't be able to sleep.'

'Oh, it's decaf. I figured you wouldn't want the real thing.'

Toby smiled. 'In that case, thanks. I'd love a cup.'

Pale morning light shone in through the window as they sat at the kitchen table, drinking their coffee. Ellen wasn't awake yet, and Toby felt almost guilty about how glad she was for the reprieve, how much she was enjoying this moment of peace. She leaned back and inhaled the steam rising from her cup. 'This is heaven.'

'Actually, it's only a cup of Colombian roast.'

'Yes, but I didn't have to grind it. I didn't have to pour it. And I can just sit here and actually drink it.'

Jane shook her head in sympathy. 'It sounds like you had a bad night.'

'It was so bad I don't even want to talk about it.' Toby set the cup down and rubbed her face. 'And how was your night?'

'A little chaotic. Your mother had trouble going to sleep. She was up and down, up and down, wandering the house.'

'Oh no. Why?'

'She told me she had to go pick you up at school. So she searched all over for the car keys.'

'She hasn't driven a car in years. I have no idea why she'd start looking for car keys now.'

'Well, it seemed really important to her that you not be kept waiting at school. She was worried you might be cold.' Jane smiled. 'When I asked her how old you were, she said you were eleven.'

Eleven, thought Toby. *That was the year Dad died. The year everything fell on Mom's shoulders.*

Jane rose from the table and washed her cup in the sink. 'Anyway, I gave her a bath last night, so you needn't bother with that. And we had a big snack at midnight. I expect she'll stay in bed for a while. Maybe all day.' She set her cup on the sideboard and turned to look at Toby. 'She must have been a wonderful mother.'

'She was,' Toby murmured.

'Then you're lucky. Luckier than I was . . .' Jane's gaze shifted sadly to the floor. 'But we can't all have the parents we want, can we?' She took a breath, as though to say something else, then simply smiled and reached for her purse. 'I'll see you tomorrow night.'

Toby heard her walk out of the house, shutting the front door behind her. Without Jane's presence, the kitchen seemed empty. Lifeless. She rose from the kitchen table and walked up the hall to her mother's room. Peeking inside, she saw that Ellen was sleeping. Quietly Toby entered the room and sat down on the bed.

'Mom?'

Ellen rolled onto her back. Slowly her eyes opened and focused on Toby.

'Mom, are you feeling all right?'

'Tired,' Ellen murmured. 'I'm tired today.'

Toby lay her hand on Ellen's forehead. No fever. She brushed a strand of silver hair away from her mother's eyes. 'You're not sick?'

'I just want to sleep.'

'Okay.' Toby dropped a kiss on Ellen's cheek. 'You sleep, then. I'm going to bed too.'

'Good night.'

Toby walked out, leaving Ellen's door open. She decided to leave her own bedroom door open, so she'd be able to hear if her mother called out. She took a shower and changed into a T-shirt, her usual sleeping attire. As she sat down on the bed, the phone rang.

She picked it up. 'Hello?'

A man's voice, vaguely familiar, said: 'May I ask who I'm speaking to?'

Taken aback by the man's rudeness, she answered: 'If you don't know who you're calling, sir, I can't help you. Good-bye.'

'Wait. This is Detective Sheehan, Boston PD. I'm just trying to find out whose number this is.'

'Detective Sheehan? This is Toby Harper.'

'Dr. *Harper*?'

'Yes. You've dialed my home phone number. Didn't you know that?'

There was a silence. 'No.'

'Well, how did you get this number?'

'Redial.'

'What?'

'There was a cell phone under the seat in Dr. Brace's car. I found it just a few minutes ago, and I punched in redial.' Sheehan paused. 'You were the last person he called.'

It took a half hour for Vickie to arrive at the house to watch Ellen, and another forty minutes for Toby to fight her way through morning traffic into Boston. By the time she'd sat through another questioning session with Detective Sheehan, she was tired and edgy enough to bite the head off the first person who crossed her. What she should have done was driven straight home and climbed into bed.

Instead she used her car phone to call Vickie and tell her she had one more stop to make.

'Mom doesn't look too well,' said Vickie. 'What's going on with her?'

'She was fine yesterday,' said Toby

'Well, she threw up a while ago. I got her to drink some juice, and I think she's a little better now. But she just wants to sleep.'

'Does she have any other complaints?'

'Mainly the upset stomach. I think you should take her to a doctor.'

'I am a doctor.'

'Well, of course *you* know best,' said Vickie.

Toby hung up, irritated with her sister and vaguely troubled by the report of Ellen's illness. Just some gastrointestinal bug, she thought. Mom will bounce back in a few days.

She left the police station and drove directly to 720 Albany Street. The ME's office.

Dvorak seemed to sense her ugly mood at once. Politely he ushered her into his office, poured her a cup of coffee, and set it down in front of her without asking if she wanted it. She did; she needed the caffeine.

She took a few quick gulps and then met his gaze head-on. 'I want to know why Sheehan's fixated on me. Why he's harassing me.'

'Is he?'

'I just wasted the last hour with him. Look, I don't know *why* Robbie called my house. I wasn't home last night – my mother's sitter took the call. I just found out about it.'

'Did the sitter know why Brace called?'

'She didn't understand the message. He told her he was driving to the hospital to see me, so she didn't bother to tell me about it. Believe me, Dan, there was nothing going on between Robbie and me. No romance, no sex, no nothing. We were barely friends.'

'Yet you seemed extremely upset about his death.'

'Upset? Robbie bled out in front of me! I had his blood all over my hands, my arms. I had my fingers around his heart, trying to keep it going, trying to keep him alive. Why the fuck *wouldn't* I be upset?' She took a breath, fighting back tears. 'But you don't work with living people, so you wouldn't know. You just get the corpses.'

He said nothing. The silence seemed to magnify the anguish, the rage of her last words.

She sank back in the chair and covered her face with her hand.

'You're right,' he said quietly. 'I wouldn't know. I don't have to watch people die in front of me. And maybe that's why I chose the field I did. So I wouldn't have to watch.'

She raised her head but didn't feel like meeting his gaze. So she stared at a corner of his desk. 'I don't suppose you've done the autopsy yet.'

'We did it this morning. There were no un-expected findings.'

She nodded, still not looking at him.

'And Mr. Parmenter? Did the neuropathologist confirm the diagnosis?'

'It was Creutzfeldt-Jakob disease.' He said it without inflection, without a hint of the personal devastation that diagnosis must have wreaked.

She looked at him, her attention suddenly focused on Dvorak's crisis, on his fears. She could see he hadn't been sleeping well; his eyes seemed sunken, feverish.

'It's just something I'll have to live with,' he said. 'The possibility of getting sick. Not knowing if I'll live another two years or forty years. I keep telling myself, I could walk outside and get hit by a bus. That's the way life is. Just surviving another day comes with its own risk.' He straightened, as though trying to shake off the gloom. Then, unexpectedly, he smiled. 'Not that I live such a thrilling life.'

'Still, I hope it's a long one.'

They both stood up and shook hands, a gesture that felt too formal for friends. While their relationship had not quite passed over into friendship, that was the direction in which she felt it moving. In which she wanted it to move. Now, as she looked at him, she felt confused by her sudden attraction to him, by her response to the warmth of his grasp.

He said, 'The night before last, you invited me over for a glass of brandy.'

'Yes.'

'I didn't take you up on it because I – well, I was still in a state of shock about the diagnosis. I would have ruined the evening for both of us.'

She remembered how she'd spent that night,

sitting alone and depressed on the sofa, leafing through medical journals while gloomy Mendelssohn played on the stereo. *You could hardly have ruined that evening*, she thought.

'Anyway,' he said, 'I wondered if I could reciprocate. It's almost noon. I've been here all morning, and suddenly I can't wait to get out of this damn building. If you're free – if I could interest you—'

'You mean . . . now?'

She hadn't expected this. She looked at him for a moment, thinking how much she'd wanted this to happen, yet afraid that she was reading too much into the invitation.

He seemed to interpret her hesitation as reluctance. 'I'm sorry, I guess it's pretty short notice. Maybe another time.'

'No. I mean, yes. Now is fine,' she said quickly.

'It is?'

'On one condition. If you don't mind.'

He cocked his head, uncertain what to expect.

'Could we sit in the park?' she asked wistfully. 'I know it's a little brisk outside, but I haven't seen the sun in a week. And I'd really love to feel it on my face right now.'

'You know what? So would I.' He grinned. 'Let me get my coat.'

Fourteen

They sat with scarves draped around their necks, huddling close together on a park bench while they ate steaming slices of pizza straight from the take-out box. The topping was Thai chicken with peanut sauce – the surprising first choice of both of them. 'Great minds think alike,' Dvorak had said, laughing, as they'd walked beneath leafless trees to this bench beside the pond. Though the wind was cold, the sun shone down from a bright, clear sky.

This isn't the same man, Toby thought, looking up at Dvorak's face, his hair ruffled, his cheeks ruddy from the wind. Take him out of that depressing building, away from his corpses, and he becomes someone entirely different. Someone with laughing eyes. She wondered if *she* looked different, as well. The wind had tossed her hair in all directions, and she was making a mess of her hands with the pizza, but at that moment she felt more attractive than she had in a long time. Perhaps it was because of the way he looked at her; the most potent of beautifiers, she thought, is to be smiled at by a desirable man.

She turned her face upward, savoring the brightness of the day. 'I'd almost forgotten how nice it is to feel the sun.'

'Has it been that long since you've seen it?'

'It feels like weeks. First we had all that rain. And then the few sunny days we did have, I slept right through them.'

'So why did you choose the night shift, anyway?'

She finished off the last bite of pizza and fastidiously wiped the sauce from her hands. 'It didn't start off as a choice, really. When I finished my ER residency, that was the only time slot I could get at Springer. At first, it made a lot of sense. The ER gets quiet after midnight, and sometimes I'd manage to catch a few hours of sleep. Then I'd go home, take a long nap, and have the rest of the day to play.' She shook her head at the memory. 'That was ten years ago. When you're in your twenties, you can get by on a lot less sleep.'

'Middle age is hell.'

'Middle age? Speak for yourself, buster.'

He laughed, his eyes narrowed against the sunlight. 'So now it's ten years later and you're an old lady in her, what? Thirties? Yet you're still working the graveyard shift.'

'It got to feel pretty comfortable, after a while. Working with the same nurses. People I could trust.' She sighed. 'Then my mom's Alzheimer's got worse. And it seemed important for me to be home during the day. To do things for her. So now I hire someone to sleep at my house at night. And then I get home from work in the morning and take over.'

'Sounds like you're burning the candle at both ends.'

She shrugged. 'There's not much choice, is there? Really, I'm lucky. At least I can afford to hire help and keep working, unlike so many other women. And my mother – even at her most exasperating – she never stops being . . .' She paused, searching for the one word that would describe Ellen's essence. 'Kind,' she said. 'My mother has always, always been kind.'

Their eyes met. She shivered as a biting wind swept across the pond and rattled the bare branches overhead.

'I have a feeling you're very much like your mother,' he said.

'Kind? No. I wish I was.' She looked across the pond, where ripples danced. 'I think I'm too impatient. Too intense to be kind.'

'Well, you are intense, Dr. Harper. I knew that from the first conversation we had. And I can see every emotion playing right across your face.'

'Scary, isn't it?'

'Probably healthy for the soul. At least you let it all out. Frankly, I could use some of your intensity.'

She admitted, ruefully, 'I could use some of your reserve.'

The last slice of pizza was gone. They threw the

box in the rubbish bin and began to walk. Dvorak seemed not to notice the cold; he moved with easy, long-limbed grace, his coat unbuttoned, his scarf trailing like an afterthought over his shoulder.

'I don't think I've ever met a pathologist who wasn't reserved,' she said. 'Are you all such good poker players?'

'Meaning, do we all have personalities bordering on the comatose?'

'Well, the ones I know seem so quiet. But also competent, as if they know all the answers.'

'We do.'

She looked at his deadpan face and laughed. 'It's a good act, Dan. You have me convinced.'

'Actually, they teach you that in pathology residency. How to look intelligent. The ones who flunk out become surgeons.'

She tossed back her head and laughed harder.

'It's true, though, what you say,' he admitted. 'The quiet ones go into pathology. It attracts people who like working in basements. Who feel more comfortable looking into microscopes than talking to live people.'

'Is that true for you?'

'I'd have to say yes. I'm not very adept with people. Which probably explains my divorce.'

They walked for a moment in silence. The wind had dragged a few clouds overhead, and they moved through intermittent patches of shadow, then sunlight.

'Was she a doctor, too?' asked Toby.

'Another pathologist. Very brilliant, but also

very reserved. I didn't even notice there was anything wrong between us. Not until she left me. I guess that proves we were both pretty good poker players.'

'Which doesn't work very well in a marriage, I imagine.'

'No, it didn't.' He suddenly halted and glanced down at his belt. 'Someone's paging me,' he said, frowning at the beeper readout.

'There's a pay phone right over there.'

As Dvorak made his call, Toby stood outside the phone booth, eyes closed as she drank in a brief moment of sunshine between passing clouds. A moment of pleasure in just being alive. She was scarcely listening to Dvorak's conversation. Only when she heard the words *Brant Hill* did she suddenly turn and look at him through the Plexiglas.

He hung up and came out of the booth.

'What?' she said. 'It's about Robbie, isn't it?'

He nodded. 'That was Detective Sheehan. He's been over at Wicklin Hospital, interviewing the staff. They told him Dr. Brace was there yesterday evening. He visited Medical Records and Pathology, inquiring about an old file on a Brant Hill resident. A man named Stanley Mackie.'

She shook her head. 'I've never heard the name.'

'According to Wicklin, Mackie died this past March of head injuries from a fall. What Sheehan found interesting was the diagnosis found on autopsy. A disease he remembered hearing about only last night.'

Overhead, the sun vanished behind a cloud. In the sudden pall, Dvorak's face looked gray. Distant.

'It was Creutzfeldt-Jakob disease.'

From the window of the twentieth-floor conference room, Carl Wallenberg could see the ornate dome of the old Boston State House, and beyond that, the trees of the Common, their branches skeletal under a hard blue sky. So this is the view the suits enjoy, he thought. While the rest of us do the real work out in Newton, keeping Brant Hill's clients alive and well, Kenneth Foley and his staff of accountants sit in this plush downtown office and keep Brant Hill's money alive and well. And growing, by leaps and bounds. *Foley's Armani clones*, thought Wallenberg, looking at the other people sitting around the table. Wallenberg remembered their names and titles only vaguely. The man in the blue pinstripes was a senior vice president; the snooty redheaded woman was a financial officer. Except for Wallenberg and Russ Hardaway, the corporate attorney, this was a gathering of glorified pencil pushers.

A secretary brought in a carafe of coffee, gracefully poured it into five bone china cups, and set the cups down on the table, along with the crystal sugar bowl and creamer. No messy paper sugar packets at this meeting. She paused, waiting discreetly for any further instructions from Foley. There were none. The five people seated at the table waited until the secretary withdrew, closing the door behind her.

Then Kenneth Foley, Brant Hill's CEO, spoke. 'This morning, I got another call from Dr. Harper. Once again, she reminded me that Brant Hill isn't doing its job. That more of our residents may be getting sick. This could turn into a far more serious problem than I thought.' He looked around the table, and his gaze settled on Wallenberg. 'Carl, you assured me this issue was resolved.'

'It *is* resolved,' said Wallenberg. 'I've discussed it with Dr. Dvorak. And I've met with the people from Public Health. We all agree now that there's no reason for alarm. Our dining facility is in total compliance with regulations. Our water supply comes off the municipal line. And those hormone injections everyone got so excited about – we have documentation to prove they're from recent lot numbers. Perfectly safe. Dr. Dvorak is convinced these cases are purely coincidental. "Statistical cluster" is the scientific term for it.'

'You're sure both Public Health and the ME's office are satisfied, then?'

'Yes. They've agreed not to make any public disclosure, since there's no cause for alarm.'

'Yet Dr. Harper knows about this. We need to know how to respond to her questions. Because if she knows about it, the public will soon know about it as well.'

'Have there been inquiries from the media?' asked Hardaway.

'So far, none. But there may be unwanted attention coming our way.' Foley refocused on

Wallenberg. 'So tell us again, Carl, that we have nothing to worry about with this disease.'

'You have nothing to worry about,' said Wallenberg. 'I'm telling you, these two cases are unrelated. Coincidences happen.'

'If more cases turn up, it won't seem like just a coincidence,' said Hardaway. 'It will turn into a PR disaster, because it'll look like we didn't bother to pursue the problem.'

'That's why Dr. Harper's call worries me,' said Foley. 'Essentially, she's put us on notice that she knows. And that she's watching us.'

Hardaway said, 'This makes it sound like a threat.'

'It is a threat,' said the financial officer. 'Our shares climbed another three points this morning. But what'll happen if investors hear our residents are dying – and we did nothing to stop it?'

'But there's nothing to *stop*,' said Wallenberg. 'This is pure hysteria, with no basis in fact.'

'Dr. Harper sounded quite rational to me,' said Foley.

Wallenberg snorted. 'That's the problem. She sounds rational, even when she's not.'

'What's she after, anyway?' asked the financial officer. 'Money, attention? There's got to be a motive we can address here. Did you get any hint of it when you spoke to her this morning, Ken?'

Foley said, quietly: 'I think this is really about Dr. Brace. And the unfortunate timing of his death.'

At the mention of Robbie Brace, everyone fell

momentarily silent and looked down at the table. No one wanted to talk of the dead.

'She and Dr. Brace were acquainted,' said Foley.

'Maybe more than just acquainted,' added Wallenberg with a note of disgust.

'Whatever their relationship,' said Foley, 'Dr. Brace's death has upset her enough to inspire these questions. And she seems to have the inside track on his murder investigation. Somehow she knew about Dr. Mackie's diagnosis. She knew he lived at Brant Hill. None of this was released to the public.'

'I know how she found out,' said Wallenberg. 'The ME's office. She had lunch with Dr. Dvorak.'

'Where did you hear that?'

'I hear things.'

'Shit,' said the financial officer. Leave it to the only woman in the group to utter the first four-letter word. 'Then she has names and facts she could leak. So much for the three-point stock gain.'

Foley leaned forward, his gaze hard on Wallenberg. 'Carl, you're the medical director. So far we've deferred to your judgment. But if you're wrong, if one other patient comes down with this disease, it could kill all our expansion plans. Hell, it could wreck what we already have.'

Wallenberg had to suppress the irritation in his voice. He managed to sound perfectly calm and perfectly confident, which he was. 'I'll say it a third time. I'll say it a dozen times if I have to. This is not an epidemic. The disease is not going to turn up in any more of our residents. If it does, I'll hand over my goddamn stock options.'

'You're that certain?'

'I'm that certain.'

Foley leaned back with a look of relief.

'Then all we have to worry about,' said the financial officer, 'is Dr. Harper's big mouth. Which, unfortunately, could do us a lot of damage, even if nothing she says can be proved.'

No one spoke for a moment as they all considered the options.

Wallenberg said, 'I think we should just ignore her. Don't take her calls, don't give her any validation. Eventually she'll hurt her own credibility.'

'In the meantime she hurts *us*,' said the financial officer. 'Isn't there some . . . pressure we can bring to bear? Her job, for instance. I thought the Springer board was pushing for termination.'

'They tried,' said Wallenberg. 'But that ER chief dug in his heels, and they backed down. Temporarily, at least.'

'What about your friend, the surgeon? I thought he had her termination sewn up.'

Wallenberg shook his head. 'Dr. Carey's like every other surgeon I know. Too damn overconfident.'

The financial officer gave a sigh of impatience. 'All right, so how *do* we handle her?'

Foley looked at Wallenberg. 'Maybe Carl's right,' he said. 'Let's not do anything at all. She's already fighting to keep her job, and I think she's losing that battle. We'll let her self-destruct.'

'With a little help, maybe?' the financial officer suggested softly.

'I doubt that'll be necessary,' said Wallenberg. 'Believe me, Toby Harper is her own worst enemy.'

From the other side of the freshly dug grave, Toby spotted him, his head slightly bowed, his gaze cast downward at the coffin. Robbie's coffin. Even without the mantle of his white coat, Dr. Wallenberg looked every inch the part of the compassionate and godly physician. What ungodly thoughts does he hide? Toby wondered. The small gathering of doctors and administrators from Brant Hill all seemed to wear the identical expression, as though they'd donned the same rubber masks of mourning. Who among them had truly been Robbie's friend? She could not tell by looking at their faces.

Wallenberg seemed to sense that he was being watched, and he raised his head and looked at Toby. For a moment they stared at each other. Then he looked away.

A cold wind swept the gathering, tumbling dead leaves into the trench. Robbie's daughter began to wail in Greta's arms, not sobs of grief, but frustration at being confined too long among adults. Greta set her daughter down, and the girl was off in a flash, giggling as she weaved through the jungle of grown-up legs.

The minister could not compete with a laughing

child. With a look of resignation he cut short his final words and closed his Bible. As the mourners began to file toward the widow, Toby lost sight of Wallenberg. Only as she circled around to the other side of the trench did she spot him walking away toward the parked cars.

She followed him. She had to call out his name twice before he finally stopped and turned to look at her.

'I've been trying to reach you for almost a week,' she said. 'Your secretary never puts me through.'

'I've been busy with a number of matters.'

'May we talk now?'

'It's not a good time, Dr. Harper.'

'When *is* a good time?'

He didn't answer. Instead he turned and walked away.

She followed him. 'Brant Hill has had two documented cases of Creutzfeldt-Jakob,' she said. 'Angus Parmenter and Stanley Mackie.'

'Dr. Mackie died from a fall.'

'He also had CJD. Which is probably why he jumped out that window in the first place.'

'You're talking about an untreatable illness. Am I supposed to feel somehow negligent about this?'

'Two cases in one year—'

'Statistical cluster. This is a large population base, Dr. Harper. One can expect several such cases in the greater Boston area. Those two men just happened to reside in the same neighborhood.'

'What if this is a more infectious strain of prion?

You could have new cases incubating right now at Brant Hill.'

He turned to her, his expression so ugly she retreated a step. 'You listen to me, Dr. Harper. People buy into Brant Hill because they want a life free of worries, free of fears. They've worked hard all their lives, and they deserve the luxury. They can afford it. They know they'll get the best medical care in the world. They do not need to hear some crackpot theory about a killer brain disease in their food.'

'Is that all you're concerned about? Your patients' ease of mind?'

'Ease of mind is what they pay for. If they lose trust in us, they'll start packing up and selling out. It would turn Brant Hill into a ghost town.'

'I'm not trying to tear down Brant Hill. I just think you should be monitoring your residents for symptoms.'

'Think of the panic *that* would cause. Our food is safe. Our hormones come from reputable drug companies. Even the Public Health Department agrees there's no reason to be monitoring any symptoms. So stop trying to scare our residents, Dr. Harper. Or you'll find an attorney knocking at your door.' He turned and began to walk away.

'What about Robbie Brace?' she blurted out.

'What about him?'

'I find it very disturbing that he was killed right after he learned about Mackie's diagnosis.' There, she had said it. She had come right out and voiced her suspicions, and she fully expected Wallenberg to lash back in defense.

Instead, he turned and looked at her with an eerily unruffled smile. 'Yes, I hear you've been pushing that angle on the police. But they've dropped the theory because they can find no evidence whatsoever of any connection.' He paused. 'By the way, they asked me a number of questions about *you*.'

'The police? What questions?'

'Whether I was aware of any relationship between you and Dr. Brace? Did I know he'd brought you into our clinic building late at night?' The smile deepened until it looked more like a snarl. 'I find it fascinating, the sexual attraction you women have for black men.'

Toby's chin jerked up in startled rage. She stepped toward him, her fury propelling her forward. 'Goddamn you. You have no right to say that about him.'

'Is everything all right, Carl?' a voice said.

Toby turned sharply to see a man, tall and almost completely bald, standing nearby. He was the same elegantly dressed man who'd stood beside Wallenberg during the graveside services. He was staring at her with some trepidation, and she realized her face was flushed with rage, her hands bunched into fists.

'I couldn't help overhearing,' the man said. 'Would you like me to call someone, Carl?'

'There's no problem here, Gideon. Dr. Harper was just feeling a bit' – again, that nasty, satisfied smile – '*distraught* over Robbie's death.'

307

You bastard, thought Toby.

'We have a board meeting in half an hour,' said the bald man.

'I haven't forgotten.' Wallenberg looked at Toby, and in his eyes she saw the glint of triumph. He had pushed her over the edge, had made her lose her temper, and this man named Gideon had witnessed it. Wallenberg was the one in control, not her, and he was communicating that fact by his smile.

'I'll see you at the meeting,' said the bald man. And with a last, concerned glance at Toby, he walked away.

'I think there's nothing more to discuss,' said Wallenberg, and he too started to leave.

'Only until the next case of CJD shows up,' she said.

He turned and gave her one last, pitying look. 'Dr. Harper, can I give you some advice?'

'What advice?'

'Get a life.'

I have a life, thought Toby as she angrily gulped coffee in the ER staff room. *Goddammit, I do have a life*. Maybe it was not the life she'd visualized as a young doctor in training, not the life she would have chosen. But sometimes one could not choose, sometimes one was handed difficult circumstances. Duties, obligations.

Ellen.

Toby drained her coffee and poured another, hot and black. It was like tossing more acid into her stomach, but she desperately needed the caffeine. Robbie's funeral had cut into her usual sleep schedule, and she had managed to catch only a few hours of rest before coming to work last evening. It was now six in the morning and she was functioning purely on automatic reflexes and occasional bursts of primitive emotion. Anger. Frustration. She was feeling both at the moment, knowing that even when this shift was over, when she finally did walk out the hospital doors in an hour and a half, it would be to walk into another set of responsibilities and worries.

Get a life, he'd said. And this was the life she happened to have, the one that had been placed on her shoulders.

Yesterday evening, as she'd gotten dressed for work, she'd looked in the mirror and realized some of her hairs were not blond, but white. When had that happened? When had she passed over from youth into the frontiers of middle age? Even though no one else would have noticed those hairs, she had plucked them out, knowing they would grow back just as white. Dead melanocytes don't regenerate. There is no fountain of youth.

At seven-thirty, she finally stepped out the ER doors and paused to inhale a breath of morning air. Air that didn't smell of rubbing alcohol and disinfectant and stale coffee. It looked like it would be a fair day. Already the mist was thinning, revealing faint patches of blue sky. It made her feel better, just to see that. She had the next four days off to catch up on her sleep. And next month, she had two weeks' vacation scheduled. Maybe she could leave Ellen with Vickie, make it a real vacation. A hotel on a beach. Cold drinks and hot sand. Perhaps even a fling at romance. It had been a long time since she'd slept with a man. She'd hoped it would happen with Dvorak. She'd been thinking about him a lot lately, in ways that could bring an unexpected flush to her cheeks. Since their one and only lunch, they'd spoken on the phone twice, but their conflicting schedules made it hard to meet.

And the last time they'd talked, he'd sounded distant. Distracted. *Have I scared him off so quickly, then?*

She forced Dvorak out of her mind. It was back to thinking about fantasy men and tropical destinations.

She crossed the parking lot and got into her car. *I'll call Vickie this afternoon,* she thought as she drove home. *If she can't or won't watch Mom, then I'll hire someone for the week.* To hell with the cost. For years Toby had faithfully set aside money for her retirement. It was time to start spending it now, enjoying it now.

She turned onto her street and felt her heart suddenly do a flip-flop of panic.

An ambulance and a police car were parked in front of her house.

Before she could turn into her own driveway, the ambulance drove off with lights flashing and sped away down the street. Toby parked the car and ran into the house.

310

There was a uniformed cop standing in her living room, writing in a spiral notebook.

'What happened?' said Toby.

The cop looked at her. 'Your name, Ma'am?'

'This is my house. What are you doing here? Where's my mother?'

'They just took her to Springer Hospital.'

'Was there an accident?'

Jane's voice said, 'There was no accident.'

Toby turned to see Jane standing in the kitchen doorway. 'I couldn't wake her up,' said Jane. 'So I called the ambulance.'

'You couldn't *wake* her? Did she respond at all?'

'She couldn't seem to move. Or speak.' Jane and the policeman exchanged glances, a look that Toby couldn't interpret. Only then did the question occur to her: *Why was a policeman in her house?*

She was wasting time here. She turned to leave, to follow the ambulance to Springer.

'Ma'am?' the cop said. 'If you'll wait, someone'll be here to talk to you—'

Toby ignored him and walked out of the house.

By the time she pulled into the Springer Hospital parking lot, she'd already imagined the worst. A heart attack. A stroke. Ellen comatose and on a ventilator.

One of the day shift nurses met her at the front desk. 'Dr. Harper—'

'Where's my mother? An ambulance was bringing her in.'

'She's in room two. We're stabilizing her now. Wait, don't go in yet—'

Toby pushed past the front desk and opened the door to room two.

Ellen's face was hidden from view by the crowd of medical personnel working around the gurney. Paul Hawkins had just finished intubating. A nurse was hanging a fresh IV bottle, another was juggling blood tubes.

'What happened?' said Toby.

Paul glanced up. 'Toby, can you wait outside?'

'*What happened?*'

'She just stopped breathing. We had severe bradycardia, but the pulse is back up—'

'An MI?'

'Can't see it on EKG. We're still waiting for cardiac enzyme results.'

'Oh my God. Oh my God . . .' Toby squeezed forward to the gurney and took her mother's hand. 'Mom, it's me.'

Ellen didn't open her eyes, but her hand moved, as though to pull away

'Mom, it's going to be all right. They're going to take good care of you.'

Now Ellen's other hand began to move, thrashing against the mattress. A nurse quickly snatched Ellen's wrist and looped a restraint around it. The sight of that frail hand trapped and struggling against the cloth cuff was more than Toby could bear. 'Does it have to be so tight?' she snapped. 'You've already made a bruise—'

'We'll lose the IV.'

'You're cutting off her circulation!'

'Toby,' said Paul, 'I want you to wait outside.

We've got everything under control.'

'Mom doesn't know any of you—'

'You're not letting us do our job. You have to *leave*.'

Toby took a step back from the gurney and saw that they were all looking at her. She realized Paul was right; she was getting in the way, making it difficult for them to make the necessary decisions. When she was the physician in charge of a critical case, she never allowed the patient's family to remain in the room. Neither should Paul.

She said, softly, 'I'll be outside,' and she walked out.

In the hallway, a man was waiting for her. Early forties, unsmiling. A monk's haircut. 'Dr. Harper?' he said.

'Yes.'

Something about the way he approached her, the way he seemed to be sizing her up, told her this was a cop. He confirmed it by showing her his badge. 'Detective Alpren. May I ask you about your mother?'

'I want to ask *you* a few questions. Why was a cop in my house? Who called you people?'

'Ms. Nolan did.'

'Why would she call the police for a medical emergency?'

Detective Alpren pointed toward an empty exam room. 'Let's step in there,' he said.

Bewildered, she followed Alpren into the room. He closed the door.

'How long has your mother been ill?' he asked.

'Are you referring to her Alzheimer's?'

'I mean her current illness. The reason she's here right now.'

Toby shook her head. 'I don't even know what's wrong with her yet . . .'

'Does she have any chronic illnesses other than the Alzheimer's?'

'Why are you asking me these questions?'

'I understand your mother's been ill for the last week. Lethargy. Nausea.'

'She's seemed a little tired. I assumed it was a virus. Some sort of gastrointestinal upset—'

'A virus, Dr. Harper? That's not what Ms. Nolan thinks.'

She stared at him, not understanding any of this. 'What did Jane tell you? You said she called you—'

'Yes.'

'I'd like to talk to her. Where is she?'

He ignored the question. 'Ms. Nolan mentioned certain injuries. She said your mother complained about burns on her hands.'

'They healed weeks ago. I told Jane what happened.'

'And the bruises on her thigh? How did she get those?'

'What bruises? I'm not aware of any bruises.'

'Ms. Nolan says she asked you about them two days ago. That you couldn't explain them.'

'*What?*'

'*Can* you explain the bruises?'

'I want to know why the hell she's saying these things,' said Toby. 'Where is she?'

Alpren studied her for a moment. Then he shook his head. 'Given the circumstances, Dr. Harper,' he said, 'Ms. Nolan doesn't wish to be contacted.'

After the CT scan, Ellen was admitted to a bed in the medical ICU, and Toby was allowed to visit her again. The first thing she did was peel back the sheets and look for the bruises. There were four of them, small, irregular blotches on the outer left thigh. She stared at them in disbelief, silently railing at herself for being so blind. How and when did this happen? Did Ellen injure herself? Or were those the marks left by someone else's hand, repeatedly pinching that fragile skin? She covered her mother's legs with the sheet and for a long time stood gripping the siderail in silent fury; trying not to let rage cloud her judgment. But she couldn't suppress the thought: *If Jane did this, I'm going to kill her.*

There was a tap on the window, and Vickie came in. She didn't say anything as she took her place across from Toby.

'She's in a coma,' said Toby. 'They just did the head scan. It appears she's had a massive intracerebral bleed. Nothing they can drain. We just have to watch. And wait.'

Vickie remained silent.

'Everything's been so crazy this morning,' said Toby. 'They noticed bruises on Mom's thigh.

315

Jane's telling the police I did it. She's actually got them thinking—'

'Yes, she told me.'

Toby stared at her, dismayed by the flatness of her sister's voice. 'Vickie—'

'Last week, I *told* you Mom was sick. I told you she was throwing up. But you didn't seem at all concerned.'

'I thought it was a virus—'

'You never took her to a doctor, did you?' Vickie looked at her as though studying a creature she'd never seen before. 'I didn't tell you, but Jane called me yesterday. She asked me not to mention it to you. But she was worried.'

'What did she say? Vickie, *what did she say?*'

'She said . . .' Vickie released a shaky breath. 'She said she was concerned about what was happening. When she first took the job, she noticed bruises on Mom's arms, as if she'd been grabbed. Shaken around. Those bruises faded, but then this week, new ones appeared, on the thighs. Did you see them?'

'Jane's been the one bathing her every day—'

'So you didn't see them? You don't even know about them?'

'She never asked *me* about them!'

'And the burns? What about the burns on Mom's hands?'

'That happened weeks ago! Mom picked up a hot dish from the stove.'

316

'So there *was* a burn.'

'It was an accident! Bryan was there when it happened.'

'Are you saying Bryan's responsible?'

'No. No, that's not what I'm saying—'

'Then who is responsible, Toby?'

The two sisters stared at each other across Ellen's sleeping form.

'I'm your sister,' said Toby. 'You know me. How can you believe a complete stranger?'

'I don't know.' Vickie ran her hand through her hair. 'I don't know what to believe. I just want you to tell me what really happened. I know Mom's hard to deal with. She's worse than a child sometimes, and it's not easy to—'

'What do *you* know about it? You've never offered to help.'

'I have a family.'

'Mom *is* family. Something your husband and kids can't seem to grasp.'

Vickie's chin lifted. 'You're turning it into another one of your guilt trips, the way you always do. Who suffers the most, who's most deserving of sainthood. Saint Toby.'

'*Don't.*'

'So when did you lose your temper? When did you finally crack and start hitting her?'

Toby jerked back, too shocked to speak, too angry to trust anything she *did* say.

Vickie's mouth was trembling. Her eyes filling with tears, she said, 'Oh, God. I didn't mean that.'

Toby turned and walked out of the cubicle. She

didn't stop until she'd left the building and crossed the parking lot to her car.

The first place she drove was to Jane Nolan's house. She had her address book in her purse, and she looked up the entry for Jane. It was in Brookline, east of Springer Hospital.

A four-mile drive brought her to the address, a green-shingled duplex on a sterile, treeless street. There were planters on the front porch with hard-baked soil and a few dying weeds. The curtains were closed over the windows, shutting off all view of the interior.

Toby rang the bell. No one answered. She knocked, then pounded on the door. *Open up, damn you. Tell me why you're doing this to me!*

'Jane!' she yelled.

The next-door neighbor's door opened and a woman cautiously poked her head out.

'I'm looking for Jane Nolan,' said Toby.

'Well stop pounding. She's not there.'

'When will she be back?'

'Who're you?'

'I just want to know when Jane will be back.'

'How should I know? I haven't seen her in days.' The woman shut the door.

Toby felt like hurling a rock through Jane's window. She gave the door one last pound of her fist, then got back into her car.

That's when it all crashed down on her. Ellen in a coma. Vickie turning into a spiteful stranger. She rocked forward and struggled not to cry, not to shatter. It was the blare of her own car horn that snapped her back up. She'd leaned too heavily on the steering wheel. A mailman, passing by on the street, stopped to stare at her.

She drove away. *Where do I go? Where do I go?*

She headed for Bryan's house. He would back her up. He had been there the day Ellen burned her hand; he'd be her character witness, the one person who knew how devoted she'd been to Ellen.

But Bryan wasn't home; he'd be at work until four-thirty, according to his companion, Noel, who answered the door. Would Toby like to come in for coffee? A drink? *You look like you need to sit down.*

What he meant was she looked like hell.

She refused the offer. For want of any other destination, she drove home.

The police car was gone. Three of her neighbors stood conversing on the sidewalk in front of her house. As Toby's car approached, they turned and stared at her. By the time she pulled into her driveway, they had walked off in three different directions. Cowards. Why didn't they just ask her to her face if she'd beaten up her own mother?

She stormed into the house and slammed the door shut.

Silence. No Ellen. No one wandering in the garden, no one watching the morning cartoons.

She sat down on the couch and dropped her head in her hands.

Fifteen

'Mine's a baby girl,' said Annie, her fingers skimming over the bedcovers, caressing her belly. 'I want her to be a girl, 'cause I wouldn't know what to do with a boy. Wouldn't know how to make him turn out right. Hardly meet a man these days who's turned out right.'

They were lying side by side in the darkness on Annie's bed. The only light was the glow of the streetlamp outside the window. Every so often there'd be moving fragments of light from a passing car, and Molly would catch a glimpse of Annie's face, head resting on the pillow as she serenely gazed up at the ceiling. It was warm in the bed with Annie. They had put on fresh sheets today, had sat together in the laundromat giggling and leafing through old magazines while the linens had spun round and round in the dryer. Now whenever Molly turned, she smelled that clean scent of laundry soap. And Annie's scent as well.

'How can you tell if it's a girl?' asked Molly.

'Well, a doctor can tell for sure.'

'Did you see a doctor?'

'I didn't want to go back to *that* one. Didn't like that place.'

'So how do you know it *is* a girl?'

Annie's hands began to move over her abdomen again. 'I just know. This nurse I met, she told me that when a mother gets to feeling like that, a real strong feeling, she's never wrong. This one's a girl.'

'I don't have no feeling 'bout mine.'

'Maybe it's too early for yours, Molly.'

'I don't have no feeling 'bout it one way or the other. See, it doesn't seem like a person yet. It seems like just a lot of fat poochin' out here. Shouldn't I be feeling love or somethin'? I mean, isn't that what's supposed to happen?' She turned and looked at Annie's face, silhouetted against the window's glow.

'You must feel something for it,' said Annie softly. 'Why else would you be keeping it?'

'I don't know.'

Molly felt Annie's hand reach for hers under the covers. They lay with fingers entwined, their breathing in perfect synchrony.

'I don't know what I'm doing or why I'm doing it,' said Molly. 'I kind of got all mixed up. And then, when Romy knocked me around, I got so pissed at him I wasn't gonna do nothin' he told me to do. So I didn't go to that place.' She paused and looked at Annie again. 'How do they do it?'

'Do what?'

'Get rid of it?'

Annie shuddered. 'I only had it done once. Last

321

year, when Romy sent me to that place. Had these people all dressed in blue. Wouldn't talk to me, just told me to get on the table and shut up. They gave me something to breathe, and after that, I just remember waking up. All skinny again. Empty . . .'

'Was it a girl?'

Annie sighed. 'I don't know. They put me in the car and sent me back to him.' Annie released Molly's hand, and her withdrawal seemed more than just physical. She had retreated into some private compartment. A place for just her and her baby.

'Molly,' said Annie, after a long silence. 'You know you can't stay here much longer.' The words, spoken so softly, delivered a stunning blow.

Molly turned on her side to face Annie. 'What did I do wrong? Tell me what I did wrong.'

'Nothing. It just can't keep going on this way.'

'Why not? I'll do more. I'll do whatever you—'

'Molly, I said you could stay for a few days. It's been over two weeks. Honey, I like you and all, but Mr. Lorenzo, he came up to see me today. Complained that I had someone living here with me. Says that's not in our rental agreement. So I can't let you stay. It's small enough, with you and me here. When my baby comes—'

'That won't be for another month.'

'Molly.' Annie's voice had steadied. Turned unyielding. 'You have to find your own place to live. I can't keep you here.'

Molly turned her back to Annie. *I thought we could be a family: You and your baby. Me and mine. No men, no assholes.*

'Molly? You okay?'

'I'm fine.'

'You understand, don't you?'

Molly gave a weary shrug of one shoulder. 'I guess.'

'It's not like right away. You can take a few days, figure out where you're going. Maybe you could try calling your mama again.'

'Yeah.'

'She's bound to take you back. She's your mama.'

When there was no reply, Annie reached over and slung an arm around Molly's waist. The warmth of the other woman's body, the other woman's swollen belly pressing against her back, filled Molly with such a sense of longing that she couldn't resist the impulse. Turning to face Annie, she wrapped her arms around Annie's waist and pulled her close, felt their bellies press together like ripening fruit. And suddenly she wished that *she* was in Annie's womb, that *she* was the child who would find its home in Annie's arms.

'Let me stay,' she whispered. 'Please let me stay.'

Firmly Annie pushed away Molly's hands. 'You can't. I'm sorry, Molly, *but you can't.*' She turned and scooted to the far side of the bed. 'Now good night.'

Molly lay very still. *What did I say? What did I*

do wrong? Please, I'll do whatever you want me to do. Just tell me what it is! She knew Annie was not sleeping; the darkness between them was too charged with tension. She sensed that Annie was coiled up as tightly as she was.

But neither one of them spoke.

The sound of groaning awakened her. At first Molly was confused by the last shreds of her dream. A baby floating in a pond, making strange noises. Frog noises. Then she opened her eyes, and it was still night and she was in Annie's bed. A light was shining under the bathroom door.

'Annie?' she said but heard no answer.

She rolled over and closed her eyes, trying to shut out that disturbing sliver of light.

A thump jolted her fully awake.

She sat up and squinted at the bathroom. 'Annie?' Hearing no reply, she climbed out of bed and went to knock on the door. 'Are you okay?' She turned the knob and pushed, but the door wouldn't open; something was blocking it. She pushed harder and felt the barrier give way slightly, allowing the door to open. She peered through the crack, at first not understanding what she saw.

A rivulet of blood on the floor.

'Annie!' she cried. Pushing with all her strength, she finally managed to open the door wide enough to squeeze through. She found Annie crumpled in the corner, her shoulder wedged against the door, her cheap nightgown gathered above her waist.

Blood was splattered across the toilet seat, and the water in the bowl was a silky crimson. A warm stream suddenly gushed out from between Annie's thighs and lapped at Molly's bare toes.

In horror, she backed away and collided with the sink.

Oh God, oh God, oh God.

Though Annie wasn't moving, her belly was; it was squirming, the bare skin bunching into a tight ball of flesh.

More blood gushed out, streaming across the linoleum. The warmth of the blood trickled around her chilled feet, shaking Molly out of her trance. She forced herself to step through the crimson pool, to cross to Annie's coiled-up body. She had to move her out from behind the door. She grasped Annie's arm and pulled, but her feet kept slipping in the blood. Annie made a noise, a high, soft whine, like the hiss of air escaping from a balloon. Molly pulled harder, finally managing to drag Annie a few feet across the linoleum. Now she placed her feet against the door jamb and, using that as an anchor, heaved at Annie's body.

Annie slid out of the bathroom.

She grabbed both arms now and pulled her completely through the doorway. Then she turned on the bedroom lights.

Annie was still breathing, but her eyes were rolled back, and her face was white.

Molly ran out of the flat and down the stairs. She pounded on the door of the ground-floor apartment. '*Help me!*' she cried. 'Please, help me!' No one answered.

She ran out of the building, to the pay telephone on the street, and dialed 911.

'Emergency operator.'

'I need an ambulance! She's bleeding—'

'Your name and address?'

'My name's Molly Picker. I don't know the address. I think I'm on Charter Street—'

'What's the cross street?'

'I can't see it! She's going to die—'

'Do you know the nearest address number?'

Molly turned and frantically scanned the building. '1076! I see a 1076.'

'Where is the victim? What is her condition?'

'She's in the upstairs apartment – she's bleeding all over the floor—'

'Ma'am, I'm dispatching an ambulance now. If you'll wait on the line—'

Fuck this, thought Molly. She left the phone hanging and ran back into the building.

Annie was lying where she'd left her on the bedroom floor. Her eyes were open but unfocused and glassy.

'Please, you have to stay awake.' Molly grasped Annie's hand, but there was no answering squeeze. No warmth at all. She stared at the chest, saw it expand in a shallow breath. *Keep breathing. Please keep breathing.*

Then another movement caught her eye. Annie's abdomen seemed to swell upward, as though some alien creature inside her body was straining to burst free. A gush of blood spilled out from between her thighs.

So did something else. Something pink.

The baby.

Molly knelt between Annie's knees and eased the thighs apart. Fresh blood, mixed with water, dribbled out around the protruding arm. At least Molly *thought* it was an arm. Then she saw there were no fingers, no hand, just that glistening pink flipper writhing slowly back and forth.

There was another contraction, a final gush of blood and fluid as the flipper slid out, followed by the rest of the body. Molly jerked backward, shrieking.

It was not a baby.

But it was alive and moving, the two flippers writhing in agonal struggles. It had no other limbs, just those two pink stubs waving from a single mass of raw flesh attached to an umbilical cord. She could see clumps of hair, coarse and black, a protruding tooth, and a single eye, unblinking, lashless. Blue. The flippers were thrashing, and the whole organism began to move with almost purposeful direction, like an amoeba swimming in a pool of blood.

Sobbing, Molly scrambled on hands and knees as far away as she could get. She pressed herself into a corner and watched in disbelief as the thing struggled to live. The paddle-arms began to twitch in erratic seizurelike spasms. The body had ceased its amoebic gliding and was only quivering now. When at last the flippers fell still, and the flesh stopped twitching, that eye was still open and staring at her.

Another gush of blood, and the placenta slid out.

Molly buried her face against her knees and curled into a ball.

As though from a great distance, she heard a whining sound. Then, a moment later, someone was banging at the door.

'Paramedics! Hello? Did someone call an ambulance?'

'Help her,' whispered Molly. In a sob, louder: 'Help her!'

The door opened and two uniformed men burst into the flat. They stared at Annie's body, and then their gazes followed the glistening trail of blood leading from between her thighs.

'Holy shit,' one of them said. 'What the hell is *that* thing?'

The other man knelt beside Annie. 'She's not breathing. Ambubag—'

There was a whoosh as one of the men squeezed air through a mask into Annie's lungs.

'No pulse. I'm not getting a pulse.'

'Okay, go! One-one thousand, two-one thousand . . .'

Molly watched them, but none of it seemed real to her. It was a movie, a TV show. It was not Annie but an actress playing dead. The needle was not really going into her arm. The blood on the floor was ketchup. And the thing – the thing lying a few feet away from her . . .

'Still not getting a pulse—'

'Flatline EKG.'

'Pupils?'

'Fixed.'

'Shit, don't stop.'

A radio crackled. 'City Hospital.'

'This is Unit Nineteen,' said the paramedic. 'We have a white female in her twenties, looks like massive vaginal hemorrhage – possible abortion attempt. Blood looks fresh. No respirations, no pulse, pupils fixed and midposition. We have an IV line, Ringer's lactate. Flatline on EKG. We are now doing CPR, without response. Should we call it?'

'Not yet.'

'But she's flatline—'

'Stabilize and transport.'

The paramedic shut off the radio and looked at his partner. 'Stabilize *what?*'

'Just get her tubed and moved.'

'What about the . . . thing?'

'Hell, I'm not *touching* that.'

Molly was still watching that TV show with ketchup blood. She saw the tube go down actress-Annie's throat. Saw the actor paramedics lift her onto a rolling stretcher and continue pumping on her chest.

One of the men glanced at Molly. 'We're taking her to City Hospital,' he said. 'What's the patient's name?'

'What?'

'Her name!'

'Annie. I don't know her last name.'

'Look, don't leave the apartment. Did you hear me? You have to stay right here.'

'Why?'

'The police will be coming to talk to you. Don't leave.'

'Annie – what about Annie?'

'You check with City Hospital later. She'll be there.'

Molly listened to them carry the stretcher down the stairs. She heard the wheels clatter out the front door, and the single whoop of the siren as the ambulance pulled away.

The police will be here to talk to you.

The words finally sank in. She didn't want to talk to the police. They would ask for her name and then they would find out she'd been arrested last year for soliciting a cop. Romy had bailed her out, had given her a few good slaps for being such an idiot.

The police will say it's my fault. Somehow, this will all be my fault.

She rose, shaking, to her feet. The *thing* was still lying there, still glistening, but the blue eye had turned dry and dull. She stepped around it, avoiding the puddles of blood, and crossed to the dresser. There was money in the top drawer – Annie's money – but Annie wouldn't be needing it now. That much Molly had understood from the paramedics. Annie was dead.

She pulled out a wad of twenty-dollar bills. Then she quickly dressed in Annie's clothes, a pair of stretch pants with an elastic belly, a giant T-shirt with *Oh, Baby!* printed across the chest. Black sneakers. She pulled on Annie's giant raincoat, stuffed the cash in her purse, and fled the apartment.

She was on the other side of the street when she saw the police car pull up in front of the building, its blue dome light twirling. Two cops entered the building. Seconds later, she saw their silhouettes move past Annie's upstairs window.

They were looking at the *thing*. Wondering what it was.

One of the cops crossed to the window and glanced outside.

Molly slipped around the corner and began to run. She kept running until she was out of breath, until she was stumbling. She ducked into a doorway and sank onto the front step. Her heart was skipping; she could feel it flutter in her throat.

The sky was starting to get light.

She huddled on that front stoop until morning came and a man emerged through the front door and told her to move on. So she did.

A few blocks away, she stopped at a pay phone to call City Hospital. 'I want to find out about my friend,' she said. 'An ambulance brought her in.'

'Your friend's name?'

'Annie. They took her from the apartment – they said she wasn't breathing—'

'May I ask if you're a relative?'

'No, I'm just – I mean—'

Molly froze, staring at a police car driving by. It

seemed to slow down as it passed Molly, then continued up the street.

'Hello, Ma'am? Could I have your name?'

Molly hung up. The police car had turned the corner and was now out of sight.

She left the phone booth and swiftly walked away.

Detective Roy Sheehan settled his ample behind onto the stool next to Dvorak's lab bench and asked: 'Okay, so what's a prion?'

Dvorak looked up from the microscope, refocusing his eyes on the cop. 'What?'

'I just been talking to your girl, Lisa.'

Of course you have, thought Dvorak. Despite Dvorak's advice, Sheehan had been making regular visits to the morgue for several days now, his real purpose not to view dead bodies but to ogle a live one.

'Real smart girl, by the way,' said Sheehan. 'Anyway, she says this Creutzfeldt-Jakob thing – am I saying it right – it's caused by something called a prion.'

'That's correct.'

'So can people catch it? Is it, like, floating around in the air?'

Dvorak looked down at his finger, where the cut had recently healed. 'You can't *catch it* in the usual sense.'

'Toby Harper's saying there's an epidemic in the making.'

Dvorak shook his head. 'I've spoken to both

CDC and the Department of Public Health. They say there's no reason for concern. That hormone protocol Wallenberg's testing is perfectly safe. And Public Health can't find any violations at the Brant Hill facility.'

'So why's Dr. Harper up in arms against Brant Hill?'

Dvorak paused. Reluctantly he said, 'She's under a lot of pressure right now. She faces a possible lawsuit over that patient of hers who vanished. And Dr. Brace's death shook her up pretty badly. When everything goes wrong in our lives, it's natural to look around for someone – or something – to blame.' He reached for a different slide and inserted it under the lens. 'I think Toby's been stressed out for a very long time.'

'You heard what happened to her mother?'

Again Dvorak hesitated. 'Yes,' he said quietly. 'Toby called me yesterday.'

'She did? You two are still talking?'

'Why shouldn't we? She needs a friend right now, Roy.'

'There may be criminal charges filed. Alpren says it looks like elder abuse. The nanny blames Dr. Harper. Dr. Harper blames the nanny.'

Dvorak bent his head back to the microscope. 'The mother had an intracerebral bleed. That's not necessarily abuse. It doesn't make either one of them a granny basher.'

'But there are bruises on the legs.'

'The elderly often bruise themselves. Their vision's not so good. They run into coffee tables.'

Sheehan grunted. 'You're sure doing your best to defend her.'

'I'm giving her the benefit of the doubt.'

'But she *is* wrong about this so-called epidemic?'

'Yes, she's wrong about that. Catching CJD isn't like catching the flu. It's transmitted in only a few specific ways.'

'Like eating mad cows?'

'The U.S. herd doesn't have mad cow disease.'

'But people here *do* come down with the human version.'

'Creutzfeldt-Jakob occurs in one in a million people, with no obvious history of exposure.'

Both men glanced up as the object of Sheehan's affection strolled into the lab, flashed them both a smile, and bent over to open a small specimen refrigerator. Sheehan stared, transfixed by that luscious rear-end view. Only when Lisa straightened and walked out again did Sheehan seem able to draw another breath.

'Is that natural?' he murmured.

'Is what natural?'

'That hair. Is she a real blond?'

'I really wouldn't know,' said Dvorak, and he focused his gaze back on the microscope slide.

'There's one way to find out, you know,' said Sheehan.

'Ask her?'

'You check out the hair no one sees.'

Dvorak leaned back and squeezed the bridge of his nose. 'Did you have something else to ask me, Roy?'

'Oh. Oh, yeah. I've heard about viruses, and I've heard about bacteria. But what the hell's a prion?'

Resignedly Dvorak turned off the microscope lamp. 'A prion,' he said, 'isn't what we'd normally call a living thing. Unlike a virus, it has neither DNA nor RNA. In other words, it has no genetic material – or what we *think* of as genetic material. It's an abnormal cellular protein. It can transform the host's proteins into the same abnormal form.'

'But it can't be caught like the flu.'

'No. It has to be introduced by direct tissue exposure, like brain or spinal cord implants. Or by extractions from neural tissue, like growth hormone. For example, you can catch it from contaminated brain electrodes.'

'Those English people got it from eating beef.'

'Okay, it's also possible to catch it by eating infected meat. That's how cannibals get it.'

Sheehan's eyebrows shot up. 'Now *this* starts to get interesting. What's this about cannibals?'

'Roy, this is completely irrelevant—'

'No, I wanna hear this. What about cannibals?'

Dvorak sighed. 'There've been villages in New Guinea where eating human flesh is part of a sacred ritual. The only people who caught CJD were the women and children.'

'Why only women and kids?'

'The men got the choicest cuts – the meat of the corpse. The muscle. The women and kids had to be satisfied with the parts no one else wanted. The brain.' He watched for a disgusted reaction on

Sheehan's face, but the cop only leaned closer. In some ways, he was like a cannibal himself, eager to devour the most appalling morsels of information.

'So eating a human brain would do it,' said Sheehan.

'An infected human brain.'

'Can you tell it's infected by looking at it?'

'No, it's a microscopic diagnosis. And this is a stupid conversation.'

'It's the big city, Doc. Weirder stuff happens. We get reports of vampires, werewolves—'

'People who *think* they're werewolves.'

'Who knows? All this crazy cult shit going on these days.'

'I hardly think there's some cannibalistic cult at Brant Hill.'

Sheehan glanced down as his beeper went off. 'Excuse me,' he said and left to make the call.

Now I can finally get some work done, thought Dvorak.

A moment later, though, Sheehan returned. 'I'm headed out to the North End. Think maybe you should come see this one.'

'What is it? A homicide?'

'They're not sure.' Sheehan paused. 'They're not even sure it's human.'

336

Sixteen

The smell of blood, cloying and metallic, had wafted even into the hallway. Dvorak nodded to the patrolman standing watch, ducked under the police tape, and stepped into the flat. Sheehan and his partner, Jack Moore, were already inside, as was the CSU crew. Moore was squatting by something near the corner. Dvorak didn't cross toward him right away but held back near the doorway, his gaze carefully scanning the floor.

It was yellow and white linoleum, in a pattern of random squares with a ratty throw rug by the bed. Blood was still drying on the floor near the bathroom – a great deal of blood. There were smear marks, as though something had been dragged across the floor, as well as a confusing collage of bloody shoeprints. He also saw the distinct imprints of bare feet, small ones, tracking toward the dresser, then fading out.

He looked at the walls and saw no arterial splatter. In fact, there was very little splatter at all, just that congealing lake. Whoever had bled in this room had done so while lying quietly on the floor, and not in a panicked frenzy.

'Doc,' said Moore. 'Come and look at this.'

'You got shots of these footprints already?'

'Yeah, those are from the EMTs. It's all been photographed and videotaped. Just step around that way. Watch out for that set of footprints there.'

Dvorak stepped carefully around the imprints of the bare feet and circled around to where Moore and Sheehan were squatting.

'What do you think?' said Moore, moving aside to let Dvorak see what lay on the floor.

'*Jesus.*'

'That was our reaction, too. So what *is* it?'

Dvorak didn't know what to say. Slowly he dropped down for a closer look.

His first impression was that it was a leftover Halloween gag, a one-eyed, flesh-colored monster fashioned from rubber and nightmares. Then he saw the streaks of blood drying on its surface, and the fragment of attached placenta, connected by an umbilical cord. This *thing* was not made of rubber, but flesh.

He pulled on a pair of gloves and gingerly touched the surface of the Thing. It felt like real skin – cold, but yielding. The single eye was a pale blue, with a rudimentary flap of skin for an eyelid, but no lashes. Below it were two small holes, like nostrils, then an open cleft. The mouth? He could scarcely identify any normal anatomy on this lump of flesh. Tufts of hair sprang out at crazy

338

angles. And – dear God – was that a tooth poking out by the flipper?

He recalled a tumor he'd once seen removed from a woman's abdomen. A teratoma. It had been the result of an ovum gone crazy, turning into a cancer made up of wildly differentiating cells. The tumor had had teeth and tufts of hair connected in a ball of skin.

Suddenly he focused on the pattern of dried blood on the floor, on the irregular smear leading from the larger pool, and the umbilical cord, stretched out straight. The realization of what he was looking at made him pull his hand away in horror.

'Shit,' he said. 'It *moved*.'

'I didn't see it move,' said Moore.

'Not now. *Before*. It left that trail.' He pointed to the flip-flop pattern of blood.

'You mean – it was actually *alive?*'

'It seems to be more than just a random collection of cells. It has rudimentary limbs. It moves, so it has some sort of skeletal structure and muscle attachments.'

'And an eye,' murmured Sheehan. 'A fucking cyclops. And it's looking at me.'

Dvorak glanced at Moore. 'So what's the story here? How did you get involved?'

'EMTs notified us. Ambulance was dispatched here around five A.M. after a female called in a medical emergency. They found a woman bleeding on the floor over there. There's a lot more blood in the bathroom, in the toilet bowl.'

'Bleeding from where?'

'The vagina, I guess. They didn't know whether to call it an unattended birth. Or an attempted abortion.' Moore looked down at the thing with flippers. 'I mean, do you call that a *baby*? Or just part of a baby?'

'I think it's multiple congenital malformations. But I've never seen anything like it.'

'Yeah, well, I hope I never see another one. Can you imagine what it'd be like, to be Daddy in the delivery room? And to see *that* come out? It'd give me a fucking coronary.'

'What happened to the victim?'

'The woman was DOA at City Hospital, which makes her an ME case. We think her name is Annie Parini – at least, that's the name the neighbors know her by.'

'What about the other female? The one who made the call?'

'She skipped out before the first patrol car arrived. EMTs said she looked pretty young. Teenager. The name she gave to the emergency operator was Molly Picker.'

Dvorak crossed to the bathroom doorway and looked inside. He saw more blood, splattered across the toilet and the shower tiles. A lake of it on the floor. 'I need to talk to the girl.'

'You think she contributed to the death?'

'I just want to know what she saw. What she knows about the victim.' He turned and frowned at the Thing. 'If Annie Parini was taking some drug – and if it caused *that* – then we're dealing with a devastating new teratogen.'

'Could a drug do that?'

'I've never seen a malformation this severe. I'll send it out for genetic analysis. In the meantime, I'd really like to talk to this Molly Picker. If that's her name.'

'We've got fingerprints. She left them all over the place.' He pointed to one bloody set on the bathroom doorframe, another set on the wall near the Thing. 'We'll confirm the name.'

'Find her for me. Don't scare her – I just want to talk to her.'

'What about Annie Parini?' asked Sheehan. 'You gonna do a post on her?'

Dvorak looked down at the blood on the floor. And he nodded. 'I'll see you both in the morgue.'

The body on the autopsy table was now nothing but a hollowed-out cavity, gutted of its organs. Throughout the autopsy, Detectives Sheehan and Moore had said very little. Judging by the pallor of their faces, both cops would rather be just about anywhere else. What made this victim more up-setting than usual was her age and her sex. A woman this young should not be lying on an autopsy table.

Dvorak had worked with a minimum of con-versation, reserving his comments for the tape recorder. Heart and lungs unremarkable. The stomach empty. Liver and pancreas of normal size and appearance. All in all, a youthful, undiseased body.

He turned his attention to the enlarged uterus, which had been removed in one piece and was lying on the cutting board under a bright light. He slit it open, through the myometrial and endometrial layers, to reveal the cavity.

'We have our answer.'

Both cops reluctantly stepped closer.

'Abortion?' asked Moore.

'Not what I'm seeing here. There's no uterine perforation. No evidence of instrumentation. In the old days, before *Roe vs. Wade*, the back room abortionists would usually insert some sort of catheter through the cervix to dilate it, and then leave packing or a tampon to hold the catheter in place. But there's nothing here.'

'Could she have passed it? Flushed it down the john?'

'Possibly. But I don't think that's what happened.' He touched a probe to a mass of bloody tissue. 'That's a placental fragment that didn't completely separate from the uterus. It's called placenta accreta. It would account for the bleeding.'

'Is that, like, an unusual condition?'

'Not all that unusual. What makes this one especially dangerous was the fact the placenta implanted itself in the lower uterus. That can lead to premature labor. Massive hemorrhage.'

'So we've got a natural death here.'

'I would say so.' Dvorak straightened. 'She probably had pain and went into the bathroom, thinking she had to move her bowels. Bled into the toilet bowl, got dizzy, fell on the bathroom floor. Lord knows how long she was lying there before anyone noticed.'

'That makes it easier for us,' said Sheehan gratefully, stepping away from the cutting board. 'No homicide.'

'I still need to talk to the other female in the apartment. Those fetal abnormalities were unlike anything I've seen. I don't like the idea of some new teratogenic drug floating around on the streets.'

'We got a hit on the name Molly Picker,' said Sheehan. 'Arrested last year for soliciting. Bailed out by a guy we assume was her pimp. We'll talk to him – he probably knows where to find her.'

'Don't scare her, okay? I just need some history on this victim.'

'If we don't scare her just a little,' said Sheehan, 'she may not talk at all.'

Romy had had a shitty day, and now it was turning into a shitty night. He paced the street corner at Montgomery and Canton, trying to stay warm. Should've grabbed a jacket on the way out, he thought, but the sun hadn't yet gone down when he'd left the apartment, and he hadn't counted on this wind, knifing between the buildings. Nor had he counted on waiting around this long.

Fuck it. If they wanted to talk, they could come see him on *his* territory.

He left the street corner and began to walk with his shoulders hunched forward, his hands thrust in his jeans pockets for warmth. He'd gone only half a block when he realized a car had pulled over beside him.

'Mr. Bell?' the man said through the crack in the tinted window.

Romy glowered at the car. 'You're late, man.'

'I would have come earlier, except for the traffic.'

'Yeah, right. Well, fuck off.' He turned and kept walking.

'Mr. Bell, we need to talk about this little problem.'

'I got nothing to say.'

'It's in your best interests to step into the car. If you want to keep doing business with us.' There was a pause. 'And if you want to get paid.'

Romy stopped and stared up the street, the wind lashing his face, the chill cutting straight through his silk shirt.

'It's warm in here, Mr. Bell. I'll take you home afterward.'

'What the fuck,' muttered Romy, and he stepped into the rear of the car. As he settled back for the ride, his attention was focused more on the plush interior than on the man sitting in the driver's seat. As usual, it was the guy with the white-blond hair, the guy who never looked at Romy.

'You need to find that girl.'

Romy gave an irritated grunt. 'I don't need to do nothing till you pay me.'

'She should have been delivered to us two weeks ago.'

'Yeah, well, she wasn't one of my most co-operative bitches, you know? I'll get you some others.'

'Annie Parini was found dead this morning. Did you know that?'

Romy stared at him. 'Who offed her?'

'Nobody. It was a natural death. Nevertheless, the body went to the authorities.'

'So?'

'So they already have their hands on one specimen. We can't let them find another. The girl has to be brought in.'

'I don't know where she is. I been looking.'

'You know her better than anyone else does. You have contacts on the street, don't you? Find her before she goes into labor.'

'She's still got time.'

'The pregnancy was never meant to go to term. We have no idea if it will last a full nine months.'

'You mean she could pop it any time?'

'We don't know.'

Romy laughed and looked out the window as the buildings glided by. 'Man, you guys crack me up. You're way behind on this. They already come by, asking about her.'

'Who?'

'Police. Dropped by this afternoon, wanting to know where she was.'

The man went silent for a moment. In the rearview mirror, Romy glimpsed a flash of panic in the man's face. *Molly Wolly*, he thought, *you got 'em scared*.

'It'll be worth it to you,' the man said.

'You want her whole? Or in Reese's Pieces?'

'We want her alive. We need her alive.'

'Alive's harder.'

'Ten. On delivery.'

'Twenty-five, half now, or fuck it.' Romy reached for the door handle.

'All right. Twenty-five.'

Romy felt like laughing. These guys were scared shitless, and all because of stupid Molly Wolly. She wasn't worth twenty-five thousand. In his humble opinion, she wasn't worth twenty-five cents.

'Can you deliver?' the man asked.

'Maybe.'

'If you can't, I'm going to have some very unhappy investors. So *find* her.' He handed Romy an envelope. 'There'll be more.'

Glancing inside, Romy caught a flash of fifty-dollar bills. It was a start.

The car pulled over at Upton and Tremont – Romy's home turf. He hated to leave those nice leather seats, to step out into the slicing wind. He waved the envelope. 'What about the rest?'

'On delivery. You can deliver?'

String him along, thought Romy. *Make it sound harder than it really is. Maybe the price will go up.* He said, 'I'll see what I can do,' and he climbed out and watched the car drive away. *Scared. The man looks scared.*

The envelope felt nice and thick; Romy stuffed it in his jeans pocket.

Better hide, Molly Wolly, he thought. *Ready or not, here I come.*

Bryan invited her into the house and offered her a glass of wine. It was the first time Toby had been inside his home. She felt uneasy about it, not because of the unconventional nature of Bryan's household, which consisted of two men, happily mated to each other. Rather, it was because she realized, as she sat on the couch in his living room, that she had never really spent time with Bryan as a friend. He had come into her home to care for her mother, had fed Ellen, bathed her. In return, Toby had written him a check every two weeks, *pay to the order of*. Friendship had never been part of the job description.

And why not? she wondered as Bryan set down a napkin and a glass of white wine on the coffee table in front of her. Why had the simple act of writing a check every two weeks made real friendship between them so impossible?

She sat sipping the wine and feeling guilty about never having made the effort. And embarrassed that only now, when she truly needed him, had she even thought to set foot in his house.

He sat down across from her, and a moment passed. They sipped wine, fussed with damp napkins. The lampshades threw arching shadows on the cathedral ceiling. On the wall across from Toby hung a black and white photo of Bryan and Noel on a crescent of beach, their arms slung around each other's shoulders. They wore the smiles of two men who knew how to enjoy life. A knack Toby had never picked up.

Bryan said, 'I guess you know the Newton police have already talked to me.'

'I gave them your name. I thought you could back me up. They seem to think I'm the daughter from hell.' She set down her wineglass and looked at him. 'Bryan, you know I'd never hurt my mother.'

'And that's what I told them.'

'Do you think they believed you?'

'I don't know.'

'What did they ask?'

He paused to take a sip, and she recognized it as his way of delaying an answer.

'They asked about medications,' he finally said. 'They wanted to know if Ellen was taking any prescription drugs. And they asked about the burn on her hands.'

'You explained what happened?'

'I repeated it several times. They didn't seem to like my answer. What is going on, Toby?'

She sank back, drawing both hands through her hair. 'It's Jane Nolan. I don't know why she's doing this to me . . .'

'Doing what to you?'

'It's the only way I can explain it. Jane comes into my home, and she seems like a – a gift from heaven. She's bright, she's kind. She's perfect. She sweeps in and fixes my life for me. Then everything goes wrong. *Everything*. And Jane is telling the police it's my fault. It's almost as if she *meant* to ruin my life.'

'Toby, this sounds so bizarre—'

'People *are* bizarre. They do crazy things to get attention. I keep telling the police she's the one they should focus on. The one they should arrest. But they're not doing anything.'

'I don't think attacking Jane Nolan is in your best interests.'

'She's attacking *me*. She's accused me of trying to hurt my own mother. Why call the police? Why didn't she just ask *me* about the burn on Mom's hands? And why pull Vickie into this? She's turned my own sister against me.'

'For what reason?'

'I don't know why! She's *crazy*.'

She saw Bryan avert his gaze, and she realized that *she* was the one who sounded ill, the one who needed psychiatric help.

'I've gone over this again and again in my head, trying to understand how it happened,' she said. 'How I could have *let* it happen. I didn't look at Jane as carefully as I should have.'

'Don't hog all the blame, Toby. Didn't Vickie help make the choice?'

'Yes, but she's so superficial about these things. It was really my responsibility. After you quit, I was in a panic. You gave me so little time to find . . .' She paused, a thought suddenly occurring to her. *That's why Jane came into my life. Because Bryan quit.*

'I would have given you more notice,' he said. 'But they wanted me to start immediately.'

'Why did they choose *you*, Bryan?'

'What?'

'You said you weren't *looking* for a new job. Then suddenly you were hired. How did that happen?'

'They called me.'

'Who did?'

'Twin Pines Nursing Home. They wanted a recreational art therapist. They knew I'd been a nurse's aide. And they knew I was an artist. That I had paintings for sale in three galleries.'

'How did they know?'

He shrugged. 'I guess someone gave them my name.'

And hired you away from me, she thought. *Leaving me scrambling for a replacement.*

She left Bryan's house with more unanswered questions than when she'd arrived.

She drove to Springer Hospital to check on her mother.

It was 10 P.M. and visiting hours were already over, but no one stopped her from entering Ellen's ICU cubicle. The lights had been dimmed, and Ellen lay in semidarkness. Toby sat down by the bed and listened to the cycling of the ventilator. On the oscilloscope above the bed, a neon green line traced the rhythm of Ellen's heart. The nurse's clipboard hung at the foot of the bed. Toby reached for it and turned on the small reading light to scan the most recent entries.

1545: skin warm, dry; no response to painful stimuli.
1715: daughter Vickie in to see her.

1903: vitals stable; still unresponsive.

She flipped to the next sheet and saw the most recent entry:

2030: lab tech here to draw blood for 7-dehydroxywarfarin screen.

At once she left the cubicle and crossed to the nurses' station. 'Who ordered this test?' she asked, handing the clipboard to the ward clerk. 'The hydroxywarfarin screen?'

'This is on Mrs. Harper?'

'Yes, on my mother.'

The ward clerk pulled Ellen's medical chart from the rack and turned to the order sheets. 'Dr. Steinglass did.'

Toby picked up the telephone and dialed. It rang twice. Dr. Steinglass barely got out his 'hello' when Toby snapped:

'Bob, why did you order a warfarin screen on my mother? Do you have reason to think she's been given Coumadin? Or rat poison?'

'It was . . . because of the bruises. And that intracerebral bleed. I told you her prothrombin time came back severely prolonged—'

'Yesterday you said you thought it might be due to liver inflammation.'

'The PT was too abnormal. Hepatitis wouldn't explain it.'

'So why the warfarin screen? She hasn't been getting warfarin.'

There was a long silence. 'They asked me to order the test,' Steinglass said at last.

'Who?'

'The police. They told me to call the medical examiner for advice. He suggested the warfarin screen.'

'Who did you talk to? Which doctor?'

'It was a Dr. Dvorak.'

Barely awake, Dvorak fumbled in the darkness for the phone, finally picking it up on the fourth ring. 'Hello?'

'Why, Dan? Why are you doing this?'

'Toby?'

'I thought we were friends. Now I find out you're on the other side. I don't understand how I could have been so wrong about you.'

'Listen to me, Toby—'

'No, you listen to *me*!' Her voice cracked. A sob spilled out, but was ruthlessly choked back. 'I didn't hurt my mother. I didn't poison her. If anyone hurt her, it was Jane Nolan.'

'No one's saying you did anything wrong. I'm not saying it.'

'Then why didn't you tell me you're checking her blood for warfarin? Why are you doing this behind my back? If you have information that she's been poisoned, you should have talked to *me*. Told me. Not slipped in this test while I wasn't looking.'

'I tried to call you earlier, to explain, but you weren't home.'

'I've been at the hospital. Where else would I be?'

'Okay, I guess I should have tried calling you at Springer. I'm sorry.'

'Sorry doesn't cut it. Not when you're working behind my back.'

'That's not how it happened. I got a call from Detective Alpren. He said your mother's clotting times came back abnormal. He asked me what could cause that and would I talk to her doctor about it. A screen for warfarin is just the next logical step.'

'Logical.' She gave a bitter laugh. 'Yes, that sounds like you.'

'Toby, there are half a dozen other reasons why her clotting times might be abnormal. A warfarin screen is part of the workup. The police asked for my advice, and I gave it. It's my job.'

She said nothing for a moment, but he could hear her shaky exhalation, and he knew she was struggling not to cry.

'Toby?'

'I suppose it'll also be your job to testify against me in court.'

'It won't come to that.'

'If it did. If it *did* come to that.'

'Jesus, Toby.' He sighed in exasperation. 'I'm *not* going to answer that question.'

'Never mind,' she said just before she hung up. 'You already did.'

* * *

353

Detective Alpren had eyes like a marmoset's, bright, inquisitive, quick to pick up details. He couldn't seem to stand in one spot for more than a minute, had paced back and forth in the autopsy lab, and when not pacing, would rock from foot to foot. The dead body on the table interested him not at all; it was Dvorak he'd come to see, and for ten minutes he'd been waiting impatiently for the autopsy to end.

At last, Dvorak shut off his cassette recorder, and Alpren said, 'Now can we talk about it?'

'Go ahead,' said Dvorak, not looking up from the table, his gaze still contemplating the corpse. It was a young man's, the torso hollowed out from neck to pubis. Inside we are all the same, he thought as he looked at the empty cavity. We're just identical sets of organs, packaged in various shades of skin. He picked up a needle and suture and began to sew the cavity shut, taking deep bites of flesh with his needle. There was no need to be elegant; this was merely a cleanup task, to prepare the body for transfer to the mortuary. A job Lisa normally performed.

Alpren, oblivious to the gruesome needlework, stepped up to the table. 'The test came back,' he said. 'That – what do you call it? RHPLC?'

'Rapid high-performance liquid chromotography.'

'Right. Anyway, the hospital lab just called me. The test is positive.'

Dvorak momentarily froze. He forced himself to keep stitching, to close the skin over the empty cavity. Had Alpren noticed? he wondered.

'So what does that mean?'

Dvorak kept his gaze tightly focused on the task. 'The RHPLC is a screening test for the presence of 7-hydroxywarfarin.'

'Which is?'

'A metabolite of warfarin.'

'Which is?'

Dvorak tied a knot and reached for another length of suture. 'A drug that affects normal clotting. It can lead to excessive bruising. Bleeding.'

'Into the brain? Like Mrs. Harper?'

Dvorak paused. 'Yes. It may explain the bruises on her legs as well.'

'So that's why you suggested the test.'

'Dr. Steinglass told me about the abnormal prothrombin time. Warfarin poisoning is on the differential diagnosis.'

Alpren was busy scribbling notes as he asked the next question. 'And how do you get this drug, warfarin?'

'It can be found in certain rat poisons.'

'Makes them bleed to death?'

'It takes some time to be effective. But eventually they hemorrhage internally.'

'Pleasant image. Where else can you get warfarin?'

Again Dvorak paused. He didn't want to be having this conversation, didn't want to be considering the possibilities. 'It can be given as a prescription medication called Coumadin. For use as a blood thinner.'

'Only by prescription?'

'Yes.'

'So you'd need a doctor to order it, and a pharmacy to fill it.'

'That's right.'

The pen was scribbling faster. 'That gives me something to work on.'

'What?'

'Area pharmacies. Who's had Coumadin prescribed for them and which doctors ordered it.'

'It's not that unusual a prescription. You'd find a number of doctors ordering it.'

'I'm screening for one particular name. Dr. Harper's.'

Dvorak set down the needle holder and looked at Alpren. 'Why focus solely on her? What about the mother's caregiver?'

'Jane Nolan has a spotless record. We've checked with her last three employers. And remember, *she* was the one who called us and raised the question of abuse.'

'To cover her own ass, maybe?'

'Look at it from Dr. Harper's point of view. She's a nice-looking woman, but no husband, no family of her own. Probably never even dates. She's trapped with a senile old mother who refuses to die. Then she starts screwing up at work and the stress builds.'

'Leading to attempted murder?' Dvorak shook his head.

'Number one rule: look at the family first.'

Dvorak tied the final knot on the corpse and snipped the suture.

Glancing at the stitched torso, Alpren gave a grunt of disgust. 'Jesus. Frankenstein.'

'It'll all be hidden under a dress suit. Even a beggar is allowed to look distinguished in his coffin.' Dvorak stripped off the gown and gloves and washed his hands in the sink. 'What about accidental poisoning?' he said. 'The mother has Alzheimer's. There's no telling what she may have put in her mouth. There could be rat poison in the house.'

'Which the daughter conveniently left out for old Mom to find. Right.'

Dvorak just kept washing his hands.

'I find it interesting that Dr. Harper now refuses to talk to me without her attorney,' said Alpren.

'That's not suspicious. That's smart.'

'Still, it makes you wonder.'

Dvorak dried his hands, not looking at Alpren, not really daring to. *I shouldn't be commenting on this investigation*, he thought. *I'm not detached enough. I don't have the heart to build a criminal case against Toby Harper.* Yet that's what he *should* be doing, what his job required of him. Examine the evidence. Draw the logical conclusions.

He didn't like what the evidence was telling him.

Clearly the old woman had been poisoned, but whether by accident or by intention was impossible to determine at this point. He could not believe Toby was responsible. Or was he simply refusing to believe? Had he lost his objectivity simply because he was attracted to her?

All last night he'd fought the urge to call her back. Twice he had even picked up the phone but then had hung up, reminding himself he could not discuss the evidence with a possible suspect. Then this morning, *she* had tried calling *him*. He'd used his secretary as a barrier, had asked her to screen out Toby's calls. He felt sick about it, but he had little choice. As friendless and vulnerable as Toby was right now, he could offer no comfort to her.

After Alpren left, Dvorak retreated to the lab next door. Boxes of tissue slides were stacked up on the countertop, waiting to be interpreted. It was quiet, solitary work, and he was grateful for it. For an hour he sat hunched over his microscope, the world shut out, the silence broken only by the occasional clink of glass slides. The hermit in his cell, shut off from the rest of the world. Normally he enjoyed working in isolation, but today he felt miserable and unable to concentrate.

He looked down at his finger, where the scalpel nick had healed, leaving a tiny scar. It was a reminder of his own mortality, of the seemingly trivial events that can lead to catastrophe. Stepping off a curb too soon. Catching an earlier plane flight. Smoking one last cigarette before bed. The specter of death is always watching, waiting for its chance. He gazed at the scar, and he imagined his own neurons imploding even now, driven to self-destruction by a horde of alien prions.

There was nothing to be done about it, nothing that could be done except to wait and watch for the signs. A year, two years at the most. Then he'd be home free. He'd have his life back.

He closed the slide box and stared at the blank wall in front of him. *When did I truly have a life?*

He wondered if it wasn't already too late to start one.

He was forty-five, his ex-wife was happily remarried, and his only son had already made the leap to independence. Dvorak's last vacation six months ago had been taken alone, a driving tour through Ireland, pub to pub, enjoying the occasional human contact, however brief and superficial. He had not considered himself a man in need of companionship until he'd arrived one evening in a small village in the west and found that the only pub was closed. Standing on that deserted road, in a place where no one knew his name, he had felt such deep and unexpected despair that he had climbed into his car and driven straight to Dublin.

He could feel that same despair coming on now as he stared at the wall.

The intercom buzzed. Startled, he rose to his feet and picked up the phone. 'Yes?'

'You have two calls. On line one's Toby Harper. Do you want me to keep brushing her off?'

It took all his willpower to say, 'Tell her I'm unavailable indefinitely.'

'The other call is Detective Sheehan, line two.'

Dvorak punched the button for line two. 'Roy?'

'We have some follow-up on that dead baby. Or whatever it was,' said Sheehan. 'You know that young female who called for the ambulance?'

'Molly Picker?'

'Yeah. We found her.'

Seventeen

'I'm sorry, but Dr. Dvorak is unable to take your call.'

Toby hung up and glanced in frustration at her watch. She'd been trying to reach Dvorak all day. Every call had been refused. She knew the police were building some kind of case against her, and if she could just talk to Dvorak, she might convince him, as a friend, to reveal what the evidence was.

But he wouldn't accept her calls.

She left the ICU nurses' station and crossed to her mother's cubicle. She stood outside the window, watching Ellen's chest rise and fall. The coma had deepened, and Ellen had no spontaneous respirations. The last CT scan had shown the hemorrhage had extended, and there was now a question of a pontine bleed as well. A nurse was at the bedside, adjusting the IV infusion rate. Sensing she was being watched, the nurse turned to the window and saw Toby. Too quickly, she looked away again. That lack of acknowledgment, of even a courteous nod, spoke volumes.

The staff no longer trusted Toby. Nobody did.

She left the hospital and got into her car but didn't start the engine. She didn't know where to go. Home was out of the question – too empty, too silent. It was four o'clock, not time yet for dinner, even if she had an appetite. Her body's circadian rhythm was askew, still in transition to a daytime schedule, and she never knew when hunger or fatigue would strike. She knew only that her mind was fuzzy, that nothing felt right. And that her life, once so well ordered, was now totally and irretrievably screwed up.

She opened her purse and took out Jane Nolan's résumé. She'd been carrying it around, intending to call all four of Jane's former employers for more information, any hint that their 'perfect' nurse was not so perfect. She'd already spoken to three nursing directors over the phone, and all had given Jane glowing evaluations.

You pulled one over on them. But I know the truth.

The one employer she hadn't spoken to was Wayside Nursing Home. The address was only a few miles away.

She started the car.

'We'd welcome Jane back in a heartbeat,' said Doris Macon, the nursing supervisor. 'Of all our nurses, she was the one our patients seemed to love the most.'

It was suppertime at Wayside Nursing Home, and the meal cart had just rattled into the dining room. Patients in various states of awareness sat at the four long tables, saying little. The only voices in the room were those of the staff as they set down the trays: *There's your supper, dear. Do you need help with that napkin? Let me cut your meat for you . . .*

Doris surveyed the gathering of gray heads and said, 'They get so fond of particular nurses, you know. A familiar voice, a friendly face, it means everything to them. When a nurse leaves, some of our patients actually go into mourning. They don't all have families, so we become their families.'

'And Jane was good with them?'

'Absolutely. If you're thinking of hiring her, you're lucky to have such a wonderful applicant. We were so sorry when she left us to take that job with Orcutt Health.'

'Orcutt? I didn't see that on her résumé.'

'I know she worked for them at least a year after she left us.'

Toby unfolded Jane's résumé. 'It's not here. After you, she lists Garden Grove Nursing Home.'

'Oh, that's part of the Orcutt chain. It's a group of nursing homes, owned by the same corporation. If you work for Orcutt, you can be assigned to any one of their facilities.'

'How many do they have?'

'A dozen? I'm not sure. But they're one of our biggest competitors.'

Orcutt, thought Toby. Why did the name sound familiar?

'I didn't realize Jane was back in Massachusetts

looking for a job,' said Doris. 'I'm sorry she didn't call us.'

Toby refocused her attention on Doris. 'She left the state?'

'A few months ago, she sent us a postcard from Arizona, telling us she'd gotten married. Living the life of leisure now. That's the last I heard. I guess she's moved back.' Doris looked curiously at Toby. 'If you're thinking of hiring her, why don't you just talk to her? She'll explain the résumé.'

'I'm double-checking,' lied Toby. 'I'm thinking of hiring her, but something about her makes me uncomfortable. It's for my mother, who really can't fend for herself. I have to be careful.'

'Well, I can vouch for Jane. She was wonderful with our patients.' Doris moved to one of the dining tables, where she rested a hand on an elderly woman's shoulder. 'Miriam, dear. You remember Jane, don't you?'

The woman smiled, a spoonful of mashed potatoes hovering at her dentureless mouth. 'Is she coming back?'

'No, dear. I just want you to tell this lady whether you liked Jane or not.'

'I *love* Janey. She hasn't been to see me in a long time.'

'Jane's been away, dear.'

'And the baby! I wonder how big the baby is. Tell her to come back.'

Doris straightened and looked at Toby. 'I'd call that a pretty good recommendation.'

364

Back in her car, Toby sat staring at the dashboard in frustration.

Why did no one recognize the truth? Jane's former patients loved her. Her ex-employers loved her. She was a dear woman, a saint.

And I've become the devil.

She reached for the ignition and was about to turn the key when she suddenly remembered where she'd heard the name Orcutt.

From Robbie Brace. That night, in the medical records room at Brant Hill, he had told her their building served as central records storage for Orcutt Health's other nursing homes.

She got out of the car and went back into the building.

Doris Macon was in the nurses' station, taking off order sheets. She looked up, obviously surprised to see Toby had returned.

'I have another question,' said Toby. 'That woman in the dining room. She said something about a baby. Did Jane have a child?'

'A daughter. Why?'

'She never said anything about . . .' Toby paused, her thoughts scattering in a dozen different directions at once. Had the baby since died? Had there ever been a child? Or had Jane simply not bothered to mention the fact she had a daughter?

Doris was looking at her with a puzzled expression. 'Excuse me, but is this relevant to your hiring her?'

Why was a baby never mentioned? Toby

suddenly straightened. 'What does Jane look like?'

'Didn't you interview her? You've seen her yourself—'

'*What does she look like?*'

Taken aback by Toby's sharp tone, Doris stared at her for a moment. 'She – uh – she's quite average-looking. Nothing particularly unusual about her.'

'How tall is she? What color's her hair?'

Doris rose to her feet. 'We have group photos of our staff. We take one every year. I can point her out to you.' She led Toby to the hallway, where a series of framed photos were hanging, each one labeled with the date it was taken. The series went back to 1981 – presumably the year Wayside Nursing Home opened. Doris paused in front of the color photo from two years before and scanned the faces.

'There,' she said, pointing to a woman in a white uniform. 'That's Jane.'

Toby stared at the face in the photograph. The woman was standing at the far left edge of the group, her pudgy face smiling, her uniform top a shapeless tent over a massively obese body.

Toby shook her head. 'That's not her.'

'Oh, but I can assure you,' said Doris. 'And so can our patients. That is definitely Jane Nolan.'

'We picked the girl up over in the North End,' said the patrol man. 'Witnesses saw some guy slapping her around, trying to drag her into a car. She was screaming her bloody head off, and they stepped in to help. We were the first officers on the scene. Found the girl sitting on the curb with a cut lip and a black eye. She gave her name as Molly Picker.'

'Who was the guy beating up on her?' asked Dvorak.

'Her pimp, I guess. She wouldn't tell us. And the guy left the scene.'

'Where's the girl now?'

'Sitting in the cruiser. Didn't want to come in here. Doesn't want to talk to anyone. All she wants is back out on the street.'

'So the pimp can rough her up again?'

'She's not big in the IQ department.'

Dvorak sighed as they walked out the front entrance to Albany Street. He wasn't optimistic about this interview. A sullen teenager, probably uneducated as well, was a poor source for a medical history The girl wasn't under arrest, and she could walk out any time, but she probably didn't know that. He was certainly not going to enlighten her, not until he had a chance to pick her brains. What brains she had.

The patrolman pointed to the cruiser, where his partner was waiting in the front seat. In the back-seat was a girl with stringy brown hair and a cut lip. She sat huddled under a giant raincoat. She was clutching a cheap patent leather purse in her lap.

The cop opened the back door. 'Why don't you step on out, miss? This is Dr. Dvorak. He'd like to speak to you.'

'Don't need no doctor.'

'He's with the medical examiner's office.'

'Don't need no exam neither.'

Dvorak leaned in and smiled at the girl. 'Hi, Molly. We're going inside to talk. It's cold out here, don't you think?'

'Wouldn't be if you'd shut the door.'

'I can wait all day. We can talk now, or we can talk at midnight. It's up to you.' He stood looking in at her, waiting to see how long it would take her to get tired of being stared at. All three men were watching her, the two cops and Dvorak, no one saying a thing.

Molly took a deep breath and let it out in a snort of frustration. 'You got a bathroom?' she said.

'Of course.'

'I gotta go real bad.'

Dvorak stepped aside. 'I'll show you the way.'

She struggled out of the patrol car, the oversize raincoat dragging after her like a giant cape. Only when she straightened did Dvorak suddenly focus on the girl's abdomen. She was pregnant. At least six months, he estimated.

The girl noticed the direction of his gaze. 'Yeah, so I'm knocked up,' she snapped. 'So what?'

'I think we should get you inside. Pregnant ladies need to sit down.'

She flashed him a *That's a joke, right?* look and walked into the building.

'Nice girl,' grunted the cop. 'You want us to hang around?'

'You can leave. I'll just put her in a taxi when I'm done.'

Dvorak found the girl waiting for him just inside the door.

'So where's the bathroom?' she said.

'There's one upstairs, next to my office.'

'Well come *on*. I gotta pee.'

She didn't say anything as they rode the elevator; judging by the look of concentration on her face, all her attention was focused on her bladder. He waited for her outside the staff rest room. She took her time, emerging ten minutes later, smelling of soap. She'd washed her face, and the swollen lip seemed to stand out alarmingly purple against that white face.

He led her into his office and shut the door. 'Sit down, Molly.'

'This gonna take long?'

'It depends on whether you help me out. Whether you know anything.' Again he gestured to the chair.

Sullenly she sat down, pulling the raincoat around her like a protective mantle. Her bottom lip stuck out, bruised and stubborn.

He stood with the back of his thighs against the desk, looking down at her. 'Two days ago you made an emergency call. The operator recorded your voice requesting an ambulance.'

'Didn't know it was a crime to call an ambulance.'

'When the team got there, they found a woman had bled to death. You were in the apartment with her. What happened, Molly?'

She said nothing. Her head drooped, the lank hair spilling across her face.

'I'm not saying you did anything wrong. I just need to know.'

The girl wouldn't look at him. Bringing her arms up, she hugged herself and began to rock in the chair. 'Wasn't my fault,' she whispered.

'I know that.'

'I wanna go. Can't I just go?'

'No, Molly. We need to talk first. Can you look at me?'

She wouldn't. She kept her head down, as though meeting his gaze would somehow signify a defeat.

'Why don't you want to talk?'

'Why should I? I don't know you.'

'You don't have to be afraid of me. I'm not a cop, I'm a doctor.'

His words had the opposite effect of what he'd intended. She shrank deeper into her chair and shuddered. He could not figure out this girl. She was an alien species to him. All teenagers were. He was unsure how to proceed.

His desk intercom buzzed.

'Dr. Toby Harper's here,' said his secretary.

'I'm unavailable.'

'I don't think she's going to leave. She insists on going upstairs to see you.'

'Look, I really can't talk to her right now.'

'Should I have her wait?'

He sighed. 'All right. Have her wait. But it may be a while.'

Dvorak turned back to Molly Picker, his irritation more acute than ever. He had one female demanding to talk to him, and another female refusing to say a word.

'Molly,' he said, 'I need to know about your friend, Annie. The woman who died. Was she using any drugs? Was she taking any medications?'

The girl gave another shudder and curled into a ball.

'This is very important. The woman had a severely deformed fetus. I need to know what she was exposed to. It could be vital information for other pregnant women as well. Molly?'

The girl began to shake. At first Dvorak did not understand what was happening. He thought she was cold, shivering. Then she toppled forward and her head slammed against the floor. Her limbs began to jerk, her whole body wracked by convulsions.

Dvorak knelt down beside her and frantically tried to loosen the raincoat, which had bunched up around her neck, but her limbs were flailing with superhuman strength. At last he got the collar open. She was still seizing, her face a shocking purple, her eyes rolled back. *What do I do now? I'm a pathologist, not an ER doctor . . .*

He sprang to his feet and hit the intercom button. 'I need Dr. Harper! Send her up *now*!'

'But I thought you said—'

'I have a medical emergency!'

He turned his attention to Molly. The girl's

flailing had stopped, but her face was still a deep red, and a lump was forming on her forehead, where she'd bumped the floor.

Don't let her aspirate. Turn her on her side.

Remembered lessons from his medical school years were finally filtering through his panic. He dropped down beside the girl and quickly rolled her onto her left side, her face slightly downward. If she vomited, her gastric contents would not spill into her lungs. He felt her pulse – it was rapid, but strong. And she was still breathing.

Okay. Okay, we've got an airway. We've got respirations. And we've got circulation. What am I forgetting?

The office door opened. He glanced up as Toby Harper stepped into the room. Her gaze fell at once to the girl, and she knelt down.

'What happened?'

'She had some sort of seizure—'

'Any medical history? Epileptic?'

'I don't know. She's got a pulse and she's breathing.'

Toby glanced at the bruise. 'When did she hit her head?'

'After the seizure started.'

Toby pulled open the raincoat to expose the girl's torso. There was a one-beat pause, then a dismayed: 'She's pregnant.'

'Yeah. I don't know how far along she is.'

'Do you know *anything* about her?'

'She has a police record. Prostitution. Her pimp roughed her up today. That's all I know.'

372

'You have a medical bag?' asked Toby.

'In my desk drawer—'

'Get it.'

The girl was groaning, moving her head.

While Toby rummaged in the bag for instruments, Dvorak eased the girl's arm out of the raincoat sleeve. She opened her eyes and looked at him. At once she began to struggle, pulling away from his grasp.

'It's all right,' he said. 'Take it easy—'

'Let her go,' ordered Toby. 'She's post-ictal and confused. You're scaring her.'

Dvorak released the pitifully thin arm and backed away.

'Okay, honey,' murmured Toby. 'Look at me. I'm right here.'

The girl shifted her gaze to Toby's face, hovering above hers. 'Mama,' she said.

Toby spoke slowly and softly. 'I'm not going to hurt you. I just want to shine a little light in your eyes. All right?' The girl kept staring at her, as though in wonder. Toby turned a penlight beam at the girl's pupils. 'Equal and reactive. And she's moving all her limbs.' Toby reached for the blood pressure cuff. The girl made a feeble whimper of protest as the cuff squeezed her arm, but she kept her gaze on Toby and seemed to be comforted.

Toby frowned as the sphygmomanometer needle slowly pulsed downward. Quickly she released the pressure and peeled off the cuff. 'She needs to be admitted.'

'Boston City's right across the street.'

'Let's get her to their ER. Her pressure's two-ten over one-thirty, and she's pregnant. I think that explains the seizure.'

'Eclampsia?'

Toby gave a quick nod and closed the black bag. 'Can you carry her?'

Dvorak bent down and gathered the girl in his arms. Despite her pregnancy, she felt frail, weightless. Or maybe he was too pumped up on adrenaline to feel the burden. With Toby leading the way, opening doors for him, they made it out the building's front entrance to Albany Street.

Wind whipped between the buildings, stinging their faces with grit as they crossed the street. The girl struggled in his arms, and with her raincoat lashing his legs, her hair flying in his face, Dvorak stumbled onto the opposite curb and up the ramp to the ER entrance. The double doors slid open.

Behind the admitting window, a male triage nurse looked up and saw the girl in Dvorak's arms. 'What happened?'

It was Toby who answered, stepping up to the window and opening Molly Picker's cheap little purse for ID. 'Pregnant girl with seizures, now post-ictal. BP two-ten over one-thirty.'

At once the triage nurse understood, and he called for a gurney.

The stab of a needle jolted Molly fully awake. She thrashed, fighting to free herself from the hands holding her down, but there were too many of them, all trapping her, torturing her. She could not remember how she'd arrived in this terrible place, nor did she know what she'd done wrong to deserve this punishment. *I'm sorry, whatever I did wrong, I'm sorry. Please stop hurting me.*

'Shit, I blew the vein! Toss me another eighteen gauge—'

'Try the other arm. Looks like a nice vein there.'

'You have to hold her down. She keeps yanking around here.'

'Is that a seizure?'

'No, she's fighting us—'

Hands trapped her face; a voice commanded, 'Miss, you have to hold still! We need to get the IV in!'

Molly's panicked gaze focused on the face staring down at her. It was a man dressed in blue. A stethoscope was looped like a snake around his neck. A man with angry eyes.

'She's still out of it,' he said. 'Just get the IV in.'

Another pair of hands grasped her arm, trapping it against the mattress. Molly tried to jerk free, but the hands only squeezed tighter, pinching and twisting her skin. Again the needle stabbed. Molly shrieked.

'Okay, it's in! Get it connected. Come on, come on.'

'How fast a drip?'

'TKO it for now. I want five milligrams Hydralazine IV. Let's hang some mag sulfate. And get those bloods drawn.'

'Doc, a chest pain just rolled in the door.'

'Why the fuck won't they leave me alone?'

Another needle, another lance of pain. Molly bucked against the gurney. Something crashed and shattered on the floor.

'Goddamn it, she won't lie still!'

'Can't we sedate her?'

'No, we need to follow mental status. Talk her down.'

'I've tried.'

'Get that woman back in here. The one who brought her in. Maybe she can calm her down.'

Molly twisted against the restraints, her head aching, pounding with every new explosion of sound. The rapid-fire voices, the clang of metal cabinets slamming shut.

Go away, go away, go away.

Then a voice called to her, and she felt a hand settle gently on her hair.

'Molly, it's me. Dr. Harper. It's all right. Everything is all right.'

Molly focused on the woman's face, a face she recognized, though she couldn't remember where she'd seen it before. She knew only that it was a face unassociated with pain. Those calm eyes spoke to her of safety.

'You need to lie very still, Molly. I know it hurts, all these needles. But they're trying to help you.'

'I'm sorry,' whispered Molly.

'For what?'

'For whatever I did that was bad. I don't remember.'

The woman smiled. 'You didn't do anything

376

bad. Now they're going to poke you, all right? A little stick.'

Molly closed her eyes and stifled a whimper as a needle pierced her arm.

'There, that's a good girl. It's all over now. No more needles.'

'You promise?'

A pause. 'I can't promise that. But from now on, no one will poke you without warning you first, okay? I'll tell them that.'

Molly reached for the woman's hand. 'Don't leave me . . .'

'You'll be fine. These people are taking good care of you.'

'But I don't know *them*.' She looked straight at the woman, who finally nodded.

'I'll stay as long as I can.'

Someone else was speaking now; the woman turned to listen, then looked back down at Molly.

'We need to know about your health. Do you have a doctor?'

'No.'

'Take any medicines?'

'No. Oh, yeah. They're in my purse.'

Molly heard the woman unsnap the patent leather clutch, heard the clatter of pills in a bottle. 'These, Molly?'

'Yeah. I take one when my stomach gets upset.'

'There's no pharmacy label on this bottle. Where did you get it from?'

'Romy. A friend. He gave the pills to me.'

'Okay, what about allergies? Are you allergic to anything?'

'Strawberries.' Molly sighed. 'And I like strawberries so much . . .'

Another voice intruded: 'Dr. Harper, the ultrasound tech is here.'

Molly heard the rattle of machinery being rolled into the room, and her gaze shot sideways. 'What are they gonna do? They gonna poke me again?'

'It won't hurt. It's just an ultrasound test, Molly. They need to check your baby. They're going to use sound waves to look at it.'

'I don't want the test. Can't they just leave me alone?'

'I'm sorry, but it has to be done. To see if the baby's all right. How big it is and how developed it is. You had a seizure today, in Dr. Dvorak's office. You know what a seizure is?'

'Like a fit.'

'That's right. You had a fit. You were unconscious and your body was shaking all over. That's very dangerous. You need to stay in the hospital so they can get your blood pressure under control. And to see if there's any way to save the baby.'

'Is something wrong with it?'

'Your pregnancy is the reason you had the seizure, the reason your blood pressure is high.'

'I don't want any more tests. Tell them I want to leave—'

'Listen to me, Molly.' Dr. Harper's voice was quiet but firm. 'Your condition can be fatal.'

Molly was silent. She stared at the other woman's face and saw the unflinching truth in her eyes.

Dr. Harper nodded to the technician. 'Go ahead and do the sonogram. I'll wait outside.'

'No,' said Molly. 'Stay with me.' She held out her hand in a silent plea.

After a hesitation, Toby once again grasped Molly's hand and sat down on the stool by the gurney.

The technician draped a modesty sheet over Molly's thighs and pubic hair, then raised the hospital gown, baring the patient's swollen abdomen. 'This'll be a little chilly,' he said as he squeezed out a gob of clear gel onto her skin. 'This stuff makes the sound waves easier to read.'

'It won't hurt? You promise it won't hurt?'

'Not a bit.' He held up a squarish device that fit neatly into his hand. 'I'm going to rub the edge of this thing over your stomach, okay? And we can see the images on this screen here.'

'You can see my baby?'

'That's right. Watch.' He dabbed the handheld device in the gob of gel, then placed it on her skin.

'That tickles,' said Molly.

'But it doesn't hurt, does it? Admit it doesn't hurt.'

'No, it doesn't.'

'So now you just relax and watch the show, okay?' Slowly he slid the device across her abdomen, his gaze focused on the monitor. Molly, too, watched the screen and saw a jumble of shadows flicker past. Where was the baby? She'd expected to see a real picture, like a photograph, not just a bunch of gray blots.

'Where is it?' she said.

The technician didn't answer. Molly looked at him and saw that he was staring at the monitor, his expression frozen.

'Do you see it?' asked Molly.

The technician cleared his throat. 'Let me just finish the test.'

'Is it a boy or a girl? Can you tell?'

'No. No, I can't . . .' He slid the device first in one direction, then another, his gaze focused on the images flickering across the screen.

Nothing but blips of gray, thought Molly. There was one larger blob surrounded by smaller blobs. She looked at Dr. Harper. 'Do *you* see it?'

Her question was met with silence. Dr. Harper kept glancing back and forth between the screen and the technician. Neither one of them was looking at Molly. Neither one of them said a word.

'Why aren't you talking to me?' whispered Molly. 'What's wrong?'

'Just hold still, hon.'

'Something's wrong, isn't it?'

Dr. Harper squeezed her hand. 'Don't move.'

At last the technician straightened and wiped the gel off Molly's abdomen. 'I'm going to show the film to one of our doctors, okay? You just rest.'

'But *she's* a doctor,' said Molly, looking at Dr. Harper.

'I'm not trained to read this. It takes a specialist.'

'Well what *did* you see? Is something wrong?'

Dr. Harper and the technician exchanged glances. And the technician said, 'I don't know.'

Eighteen

'Freeze that frame,' said Dr. Sibley. He took off his glasses and stared at the monitor, his attention transfixed by the sonogram image. For a moment there was only silence in the room. Then Sibley murmured, 'What the hell is that . . .'

'What do you see?' asked Toby.

'I don't know. I honestly don't know what I'm looking at.' Sibley turned to the ultrasound technician. 'This shadow here is what you're referring to?'

'Yes, sir. That mass right there. I didn't know what it was.'

'Is it fetal tissue?' asked Toby.

'I can't tell.' He nodded to the technician. 'Okay, unfreeze it. Let's see the rest.'

As shadows flickered across the monitor, Sibley bent even closer. 'There's alternating density of tissue, both solid and cystic.'

'It looks like a head,' said Toby.

'Yes, it has a vaguely cranial shape. And see that calcification?'

'A tooth?'

'That's what I think it is.' Sibley paused as the view shifted to a new field. 'Where's the thorax?' he murmured. 'I don't see a thorax.'

'But it has teeth?'

'A single tooth.' Sibley sat frozen, watching the interplay of light and shadow on the monitor. 'Limbs,' he said softly. 'One there, and one there. Solid appendages. But no thorax . . .' Slowly he sat back and put on his glasses. 'It's not a fetus. It's a tumor.'

'Are you certain?' asked Toby.

'It's a ball of tissue. Primitive germ cells gone crazy, manufacturing teeth, maybe hair. It has no heart, no lungs.'

'But there's a placenta.'

'Yes. The patient's body *thinks* it's pregnant, and it's nurturing that tumor, helping it gain mass. I suspect this is a type of teratoma. Those tumors are known to form all sorts of bizarre structures, from teeth to hormone-producing glands.'

'Then it's not a congenital malformation.'

'No. It's disorganized tissue. A hunk of meat. It should be removed from the patient as soon as——' Suddenly Sibley jerked backward, his gaze sharp on the screen. 'Run that back! Do it!' he snapped to the technician.

'What did you see?'

'Just run it back!'

The monitor went blank for a moment, then lit up again in a replay of images.

'This is impossible,' said Sibley.

383

'What?'

'*It moved.*' He looked at the technician. 'Did you manipulate the abdomen?'

'No.'

'Well *look* at that. The appendage – see how it shifts position?'

'I didn't touch the abdomen.'

'Then the patient must have shifted position. A tumor doesn't move on its own.'

'It's not a tumor,' said Dvorak.

Everyone turned to look at him. He had been so quiet Toby had not realized he'd entered the room and was now standing behind her. Slowly he moved toward the monitor, his gaze fixed on the freeze-frame image. 'It does move. It has arms. It has an eye. It has teeth. Maybe it can even think . . .'

Sibley snorted. 'That's ridiculous. How could you possibly know that?'

'Because I've seen one just like it.' Dvorak turned and looked at them, his expression stunned. 'I have to make a phone call.'

In the darkness of Molly's room, Toby could see the red light on the IVAC machine blinking on and off, silent confirmation that the medication was dripping into the patient's vein. Toby let the door swing shut, and she settled into a chair by the bed. There she sat and listened to the sound of the girl's breathing. The red IVAC light blinked a hypnotic rhythm. Toby allowed her limbs to relax and her mind to drift for the first time all day. She had just called Springer Hospital to check on her mother's condition and had been assured there were no changes. *At this moment, in a different bed, in a different hospital,* she thought, *my mother is sleeping while the red light of her IVAC pulses, like this girl's, in the darkness.*

Toby glanced at her watch and wondered when Dvorak would return. Earlier tonight, she'd tried to tell him about Jane Nolan and had been frustrated by his obvious reluctance to hear her out. He'd had so many distractions as well – the crisis with Molly. His beeper going off. And then he had left, to meet someone in the hospital lobby.

She settled back in the chair and was considering a short nap when Molly's voice suddenly said, through the gloom: 'I'm cold.'

Toby straightened. 'I didn't realize you were awake.'

'I've been lying here. Thinking . . .'

'Let me find you a blanket. Can I turn on the light?'

'Okay.'

Toby switched on the bedside lamp, and the girl recoiled from the sudden glare. The bruise on her forehead was black against the pallor of her face. Her hair looked like dirty streaks across the pillow.

On the shelf in the closet, Toby found an extra hospital blanket.

She shook it out and spread it over the girl's

bed. Then she turned off the lamp and felt her way back to the chair.

'Thank you,' whispered Molly.

They shared the darkness, neither one speaking, the silence both calming and comfortable for them both.

Molly said, 'My baby's not normal. Is she?'

Toby hesitated. Decided that the kindest answer was the truth. 'No, Molly,' she said. 'It's not normal.'

'What does it look like?'

'It's difficult to say. The sonogram's not like a regular picture. It's not easy to interpret.'

Molly considered this in silence. Toby steeled herself for more questions, wondering just how graphic she should be. *Your baby isn't even human. It has no heart, no lungs, no torso. It's nothing but a frightening ball of flesh and teeth.*

To Toby's relief, the girl didn't pursue the issue. Perhaps she was afraid to hear the whole truth, the whole horror of what was now growing in her womb.

Toby leaned forward. 'Molly, I've been talking to Dr. Dvorak. He says there was a woman – someone you knew – who also had an abnormal child.'

'Annie.'

'That was her name?'

'Yes.' Molly sighed. Though darkness hid the girl's face, Toby could hear the weariness in that sigh, an exhaustion that was more than physical.

Toby's gaze focused on the vague shadow that

formed the girl's face. Her vision was adjusting to the darkness, and she could just make out the gleam of her eyes. 'Dr. Dvorak is concerned that you and Annie may have been exposed to the same toxin. Something that caused both your babies to be abnormal. Is that possible?'

'What do you mean . . . toxin?'

'Some kind of drug or poison. Did you and Annie take anything? Pills? Injections?'

'Just the pills I told you about. The ones Romy gave me.'

'This Romy, did he give you any other drugs? Anything illegal?'

'No. I didn't do that stuff, you know? I never saw Annie do it, either.'

'How well did you know her?'

'Not very well. She let me stay with her for a few weeks.'

'You were together only a few weeks?'

'I just needed a place to sleep.'

Toby gave a sigh of frustration. 'Then this doesn't add up.'

'What do you mean?'

'Whatever caused the abnormalities in your babies happened very early in pregnancy. During the first three months.'

'I didn't know Annie then.'

'When did you find out you were pregnant?'

The girl thought it over. In the lull of conversation, they heard the squeak of a medication cart being wheeled down the hall, and the murmur of nurses.

'It was in the summer. I was sick.'

'Did you see a doctor?'

A pause. Toby saw the white blanket ripple, as though moved by a shudder. 'No.'

'But you knew you were pregnant?'

'I could tell. I mean, it wasn't hard to see, after a while. Romy told me he'd take care of it.'

'What do you mean by *take care of it*?'

'Get rid of it. Then I got to thinking how nice it'd be to hold a baby. To play with it. Have it call me Mama . . .' The sheets rustled as the girl's arms moved beneath the blankets, caressing her belly. Her unborn child.

Only it was not a child.

'Molly? Who is the father?'

There was another sigh, this one wearier. 'I don't know.'

'Could it be your friend Romy?'

'He's not my friend. He's my pimp.'

Toby said nothing.

'You know about me, don't you? What I do? What I been doing . . .' Molly rolled over in bed, turning her back to Toby. Her voice was now faint, as though it came from a great distance. 'You get used to it. You learn not to think about it too much. You can't think about it. It's like your mind sort of fuzzes out, you know? Sort of drifts someplace else. And what's going on down there between your legs, it's not really happening to *you* . . .' She gave a self deprecating laugh. 'It's an interesting life.'

'It's not a healthy life.'

388

'Yeah. Well.'

'How old are you?'

'Sixteen. I'm sixteen.'

'You're from the South, aren't you?'

'Yes, Ma'am.'

'How did you get all the way up here to Boston?'

A long sigh. 'Romy brought me. He was down in Beaufort, staying with some friends. Had this way about him, you know? These real dark eyes. Never saw a white boy with eyes that dark before. Treated me so nice . . .' She cleared her throat, and Toby heard the rustle of the sheet as Molly brought it up to wipe her face. The IV tube dangled, silvery, over the bed.

'I take it he wasn't so nice to you after he brought you to Boston.'

'No, Ma'am. He wasn't.'

'Why didn't you go home, Molly? You can always go home.'

There was no answer. Only by the shuddering of the bed did Toby realize the girl was sobbing. Molly herself made no sound; it was as though her grief was trapped in a jar, her cries inaudible to anyone but her.

'I can help you go home. If all you need is the money to get there—'

'I can't.' The answer was barely a whisper. The girl rolled into a tight lump under the covers. Toby became aware of a soft keening, the sound of Molly's grief at last escaping from the vacuum of the jar. 'I can't. I can't . . .'

'Molly.'

'They don't want me back.'

Toby reached out to touch her and could almost feel the girl's pain seeping through the blanket.

There was a knock, and the door opened.

'Can I talk to you, Toby?' said Dvorak.

'Right now?'

'I think you should come out and hear this.' He hesitated, and glanced at Molly's bed. 'It's about the sonogram.'

Toby murmured to the girl, 'I'll be back.' She followed Dvorak into the hall and closed the door behind her.

'Did she tell you anything?' he asked.

'Nothing that sheds any light on this.'

'I'll try talking to her later.'

'I don't think you'll get anything. She doesn't seem to trust men, and the reason's pretty clear. Anyway, there are too many factors that can cause fetal abnormalities. The girl can't pinpoint anything.'

'This is more than just a fetal abnormality.'

'How do you know?'

He gestured toward a small conference room at the end of the hall. 'I want you to meet someone. She can explain it better than I can.'

Dvorak had said *she*, but as Toby walked into the room, the person she saw sitting in front of the video monitor looked more like a man from behind – steel gray hair, closely cropped. Broad shoulders in a tan Oxford shirt. Cigarette smoke forming a drifting wreath above the squarish head. On the monitor, the sonogram of Molly Picker's womb was slowly replaying.

'I thought you gave up the cigarettes,' said Dvorak.

The person swiveled around, and Toby saw that it *was* a woman sitting in the chair. She was in her early sixties, her blue eyes startlingly direct, her plain features unadorned by even a hint of makeup. The offending cigarette was mounted in an ivory holder, which she wielded with comfortable elegance.

'It's my one and only vice, Daniel,' the woman said. 'I refuse to give it up.'

'I guess the scotch doesn't count.'

'Scotch is not a vice. It's a tonic.' The woman turned to Toby and regarded her with a raised eyebrow.

'This is Dr. Toby Harper,' said Dvorak. 'And this is Dr. Alexandra Marx. Dr. Marx is a developmental geneticist at Boston University. One of my professors from medical school.'

'A very long time ago,' said Dr. Marx. She reached out to shake Toby's hand, a gesture one didn't expect from another woman, but one which seemed perfectly natural coming from Alex Marx. 'I've been replaying the sonogram. What do we know about this girl?'

'I just spoke to her,' said Toby. 'She's sixteen. A prostitute. She doesn't know who the father is. And she denies any history of exposure to toxins. The only med she was taking was that bottle of pills.'

Dvorak said, 'I checked with the hospital pharmacist. He identified the code stamped on the tablets. Prochlorperazine.' He looked at Dr. Marx. 'They're usually prescribed for nausea. There's no evidence they cause fetal abnormalities. So we can't blame this on the pills.'

'How did the pimp get his hands on a prescription drug?' asked Toby.

'You can get anything on the streets these days. Maybe she's not telling you about all the other drugs she's taking.'

'No, I believe her.'

'How far along is the pregnancy?'

'Based on her recall, maybe five or six months.'

'So we're looking at what should be a second trimester fetus.' Dr. Marx swiveled around to face the monitor. 'There's definitely a placenta. There's amniotic fluid. And I believe that's an umbilical cord I see here.' Dr. Marx leaned forward, studying the images flickering across the monitor. 'I think you're right, Daniel. This is not a tumor.'

'So it's a fetal abnormality?' asked Toby.

'No.'

'What else *is* there?'

'Something in between.'

'A tumor *and* a fetus? How is that possible?'

Dr. Marx took a drag from her cigarette and exhaled a cloud of smoke. 'It's a brave new world.'

'All you've got is a sonogram. A bunch of gray shadows. Dr. Sibley, the radiologist, thinks this is a tumor.'

'Dr. Sibley has never seen one of these before.'

'And you have?'

'Ask Daniel.'

Toby looked at Dvorak. 'What's she talking about?'

He said, 'The woman who died giving birth – Annie Parini – I sent her fetus to Dr. Marx for genetic analysis.'

'I've done only preliminary studies,' said Dr. Marx. 'We've done the tissue sections and staining. It will take months to complete the DNA analysis. But based purely on the histology of the . . . thing, I have a few theories.' Dr. Marx turned her chair around to face Toby. 'Sit down, Dr. Harper. Let's talk about fruit flies.'

What on earth is this leading up to? Toby wondered as she sank into a chair at the conference table. Dvorak, too, sat down. Dr. Marx, at the head of the table, regarded them with the severe demeanor of a professor confronting two remedial students. 'Have you heard about the studies coming out of the University of Basel using *Drosophila melanogaster*? The common fruit fly?'

'Which research are you talking about?' said Toby.

'It had to do with ectopic eyes. Scientists have already identified a master gene that activates the entire cascade of twenty-five hundred genes needed to form a fruit fly's eye. The gene is called "eyeless" because when it's missing, the fly is born without any eyes. The Swiss scientists managed to activate the "eyeless" gene in various parts of the fly embryo. With fascinating results. Eyes popped up in bizarre places. On wings, on knees, on antennae. Fourteen eyes grew on *one* fly! And this was merely from the activation of a *single gene*.' Dr. Marx paused to stub out her cigarette. She inserted a fresh one into the ivory holder.

'I don't see the relevance of fruit fly research to this situation,' said Toby.

'I'm getting to that,' said Dr. Marx, lighting up. She inhaled and leaned back with a satisfied sigh. 'Let's leap across species lines now. To mice.'

'I still don't see the relevance.'

'I'm trying to start off on a very elementary level here. You and Daniel aren't developmental biologists. You probably aren't aware of the advances that have occurred since you left medical school.'

'Well, that's true,' admitted Toby. 'It's hard enough keeping up with clinical medicine.'

'Then let me catch you up. Briefly.' Dr. Marx tapped off a cigarette ash. 'I was talking about mice. Specifically, mice pituitary glands. Now, the pituitary is crucial to a newborn mouse's survival. There's a reason they call it "the master gland." All those hormones it produces regulate everything from growth to reproduction to body temperature. It secretes hormones whose purpose we don't know. Hormones we haven't even identified. Mice born without a pituitary die within twenty-four hours – that's how vital the gland is.'

'And here's where the research comes in. At NIH, they're studying the pituitary's embryonic development. They know that all the different cells that form the gland arise from a single primordium. Precursor cells. But what induces those precursor cells to make a pituitary gland?' She looked back and forth at her two remedial students.

'A gene?' ventured Toby.

'Naturally. It all gets back to DNA. Life's building block.'

'Which gene?' asked Dvorak.

'In the mouse, it's Lhx3. An LIM homobox gene.'

He laughed. 'That's perfectly clear.'

'I don't expect you to completely understand it, Daniel. I just want you to grasp the concept here. Which is that there are master genes that make primoridal cells develop in certain ways. A master gene to make an eye, another to make a limb, another to make a pituitary gland.'

'All right,' said Dvorak. 'I think we understand that much. Sort of.'

Dr. Marx smiled. 'Then the next concept should be easy for you. I want you to combine these two pieces of research and consider what they mean *together*. A master gene that kicks off the formation of a pituitary gland. And a fruit fly born with fourteen eyes.' She looked at Toby, then at Dvorak. 'Do you see what I'm getting at?'

'No,' said Toby.

'No,' said Dvorak, almost simultaneously.

Dr. Marx sighed. 'All right. Let me just tell you what I found on tissue section. I dissected that specimen Daniel sent to me – what he thought was a malformed fetus. I'd never seen anything like it, and I've examined thousands of congenital abnormalities. Now, the human genome is made up of a hundred thousand genes. This *thing* appears to possess only a fraction of the normal genome. And what was present was greatly disrupted. Something catastrophic happened to that entire genome. The result? It's as if you took apart a fetus and then tried to reconstitute it in no particular order. Arms, teeth, cerebrum, all lumped together.'

Toby felt queasy. She looked at Dvorak and saw that he had paled. The image conjured up by Dr. Marx sickened them both.

'It wouldn't survive. Would it?' asked Toby.

'Of course not. Its cells were kept alive purely by placental circulation. It was using the mother as its nutrient source. It was a parasite, if you will. But then, all fetuses are parasites.'

'I never thought of it that way,' murmured Toby.

'Well, they are. Mother is the host. Her lungs oxygenate the blood, her food intake provides glucose and protein. This particular parasite – this thing – could stay alive only as long as it remained in the womb, connected to the mother's circulation. Within moments of being expelled, its cells began to die.' Dr. Marx paused, her gaze drifting upward to the rising coil of cigarette smoke. 'It was not, in any way, an independent organism.'

'If it's not a fetus, what *would* you call this thing?' asked Toby.

'I'm not sure. We prepared multiple sections of tissue. The slides were stained and examined by myself as well as by a pathologist in my department. We both concurred. One particular type of tissue appeared again and again, in organized clusters of cells. Oh, there were other tissues as well – muscle and cartilage, for instance, even an eye. But those seemed random. What was organized, and well differentiated, was the repetitive cell clusters. Glandular tissue we haven't yet identified. Identical clusters, all apparently in the midgestational stage.' She paused. 'This thing, in short, looked like a tissue factory.'

Dvorak shook his head. 'I'm sorry, but this sounds pretty crazy.'

'Why? It's been done in a lab. We can make eyes grow on fruit fly wings! We can turn on or turn off a pituitary master gene! If it can happen in a lab, it can happen in nature. Somehow, in this girl, human embryonic cells developed multiple copies of the same gene. It meant, of course, that the embryo didn't differentiate properly. So there are no legs, there's no torso. What's growing instead are these specific cell clusters.'

'What could cause this abnormality?' asked Toby.

'Outside of the lab? Something devastating. A teratogenic agent we've never seen before.'

'But Molly doesn't remember any exposure. I

397

asked her several times—' Toby paused, her gaze swerving toward the door.

Someone was screaming.

'It's Molly!' said Toby, and she shot to her feet. Dvorak was right on her heels as she pushed out of the room and sprinted down the hallway. By the time she reached Molly's room, a nurse was already at the bedside, trying to calm the girl.

'What happened?' asked Toby.

'She says someone was in her room,' the nurse said.

'He was standing right here by the bed!' said Molly. 'He knows I'm here. He followed me—'

'Who?'

'Romy.'

'The lights were off,' the nurse calmly pointed out. 'You could have been dreaming.'

'He *talked* to me!'

'I didn't see anyone,' said the nurse. 'And my desk is right around the corner—'

The slam of a door echoed in the hallway.

Dr. Marx poked her head in the room. 'I just saw a man run into the stairwell.'

'Call Security,' Dvorak said to the nurse. 'Have them check the lower levels.'

Toby was right behind Dvorak as he ran into the hall. 'Dan, where are you going?'

He pushed through the stairwell door.

'Let Security handle this!' She followed him into the stairwell.

Somewhere below, Dvorak's footsteps pounded down concrete steps.

She started down after him, tentatively at first, then picked up her pace as determination took hold. She was angry now, at Dvorak for this insanely reckless pursuit, and at Romy – if it *was* Romy – for daring to pursue the girl into the sanctuary of a hospital. How had he tracked her down? Did he follow them from Dvorak's office?

She picked up her pace, flying past the second-floor landing. She heard a door bang open, then slam shut again.

'Dan!' she yelled. No answer.

At last she hit the first floor, pushed through the door, and emerged next to the ER loading platform facing Albany Street. The blacktop was glistening with rain. She squinted as wind gusted at her face, lifting the tang of wet pavement.

Off to her left, through a soft drizzle, a silhouette appeared. It was Dvorak. He halted beneath a streetlamp, glancing left, then right.

She jogged up the sidewalk to join him. 'Where did he go?'

'I caught a glimpse of him in the stairwell. Lost him right after he left the building.'

'You're sure he *did* leave the building?'

'Yes. He's got to be around here somewhere.' Dvorak started across the street, toward the hospital power plant.

The squeal of tires made them both swing around.

The van came straight at them, barreling out of the darkness.

Toby froze.

It was Dvorak who shoved her sideways, who sent her tumbling, scraping across the blacktop.

The van roared past, taillights fading away down Albany Street.

As she struggled back to her feet, she found Dvorak already reaching for her arm, steadying her as he helped her back to the sidewalk. The impact of her fall was just beginning to register as pain, first as a vague throbbing in her knees, then the sting of nerve endings scraped raw. They stood beneath the streetlight, both of them too shaken at first to speak.

Dvorak said, 'I'm sorry I shoved you so hard. Are you all right?'

'Just a little banged up.' She glanced up the street, in the direction the vehicle had just vanished. 'Did you get the license number?'

'No. I didn't get a look at the driver, either. It all happened so fast – I was trying to get *you* out of the way.'

They both turned as an ambulance pulled up to the ER loading dock, lights flashing. Somewhere in the distance, the wail of a second ambulance was drawing closer.

'It's going to be chaos in that ER,' said Dvorak. 'I've got a first aid kit in my office. Let's go there and clean up your knees.'

With Dvorak holding her by the arm, she limped across the street, the pain worsening with every step. By the time they'd made it upstairs to his office, she was dreading the first dab of antiseptic.

He moved aside his papers and sat her down on the desk, next to the photo of his fisherman son. The smell of rubbing alcohol and iodine rose up from the open first aid kit. Crouching in front of her, he moistened a cotton ball with peroxide and gently dabbed the abrasion.

She gave a start of pain.

'Sorry,' he said, glancing up. 'There's no way to do this without hurting you.'

'I'm such a wimp,' she muttered, clutching the edge of the desk. 'Go ahead, just do it.'

He continued dabbing her knees, one hand resting on her thigh, the other gently cleaning off dirt and gravel. As he worked, she focused on his head, bent in concentration, his dark hair close enough to ruffle with her hands. His breath felt warm against her skin. *At last I have him alone,* she thought. *No crises, no distractions. This may be my only chance to make him listen. To make him believe me.*

She said, 'You think I hurt my mother, don't you? That's why you won't talk to me. Why you've avoided my calls.'

He said nothing, just reached for another ball of cotton.

'I'm being set up, Dan. They're using my mother to get back at me. And you're helping them, without even listening to my side.'

'I've been listening to you, Toby.' He'd finished cleaning her abrasions. Now he took out a roll of adhesive tape and began tearing off strips of it, taping squares of gauze on her knees.

'Then why won't you tell me if you believe me?'

'What I think you should do,' he said, 'is talk to your attorney. Lay it all out, everything you know. And let him discuss it with Alpren.'

'I don't trust Alpren.'

'And you think you can trust me?' He looked up at her.

'I don't know!' She exhaled, her shoulders drooping forward as she realized it was hopeless, trying to make him *care*. 'I did talk to Alpren, this afternoon,' she said. 'I told him what I told you. That Brant Hill's getting back at me. They're trying to ruin me.'

'Why would they bother?'

'Somehow I've scared them. I've done something, said something to make them feel threatened.'

'You have to stop blaming Brant Hill as the source of all your problems.'

'But now I have proof.'

He shook his head. 'Toby, I *want* to believe you. But I don't see how your mother's condition is connected to Brant Hill.'

'*Listen* to me. Please.'

He snapped the first aid kit shut. 'All right. All right, I'm listening.'

'The woman I hired to take care of my mother isn't who she says she is. Today I spoke to someone who worked with Jane Nolan years ago – the *real* Jane Nolan.'

'As opposed to what?'

'The fake one. The one I hired. They're completely different people. I'll get Vickie to back me up.'

He remained silent, closed off, his gaze focused stubbornly on the first aid kit.

'I saw a photograph, Dan. The real Jane was about a hundred pounds overweight. That's not the woman I hired.'

'Then she's lost weight. Isn't that possible?'

'There's more. Two years ago, the real Jane worked for a nursing home run by the Orcutt Health chain. I just learned that Orcutt is part of an umbrella corporation – owned by *Brant Hill*. If Jane was Brant Hill's employee, then they had her résumé in their files. They'd know she left Massachusetts. It'd be easy for them to slip another woman into my house under Jane's name. With Jane's credentials. If I hadn't seen that photograph, I *never* would have guessed the truth.'

He said nothing, but his gaze had lifted to hers now. *At last he's listening to me. At last he's considering my side of it.*

'Have you told all this to Alpren?' he asked.

'Yes. I told him that all he had to do was talk to the *real* Jane Nolan. The problem is, no one knows where she's living or what her married name is. I've tried to track her down, but I can't even find out if she's still in the country. Obviously Brant Hill chose someone they knew would be hard to find. If she's even still alive.'

'Social Security records?'

'I suggested that to Alpren. But if Jane's not currently employed, it could take weeks to track her down. I'm not sure Alpren wants to put out the effort. Since he doesn't believe me in the first place.'

Dvorak rose to his feet. He stood looking at her for a moment, as though seeing her, really *seeing* her, for the first time. He nodded. 'For what it's worth, I'll talk to him.'

'Thank you, Dan.' She gave a sigh, the tension leaving her body in one exhilarating rush. 'Thank you.'

He held out his hand to help her off the desk. She grasped his arm and allowed him to steady her as she rose to her feet. Still holding on to him she looked up and met his gaze.

That's all it took, that meeting of gazes. She felt his other hand come up to touch her face, his fingers slowly gliding down her cheek. And she saw, in his eyes, the same longing she felt.

The first kiss was too brief, merely a brushing of each other's lips. A timid first meeting. His arm wrapped around behind her back, drawing her closer. She gave a murmur of pleasure as their lips met again, and then again. She swayed backward, and her hips bumped against the desk. He kept kissing her, matching her whimpers with murmurs of his own. She tipped backward, falling onto the desk, pulling him down with her. Papers scattered everywhere. He trapped her face in his hands, his mouth seeking hers in deeper exploration. She reached out to grasp his waist and instead knocked something away.

Glass shattered.

They both gave a start and looked at each other, their breathing hard and fast. Their faces flushed at the same time. He pulled away, helping her back to her feet.

The photo of Dvorak's son had landed face-down on the floor.

'Oh no,' murmured Toby, looking at the broken glass. 'I'm sorry, Dan.'

'No problem. All it needs is a new frame.' Kneeling down, he gathered up the pieces of glass and dropped them in the rubbish can. He stood up, and his face flushed again as he looked at her. 'Toby, I . . . didn't expect . . .'

'I didn't, either—'

'But I'm not sorry it happened.'

'You're not?'

He paused, as though reconsidering the truth of that last statement. He said again, firmly: 'I'm not sorry at all.'

They stared at each other for a moment.

Then she smiled and pressed her lips to his. 'You know what?' she whispered. 'Neither am I.'

They held hands as they walked back across Albany Street to the hospital. Toby was moving in a daze, her bruises and scrapes now forgotten, her attention focused instead on the man holding her hand. In the elevator they kissed again, were still kissing when the door slid open.

They stepped out just as a crash cart rattled by, wheeled by a panicked-looking nurse.

Now what? thought Toby.

The nurse with the cart rounded the corner and vanished into the next hallway. An announcement crackled over the public address system:

'Code Blue, room three eleven . . .'

Toby and Dvorak glanced at each other in alarm.

'Isn't that Molly's room?' she asked.

'I don't remember—'

He was in the lead as they chased the nurse around the corner. Toby, her knees stiff from the bandages, couldn't keep up with him. He halted outside one of the rooms and stared into the doorway. 'It's not Molly,' he said as Toby caught up. 'It's the patient next door.'

Toby glanced past him and caught a glimpse of chaos.

Dr. Marx was performing CPR. A scrub-suited resident barked out orders as a nurse scuffled through the drawers of the crash cart. The patient was almost lost from view in the press of personnel; all Toby could see through the crowd was one gaunt foot, anonymous, sexless, lying exposed on the sheet.

'They don't need us,' murmured Dvorak.

Toby nodded. She turned to Molly's room. Knocking softly, she opened the door.

Inside, the lights were on. The bed was empty.

Her gaze shot to the bathroom, also empty. She looked at the bed again and suddenly realized the IV pole was there, the plastic tube dangling free, the end still attached to the intravenous catheter. A small pool of dextrose and water glistened on the floor.

'Where is she?' said Dvorak.

Toby crossed to the closet and opened the door. Molly's clothes were gone.

She ran back into the hall and poked her head into Room 311, where the code was still in progress.

'Molly Picker's left the hospital!' said Toby.

The charge nurse glanced up, obviously overwhelmed. 'I can't leave now! Call Security.'

Dvorak pulled Toby out of the room. 'Let's check the lobby.'

They ran back to the elevator.

Downstairs, they found a security guard manning the front entrance.

'We're looking for a girl,' said Dvorak. 'About sixteen – long brown hair, wearing a raincoat. Did you see her leave?'

'I think she walked out a few minutes ago.'

'Which way did she head?'

'I don't know. She just walked out that front door. I didn't watch where she was going.'

Toby stepped out the lobby entrance, and rain gusted at her face. The wet pavement stretched like a glistening ribbon.

'It's only been a few minutes,' said Dvorak. 'She can't have gotten very far.'

'Let's take my car,' said Toby. 'I've got a phone in there.'

Their first swing around the block turned up no glimpse of Molly. They drove without speaking,

407

both of them scanning the sidewalks as the windshield wipers squeaked back and forth.

On their second circle around the block, Dvorak said, 'We should call the police.'

'They'll scare her off. If she sees a cop, she'll run.'

'She's *already* running.'

'Are you surprised? She's afraid of that Romy guy. She was a sitting duck in the hospital.'

'We could've arranged for police protection.'

'She doesn't trust the police, Dan.'

Toby circled the block one more time then decided to widen the search. Slowly she drove northeast along Harrison Street. If the girl was seeking the safety of crowds, this was the direction she'd take – toward the busy streets of Chinatown.

Twenty minutes later, she finally pulled over to the curb. 'This isn't working. The girl doesn't want to be found.'

'I think it's time to call the police,' said Dvorak.

'To arrest her?'

'You'd agree she's a danger to herself, wouldn't you?'

After a pause, Toby nodded. 'With that blood pressure, she could have another seizure. A stroke.'

'Enough said.' Dvorak picked up the car phone.

As he made the call, Toby stared out the window and thought about the misery of trudging through that rain, icy water seeping into your shoes, trickling under your collar. She thought about her own relative comfort here in the car.

Leather seats. Warm air whispering out of the heater.

Sixteen. Could I have survived the streets at sixteen?

And the girl was pregnant, with a blood pressure lethal as a time bomb.

Outside, the rain began to fall harder.

Nineteen

Four blocks away, in an alley behind an Indian restaurant, Molly Picker huddled inside a cardboard box. Every so often, she caught a whiff of cooking smells – strange, spicy scents she could not identify but that made her mouth water. Then the wind would shift and she'd smell the nearby Dumpster instead and would gag on the stench of rotting food.

Her stomach veering between hunger and nausea, she hugged herself tighter. Rain had seeped into the box, and it was beginning to sag, collapsing onto her shoulders in a mantle of soggy cardboard.

The back door of the Indian restaurant opened and Molly blinked as light spilled into the alley. A man with a turban came out, lugging two trash bags, which he carried to the Dumpster. He lifted the metal lid, tossed the trash inside, and let the lid slam back down again.

Molly sneezed.

She knew from his abrupt silence that the man

had heard her. Slowly his silhouette appeared at the box opening, the turbaned head frighteningly enormous. He stared at her and she at him.

'I'm hungry,' she said.

She saw him glance toward the kitchen, then he nodded.

'You wait,' he said, and went back inside.

A moment later he reemerged with a warm napkin-wrapped bundle. Inside was bread, fragrant and soft as a pillow.

'You go now,' he said, but not unkindly. Rather than a command, it was a gentle suggestion. 'You cannot stay here.'

'I don't have anywhere to go.'

'You wish me to call someone?'

'There's nobody to call.'

He glanced up at the sky. The rain had eased to a slow drizzle, and his brown face gleamed with moisture. 'I cannot bring you inside,' he said. 'There is a church three blocks from here. They have beds for people when it is cold.'

'Which church?'

He shrugged, as if one Christian church was the same as another. 'You go on that street. You will see it.'

Shivering, her limbs stiff from the box, she rose to her feet. 'Thank you,' she murmured.

He didn't answer. Before she'd even made it out of the alley, she heard the door shut as he went back into the restaurant.

It began to rain again.

She headed in the direction the man had told her

411

to go, devouring the bread as she walked. She could not remember tasting bread so wonderful; it was like eating clouds. Someday, she thought, someday, I'll pay him back for being nice to me. She always remembered the people who'd been nice to her; she kept a list in her head. The woman at the liquor store who'd given her a day-old hot dog. The man in the turban. And that Dr. Harper. None of them had a reason to be nice to Molly Picker, but they had been. They were her personal saints, her angels.

She thought of how nice it would be someday to have money. To slip a bundle of cash in an envelope and hand it to that man in the turban. Maybe he would be old by then. She would stick a note inside: *Thanks for the bread.* He would not remember her, of course. But she would remember him.

I won't forget. I'll never forget.

She came to a halt, her gaze focused on the building across the street. Beneath the large white cross were the words: MISSION SHELTER. WELCOME. Over the doorway a light shone, warm and inviting.

Molly stood momentarily transfixed by the vision of that light glowing in the drizzle, beckoning her to come out of the darkness. She felt a strange sense of happiness as she stepped off the curb and started across the street.

A voice called out: 'Molly?'

She froze. Her panicked gaze darted toward the sound. It was a woman's voice, and it came from a van parked near the church.

412

'Molly Picker?' the woman called. 'I want to help you.'

Molly took a step backward, on the verge of fleeing.

'Come here. I can take you to a warm place. A safe place. Won't you get in the van?'

Molly shook her head. Slowly she backed away, her attention focused so completely on the woman that she didn't hear the footsteps closing in behind her.

A hand clapped over her mouth, muffling her scream, yanking her head back with such force her neck felt as if it would snap. She smelled him, then – Romy, his aftershave gaggingly sweet.

'Guess who, Molly Wolly?' he murmured. 'I been chasing after you all fucking afternoon.'

Squirming, fighting, she was dragged across the street. The van door slid open and another pair of hands hauled her inside and shoved her to the floor, where her wrists and ankles were quickly bound with tape.

The van lurched forward, screeching away from the curb. As they passed under a streetlight, Molly caught a glimpse of the woman sitting a few feet away – a small woman with quick eyes and short dark hair. She lay her hand on Molly's swollen abdomen and gave a soft sigh of satisfaction, her smile like the rictus of a corpse.

'We should go back,' said Dvorak. 'We're not going to find her.'

They had been driving in circles for an hour, had

scanned every street in the neighborhood at least twice. Now they sat in her parked car, too weary to converse, their breath fogging the windows. Outside, the rain had finally stopped and puddles glistened in the road. *I hope she's safe*, thought Toby. *I hope she's somewhere warm and dry.*

'She knows the streets,' said Dvorak. 'She'll know enough to find shelter.' He reached over and squeezed her hand. They studied each other in the dark, both of them tired, but neither one quite ready to end the night.

He leaned toward her and had just touched his lips to hers when his pager went off.

'That could be about Molly,' she said.

He picked up her car phone. A moment later he hung up and sighed. 'It's not about Molly. But it does put an end to our evening.'

'Is it back to work for you?'

'Unfortunately. Could you drop me off? I need to get to an address right up this street.'

'What about your car?'

'I'll catch a ride back in the morgue van.'

She started the engine. They drove north, toward Chinatown, along streets wet and shimmering with the multicolored reflections of city lights.

Dvorak said: 'There – it's up ahead.'

She'd already spotted the flashing lights. Three Boston police cruisers were parked at haphazard angles by the curb outside a Chinese restaurant. A white morgue van with COMMONWEALTH OF

414

MASSACHUSETTS stenciled on the side was backing into Knapp Street.

She pulled to a stop behind one of the cruisers, and Dvorak stepped out.

'If you hear any news about Molly, will you call me?' she said.

'I will.' He gave her a smile, a wave, and walked toward the barrier of crime tape. A patrolman recognized him and waved him through.

Toby reached for the gearshift but then left it in park and sat back for a moment, watching the crowd that had gathered on the street. Even at midnight, the ranks of the curious had assembled. There was a bizarre frivolity in the air, two men slapping palms, women laughing. Only the cops looked grim.

Dvorak was standing just beyond the crime tape, conversing with a man in plainclothes. A detective. The man pointed toward an alley, then flipped through a notebook as he talked. Dvorak nodded, his gaze scanning the ground. Now the detective said something that made Dvorak glance up with a look of surprise. At that moment he seemed to notice that Toby was still parked. The detective stared as Dvorak abruptly walked away from him, ducked under the tape, and crossed back to Toby's car.

She rolled down the window. 'I just wanted to watch for a moment,' she said. 'I guess I'm as morbidly curious as the rest of these people. It's a strange crowd.'

'Yeah, it's always a strange crowd.'

'What happened in the alley?'

He leaned into the window. Quietly he said, 'They found a body. The ID says his name's Romulus Bell.'

She responded with a blank look.

'He goes by the name of Romy,' said Dvorak. 'It's Molly Picker's pimp.'

The body was sprawled on the pavement, almost hidden behind a parked blue Taurus. The left arm was bent under the body, the right was flung out, as if pointing toward the restaurant at the end of the alley. An execution, thought Dvorak, eyeing the bullet's entry wound in the corpse's right temple.

'No witnesses,' said Detective Scarpino. One of the older cops, close to retirement, he was famous for his bad hairpieces. Tonight, the pelt looked as if it had been slapped on backward in haste. 'Body was spotted about eleven-thirty by a couple coming out of that Chinese restaurant. That's their car.' Scarpino pointed to the blue Taurus. 'The upstairs tenant came into the alley to toss out some trash around ten o'clock or so, didn't see the body, so we're guessing it happened after ten. ID was in the victim's wallet. One of the patrolmen recognized the name. He'd talked to the victim yesterday, when he asked him about that girl you were looking for.'

'Bell was seen at Boston City Hospital around nine o'clock tonight.'

'Who saw him there?'

'The girl, Molly Picker. He came into her hospital room.' Dvorak pulled on a pair of latex gloves and bent down for a closer look at the corpse. The victim was in his early thirties, a slim man with straight black hair pomaded into an Elvis helmet. His skin was still warm; the arm that lay stretched out was tanned and muscular.

'If you'll excuse me for saying so, Doc, it just doesn't look right.'

'What doesn't?'

'You driving around with that doctor.'

Dvorak straightened and turned to face Scarpino. 'Excuse me?'

'She's under active investigation. The word I hear is, her mother's not going to make it.'

'What else have you heard?'

Scarpino paused, glancing up the alley at the crowd. 'That there's new evidence being developed. Alpren's guys are checking pharmacies around town. He's chasing something solid. If the mother dies, it goes to Homicide, and that makes this look *real* awkward. You and her, driving up to a crime scene together.'

Dvorak stripped off his gloves, suddenly furious at Scarpino. The hours he'd just spent with Toby Harper made him doubt she was capable of violence, much less violence against her own mother.

'Shit, there are reporters standing right over there,' said Scarpino. 'They all recognize you. And soon they'll know Dr. Harper's face as well. They'll remember seeing you two together and pow! Fucking front page.'

He's right, thought Dvorak. Which made him only angrier.

'It just doesn't look right,' Scarpino said, emphasizing every word.

'She hasn't been charged with a crime.'

'Not yet. You talk to AIpren.'

'Look, can we focus on this case?'

'Yeah, sure.' Scarpino threw a disgusted look at the corpse of Romulus Bell. 'I just thought I'd pass on a little advice, Doc. Guy like you doesn't need that kind of trouble. A woman who beats up on her own mother—'

'Scarpino, do me a favor.'

'Yeah?'

'Mind your own fucking business.'

Toby slept in Ellen's bed that night. After driving home from that garish scene in Chinatown, she'd walked into her house and felt she was entering an airless, silent chamber. She felt walled away. Buried.

In her own bedroom, she turned on the radio to a late-night classical station, playing it loudly enough to hear even in the shower. She desperately needed music, voices – anything.

By the time she came out of the bathroom, drying her wet hair with a towel, the music had sputtered to static. She turned it off. In the abrupt silence, she felt Ellen's absence as acutely as a physical pain.

She went down the hall, to her mother's room. She didn't turn on the light but simply stood in

418

the semidarkness, inhaling Ellen's scent, faintly sweet, like the summer flowers she so lovingly tended. Roses and lavender.

She opened the closet and randomly touched one of the dresses hanging there. Just by its texture she recognized it: her mother's linen summer shift, a dress so old that Toby could remember Ellen having worn it to Vickie's college graduation. And here it was, still hanging in the closet with all the other dresses Ellen had kept through the years. *When was the last time I took you shopping? I can't remember. I can't remember the last time I bought you a dress . . .*

She closed the closet door and sat down on the bed. She had changed the sheets several days ago, in hopeful anticipation of her mother's eventual return home. Now she almost wished she hadn't done so; all traces of her mother had been stripped away with the sheets, and now the bed smelled blandly of laundry soap. She lay down, thinking of the nights Ellen had occupied this same space. Wondering if the air itself had somehow been imprinted with the shadow of her presence.

She closed her eyes, inhaled deeply. And fell asleep.

Vickie's call awakened her at eight the next morning. It took eight rings before Toby managed to stumble to her own bedroom to pick up the phone. Half-drugged by sleep, she could barely focus on what her sister was trying to tell her.

'A decision has to be made, but I can't do it myself, Toby. It's just too much on my shoulders.'

'What decision?'

'Mom's ventilator.' Vickie cleared her throat. 'They're talking about turning it off.'

'No.' Toby came fully awake. '*No.*'

'They did the second EEG and they said it's just as—'

'I'm coming in. Don't let them touch a thing. Do you hear me, Vickie? Don't let them touch one goddamn thing.'

Forty-five minutes later, she walked into the ICU at Springer Hospital. Vickie was standing in Ellen's cubicle; so was Dr. Steinglass. Toby went straight to her mother's side and, bending down, whispered: 'I'm here, Mom. I'm right here.'

'The second EEG was done this morning,' said Dr. Steinglass. 'There's no activity. The new pontine hemorrhage was devastating. She has no spontaneous respirations, no—'

'I don't think we should talk about this in the room,' said Toby.

'I realize it's not easy to accept,' said Steinglass. 'But your mother can't comprehend anything we're saying right now.'

'I'm not going to discuss this. Not in here,' said Toby, and she walked out of the cubicle.

In the small ICU conference room, they sat at the table, Toby grim and silent, Vickie on the verge of tears. Dr. Steinglass, whom Toby thought of as competent but detached, looked uncomfortable in his new role of family crisis counselor.

'I'm sorry to raise this issue,' he said. 'But it really does need to be addressed. It's been four days now, and we've seen no improvement. Both EEG's show no activity. The hemorrhage was massive, and there's no brain function left. The ventilator is just . . . prolonging the situation.' He paused. 'I do believe it would be the kindest thing to do.'

Vickie looked at her sister, then back at Steinglass. 'If you really think there's no chance . . .'

'He doesn't know,' said Toby. 'No one does.'

'But she's suffering,' said Vickie. 'That tube in her throat – all those needles—'

'I don't want the ventilator shut off yet.'

'I'm only thinking about what Mom would want.'

'It's not your decision. You're not the one who takes care of her.'

Vickie shrank back in her chair, eyes wide with hurt.

Toby dropped her head in her hands. 'Oh God, I'm sorry. I didn't mean to say that.'

'I think you did mean to say it.' Vickie rose from her chair. 'All right, *you* make the decision, then. Since you seem to think *you're* the only one who loves her.' Vickie walked out.

After a moment, so did Dr. Steinglass.

Toby remained in the room with her head bowed, shaking with self-disgust and anger. At herself. At the woman who'd called herself Jane Nolan. *If I could just find you. If I could have just one goddamn moment alone with you.*

* * *

421

By that afternoon, she'd run out of both anger and adrenaline. She didn't have the energy to try reaching Dvorak again; she didn't feel like talking to anyone right now. In a chair by Ellen's bed, she leaned back and closed her eyes, but she could not shut out the image of her mother lying only a few feet away. With every whoosh of the ventilator bellows, she could picture quite clearly her mother's chest rising and falling. The lungs filling with air. The oxygen-rich blood streaming from the pulmonary alveoli to the heart, and then to the brain, where it would circulate, useless and unneeded.

She heard someone enter the cubicle, and she opened her eyes to see Dr. Steinglass standing at the foot of Ellen's bed. 'Toby,' he said quietly. 'I know it's hard for you. Nevertheless, we have to make the decision.'

'I'm not ready.'

'We're faced with a difficult situation here. The ICU beds are all full. If an MI comes in, we're going to need space.' He paused. 'We'll keep her on the ventilator until you make your decision. But you understand the position we're in.'

She said nothing. She only gazed at Ellen, thinking: *How frail she looks. Every day she seems to shrink even smaller.*

'Toby?'

She looked at Dr. Steinglass. 'I need a little longer. I need to be certain.'

'I could have the neurologist speak to you.'

'I don't need another opinion.'

'Maybe you do. Maybe—'

'Please, can't you just leave me *alone*?'

Dr. Steinglass took a step back, surprised by the anger in her voice. Beyond the doorway of the cubicle, several nurses were staring.

'I'm sorry,' said Toby. 'Give me some time. I need time. One more day.' She picked up her purse and walked out of the ICU, acutely aware, with every step she took, that the nurses were watching her.

Where do I go now? she wondered as she stepped into the elevator. *How do I fight back when I'm being attacked from all sides?*

The opposition had grown too many tentacles. Detective Alpren. Jane Nolan. Her old nemesis Doug Carey.

And Wallenberg. First she had embarrassed him by requesting that autopsy. Then she'd raised troubling questions about his two Creutzfeldt-Jakob patients. She'd made an enemy, certainly, but as far as she could tell, she'd caused him no serious damage.

So why has Brant Hill worked so hard to discredit me? What are they trying to hide?

The elevator stopped on the second floor to admit a pair of billing clerks just getting off work. Toby glanced at her watch and saw it was already past five; the weekend had officially begun. She caught a glimpse of the administrative hallway and suddenly had a thought.

She squeezed out of the elevator and walked up the hall to the medical library. The door was still unlocked, but the library was deserted for the day. She went to the reference computer and turned on the power.

The Medline search screen came on.

Under 'author's name' she typed in: Wallenberg, Carl.

The titles of five articles appeared, listed in reverse chronological order. The most recent one was three years old, and it had appeared in *Cell Transplant*: 'Vascularization after Cell-Suspension Neural Grafts in Rats.' There were two co-authors also credited, Gideon Yarborough, M.D., and Monica Trammell, Ph.D.

She was about to scroll down to the next article listing when her gaze paused on that name, Gideon Yarborough. She remembered the bald man at Robbie's funeral, tall and elegantly dressed, who had tried to intercede when she and Wallenberg were arguing. Wallenberg had called the man Gideon.

She went to the reference desk and pulled the *Directory of Medical Specialists* from the shelf. She found the name listed under the section for surgical specialists:

Yarborough, Gideon. Neurosurgery.
B.A. Biology, Dartmouth. M.D. Yale University.
Residency: Hartford Hospital, General Surgery; Peter Bent Brigham, Neurosurgery. Board Certified: 1988.
Postgraduate Fellowship: Rosslyn Institute for Research in Aging, Greenwich, Connecticut.

424

Currently practicing: Wellesley, Massachusetts,
Howarth Surgical Associates.

The Rosslyn Institute. It was the same research
facility where Wallenberg had once worked.
Robbie Brace had said Wallenberg left Rosslyn
after a falling-out with one of his fellow
researchers over a woman. A romantic triangle.

Had Yarborough been the other man?

She carried the *Directory of Medical Specialists*
back to the Medline computer, and this time she
typed in Yarborough under 'author's name.'

Several articles appeared, among them the one
she'd already noted from *Cell Transplant*. She
scrolled down to the first article published, dated
six years ago, and read the abstract. It described
experiments using rat fetal brain tissue fragments,
broken up into individual cells by the enzyme
trypsin, and then injected into the brains of adult
rats. The transplanted cells had thrived and
formed functioning colonies, complete with newly
grown blood vessels.

A chill had begun to creep up her spine.

She clicked on the next article, from *Journal of
Experimental Neurobiology*. Yarborough's co-
authors were names she didn't recognize. The
title was: 'Morpho-functional Integration of
Transplanted Embryonic Brain Tissue in Rats.'
There was no abstract attached.

She scrolled up to the next article titles:

'Mechanisms of Fetal Graft Communication
with Host Brain in Rats.'

'Optional Gestational Stage for Harvest of Fetal Rat Brain Cells.'

'Cryopreservation of Fetal Rat Brain Grafts.' An abstract was attached to this one. 'After cryopreservation in liquid nitrogen for ninety days, fetal mesencephalic brain cells showed significantly decreased survival as compared to fresh cells. For optimal graft survival, immediate transplant of freshly harvested fetal brain tissue is mandatory.'

She stared at that last phrase: *Freshly harvested-fetal brain tissue*.

By now the chill had spread all the way up to the nape of her neck.

She clicked on the most recent article, dated three years ago: 'Transplantation of Fetal Pituitary Grafts in Elderly Monkeys: Implications for Prolongation of Natural Life Spans.' The authors were Yarborough, Wallenberg, and Monica Trammell, Ph.D.

It was the last article they'd published; soon after, Wallenberg and his research partners had left Rosslyn. Was it their controversial research that had forced them out?

She rose and went to the library telephone. Her heart was racing as she dialed Dvorak's home phone number. The phone kept ringing, unanswered. She glanced up at the wall clock and saw it was five-forty-five. The answering machine clicked on, and then came a recording: *This is Dan. Please leave your name and number . . .*

'Dan, pick up,' said Toby. '*Please* pick up.' She

426

paused, hoping to hear a live voice, but no one came on. 'Dan, I'm in the Springer medical library, extension two five seven. There's something here on Medline you have to see. Please, *please* call me back right—'

The library door opened.

Toby turned to see the evening security guard poking his head into the room. He looked just as startled to see her as she was to see him.

'Ma'am, I have to lock up for the night.'

'I'm making a phone call.'

'You can finish the call. I'll wait.'

In frustration she simply hung up and walked out of the library. Only as she pushed into the stairwell did she remember she'd left the computer on.

Sitting in the parking lot, she used her car phone to call Dvorak's direct line in the medical examiner's office. Again, a recording came on. She hung up without leaving another message.

With a violent twist of the ignition she started the car and pulled out of the parking lot. Driving purely by habit, she headed toward home, her mind focused on what she'd just read on the Medline computer. Neural grafts. Fetal brain cells. Prolongation of the natural life span.

So this was the research Wallenberg had been working on at Rosslyn. His associate had been Gideon Yarborough, a neurosurgeon who now practiced in nearby Wellesley . . .

She turned into a gas station, ran inside, and asked the cashier for the Wellesley telephone directory.

In the Yellow Pages, under *Physicians*, she found what she was looking for:

Howarth Surgical Associates
A multispecialty group
1388 Eisley Street

Howarth. It was a name she'd remembered seeing in Harry Slotkin's medical record. When Robbie had brought her to Brant Hill to look at Harry's chart, they'd seen the name in the M.D. order sheet:

Preop Valium and six A.M. *van transport to Howarth Surgical Associates.*

She got back in her car and drove toward Wellesley.

By the time she reached the Howarth building, she was starting to put it all together, in a way that made horrifying sense.

She parked across the street from the building and gazed through the gloom at the nondescript two-story structure. It was heavily cloaked by shrubbery, with a small parking lot in front that was currently empty of cars. The upstairs windows were dark; downstairs, the entryway and reception area were lit but no movement could be seen inside.

Toby got out of the car and crossed the street to the front entrance. The doors were locked. On the window were stenciled the doctors' names:

Merle Lamm, M.D., Obstetrics and Gynecology
Lawrence Remington, M.D., General Surgery
Gideon Yarborough, M.D., Neurosurgery

Interesting, she thought. Harry Slotkin had been
sent here from Brant Hill, supposedly for a
deviated nasal septum. Yet none of these doctors
was an ear, nose, and throat specialist.

From somewhere in the building came the faint
whine of machinery. A furnace? A generator? She
couldn't identify the sound.

She circled around to the side of the building,
but dense shrubbery hid any view through the
windows. The low whine suddenly shut off, leaving absolute silence. She rounded the corner and
found a small paved lot at the rear of the building.
Three cars were parked there.

One of them was a dark blue Saab. *Jane
Nolan's.*

The building's rear entrance was locked.

Toby returned to her car and picked up the
phone. Again she tried calling Dvorak on his
direct office line. She didn't really expect him to
answer and was startled when his voice came on
with a brisk: 'Hello?'

Her words came out in a rush. 'Dan, I know
what Wallenberg's been doing. I know how his
patients are getting infected—'

'Toby, listen to me. You have to call your
attorney at once.'

'They're not injecting hormones. They're trans-
planting pituitary cells from fetal brains! But

429

something's gone wrong. Somehow they transmitted CJD. Now they're trying to cover it up – trying to hide the disaster before it becomes public—'

'*Listen* to me! You're in trouble.'

'What?'

'I just spoke to Alpren.' He paused. Quietly he said, 'They've issued a warrant for your arrest.'

For a moment she said nothing but simply stared at the building across the street. One step ahead, she thought. They're always one step ahead of me.

'This is what I think you should do,' he said. 'Call your attorney. Ask him to accompany you to the police station, Berkley Street headquarters. The case has been transferred there.'

'Why?'

'Because of your mother's . . . condition.'

Homicide was what he meant. It would soon be considered a homicide.

'Don't make Alpren arrest you at home,' said Dvorak. 'It'll just turn into a shark-feeding for the media. Come in voluntarily, as soon as you can.'

'Why did they issue the warrant? Why now?'

'They have new evidence.'

'What evidence?'

'Toby, just come in. I can meet you first, and we'll come in together.'

'I'm not going anywhere until I know what his evidence is.'

Dvorak hesitated. 'A pharmacist near your home says he filled a prescription for your mother.

430

Sixty tablets of Coumadin. He says you called in the prescription by telephone.'

'That's a lie.'

'I'm only telling you what the pharmacist said.'

'How does he know I made the call? It could have been another woman, claiming to be me. It could have been Jane. He wouldn't know.'

'Toby, we'll straighten it out, I promise. Right now your best move is to come in. Voluntarily, and without delay.'

'And then what? I spend the night in jail?'

'If you don't come in, it could be months in jail.'

'I didn't hurt my mother.'

'Then come in and tell it to Alpren. The longer you wait, the guiltier you'll seem. I'm here for you. Please, just come in.'

She felt too defeated to say a word, and too tired to consider all the tasks that now had to be done. Call an attorney. Talk to Vickie. Arrange for bills to be paid, the house to be watched over, the car to be picked up. And money – she would have to transfer money from her retirement savings. Attorneys were expensive . . .

'Toby, do you understand what you need to do?'

'Yes,' she whispered.

'I'm going to leave my office now. Where would you like to meet me?'

'The police station. Tell Alpren I'm coming in. Tell him not to send anyone to my house.'

'Whatever you wish. I'll be waiting for you.'

She hung up, her fingers numb from clutching the receiver. So now the storm finally breaks, she

431

thought. She sat preparing herself for the ordeal to follow. Fingerprints. Mug shots. Reporters. If only she could slink away somewhere and gather up her strength. But there was no time now; the police were expecting her.

She reached for the ignition and was about to turn the key when she glimpsed the flicker of headlights. Looking sideways, she saw Jane's Saab pull out of the Howarth driveway.

By the time Toby got her Mercedes turned around, the Saab had already glided out of sight around the corner. Frantic she'd lose it, she swerved around the corner. The Saab's rear lights came into view. At once Toby eased up on the gas, letting her quarry pull ahead just far enough to stay in sight. At the next intersection, it turned left.

Seconds later, so did Toby.

The Saab headed west, winding its way into the tonier sections of Wellesley. It wasn't Jane at the wheel, but a man; she could see his head silhouetted against the glare of oncoming head- lights. Completely focused on her quarry, Toby caught only glimpses of the neighborhood: iron gates and tall hedges and lights shining from many-windowed houses. The Saab picked up speed, the taillights receding into the night. A truck pulled onto the road from a cross street and slipped between Toby and the Saab.

In frustration, Toby blew her horn.

The truck slowed down and veered right. She shot past it, finally pulling in front of it.

The road ahead was empty.

Cursing, she scanned the darkness for a glimpse of taillights. She spotted them fading off to the right. The Saab had turned onto a private drive and was weaving through a dense stand of trees.

She slammed on the brakes and swerved onto the same road. Heart pounding, she braked to a stop and gave herself time to steady her nerves and allow her pulse to slow down. The Saab's taillights vanished beyond the trees, but she was no longer worried about losing it; this road seemed to be the only way on and off the property.

A mailbox was mounted at the entrance, the red flag up. She stepped out of the car and looked inside the box. There were two envelopes inside, utility payments. The name Trammell was on the return address.

She got back in her car and took a deep breath. With the headlights off, guided only by her parking lights, she drove slowly down the road. It wound through the trees in a gentle downhill grade. She rode the brakes all the way, letting the car glide at a crawl along sharp curves that were barely visible in the dim glow of the parking lights. The road seemed endless as it wound past thickets of evergreens. She could not see what lay at the end of the road; all she could make out was intermittent twinkles of light through the branches. Moving deeper into the lair of the enemy, she thought. Yet she didn't turn back; she was forced onward by all the pain and rage of these past few weeks. Robbie's death. Soon Ellen's, as well. *Get a life*, Wallenberg had sneered at her.

This is my life now. All that's left of it.

The road widened to a driveway. She pulled off to the side, her tires skidding across pine needles, and turned off the engine.

A mansion loomed ahead in the darkness. The upstairs windows were lit, and a woman's silhouette glided past one of them, then back again in agitated pacing. Toby recognized the profile.

Jane. Did she live here?

Toby gazed up at the massive roofline, which blotted out her view of half the stars in the sky. She could make out four chimneys, as well as the gleam of third-story windows. Was Jane a guest here? Or merely an employee?

A light-haired man appeared in the upstairs window – the driver of Jane's Saab. They spoke to each other. He glanced at his watch, then made a how-should-I-know? gesture with his arms. Now Jane seemed even more agitated, perhaps angry. She crossed the room and picked up a telephone.

Toby fished a penlight out of her medical bag and stepped out of her car.

The Saab was parked near the front porch. She wanted to find out who owned it, who Jane was working for. She crossed to the Saab and shone her penlight through the car window. The interior was clean, not even a stray scrap of paper in sight. She tried the passenger door and found it unlocked. In the glove compartment were the car's registration papers, made out to a Richard Trammell. She popped open the trunk lock and circled around to the rear of the car. Leaning forward, she played her penlight on the trunk's interior.

From behind her came the snap of twigs, the rustle of something moving through the underbrush. A low, threatening growl.

Toby whirled and saw the gleam of teeth as the Doberman sprang.

The force of its attack sent her sprawling. Instinctively she brought up her hands to protect her throat. The dog's jaws clamped down on her forearm, its teeth sinking straight to the bone. She screamed, flailing at him, but the Doberman would not release her. It began to whip its head back and forth, teeth ripping at flesh. Blinded by pain, she gripped the dog by the throat with her free hand and tried to choke it into releasing her, but its teeth seemed permanently embedded in her arm. Only when she clawed at its eyes did the dog give a yelp and release her.

She rolled free and scrambled back to her feet, blood streaming down her arm, and ran toward her car.

Again the Doberman lunged.

It slammed into her back, knocking her to her knees. This time its jaws caught only her shirt, teeth shredding fabric. She flung off the animal and heard it collide with the Saab. Too soon the Doberman was back on its feet and coiling for the third attack.

A man shouted, '*Down!*'

Toby staggered to her feet but never made it to the safety of her car. This time it was a pair of human hands that captured her and slammed her facedown against the hood of the Saab.

The Doberman was barking wildly, demanding to be allowed to make its kill.

Toby twisted and tried to squirm free. The last thing she saw was the flashlight beam, tracing an arc through the night. The blow caught her in the temple, flinging her sideways. She felt herself falling, tumbling into blackness.

Cold. It was very cold.

As though surfacing through icy waters, she drifted back toward consciousness. At first she couldn't feel her limbs; she had no sense of where they were, or even if they were still attached to her body.

A door thudded shut, releasing a strangely metallic series of echoes. The sound seemed to ring like a bell in Toby's head. She groaned and rolled onto her side. The floor felt like ice. Curling into a ball, she lay shivering as she struggled to think, to make her limbs respond. Her arm was hurting now, the pain gnawing its way through her numbness. She opened her eyes and winced as light pierced her retinas.

There was blood on her shirt. The sight of it shocked her fully awake. She focused on her shredded sleeve, soaked red.

The Doberman.

As the memory of those jaws flooded back, so did the pain, returning with such intensity she felt herself slipping back toward unconsciousness. She fought to stay awake. Rocking onto her back, she collided with a table leg. Something fell loose and swung above her head. She looked up and saw a naked arm hanging over the edge of the table, its fingers dangling just above her face.

Gasping, she rolled away and scrambled to her knees. The lightheadedness lasted only a few seconds, then cleared as the image came shockingly into focus.

There was a body on the table, covered by a plastic drape. Only the arm was visible, the skin a bluish white under the fluorescent lights.

Toby rose to her feet. She was still dizzy and had to reach out to a countertop to steady herself. She refocused on the body and saw there was another table in the room, with another plastic-draped form. A blast of refrigerated air rumbled from a vent. Slowly she took stock of her surroundings – the windowless walls, the heavy steel door – and she realized where she was. The foul odor alone should have told her.

It was a cold room, for the storage of corpses.

Focusing again on the dangling arm, she approached the table and pulled aside the drape.

The man was elderly, his dark brown hair showing silver roots. A bad dye job. His eyelids were open, revealing glazed blue eyes. She peeled back the rest of the drape and saw that the nude body was unmarred by any obvious injuries. The only bruises were on his arm, and she recognized them as the aftermath of IVs. Tucked between his ankles was a manila folder with a name written on the

437

cover: James R. Bigelow. She opened it and saw it was a medical record of the man's last week of life.

The first entry was dated November 1.

Subject observed to be clumsy during breakfast – poured milk on plate instead of cup – responded with look of confusion when asked if he needed help. Patient escorted to clinic for further eval.

On exam, mild tremors. Positive cerebellar findings. No other localizing signs.

Permanent transfer sequence initiated.

The note was unsigned.

She struggled to understand what she was reading, but her headache made every word a challenge. What did that last entry mean? Permanent transfer sequence?

She flipped forward, through the next few entries, to November 3.

Patient unable to walk without assistance. EEG results nonspecific. Tremors worse, cerebellar signs more pronounced. CT scan shows pituitary enlargement, no acute changes.

November 4:

Disoriented times two. Episode of startle myoclonus. Cerebellar function continues to deteriorate. All labs remain normal.

Then, the final entry, on November 7.

438

Patient in four-point restraints. Incontinent bowel and bladder. Twenty-four-hour IV fluids and sedation. Terminal stages. Autopsy to follow.

She lay the chart down on the man's bare thighs. For a moment she gazed at the body with strangely clinical detachment, noting the silver hairs on the chest, the wrinkles on the abdomen, the limp penis in its nest of wiry hair. Had he known the risks? she wondered. Had it occurred to him that trying to live forever would exact its costs?

The old are feeding on the young.

She swayed against the table, vision blurring from the pain throbbing in her head. It took her a moment to refocus her eyes. When she did, her gaze shifted to the other corpse.

She left the first table and went to stand beside the second body, still concealed beneath its drape. She drew away the shroud. Though she'd steeled herself, she was not prepared for the horror of what lay on that table.

The man's corpse had been flayed open, the rib cage and abdomen cleanly sliced down the center and spread apart, revealing a jumble of internal organs. Whoever had autopsied the corpse had removed the organs, then replaced them again with no concern for proper anatomy.

She backed away as nausea assailed her. The odor of this corpse told her it had been dead longer than the first one.

She forced herself to step back toward it, to

look at the plastic ID wristband. The name Phillip Dorr had been written in black marker. She saw no medical record, no documentation of the man's illness.

She forced herself to look at the face. It was another elderly man, eyebrows streaked with gray, the face strangely collapsed like a rubber mask. She noticed only then that the scalp had been slit behind the ear. The flap had sagged, exposing a pearly arc of skull. Gently she tugged on the hair, gingerly peeling the scalp forward.

The top of the cranium fell off and clattered onto the floor.

She gave a cry and jerked away.

The skull gaped open like an empty bowl. There was nothing inside; the brain had been removed.

Twenty

'She'll be here,' said Dvorak, watching Alpren tap a pencil on the desk. 'Just be patient.'

Detective Alpren looked at his watch. 'It's been two hours. I think you screwed up, Doc. You shouldn't have told her.'

'And you shouldn't jump to conclusions. This arrest warrant is premature. You haven't finished the preliminary investigation.'

'Yeah, I'm supposed to waste my time searching for the *real* Jane Nolan? I'd rather arrest the *real* Dr. Harper. If we can even find her now.'

'Give her a chance to walk in here on her own. Maybe she's waiting for her attorney. Maybe she went home to square things away.'

'She didn't go home. We sent a cruiser there half an hour ago. I think Dr. Harper's put pedal to the metal and skipped town. Right now she's probably a hundred miles away, thinking about ditching the car.'

Dvorak stared at the clock on the wall. He could not picture Toby Harper as a fugitive; she didn't seem like a woman who'd run, but someone who'd turn and fight back. Now he had to question his instincts, had to rethink everything he knew, or thought he knew about her.

Clearly Alpren took some measure of satisfaction from all this. Dvorak the M.D. had screwed up; this time the cop had proved a better judge of character. Dvorak sat in silence, anger balling up in his stomach, anger at Alpren for his smugness, at Toby for betraying his trust.

Alpren answered a ringing telephone. When he put it down again, he had a glitter in his eyes, hard and self-satisfied. 'They found her Mercedes.'

'Where?'

'Logan Airport. She left it parked in the passenger loading zone. Guess she was in a hurry to catch a plane.' He stood up. 'No reason to hang around any longer, Doc. She's not coming in.'

Dvorak drove home with his radio turned off, the silence only fueling his agitation. She ran, he thought, and there was only one explanation for it: a guilty conscience, and the certainty of punishment. Yet certain details continued to trouble him. He played out the sequence of actions that a fleeing Toby would have taken. She'd driven to Logan, where she'd abandoned her car in the loading zone, hurried into the terminal, and boarded a plane, destination unknown.

But this was not logical. Leaving a car in the loading zone was simply flagging attention to it. Anyone attempting a discreet escape would have parked their car in one of the crowded satellite lots, where it might go unnoticed for days.

So she didn't board a plane. Alpren might think she was that stupid, but Dvorak knew better. The detective was wasting his time, checking the flights out of Logan.

She must be fleeing some other way.

When Dvorak walked in his front door, he headed straight for the telephone. He was angry now, stung by Toby's betrayal, and by his own stupidity. He picked up the receiver to call Alpren, then put it down again when he noticed his answering machine was blinking. He hit Play.

The electronic voice gave the message time as five forty-five. Toby's voice came on:

'I'm in the Springer medical library, extension two five seven. There's something here on Medline you have to see. Please, *please* call me back right . . .'

The last time they'd spoken was around seven-thirty, so this phone message had preceded their final conversation. He remembered she'd been trying to tell him something, that he'd cut her off before she could explain what she'd found.

Springer medical library . . . something here on Medline you have to see. Please, please call me back . . .

The pain came on like a fist crushing her abdomen, squeezing so tight it choked off any groan. Eyes closed, teeth gritted, Molly closed her hands into fists and strained against the wrist straps. Only when the contraction had ended did

443

she release a whimper of relief. She had not expected childbirth to be so silent. She had imagined herself screaming, and loudly too, had assumed that pain was a noisy affair. But when it came, when she felt the first ripples of another contraction, and then the seizing up of her womb, she bore it without uttering a sound, wanting not to scream but simply to curl up and hide in the dark.

But *they* would not leave her alone.

There were two of them, both dressed in blue surgical gowns, only their eyes visible in the narrow gap between mask and cap. A man and a woman. Neither one spoke to Molly; to them, she was an object, a dumb animal on the table, her thighs spread, her legs strapped on elevated leg rests.

At last the contraction eased, and as the haze of pain cleared, Molly became aware, once again, of her surroundings. The lights, like three blinding suns shining overhead. The hard gleam of the IV pole. The plastic tube that had been threaded into her vein.

'Please,' she said. 'It hurts. It hurts so much . . .'

They ignored her. The woman's attention was focused on the bottle dripping into the IV, the man's on Molly's parted thighs. Had he worn even the vaguest expression of lust, Molly would have felt some measure of control, some measure of power. But she saw no desire in his gaze.

Another contraction began to build. She jerked on the wrist straps, straining to curl up on her side, pain suddenly translating to fury. Enraged, she jerked back and forth, and the table shook with the rattle of steel.

'The IV's not going to last,' said the woman. 'Can't we put her under?'

The man answered: 'We'll lose the contractions. No anesthesia.'

'Let me *go*!' screamed Molly.

'I don't want to put up with this noise,' said the woman.

'Then dial up the Pitocin and let's get the god-damn thing expelled.' He bent forward, his gloved fingers probing between Molly's thighs.

'Let ... me ... go!' gasped Molly, her voice suddenly dying as the wave of pain broke and washed over her. The insertion of the man's fingers at that moment intensified the agony, and she closed her eyes, tears trickling down her face.

'Cervix is fully dilated,' the man said. 'Almost there.'

Molly's head lurched forward, and she gave an anguished grunt.

'Good, she's bearing down. Do it. Come on, girl. Push.'

Molly forced out the words: 'Fuck you.'

'Push, goddamn it, or we'll have to get it out some other way.'

'Fuck you, fuck you, fuck you . . .'

The woman slapped Molly across the face, the blow so brutal Molly's head snapped sideways. For a few seconds she lay stunned and mute, her cheek ringing, her vision dimmed. The pain of the contraction faded away. She felt hot liquid seep from her vagina, heard it drip, drip onto the paper drape beneath her buttocks. Then her vision cleared and she focused again on the man. And realized that what she saw in his face was expectation. Impatience.

They are waiting to take my baby.

'Increase the Pitocin,' said the man. 'Let's finish this.'

The woman flicked up the dial on the IV, and a moment later, Molly felt another contraction begin to build, this one accelerating so fast and so hard it shocked her by its violence. Her head lifted off the table, face straining toward her chest as she pushed. Blood gushed from between her legs; she heard it splatter the surgical drape.

'Push. Come on, *push*!' the woman commanded.

The pain crescendoed to unbearable heights. Molly gasped in a deep breath, and again strained. Her vision blackened. New pain suddenly exploded in her head. She heard herself cry out, but the sound was foreign to her, like the shriek of a dying animal.

'That's it. Come on, come on . . .' said the man.

She pushed one last time, and felt the agony between her legs suddenly give way to the pain of tearing flesh.

And then, mercifully, it was over.

Groggy, clammy with sweat, she could neither move nor utter a sound. Perhaps she fell asleep – she wasn't sure. She knew only that time had passed and there was movement in the room. The sound of splashing water, a cabinet clanging shut. It took great effort, but slowly she opened her eyes.

At first the glare of light was all she saw, the trio of bright suns shining directly overhead. Then she focused on the blurred image of the man, standing near her opened thighs, and on what he was holding in his hands.

It had hair, coarse black tufts of it clotted with blood. The flesh was pink and formless, like a clump of butchered meat lying limp in the man's gloved hands. It moved. Only a quiver at first, then a violent shudder, the flesh balling up, the hair stiffening like the fur of a startled cat.

'Primitive muscle function,' said the man. 'And we still have rudimentary follicular and dentate structures. Haven't eliminated the appendages yet, either.'

'Saline bath's ready.'

'Are we all set up next door?'

'Our patient's positioned on the table. We just need the tissue.'

'Let me get a weight on this.' The man rose and lay the clump of flesh on a table scale not far from Molly's head.

Molly stared. A single eye, lidless, soulless, stared back at her.

Her scream shattered into a thousand piercing echoes. Again and again she screamed, her horror swelling with the sound of her own voice.

'We have to shut her up!' the woman said. 'The patient might hear it!'

The man clapped a rubber mask over Molly's mouth and nose, and Molly caught a whiff of noxious gas. She jerked her face away. He grabbed her by the jaw and tried to force her to hold still, to breathe in the fumes. Molly caught the man's little finger in her teeth and bit down like a panicked animal. The man shrieked.

A blow slammed into Molly's temple with such force a hundred bright lights seemed to explode in her head.

'Bitch! Fucking bitch!' the man gasped.

'My God, your finger—'

'The syringe. Get the syringe!'

'What?'

'The potassium. Do it *now*.'

Slowly Molly opened her eyes. She saw the woman standing over her, holding a syringe and needle. She saw the needle pierce the rubber dam on the IV line.

What felt like a line of fire slowly burned its way up Molly's arm. In pain, she cried out and tried to pull free, but the strap held her wrist in place.

'All of it,' the man snapped. 'Give her the whole fucking thing.'

The woman nodded. She squeezed down on the syringe.

The count was extraordinary. Embedded in swirls of fetal brain tissue were at least thirty-three separate pituitary glands, more than any previous embryonic implant had produced. The cells appeared healthy and disease free under the microscope, and the girl's blood tests had all been normal. They could not allow any infections to be transmitted. They had made that mistake with their first group of recipients, when they'd used intact fetuses harvested from the hired wombs of women in a poor Mexican village. A village where the cattle were already dying.

This tissue had been grown from a genetically altered embryo started in his own lab. He knew it was clean.

Dr. Gideon Yarborough dissected out three of the glands and dropped them into a vial of trypsin warmed to thirty-seven degrees Centigrade. The rest of the fetus – if one could call the clump of flesh a fetus – was rinsed and placed in a jar of buffered Hanks' balanced salt solution. It bobbed in the liquid, and the blue eye surfaced, staring up at him. There was no functioning brain behind that eye, and no soul, nevertheless it gave Yarborough the willies. He covered the jar and set it aside. Later, he would harvest the remaining pituitaries. It was a valuable crop; there would be enough to implant ten patients.

Twenty minutes had passed.

He rinsed the vial containing the three pituitaries with salt solution. By now the trypsin had broken up the tissue and turbid liquid swirled in the vial, which no longer contained solid pituitaries but individual cells in suspension. The building blocks of a new master gland. Gently he aspirated the suspension into a syringe, then he carried it into the next room, where his assistant was waiting for him.

The patient, lightly sedated with Valium, lay on the table. A seventy-eight-year-old man in satisfactory health who'd been feeling his age. Who wanted his youth back and was willing to pay for it, willing to endure a minor measure of discomfort for a chance at rejuvenation.

Now the man lay with his head aligned in a Todd-Wells stereotaxic frame, his skull fixed in place. The amplified image taken by an X-ray tube was projected onto a fifteen-inch television. On the screen was a view of the sella turcica, the small bony well containing the patient's aging pituitary gland.

Yarborough sprayed a local anesthetic into the man's right nostril and swabbed it with cocaine solution. Then he inserted a long needle up the right nostril and injected more anesthetic into the mucous membrane.

The patient gave a murmur of discomfort.

'I'm just numbing up the area, Mr. Luft. You're doing fine.' He handed the syringe of anesthetic to his assistant.

And picked up the drill.

It had a simple twist bit, almost needle-fine. He inserted this up the nostril. With the image on the screen to guide him, Yarborough began to drill through bone, the bit whining through the floor of the sphenoid bone. As it broke through the other side, piercing the dura propria, the membrane lining the pituitary, the patient gave a sharp cry, his muscles tensing.

450

'It's all right, Mr. Luft. That's the worst part of it. The pain should last only a few seconds.'

As he predicted, the patient slowly relaxed, his discomfort passing. Piercing the dura always caused that brief jolt of pain in the forehead. It did not worry Yarborough.

His assistant handed him the syringe containing the ceil suspension.

Through the newly drilled hole in the sphenoid bone, Yarborough introduced the needle tip. Gently he injected the syringe contents into the sella turcica. He pictured the cells swirling into their new home, growing, multiplying into healthy new colonies. Cell factories pumping out the hormones of a young brain. Hormones Mr. Luft himself could no longer produce.

He withdrew the needle. There was no bleeding; a good, clean procedure.

'It went perfectly fine,' he told the patient. 'Now we're going to remove the head frame. We'll have you lie here for a half hour or so while we watch your blood pressure.'

'That's it?'

'It's all done. You sailed through with flying colors.' He nodded to his assistant. 'I'll stay and watch him. I'll call the van when he's ready to go back to Brant Hill.'

'What do we do about . . .' His assistant glanced toward the door. Toward the other room.

Yarborough stripped off his gloves. 'I'll take care of that too, Monica. You go back to the house and deal with the other problem.'

451

The thermometer on the wall registered thirty-five degrees Fahrenheit.

Toby huddled in a corner, her knees bent to her chest, a plastic sheet draped over her shoulders. It was a corpse's shroud, and the smell of Formalin permeated the fabric. At first it had repelled her, and she had felt nauseated by the thought of stripping the sheet off one of the dead bodies for her own use. But then she'd started shaking from the cold and she knew she had no choice. It was the only way to conserve body heat.

But it wasn't enough to keep her alive. Hours had passed, and her hands and feet had lost all feeling. At least her arm had stopped aching. But she was having trouble thinking, her mental processes slowed to the point where she could not focus on anything except staying awake.

Soon, though, she lost the will to manage even that.

Gradually her head sagged to the floor and her limbs fell limp. Twice she shook herself awake and found she was lying on her side and that the lights were still shining. After that, she slept.

And dreamed. Not in images, but in sounds. There were two people speaking – a man and Jane Nolan – their voices distorted, metallic. She felt herself floating through black liquid, felt a welcome rush of warmth against her face.

Then she was falling.

She jerked awake to find herself lying on her side in darkness. There was a carpet beneath her cheek. A faint blade of light cut through the shadows and a door squealed shut. She tried to move but found she could not; her hands were bound together behind her back. Her feet felt numb and useless. She heard another door shut, and then the sound of a car engine starting up.

A man said, 'Shouldn't you latch the gate?'

The answering voice was Jane Nolan's: 'I've tied up the dog. He won't get out. Let's just go.'

They began to drive up a bumpy road. The road from the house, thought Toby. Where were they taking her?

A sudden jolt of the van slammed her left shoulder against the floor, and she almost cried out in pain. She was lying on her injured arm, and the merciful numbness from the cold room was now wearing off. With a burst of effort she twisted and managed to roll onto her back, but she now found herself wedged up against something cold and rubbery. Light had begun to filter through the darkness from street lamps and passing cars. She turned her head to see what she had bumped up against and found herself staring into the face of one of the corpses.

Toby's shocked gasp drew the attention of her captors. The man said, 'Hey, she's awake.'

'Just keep driving,' said Jane. 'I'll tape her mouth.' She unbuckled her seat belt and crawled to the rear of the van. There she knelt beside Toby and fumbled in the semidarkness with a roll of surgical tape. 'Didn't think we'd have to hear from you again.'

Toby strained to free her hands but could not

loosen the bonds. 'My mother – you hurt my mother—'

'It's your fault, you know,' said Jane, peeling off a strip of tape. 'So obsessed, Dr. Harper. Too busy worrying about a few old men. You didn't even notice what was going on in your own home.' She slapped the tape over Toby's mouth and said, in mock disgust: 'And you call yourself a good daughter.'

Bitch, thought Toby. *You murdering bitch*.

Jane clucked as she peeled off a second strip of tape. 'I didn't *want* to hurt your mother. I was only there to keep an eye on you. Find out how far you were pushing it. But then Robbie Brace called your house that night, and everything got completely out of hand . . .' She slapped a second strip of tape over Toby's mouth. 'Then it was too late for you to have an accident. Too late to shut you up. People are so willing to believe the dead.' She tore off a final piece of tape and pressed it across Toby's face, ear to ear. 'But will they believe a woman who'd hurt her own mother? I don't think so.' She gazed down at Toby for a moment, as though evaluating her handiwork. In the van's semidarkness, cut only by the occasional gleam of passing headlights, Jane's eyes seemed to take on a glow of their own. How many times had Ellen awakened to find those same eyes staring down at her? *I should have known. I should have sensed the evil in my home.*

The van made an abrupt turn, and Jane reached out to steady herself.

No, her name is not Jane, thought Toby with sudden comprehension. *Her name is Monica Trammell.* Wallenberg's associate at the Rosslyn Institute.

The van swayed as it moved down a winding drive. The pavement gave way to the unevenness of a dirt road, and Toby could feel the old man's corpse bouncing against her, his flesh clapping against hers. They braked to a stop, and the side door slid open.

A man stood silhouetted against the moonless sky. 'Gideon's not here yet,' the man said. It was Carl Wallenberg's voice.

The woman climbed out of the van. 'He has to be here for this. We all have to be here.'

'The patient needed stabilizing. Gideon's staying with him.'

'We can't do this without him. This time the responsibility has to be shared, Carl. All of us equally. Richard and I have done too much already.'

'I don't want to do this.'

'You have to. Is the hole dug?'

The answer came out a sigh: 'Yes.'

'Then let's finish it.' The woman turned to the driver, who'd already climbed out of the van. 'Get them out, Richard.'

The driver grabbed Toby's bound feet and dragged her halfway out. As Wallenberg took hold of her shoulders, Toby squirmed.

He almost dropped her. 'Jesus Christ! She's still *alive.*'

'Just move her,' said Monica.

'My God, do we have to do it this way?'

'I didn't bring the syringes. This way is bloodless. I don't want any evidence splattered around.'

Wallenberg took a few deep breaths, then once again grasped Toby's shoulders. The two men swung her from the van and carried her through the night. At first Toby had no idea where they were bringing her. She knew only that the ground was uneven, that the men were having trouble navigating in the darkness. She caught glimpses of Richard Trammell's head, his hair white-blond under the moonlight, then she saw sky and the shadow of a construction crane arching across the field of stars. Turning her head, she noticed lights shining through the filter of a fence, and she recognized the building in the distance: the Brant Hill nursing facility. They were carrying her into the foundation pit of another new building.

Wallenberg stumbled and lost his grip on Toby's shoulders. She fell, her head thudding to the dirt so hard it slammed her jaws together. Pain sliced her tongue, and she tasted blood, felt it pooling in her mouth.

'Jesus,' Wallenberg muttered.

'Carl,' said Monica, her voice flat and metallic. 'Just get it over with.'

'Fuck this. *You* do it!'

'No, it's your turn. This time *your* hands get dirty. And Gideon does too. Now finish it.'

Wallenberg took a deep breath. Once again Toby was lifted and carried, squirming, into the pit. The two men came to a stop. Toby looked straight up into Wallenberg's face, but she could not see his expression against the moonlit sky. She saw only a dark oval, a fluttering of windblown hair as he swung her sideways, then released her.

Though she'd steeled herself for the landing, the sudden impact slammed the breath from her lungs. For a moment she saw only blackness. Gradually her vision returned. She saw a bowl of stars suspended above her and realized she was lying at the bottom of a hole. A sprinkling of dirt tumbled in from the side, stinging her eyes. She jerked her head sideways and felt gravel against her cheek.

The two men walked away. *Now*, she thought. *My one and only chance*. She fought to free herself, twisting one way, then another, dirt spilling on top of her as she thrashed against the wall of the pit. No good; her wrists and ankles were too tightly bound, and her struggles only resulted in making her hands numb. But one corner of the tape had begun to peel off her cheek. She rubbed her face against the gravel, scraping her skin raw as more of the tape lifted away.

Hurry. Hurry.

She was coughing and choking on clouds of dust. Another inch of tape peeled off, freeing her lips. She took a breath and screamed.

A figure appeared above the pit, staring down at her. 'No one can hear you,' said Monica. 'It's quite a deep hole. Tomorrow it'll be gone, smoothed over. Tomorrow they pour the gravel. Then the foundation.' She turned as the men reappeared, carrying one of the corpses. They threw it in, and it landed beside Toby, the man's head thudding against her shoulder. She recoiled against the far side of the pit, and fresh dirt sprinkled onto her face.

So this is how it ends. Three skeletons in a hole. A concrete slab to seal us in.

The men left to get the second corpse.

Again Toby screamed for help, but her voice seemed lost in that deep pit.

Monica crouched at the side of the hole, staring down. 'It's a cold night. Everyone's closed their windows. They can't hear a thing, you know.'

Toby screamed again.

Monica dropped a handful of dirt on her face. Coughing, Toby twisted sideways and found herself staring at the corpse. Monica was right. No one was listening; no one would hear her.

The men returned, both breathing heavily from exertion. They threw the last body into the pit.

It landed on top of Toby, the shroud flapping across her face, covering it. She could barely move under the weight of the corpse, but she could hear voices above her, and the sound of a shovel scraping through dirt.

The first scoop of soil fell into the pit. It landed on Toby's legs. She tried to shake it off, but then another shovelful fell, and another.

'Wait for Gideon,' said Monica. 'He has to be part of this.'

'He'll be here to finish up. Let's just get it over

with,' said her husband. He grunted, and a fresh load of dirt fell onto the top corpse, soil trickling onto Toby's hair. Again she tried to move under the corpse's weight. The shroud slipped down, uncovering her eyes. She stared straight up at the three figures standing around the pit. They seemed to sense that she was watching them, and they fell momentarily silent.

Monica said, 'All right. Fill it in now.'

Toby cried out, 'No!' but her voice was muffled by the fabric. By the weight of the corpse.

Dirt tumbled down. She blinked against the sting of grit. Another shovel of earth fell onto her hair, then more dirt, rivers of it spilling around her body, covering her limbs. She struggled to move, but the corpse, and the steadily falling soil, trapped her in place. She heard her own heartbeat roaring in her ears, heard gasps of air rushing through her lungs. She caught one final glimpse of stars as she burrowed her face under the cover of the shroud.

Then her head was buried, and she saw no light at all.

Twenty-One

It was his turn to wield the shovel.

Carl Wallenberg's hands were shaking as he gripped the handle and scooped up the first bladeful of earth. He paused at the edge of the pit, staring down into its darkness, thinking about the woman, still alive. Heart still beating, blood still pumping. A million neurons firing off in the panicked throes of death. Beneath that blanket of soil, she was dying.

He threw his load of dirt into the pit and scooped up another. He heard Monica's murmur of approval, and silently he cursed her for forcing him into this appalling act. This was the last evidence to be disposed of, the last two corpses to be covered up from an experiment gone horrifyingly wrong.

We should have been more careful with the donors. We should have screened the fetal material for more than just bacteria and viruses. We never considered the possibility of prions.

But Yarborough had been in a rush to implant

the cells. The tissue had to be fresh, he'd insisted. The cell suspensions had to be implanted within seven days of harvest or they would not survive in the brains of the new hosts. They would not colonize. And then there'd been that long waiting list of eager recipients, three dozen men and women who'd paid their deposits, who were clamoring for their second chance at youth. Risk free, they'd been assured. And it was, in truth, a benign procedure: a local anesthetic, the X-ray guided injection of fetal pituitary cells into the brain, and weeks later, the slow rejuvenation of the master gland. He and Gideon had done it dozens of times, without complications, right up until Rosslyn had shut down the project on moral grounds. If not for the necessity of using aborted human fetuses, the procedure would have been hailed as a medical breakthrough. A fountain of youth, distilled from the brains of the unborn and unwanted.

A breakthrough, yes. But one that would be forever shunned because of the politics.

He paused, breathing hard, his sweat already chilling his skin. The hole was nearly filled. By now the woman's lungs would be choking with dust, her brain cells starved of oxygen. The heart pumping its last desperate beats. He disliked Toby Harper, he agreed she needed to be silenced, but he wished her a merciful death, one that would not haunt him in the years to come.

He had never intended to kill anyone.

A few fetuses had been sacrificed, true, but only at the beginning. Now they were using cloned tissue, scarcely human at all, implanted and nurtured in wombs. He did not feel guilty about the tissue's source. Neither did his patients feel any qualms; they simply *wanted* it, and they were willing to pay for it. As long as Brant Hill knew nothing about it, his work would go on, and the private flow of money would continue.

But then Mackie had died, followed by the others. Now it wasn't just the money he could lose; it was his position, his reputation. His future.

Is it worth committing murder for?

Even as he continued to shovel dirt into the rapidly filling hole, he was painfully aware that the woman below was dying. *But then, we are all dying. Some of us more horribly than others.*

He set the shovel down. He was going to be sick.

'More dirt. Make it level,' said Monica. 'It has to blend in. We can't have the construction crew noticing.'

'You do it.' He thrust the shovel toward her. 'I've done enough.'

She took the shovel and studied him for a moment. 'Yes, I suppose you have,' she finally said. 'And now you're in just as deep as Richard and me.' She paused, her shoe on the shovel, and prepared to scoop up another bladeful of soil.

'There's Yarborough,' said Richard.

Wallenberg turned and saw headlights approaching. Yarborough's black Lincoln bounced onto the dirt road and braked to a stop at the construction fence. The driver's door opened and slammed shut again.

A bright light came on, its beam flooding the construction pit. Wallenberg stumbled backward, shielding his eyes from the sudden glare. He heard the frantic grinding of other tires over gravel, then heard two more car doors slam shut, and the sound of running footsteps.

He squinted as the silhouettes suddenly appeared before the floodlights. *Not Yarborough*, he thought. *Who are you?*

Two men walked toward them.

Fresh air flooded her lungs, so cold it seared her throat. She gasped in another breath, and another, wheezing in air between coughs. Something was pressed against her face, and she fought to escape it, thrashing out at the hands trapping her head. She heard voices, too many voices to keep track of, all of them talking at once.

'Get that oxygen back on her!'

'She's fighting—'

'Hey, I need a pair of hands here! I can't get the IV in.'

She twisted, clawing blindly. There was a light shining in the distance, and she fought to tear her way through the darkness, to reach the light before it vanished. But her arms felt paralyzed; something was pressing them down. The air she breathed in smelled of rubber.

'Toby – stop fighting us!' She felt a hand grasp hers as though to drag her from the darkness.

A black curtain suddenly seemed to tear apart

before her eyes and she surfaced into a stream of light. She saw faces staring down at her. Saw more lights now, blue and red, dancing in a circle. *Beautiful*, she thought. *The colors – so very beautiful*. Static crackled in the night. A police radio.

'Doc, you'd better come and see this,' one of the cops said.

Dvorak didn't respond; his gaze was focused on the ambulance, taillights shuddering as the vehicle drove up the dirt road, bearing Toby to Springer Hospital. She should not be alone tonight, he thought. I should be with her; it's where I want to be. Where I want to stay.

He turned to the cop and realized his legs were not quite steady, that in fact he was still shaking. The night had taken on a crazy neon quality. All the cruisers, all the lights. And there were on-lookers gathered outside the construction fence – the expected crime scene groupies, but this was an older crowd, residents of Brant Hill who'd heard the multiple sirens and, curious, had wandered out into the night still dressed in their bathrobes. They stood in a solemn line, staring through the mesh of the fence into the foundation pit, where the two bodies had been uncovered and now lay exposed on the dirt.

'Detective Sheehan's waiting for you up there,' the cop said. 'He's the only one who's touched it.'

'Touched what?'

'The body.'

'Another one?'

'I'm afraid so.'

Dvorak followed the cop out of the foundation pit, both of them stumbling their way up to the fence.

'It was in the trunk of the car,' the cop panted as he climbed.

'Which car?'

'Dr. Yarborough's Lincoln. The one we followed here from the Howarth building. Looks like he was bringing a last-minute addition to the burial. We sure didn't expect to see *that* when we popped open his trunk.'

They walked past the gathering of elderly onlookers and crossed to Yarborough's car, parked by the fence. Detective Sheehan was standing beside the open trunk. 'Tonight they come in threes,' he said.

Dvorak shook his head. 'I'm not sure I can handle much more of this tonight.'

'You feeling okay, Doc?'

Dvorak paused, thinking about the night that lay ahead. About the hours it would take him to reach Toby's bedside. The delay could not be helped; this he had to do.

He took a pair of latex gloves from his pocket. 'Let's get on with this,' he said and looked into the trunk.

Sheehan trained his flashlight beam on the face of the corpse.

For a moment Dvorak could not say a word. He stood gazing at the girl's face, at the bruise marring that fragile skin, at the gray eyes, open and soulless. Once there had been a soul there; once he had seen it, shining brightly. *Where are you now?* he wondered. *Somewhere good, I hope. Somewhere warm and kind and safe.*

He reached down and, gently, closed Molly Picker's eyes.

The sound of nurses laughing in the hallway roused Dvorak from a fitful sleep. He opened his eyes and saw daylight shining in the window. He was sitting in a chair by Toby's hospital bed. She was still asleep, her breathing slow and steady, her cheeks flushed. Most of the dirt had been wiped away from her face last night, but he could still see a few grains of sand sparkling in her hair.

He rose and stretched, trying to work the kinks out of his neck. At last a sunny day, he thought, staring out the window. Only the smallest wisp of a cloud drifted in the sky.

Behind him, a voice murmured: 'I had the worst nightmare.'

Turning, he met Toby's gaze. She held out her hand to him. He took it warmly in his and sat down beside her.

'But I didn't dream it, did I?' she said.

'No. I'm afraid it was all too real.'

She lay silent for a moment, frowning, as though trying to gather all her fragments of memory into one comprehensible whole.

'We found their medical records,' said Dvorak.

She looked at him, her eyes questioning.

'They kept data on all the brain implants. Seventy-nine files, stored in the basement of the Howarth building. Patient names, operative notes, follow-up head scans.'

'They were compiling data?'

He nodded. 'To back up their claims of success. By the look of it, the implants did have benefits.'

'And hazards too,' she added softly.

'Yes. There was a cluster of patients early last year, when Wallenberg was still using aborted fetuses. Five men received their implants from the same pooled fetal cells. They were all infected at the same time. It took a year for the first one to come down with symptoms.'

'Dr. Mackie?'

He nodded.

'You said there were seventy-nine files. What about all the other patients?'

'Alive and well. And thriving. Which presents a moral dilemma. What if this treatment really does work?'

By her troubled expression, he knew she shared his concerns. *How far do we go to prolong life? How much of our humanity do we sacrifice?*

She said, suddenly, 'I know where to find Harry Slotkin.' She looked at him with startling clarity in her eyes. 'Brant Hill – the new nursing home wing. A few weeks ago, they poured the foundation.'

'Yes, Wallenberg told us.'

'Wallenberg did?'

'They're at each others' throats now. Wallenberg and Gideon against the Trammells. lt's a race to pin the blame. Right now, the Trammells seem to be in the worst trouble.'

Toby paused, gathering the courage to ask the next question. 'Robbie?'

'It was Richard Trammell. The gun was registered to him. We expect ballistics will confirm it.'

She nodded, absorbing the painful information in silence. He saw tears flash in her eyes and decided he would wait to tell her about Molly. This was not the time to burden her with yet more tragedy.

There was a knock on the door, and Vickie stepped into the room. She looked paler than she had last night, when Dvorak had seen her visiting Toby. Paler and strangely afraid. She paused a few feet away from the bed, as though reluctant to approach.

Dvorak stood up. 'I think I'll leave you two alone,' he said.

'No. Please,' said Vickie. 'You don't have to go.'

'I'm not going anywhere.' He bent down and gave Toby a kiss. 'But I will wait outside.' He straightened and crossed to the door.

There he paused.

Glancing back, he saw Vickie suddenly break free of some invisible restraint. In three swift steps she crossed to the bed and took Toby into her arms.

Dvorak brushed his hand across his eyes. And quietly left the room.

Two Days Later

The ventilator delivered its twenty breaths per minute, each whoosh followed by a sigh, the deflation of ribs and chest wall. Toby had found the rhythm soothing as she combed her mother's hair and bathed her limbs and torso, the washcloth gliding across landmarks she had come to know so well. The star-shaped patch of pigment on the left arm. The biopsy scar on the breast. The arthritic finger, bent in a shepherd's crook. But this scar on the knee – how did Ellen get it? Toby wondered. It looked like a very old scar, well healed, almost invisible, its origins lost in the forgotten reaches of her mother's childhood. Gazing at it under the bright lights of the ICU cubicle, she thought: All these years Mom has had this scar, and I never noticed it until now.

'Toby?'

She turned and saw Dvorak standing in the cubicle doorway. Perhaps he'd been there for some time; she hadn't noticed his arrival. That was simply Dvorak's way. In the day and a half she'd been hospitalized, Toby would awaken and think she was alone. Then she'd turn her head and see that he was still sitting in her room, silent and unnoticed, watching over her. As he was doing now.

'Your sister's just arrived,' he said. 'Dr. Steinglass is on his way upstairs.'

Toby looked down at her mother. Ellen's hair was splayed across the pillow. It looked not like the hair of an old woman but the luxurious mane of a young girl, bright as windblown sheets of silver. Toby bent down and touched her lips to Ellen's forehead.

'Good night, Mom,' she whispered, and walked out of the cubicle.

On the other side of the viewing window, she took her place beside Vickie. Dvorak stood behind them, his presence felt though unseen. Through the glass they watched Dr. Steinglass enter the cubicle and cross to the ventilator. He glanced at Toby, a silent question in his eyes.

She nodded.

He turned off the ventilator.

Ellen's chest fell still. Ten seconds passed in silence.

Vickie reached for Toby's hand, held on tight.

Ellen's chest remained motionless.

Now her heart was slowing. First a pause. A stumbled beat. Then, at last, the final stillness.

From the moment we're born, death is our final destination, thought Toby. *Only the date and time of our arrival is unknown.*

For Ellen, the journey was completed at two-fifteen, on this afternoon in late autumn.

For Daniel Dvorak, death might come in two years or in forty years. It might be heralded by the tremor of his hand, or arrive without warning in the night while his grandchildren sleep in the next room. He would learn to cope with that uncertainty, as people coped with all the other uncertainties of life.

470

And for the rest of us?

Toby pressed her hand against the glass and felt her own pulse, warm and strong, in her fingertips. *I've already died once*, she thought.

This was a brand-new journey.

THE END

References

Berny, P. J., Buronfosse, T., and Lorgue, G., 'Anticoagulant Poisoning in Animals,' *Journal of Analytical Toxicology*, Nov.–Dec. 1995; 19(7): 576-80.

Boer, G. J., 'Ethical Guidelines for the Use of Human Embryonic or Fetal Tissue for Experimental and Clinical Neurotransplantation and Research,' *Journal of Neurology*, Dec. 1994; 242(1): 1–13.

Carey, Benedict, 'Hooked on Youth,' *Health*, Nov.–Dec. 1995; 68–74.

Hainline, Bryan E., Padilla, Lillie-Mae, et al., 'Fetal Tissue Derived from Spontaneous Pregnancy Losses Is Insufficient for Human Transplantation,' *Obstetrics and Gynecology*, April 1995: 85(4): 619–24.

Halder, G., Callaerts, P., and Gehring, W. J., 'Induction of Ectopic Eyes by Targeted Expression of the Eyeless Gene in Drosophila,' *Science*, Mar. 24, 1995, 267 (5205): 1788–92.

Hayflick, L., and Moorhead, P. S., 'The Cell Biology of Human Aging,' *New England Journal of*

Medicine, Dec. 2, 1976; 295(23): 1302–8.

O'Brien, Claire, 'Mad Cow Disease: Scant Data Cause Widespread Concern,' *Science*, March 29, 1996; 271 (5257): 1798.

Prusiner, Stanley, 'The Prion Diseases,' *Scientific American*, Jan. 1995; 272 (1): 48–57.

Rosenstein, J. M., 'Why Do Neural Transplants Survive?' *Experimental Neurology*, May 1995: 133 (1): 1–6.

Roush, Wade, 'Smart Genes Use Many Cues to Set Cell Fate,' *Science*, May 3, 1966; 272 (5262): 652–53.

Sheng, Hui, Zhadanov, Alexander, et al., 'Specification of Pituitary Cell Lineages by the LIM Homeobox Gene Lhx3,' *Science*, May 1996; 272 (5264): 1004–7.

Vinogradova, O. S., 'Some Factors Controlling Morpho-Functional Integration of the Transplanted Embryonic Brain Tissue,' *Zhurnal Vysshei Nervnoi Deiatelnosti Imeni I.P. Pavlova* (Moscow), May–June 1994; 44 (3): 414–30.

Weinstein, P. R., and Wilson, C. B., 'Stereotaxic Hypophysectomy, *Youmans Neurological Surgery*,' vol. 6, Julian Youmans, Ed., 3rd ed., Philadelphia: Saunders, 1990.

THE SURGEON

**In Boston, there's
a killer on the loose...**

A killer who targets lone
women and performs
terrifying ritualistic acts
of torture on them before
finishing them off. His
surgical skills lead police
to suspect he is a physician
who, instead of saving lives,
takes them.

But as homicide detective
Thomas Moore and his
partner Jane Rizzoli begin
their investigation, they make
a startling discovery. Closely linked to these
killings is Catherine Cordell, a beautiful doctor with
a mysterious past. Two years ago she was subjected
to a horrifying rape, and shot her attacker dead.

Now, the man she believes she killed seems to be stalking
her once again. And this time he knows exactly where
to find her...

'This is crime-writing at its nerve-tingling best'
HARLAN COBEN

**TESS
GERRITSEN
The Surgeon**

A RIZZOLI AND ISLES THRILLER

'A real page-turner. A read-in-one-go novel if ever there was one'
Independent on Sunday

THE APPRENTICE

I am not the only one of my kind who walks this earth. Somewhere, there is another. And he waits for me...

The Surgeon has been locked up for a year but his chilling legacy still haunts the city, and especially Boston detective Jane Rizzoli. But now a new killer is at work and Rizzoli senses something horrifyingly familiar about him.

Then the FBI starts taking an interest in the investigation and Rizzoli begins to wonder just what makes this case so different and so dangerous?

But then the unthinkable happens: the Surgeon escapes. And suddenly there are two twisted killers on the loose – master and apprentice...

'This is crime-writing at its nerve-tingling best'
HARLAN COBEN

TESS GERRITSEN
THE Apprentice
A RIZZOLI AND ISLES THRILLER

'A classic page-turner full of heightened tension'
Mail on Sunday

HARVEST

In the ward of a Boston hospital, a tale of twisted terror lies waiting...

Dr Abby DiMatteo is about to make a decision that will jeopardize her career.

A car-crash victim's healthy heart is ready to be harvested, having been cross-matched to a private patient, forty-six year-old Nina Voss. Instead Abby makes sure the transplant goes to a dying seventeen-year-old boy who is also a perfect match.

The repercussions leave her plagued with self doubt. Suddenly a new heart appears, and the transplant is completed – but Abby makes a terrible discovery. The new heart has not come through the right channels.

Defying the hospital's demands for silence, Abby begins her own investigation that reveals an intricate and murderous chain of deceptions...

'The best medical thriller I've read since _Coma_'
James Patterson

THE BONE GARDEN

A gruesome secret is about to be unearthed...

When a human skull is dug up in a garden near Boston, Dr Maura Isles is called in to investigate. She quickly discovers that the skeleton – that of a young woman – has been buried for over a hundred years. But who was the woman? And how did she die?

It is the 1930s, and an impoverished medical student, Norris Marshall, is forced to procure corpses in order to further his studies in human anatomy. It's a gruesome livelihood that will bring him into contact with a terrifying serial killer who slips from ballrooms to graveyards and into autopsy suites.

And who is far, far closer than Norris could ever imagine...

TESS GERRITSEN'S
UNPUTDOWNABLE FIRST CRIME NOVEL

GIRL MISSING

Assistant coroner
Kat Novak knows her
way around an autopsy
room better than most.

But she's at a loss to
explain what it means
when an unknown
woman is brought
in dead, clutching
a matchbook with
a phone number in it.
A few days later two more
women are carried into
her morgue, and Kat
quickly establishes that
their deaths are related.

Soon she is racing to expose both a deadly conspiracy
and a brutal killer who will stalk her from the dangerous
streets of the inner city to the corridors of power.

Because he's closer than she ever dreamt. And every move
she makes could be her last.

'You are going to be up all night'
Stephen King